I0658416

Trigger Warning

Look, I'm just going to come right out and say it: This can be a dark novel. I wish I could tell you that what you are about to read was solely a product of my wonderfully twisted mind, but the truth is that very little of this was pulled from my imagination. At this stage in the Eamon Tauk saga, the man is at war and I wrote that aspect of his tale as a horror story, as human conflict invariably ends up being, even to the victors.

To inspire the feel of these passages, I read about the atrocities of World War II. I watched graphic videos of the current war in Ukraine. To do justice to some of the more unfathomable aspects of the human condition, I tried to capture the essence of the savagery we inflict upon one another when we make that decision to dehumanize our fellow man and kill him *en masse*.

While my intention was not to create an epic work of gore porn, and I don't think that I did, if you finish parts of this novel and are not left wondering with a bit of distress about how you might act in an indescribably horrific situation, I failed in what I was trying to do.

Other than that, I hope you enjoy the story!

Contents

Title Page   VII

1. Prologue   1

2. Reckoning   4

3. Razbauten   11

4. Flight   18

5. Rendezvous   24

6. The Council   30

7. Epiphanies of Idiocy   39

8. Elia   48

9. The Proposition   57

10. Oral History   62

11. Painless   69

12. Metamorphosis   75

13. Scene of the Crime   84

14. The Cost of Victory   92

15. The Goraparasilim Factor   97

16. Guests   104

17. Bina   112

18. Vindication   119

19. Reunion   128

20. The Xun   134

21. Tradecraft   140

22. Rabaat's Bane   147

23. The Encounter   154

24. Crossing the Line   163

25. To Anga-Iskalei   168

26. A Peek into the Abyss   173

27. Gunny   180

28. Fanning Flames   187

29. Whispers of the Morghul   194

30. Seeking Salvation   201

31. One Minute to Midnight   207

32. Contact   214

33. The Saint   219

34. The Rising Xun   226

35. Sacrifice   231

36. Homecoming   237

37. Aftermath   246

38. Trek to Xaramika   251

39. Hear No Evil   255

40. A Shift in Paradigm   262

41. Turqs   269

42. The Duvani   277

43. A Forced Hand   285

44. The Big Bang   290

45. Kryndil's Lair   296

46. The Skinner's Fate   305

47. An Unwelcome Reunion   313

48. Agony   320

49. The Fall   327

50. A Final Farewell   332

51. A Toast of Death   339

52. Clarity   345

53. Transition   352

54. Fin   358

My Sincerest Thanks to...   362

Xi: The Waardan Reaper   364

About the Author   365

Also By J.E. Park   366

The Morghul

An Eamon Tauk Space Odyssey - Book 3

J.E. Park

Chapter 1

PROLOGUE

In the aftermath of the assault on the Satapadaya lines, Elia Gyanis stumbled upon her friend, looking dazed and disoriented as she stood amidst the carnage they had wrought. Idris Jatmika was shaking, in shock and confused. In one hand, she had her fingers tightly wrapped around the handle of her combat dagger. In the other, she held a large piece of flesh carved from an enemy prisoner who was writhing in the mud, shrieking in terror and agony.

Elia swallowed hard as she gawked at the Narman woman, whose hands covered her mutilated face as copious amounts of blood flowed from the space between her fingers. "Idris," Gyanis softly called out as her hand reached for her sidearm. "What are you doing?"

Jatmika looked at the gore in one hand and the knife she was holding in the other. "I-I-I...I don't know. I think I...I think I...." Unable to complete a sentence, Idris glanced up at her comrade as if she could not comprehend what she had done to the woman before them.

"Idris, put the dagger away," Elia begged her squadmate.

"Why?"

"Because you're scaring me."

Idris nodded as her lip quivered. "I'm scared, too."

Elia nodded. "I know you are."

Gyanis could not believe her eyes. Idris Jatmika was the sister Elia never had. She was always full of cheer and quick with a joke. Despite the damage she could inflict with her M2117 light machine gun, Idris always seemed immune to the effects of the fighting they had survived. A fearless Marine, she charged into combat without hesitation and left the horrors she experienced on the battlefield. No matter how hairy things got, when the violence was over, Idris returned to the same bubbly girl she had always been.

Until now. This time, something snapped, and Elia did not think Idris would be able to recover from it.

After a moment of surreal silence, Idris pointed her blade at the woman screeching in the mud. "Sh-she killed Nicola. And Ginni. They're gone. And I think I...think I....Oh, no!" Jatmika broke down as the realization of what she had done to her victim began to sink in. "I'm in trouble, aren't I?"

Elia sighed. Idris was in trouble. Big trouble. Not so much from the Marines, though. The Corps could hardly have cared less about what the grunts did to the rebels they captured. As horrific as what Idris had done was, it was nothing compared to what the Qilkorian death squads did during their interrogations.

No, the command had a place for people who snapped like Idris had — a place where they could commit all the atrocities they wanted with impunity. The problem was they could not return those broken Marines to polite society after assignments like that. They had to be put down when they outlived their usefulness, lest they unleash that sort of cruel barbarism upon the civilian population when they got home. If they found out about what Idris had done, she was doomed.

As some semblance of lucidity began returning to Jatmika, she sobbed, "What do you think Tauk's going to do when he finds out about this?"

"He's going to send you away," Elia said.

"To where?"

"You know where."

Idris sobbed again. "I'll never make it home if he does that!"

"I know, Idi," Elia cried. "I know."

"Please don't let him do it! I can come back from this! I didn't mean to do it! I just...I just...."

Elia drew her sidearm and shot the mutilated prisoner in the head. She did that not so much to cover up Idris's savagery but to end the poor woman's suffering.

"Are you turning me in?" Idris sniffled.

Gyanis shook her head. "No. But you have to promise me you'll never do anything like this ever again."

Breaking down, Idris fell to her knees and wept. "I promise! I promise! I don't know what got into me! I just...I just...I saw what they did to...and I...and I...."

Only once after Idris had dropped her dagger did Elia feel safe enough to holster her weapon. She then bent down to place her hand on her friend's shoulders. "Come on, Idi. Let's get you the hell out of here."

Weeping hysterically, Idris threw her arms around Elia's legs and squeezed them tightly. "Thank you, Elia! Thank you so much for not turning your back on me!"

Idris opened her eyes and looked at her prisoner's body. After seeing what she had done to the Narman's face, she wept even harder. "How could I have done that? What the hell's the matter with me? How could you see that and still be friends with someone capable of doing such a thing?!?"

"I'm your friend because you're like a sister to me, Idi," Elia sighed.

And right now, I'm far too terrified of you to make you my enemy.

Chapter 2

RECKONING

Despite my best efforts not to, I looked at Black Francis as if he had lost his mind. "I think that might be a bridge too far, Gunny."

Frustrated, my platoon sergeant pounded his fist on the plotting table, then started pushing his way through the Marines and liberated prisoners crowding the Mar-Sitaara's cockpit. When he was close enough to get in my face, he snapped, "We've got the momentum, sir! Section 615 doesn't know what hit them! Since this was an intelligence operation, I bet the Marine Expeditionary Force doesn't even know this mission existed! Razbauten was protected by Peeli's platoon, and they were completely wiped out! There are only two people left that could raise the alarm about what we did, and we got both of those assholes chained to each other in the cargo bay! Lieutenant, that place is now guarded by no more than a few dozen Blue Shirt militiamen! They're sitting ducks!"

I could not believe what Francis was asking me to do. We had just sat the *Niberian Hornet* down in a patch of Kanarisian rainforest we had not been to before. Seemingly every centimeter of space aboard the assault fighter was packed full of our exhausted troops, the starving survivors of a destroyed labor camp, insurgent refugees, and a couple of dozen alien beings who were still trying to figure out if we were friend or foe. Waving my hand at the unforgiving jungle just outside the cockpit's forward window, I said, "We can't take all these people with us! What're we supposed to do? Leave them here to get eaten alive by soroquids?!?"

"We'll be back."

I pointed my finger at my platoon sergeant's nose. "You don't know that, Francis! Look at everything we accomplished today! We took out the bastards that were going to lay Bazad-Yul to waste! We rescued the colonists and their Morghul allies! We hijacked another Mar-Sitaara fighter and doubled our air capability! We reduced that place to a smoldering ruin, leaving nothing behind but ash and memories! We got away with it! Section 615 ain't ever gonna piece together what went down there!"

Spinning around, I took one of the Narman colonists by the shoulder of his shirt. I was going to grab one of the Morghul, too, but having only laid eyes upon them for the first time that day, I was not sure what to make of them yet. "We got them all back! Human and alien alike. We got them all to the coordinates they gave us and only lost three people! Do you have any idea how lucky that is?!?"

Letting go of the Narman, I put my arm around the closest Portunese inmate I could find who was still standing under their own power. "We went back and rescued hundreds of people from that...that...." I was struggling to find a better word. "...that concentration camp! Francis, these folks are not in good shape! We can't just dump them off and...."

Black Francis violently shook his head in disagreement. "We aren't dumping anybody off! Lieutenant, look at these people! Stop for a second and really look at their faces! Stare into their eyes!"

Unable to help myself, I did what the sergeant told me to. I immediately wished I hadn't. The Portunese were a wretched lot. Months of unrelenting labor, malnourishment, and relentless abuse by the Blue Shirts had reduced them to little more than living skeletons. I noticed that most of those still able to stand bore expressions of unbridled rage. What they did to their Samaari tormentors at Saimsun was not enough. They hungered for much, much more.

Those sitting on the deck were a different story. They were either paralyzed with despair or so exhausted they were barely cognizant of where they were. Some of those lying down were giving up. Aware that they were at the end of the line, it seemed like they were letting go so they could at least die free, having long been denied the chance to live that way. I saw one sprawled out near our pilot who looked as if she had already expired.

"There's a lot more of those where these came from, Tauk!" Black Francis told me. "If we don't get them out of Razbauten, they're dead!"

"We accomplished far more today than we ever could have hoped, Gunny. Not everything went to plan, but when our contingencies faltered, fortune prevailed. We pushed our luck far beyond any limits we could have reasonably expected it to hold. I don't think we can stretch it even further."

"We have to try!" Francis begged.

"We don't have a plan!" I shot back. "We don't have eyes on the ground! No intel! No...."

"By the time we devise a plan, our moment will be gone! We have to act before reinforcements arrive at that mine! Now, sir!"

Haeli Deboara, the woman who initiated the uprising at Saimsun, shoved her way to Francis's side. She was one of those Portunese who stood seething on the sidelines of the command center, barely able to contain her murderous fury. Her husband, who was squeezing through behind her, should have been one of those lying on the deck. He looked horrible and was standing upright only through sheer force of will. I could see on his face that the man was in great physical pain, but it was in his soul where his real agony lay. The man had been compelled to kill his sons that day to spare them the horrors of falling back into Samaari hands. For the act of mercy that that was, it came with a burden of guilt that I was not sure Daino Deboara was equipped to survive. His wife was a different story. She bore no shame about what they had to do — only an insatiable thirst for vengeance for being pushed into a situation where they had to do it.

"There're hundreds of people at Razbauten," Haeli spat, her face red as she struggled to restrain herself from slapping me. "People who'll die if we don't take advantage of all this confusion you've sowed and go get them! I sacrificed my children to get this far, Eamon! I didn't do that just to sit here and do nothing while we wait to fucking die!"

"We can't go in there without a clear idea of what we're up against!" I fired back. "If reinforcements are already on the ground at Razbauten, we could lose everything we've gained!"

"What you *might* lose will be nothing compared to what those people in Razbauten *will* lose if you do nothing!" Haeli screamed, her voice quaking with rage and raw grief. "I know because I've already lost it!" A low murmur of assent rose from the crowd around me, signaling that the liberated inmates were united behind their leader.

I let out an exhausted sigh and once again scanned the faces around me. When we first landed in that clearing, most of those filling the cockpit thought I was a hero. I could see I was hemorrhaging that goodwill very fast. Hoping to shore up support from at least one quarter, I marched over to Melki, the alien I took to be the ranking Morghul.

"You've got an air force now, sir," I told him. "It's small, but it's deadly. We've got plasma blasters! Armor that makes us all but invisible! You've ended the day significantly stronger than when you started it! You have the capability now to inflict real damage on the League! Do you really want to risk all that?"

The Morghul cut an imposing figure. Wrapped in a hooded cloak, Melki was half a head taller than me, with red eyes so bright they almost seemed to glow. I noticed he was the only alien not wearing goggles, and he tended to squint a lot, as if the light bothered him. Melki had a large head that looked to house considerable computing power. His arms stretched abnormally far past his waist and ended at a pair of giant hands bearing freakishly long fingers. At first glance, he looked like a demon, but once you heard him speak, you got the impression that he was a pensive creature seldom prone to impulsive decisions.

Uncomfortable with being put on the spot by someone far better armed than he was, Melki diverted his eyes. As he glanced around the crowded cockpit, his gaze fell upon one of the overhead screens showing the video feed from a camera pointed at the Mar-Sitaara's egress bay.

The craft was still full of Portunese from the Saimsun mine. As the fresher inmates could disembark from the Mar-Sitaara by themselves, the video mostly showed those too weak to move.

I caught sight of Akkam Lumuk seated on the deck. He was weeping over the body of a young boy who had died in his arms. The child had survived the strife on Portuna and lived through the horrors of the Harnillium mines, only to have his heart give out just as he was rescued. That scene seemed to strike a chord in Melki, whose own son had nearly been executed in front of him that morning.

With a newfound resolve in his voice, the alien elder answered my question with one of his own. "What good is everything we've gained if we don't use it? It seems that the enemy may be off-balance at the moment, still unaware of what you accomplished in the Arad Valley. That is not going to last long. Our best chance of taking down Razbauten and rescuing those prisoners is now. We can take advantage of the enemy's arrogance. They think they broke us at the Satapadaya Front. That's why they're letting the Blue Shirts handle mine security. They will never expect an attack from the air. I think we can take them."

I let out a long sigh. Everything Melki said made sense. Judging by the glares being directed at me by my audience, I appeared to be the only one urging restraint. Even Je'Sikka Albarn nodded at me. She had had an eventful day as well. Not only did Albarn drop us off at Bazad-Yul, but she also returned to where we were supposed to land and vaporized the Killbillies lying in wait to ambush us. She then disarmed and disembarked the Marines we had that were still loyal to the League.

Unbeknownst to Albarn, that last mission was among the most critical sorties she had flown that day. It was not just an act of mercy but a way for me to slip Elia Gyanis into the lion's den to be my eyes and ears inside Narman's Pyke.

Like the rest of us, Albarn was exhausted and emotionally spent. When our gazes met, however, she signaled she was ready to fly one more mission.

I let out a long sigh. I was trying to fight a war — a prolonged battle with long-term goals. I was plotting my strategy as I had been taught my entire life. Coldly. Logically. Calculatingly. Clearly, I was the only one looking at our situation that way. For everyone else in that cockpit, this fight was intensely personal. Despite how confident I was that making strategic decisions based on emotion was suicidal, I also knew that future success would be impossible if I lost the confidence of my troops because I failed to seize the initiative.

What the hell, I thought to myself. *Our odds of success are already pretty damned long, and what do I really have to live for anyway?*

"Okay," I said, throwing my hands up and admitting defeat. The cockpit erupted into an instant uproar of cheers I had to put down before I could continue.

"We're going to land at Razbauten on the *Serpent*. That's the ship they'll be expecting to see. If things go our way, there should only be a few dozen Blue Shirts keeping order around the place. If typical, they'll be lightly armed, poorly trained, and almost entirely devoid of discipline. They were chosen for that kind of work for their sadism, not their intelligence. Two rifle squads should be sufficient to neutralize them."

I paused to stare at those gathered around the plotting table, ensuring everyone was paying attention. "If things don't go our way and we find Marines on the ground at our objective, having an entire platoon aboard the *Serpent* won't make any difference. We'll be lost, and our mission will be short. I want half our Marines to stay here to protect these civilians."

"You need me to go with you," Haeli Deboara said.

"What?!?" exclaimed her husband. "We just got out of Saimsun! We...we...we..." Daino looked distraught. He did not seem able to process that his wife wanted to drag him back into the same hopeless situation they had just escaped. It was not cowardice; the man was just all too aware of what his physical limitations were. He had given everything he had to get his wife to freedom. There was nothing left in him to give.

Haeli Deboara was a different animal. She desperately needed the distraction. If Haeli had allowed herself to think about what they had done to spare her boys further suffering, she might have fallen into a well of despair from which she might not ever have been able to climb out. Still, this was about saving the inmates at Razbauten, not saving Haeli Deboara. I could not see how she would be an asset to our mission. After a casual glance into those crazed eyes of hers, I could list dozens of ways she could end up a liability.

Shaking my head, I turned to her and said, "I'm sorry, Haeli. I can't...."

Haeli charged to my side and grabbed my arm. "You have to take me!" she snapped, her voice cracking in desperation. "Those prisoners have been brutalized by people who look just like you for weeks! Maybe even months! When they see you get off that transport and open fire, they ain't going to be running toward you, Eamon! They're going to be running to get as far from you as humanly possible! You need me and a few others to show them we're on the same side!"

Black Francis nodded in agreement. "She's got a point."

I cursed. She *did* have a point. "Alright. Go see Warrant Officer Dav and have her issue you a weapon. Do you know how to use an M72?"

Haeli shook her head. "I've never fired a gun before in my life."

I cursed again. "Get one anyway. I don't want you to use it, but I think the prisoners would find reassurance seeing one of their own under arms."

As the Deboaras left to find the *Niberian Hornet's* weapons officer, I noticed Haeli's husband could barely walk. I grabbed him by the arm as he passed. "You've been through a lot today, sir. You don't have to go with us. There's no shame in...."

Daino Deboara ripped his arm from my grip and glared into my eyes, his expression betraying he was aware of what had occurred between his wife and me. The Blue Shirts had thrown Haeli into my tent as a test. They wanted me to prove I hated people deemed enemies of the state as much as they did. Unwilling to add rapist to my growing list of character flaws, I had no intention of molesting her. Haeli sensed the potential I had to assist her, though. She also knew I would not be any help to anybody if I ended up buried in a shallow grave. Seeing me as her only hope of getting her and her family out of their predicament, she insisted I do what the Samaaris expected of me.

What we did was not born of lust. It was something we simply needed to do to survive the night and fight another day. Daino Deboara did not see it that way, though. To him, I was no ally. I was a rival. "She's not going anywhere with you!" the man snarled at me. "Not unless I'm going, too!"

•• ◄► ● ◄► ••

Chapter 3

Razbauten

The Blue Shirt foreman did not look as if he did much more at Razbauten than collect chins. He was morbidly obese, so large that the M72 slung across his chest looked like little more than a toy. With the way he had it positioned, it may as well have been. There was not enough slack in the sling for him to have done a damn thing with it had he needed to draw it in a hurry. For me, there was no greater indication that the man had absolutely no idea just how much trouble he was facing.

As we landed at the mine in the *Space Serpent*, the oversized Blue Shirt waddled across the tarmac to greet us. With him were two underlings who, even combined, would not have matched half their boss's weight. Both of them were also armed, but carried their rifles diagonally over their backs. The way the Blue Shirts wore their weapons was symptomatic of men unaccustomed to inflicting violence against foes who fought back. They were more used to wielding whips than firearms.

Black Francis and I watched the men walk through the rain toward the port side of the Mar-Sitaara. "It's going to take that fat fucker a decade to get here," laughed my platoon sergeant.

"Let them take their time," I told him. "We'll walk out and meet them once our Marines are out the starboard hatch. We'll keep them focused on us while Korman's people sneak deeper into the camp."

When the time was right, we lowered the egress ramp and marched into the downpour to approach the Blue Shirts. The chief smiled at us when we stepped within earshot. He looked like a gremlin with his tiny eyes, thin lips, and flat nose. His two minions were just as homely. The three of them cut a picture of men who would have languished at the bottom rung of any organization other than the Blue Shirts. They had no physical prowess, looked light on intellectual computing power, and were as lacking in courage as they were in empathy.

"Things must have gone well!" the boss Blue Shirt wheezed, his breath as short as the walk he had just taken. "We weren't expecting you here until tomorrow!"

Black Francis turned to look at me. With our visors down, I could not see the expression on his face, but I could only assume it was one of complete surprise at learning we had all night to take that camp. I was sure he was even more shocked when I pulled my sidearm and blew the crown off the chief's skull on the spot.

The blast knocked the big Blue Shirt backward, causing him to fall atop one of his underlings and pin him to the ground under a couple hundred kilograms of dead weight. The remaining Samaari froze in his tracks, unable to do anything but stare at us slack-jawed. Black Francis planted the butt of his rifle into the man's face and dropped him unconscious into the mud. With the trio of Samaaris neutralized, I jumped on the commlink and set my troops into motion.

"Condition Green!" I shouted over the network. "Condition Green! There are no regular troops on the ground! Proceed to plan! Bird One, come in! Bird One! Do you read!"

"Loud and clear!" answered Je'Sikka Albarn, who was circling the area of operations at the far extreme of our radio range.

"The *Serpent* was not expected back at Razbauten until tomorrow!"

"That's great!" Albarn yelled. "We got them before anyone realized they were missing!"

"Not so fast," I corrected her. "If Peeli and Takawa weren't expected here, they were expected somewhere else. When they didn't show, I'm sure they set off alarms. Razbauten could be under surveillance. Keep your eyes open for inbound bogeys."

"Roger that."

The operation to secure the mines at Razbauten went like clockwork. First Squad captured the off-shift Blue Shirts, rousting them out of their beds at gunpoint, placing them in gags and restraints, then leaving them outside in the rain, guarded by a pair of riflemen. They then repeated the process and apprehended the Tahnebaht executives who ran the facility. After that, Sergeant Korman led his Marines in breaching the space freighters on site, walking unchallenged aboard every single one of them and capturing their crews without firing a shot.

Black Francis could not comprehend the sheer incompetence of our adversaries. After Korman had reported what he had done, my platoon sergeant shook his head in disbelief. "Fucking Samaaris. You know, sometimes there's just no greater ally you can have than a mind-numbingly stupid enemy. How the hell did a people that moronic gain control of our entire government?"

"Money," I answered. "It goes to show you just how far one can go with nothing but wealth."

"And ruthlessness," Black Francis added as he saw the first inmates starting to gather on the tarmac. They looked worse than the people we lived among at Saimsun. That should not have been a surprise. With Mott Peeli's platoon quartered at Razbauten, more people were around to torment them.

My platoon's First Squad had a slightly tougher time of things. The Blue Shirts they encountered were wide awake and driving the night shift miners. Still, when the Samaaris saw Dina Tiago's troops charging into the mine, they thought we were coming to warn them of impending trouble. They did not suspect we *were* the trouble until they spotted Haeli Deboara running beside my sergeant with an M72 in her hands. "BREACH!" screamed one of the security foremen as he hit the panic button on his belt, setting off alarms throughout the entire facility. It was the Blue Shirt's last act of defiance. Corporal Kunigas blasted him through the chest before he could do anything else.

As Tiago's Marines took aim at the guards, the leader of the inmates we rescued earlier ran to a communications kiosk and grabbed the microphone to the mine's PA system. "To the prisoners of Razbauten! My name is Haeli Deboara! I was an inmate of the Saimsun facility until early this morning when we rose up and overthrew the Blue Shirts! We've come to help you do the same! The Marines you see are not the same monsters who hurt you before! They're on your side! Charge the guards! Seize their weapons! Grab your children, and get the hell out of this hole! You no longer have to fear the Samaaris! Now is the time for them to fear us!"

The prisoners did not need a lot of convincing. Haeli's voice was their first sign of hope since they were rounded up on their home planets, and they seized the opportunity. The miners rushed the guards, killing many on-site, then stampeded for the exit. Only one Blue Shirt escaped the carnage and stumbled away from the mob. One of the craftier Samaaris on the grounds, he snuck into the supervisors' quarters and got his hands on a distress flare, which he fired into the air before running for the perimeter.

"You see that?" I shouted into the Mar-Sitaara commlink.

"Affirmative," answered Je'Sikka Albarn. "I'm climbing to the cloud line to search for inbound hostiles."

"Skaigard!" I yelled. "Get the *Serpent* off the tarmac and go with her! The last thing I want is for you to be stuck on the ground if we come under attack!"

"Aye aye, Tauk! *Serpent* is going airborne!

With Kanaris's Harnillium interference limiting our radio range to just four kilometers, there had been attempts to run landlines from the remote satellite bases to the central command center at Narman's Pyke. After getting crushed at the Satapadaya Front, though, the only thing the Narmans had still been effective at was cutting those cables nearly as fast as they were laid. Without a voice link to the Pyke, the Blue Shirts could only use flares to signal they were in trouble. They had no way of specifying the nature of the threat.

Since the Narmans were not known to have air capabilities, the theater commander assumed Razbauten was under assault by ground forces. In response, they sent a fast attack company to assist the facility in four Raptor transport craft. Of course, they did not bother sending escort fighters. The Raptors never stood a chance.

"Okay, that one's a freebie," Albarn broadcast as the eastern sky lit up with fireballs born of League airships and a few hundred flaming Marines hurtling toward the ground. "They're not going to make that mistake again."

"No, they're not," I agreed. "The leader of that expedition would've had his own flares to signal back what was going on. If they don't indicate they're on the ground safely, the theater commander's going to assume they didn't make it. They won't send more Raptors next time."

"No, they won't," Skaigard told me. "They'll send Haiv fighters. Tauk, I don't have a weapons officer aboard this thing. There's no way I can win a dogfight with multiple bogeys. What do you want me to do?"

I cursed and looked at Black Francis, who shrugged his shoulders at me. After shoving him hard in the breastplate, I growled, "That's why I didn't think this was a good idea! We're going to lose our aircraft and have to march these people back to our rendezvous! Look at them, Francis! They ain't going to fucking make it!"

A glance around the growing crowd of prisoners suggested that they might not have cared. They were entertaining themselves by doing to the captured Blue Shirts what the Blue Shirts had done to them. They had thirty guards lined up in a row, keeping them on their knees with their hands tied behind their backs. The prisoners had queued up to take turns cutting small pieces of skin off them with a single dagger they shared between each other. The man currently being cut shrieked in agony as he was hacked away little by little. The rest of our captives howled in terror as they awaited their turn under the knife.

"Please!" begged the Blue Shirt who was next in line. "Please have mercy on me! I have children!"

A passing prisoner spat in his face. "So did I!" the woman wept. "You animals butchered them!"

"I didn't do anything!" bawled another man much further down the row. "I'm not a Blue Shirt! I'm not even Samaari! I'm a fucking pilot! I never left my freighter when I got here because I couldn't handle looking at what was going on! Please, don't do this to me!"

As much as the Samaaris deserved what was coming for them, I could not bear to watch it. While walking away from the unfolding atrocity, I caught sight of Haeli Deboara looking at what was going on in horror. She made no move to stop the slow-motion slaughter, but it was clear she was sickened by the spectacle.

There may be hope for you yet, young lady, I thought. *Maybe you're not as far gone as I feared.*

Turning to Francis, I said, "Let the prisoners have the Blue Shirts while we figure this shit out. Get the Tahnebaht executives out of there, though. They'll probably have information we can use. From what I heard, the Morghul have a guy who can get it out of them."

"Aye, aye," Francis said as he walked away to carry out my orders.

"Owen," I heard Albarn say over the commlink. "How comfortable are you in your evasion skills?"

"Excellent!" Skaigard excitedly replied. With much less enthusiasm, he added, "On a simulator."

"What was your best rating?" Albarn asked.

"Ninety-seven."

"Mine was ninety-three. You got this! Listen, I want you to head for the eastern horizon. We know that's where our bogeys are going to be inbound from. You grab their attention and lead them toward Razbauten."

"And what are you going to do?" Though he did his best to hide it, I could tell by Skaigard's voice that he was a bit leery of Albarn's strategy.

"I'm going to find a clearing in the canopy to lay low in. When you pass me, I'll engage them from behind."

"Where are you going to be?"

"I'll let you know when I find that clearing!"

As Skaigard and Albarn tried to formulate a plan to get us out of the mess in which we had inserted ourselves, Black Francis approached and tapped me on the shoulder. "We have a big problem."

"Really?" I asked sarcastically. "But I thought everything was going so well!"

My platoon sergeant pointed at the swelling crowd of Razbauten's inmates. "Sir, even if we come out of this with both our aircraft, we don't have a fraction of the cargo space we need to evacuate these people."

My jaw dropped open. Black Francis was right. There were far more inmates in that facility than we thought. If we filled every available centimeter of space on one of our Mar-Sitaara fighters, we might be able to fit three hundred people aboard. And we had better have a smooth flight back because if our pilots had to engage an enemy in an aerial dogfight, the maneuvering they would have to do would kill everybody not strapped into a seat with a restraining bar. That meant we could transport six hundred inmates at best. If I had to guess, a few thousand people were already gathered around the landing pads, and the crowd was still growing.

"PLEEEASE!" came a hysterical cry from the line of prisoners being cut to death by the camp survivors. "I TOLD YOU! I DIDN'T DO ANYTHING! I'M JUST A PILOT!"

Grabbing Black Francis by the arm, I rushed into the crowd, hoping to get to that prisoner before someone with a blade did. I arrived just in time. "Do you want to live?!?" I screamed at the man as I yanked him to his feet.

"Yes! Please! Don't let me die here! Not like this!" The pilot's eyes had gone wild in terror.

"Then point out the other pilots!"

The prisoner eyed me suspiciously, as if I were asking him to rat out his friends for further retribution. Not having time to bargain with him, I dragged him up the queue of the doomed so that he would be next to go under the knife. "ALRIGHT! ALRIGHT! I'LL POINT THEM OUT!"

After he identified three more men, I gathered them all together. "You have a choice," I told the freighter pilots. "You can fly us all the fuck out of here, or you can go back to that line and wait your turn."

One of the men spat at me. "Fuck you traitors! I ain't helping you do a goddamn thing! I'll take my chances with those rats you flushed out of the hole!"

I nodded at Black Francis, who yanked the Samaari out of our ranks and turned him over to the miners, who immediately went to work on him. As his shrieks rose above the ambient din, I asked, "Does anybody else feel like valiantly laying down their lives for the Samaari cause tonight?"

As I watched one of the other pilots wet himself, I took it as a sign that the surviving aviators had reached the limits of what they were willing to sacrifice for their country.

••-◆-●-◆-••

Chapter 4

FLIGHT

I t was far easier herding Razbauten's inmates onto freighters than getting those we rescued from Saimsun onto a Mar-Sitaara after they had been chased for dozens of kilometers through the Kanarisian rainforest. The people from Saimsun had been pushed past their limits and were dropping like flies before we arrived to rescue them. By the time we landed to pick them up, we had to carry more than half of them aboard.

Nearly everyone at Razbauten was still able to move under their own power. The mine's Blue Shirts instantly executed those unable to meet their quotas to make space for those who could. The result was we had very few invalids to deal with at our objective. To my surprise, one of the few exceptions was Daino Deboara. I found him hunched over on all fours, shaking in agony while his wife rushed among the other inmates, guiding them onto their rides out of the labor camp. "Are you all right?" I asked the man as I dropped down to my knees beside him.

"Does it look like I'm all right?!?" Daino cried, blowing snot down his lip. "I'm all used up, man! The fuckers broke me! I can't move any more! My hands are so messed up I can't even hold a rifle! They pushed me twelve hours a day, *every day*, for I don't know how long! I worked three times as hard as everyone else to make sure my kids met their quotas and could live just one more day! And I killed them anyway! Me!"

As Daino descended into hysterics, he dropped his face into the mud. Ever since he had arrived on Kanaris, the man had pushed himself far beyond his limits to keep his children safe. His love for his boys acted like an anesthetic, giving him almost superhuman endurance. But, with his boys gone, Daino no longer had anything to mask his pain and little reason to continue on. He was giving up.

"I had to kill my kids, man!" Daino sobbed. "I pinched their little noses and covered their mouths! I held them until they stopped moving so those fucking Marines, YOUR people, wouldn't get their hands on them! I MURDERED MY BOYS!"

"You have to pull yourself together, man," I urged him. "Your wife needs you!"

My comment made Daino Deboara unravel even faster. "My wife needs me?!? ME?!? What can I do for her? Huh? I couldn't protect her even when I was fresh! The Blue Shirts took her and passed her around themselves right in front of me! And I couldn't do a fucking thing about it! But you know all about that, don't you? DON'T YOU?!?"

Feeling very uncomfortable, I needed to end the conversation and return to my mission. Checking my forearm console, I discovered that Melyn Ashwar was the closest medic to me. I ordered him to grab two able-bodied prisoners and come to my location. When they arrived, I asked the corpsman, "Do you know who this is?"

The lance corporal nodded. "We rode in together."

"Good. Get him aboard one of the freighters. Whatever you do, don't let his wife see him like this."

No sooner had my Marines gotten Daino to his feet when I heard Warrant Officer Skaigard's voice over the commlink. "MAYDAY! MAYDAY! I GOT BO-GIES, JE'SIKKA! I GOT BOGIES!"

"Roger that," Albarn replied, her voice calm and collected. "How many?"

"AT LEAST A HALF DOZEN! THEY'RE ALL OVER MY SIX! THERE'S TOO MANY OF THEM! WHERE THE FUCK ARE YOU?!?"

"Tree top level, heading due east. I'm dark and in stealth mode. I got reads on their exhaust signatures and am coming your way. Do what you have to do to keep them from locking onto you, but continue leading them to the mine."

I craned my head toward the eastern horizon just in time to see a trio of air-to-air missiles launch from the Haiv fighters on Skaigard's tail. The Mar-Sitaara automatically detected them and deployed thermal decoys in response. The flares took out two rockets, but a third locked onto the *Serpent's* exhaust.

"Loop!" Albarn said unnecessarily. Skaigard was a capable pilot. He was already in the process of doing what the *Hornet* advised well before she advised it. Still, Albarn kept talking to him anyway. "Climb and loop! I'm almost there!"

Skaigard did not answer her. He was too busy.

The fighters were heading right for us at incredible speed. I was so focused on them I never spotted Albarn approach from the west. Not that I could have. The *Hornet* screamed past us long before I heard it, and my eardrums were nearly shattered by the sonic boom that hit us in her wake.

"THAT MISSILE'S ABOUT TO CRAWL UP MY FUCKIN' ASS!" Skaigard shrieked, suddenly breaking his silence. "IT'S ALMOST...!"

A massive explosion lit up the sky as the *Serpent* burst into a million little pieces.

"OWEN!" I heard Albarn scream. After that, I switched off the air network. There was nothing I could do for the *Hornet*. I needed her to concentrate on her job while I focused on mine.

Not long after the *Serpent* went down, another explosion lit up the eastern sky. Dina Tiago ran up to me with fear written all over her face. "Do you think that was Albarn?"

I shook my head. "I don't know. I...."

I was interrupted by another fireball erupting over the horizon. Grinning, I told Tiago, "No, that seems to be the *Niberian Hornet* getting all warmed up."

Two more Haiv fighters went down within ten minutes after that. The other two bugged out. "I'm going after them," Albarn told me.

"No!" I called back. "We're loading the inmates into freighters and need a fighter escort back to...."

I was cut off by the sound of another Mar-Sitaara flying above Razbauten at treetop level. After the second boom struck, I jumped back on the commlink and screamed, "ALBARN! ALBARN! THERE'S ANOTHER MAR-SITAARA IN THEATRE! I REPEAT THERE'S ANOTHER MAR-SITAARA IN THEATER, BEARING DOWN ON YOU FROM THE WEST!"

There was no reply. Considering how quickly Kanarisian Harnillium could scramble a radio transmission into indecipherable gibberish, odds were the *Hornet* was well out of comm range before I even sent the message.

"What are we going to do?" asked Sergeant Tiago.

"The only thing we can!" I shouted back at her. "Get these people on the fucking freighters so we can get off the ground before those fighters lose interest in Albarn and turn their attention to us!"

We probably could have fit all the inmates into one transport, but to quicken the evacuation, we loaded them onto two. With the sky still quiet above us, we initiated our ascent and climbed above the trees. There was no sign of the *Niberian Hornet* anywhere in the area.

"What do you think happened to her?" Sergeant Tiago asked as the pilot set a course for the coordinates I gave him. She wanted someone to tell her Albarn was going to be alright, but that was not a reassurance I was willing to offer.

"You okay?" Black Francis asked me.

I shook my head. "I shouldn't have done it. We needed those fighters, Francis. Not only are we less combat capable than we were before, we're burdened with thousands of people who need a level of care we can't possibly provide."

Haeli Deboara heard that comment and took great offense to it. "That's what we are to you, Eamon? A burden?"

I sighed. "You know what I meant. That rendezvous where we offloaded your people is not our final destination. We'll probably have to hike a considerable distance to get to a long-term haven. How many of your people do you think will survive that?"

Haeli's expression hardened. "I have no idea, but I can tell you those who do will be fucking warriors. The strongest of the strong. The weakest among us have been culled, and the Samaaris are going to tremble before what's left. Mark my words, Tauk. We'll never forget what those animals took from us, and we're going to make them pay it back with interest."

"Tanner-Eight-Twelve and Tanner-Thirteen-Seven," came a voice over the freighter's cockpit receiver. "Confirm conductor identity."

Our pilot's face went white. "That's us," he told me. "We're Tanner-Thirteen-Seven."

"Then fucking answer him!" I told the man. "Buy us time! Just stay the course."

"This is Tanner-Thirteen-Seven. You go first. Who am I speaking with?"

"This is APAAF-12, following four clicks past your six."

I hung my head. "It's that other Mar-Sitaara," I moaned. "It must have gotten Albarn. We're fucked."

Our pilot swallowed hard. "APAAF-12, my name is Abel Dorn. I'm currently at the helm of Tanner-Thirteen-Seven."

There was a pause while the Mar-Sitaara checked the freighter's electronic signature. "Pilot ID does not match, Tanner-Thirteen-Seven."

"Affirmative. Tanner-Thirteen-Seven was the closest flight-worthy craft to me when I evacuated the Razbauten mining facility. Manis Brayne, the craft's assigned pilot, is dead."

There was another pause while the Mar-Sitaara considered the data it had received. "Tanner-Thirteen-Seven, what is your current situation? Who do you have on board?"

Abel Dorn looked at me for guidance. I shook my head and said, "Tell them anything you want except inmates and Marines."

"APAAF-12, current manifest is surviving mine security staff, freighter and loading crew, and roughly fourteen hundred tons of unprocessed Harnillium."

"And what is your destination?"

Our pilot swallowed hard. "Uh...uh...uh...I don't know."

"What do you mean you don't know?"

Dorn cursed and slapped the control console. "I! Don't! Know! We didn't exactly have time to file a proper flight plan as we were running for our lives!"

"So, where were you going?"

"I have no idea! Anywhere but fucking Razbauten!"

"Okay. Stand by for redirect."

"Redirect?" Haeli Deboara exclaimed. "What the hell is a redirect?"

"He's telling us where to go!" Dorn told her.

"Fuck that!" Haeli cursed as she reached for the microphone. "I'll tell him where to fucking go!"

Dorn pulled the transmitter out of Haeli's reach. "Back off! You're going to get us killed!"

Haeli ripped the M72, the rifle she did not know how to use, off her shoulder and pointed it at the pilot. "We aren't going anywhere with those sons-of-bitches! I'll force them to blow us out of the sky before I let them lay their hands on me again!"

Seeing that the safety was still engaged on Deboara's weapon, I snatched it from her hands. "Settle down and shut up! Let me think, for fuck's sake! I have to figure a way out of...!"

"Hey!" Dorn exclaimed, turning toward me. "Eamon? Is that your name? Sorry, but we've never been properly introduced."

"My name's Tauk," I answered. "My friends call me Eamon. You can call me 'sir.'"

The pilot cleared his throat. "Fine, sir. That Mar-Sitaara just sent us the coordinates they want us to fly to."

"Okay," I said. "And?"

"They're the same coordinates for where we were going in the first place!"

Chapter 5

Rendezvous

O ur haven was little more than a large clearing in the rainforest shielded from aerial surveillance by a hologram ceiling. It was never meant to be a permanent refuge, just a place for us to gather so the Narmans could determine what our motivations were and where we could plot our next steps. When we returned with the inmates from Razbauten, however, it was not entirely certain we were still welcome there.

As we landed, I could see about forty Marines, *my* Marines, surrounding our LZ with their weapons at the ready, prepared to storm our freighters the second we opened the hatches. Right next to where we were to touch down were a pair of Mar-Sitaara fighters. I recognized one of them as the *Niberian Hornet*. I had no clue who the other one belonged to, nor was I aware of who had escorted us back to base and was now circling the area one last time to ensure we were not followed.

"What the hell do you make of this?" Black Francis asked me.

"I have no idea," I answered.

Once the freighter pilots cut the engines, we opened the craft's access ramps to allow my Marines to board. It made me a little nervous to do so, but we had no other choice.

As I waited for my troops to reach the cockpit, I watched my Technical Warfare Specialist step out of the *Hornet* with Albarn, Melki, and a few unfamiliar people in civilian clothes. I assumed those must have been the Narmans. Only then did I start to relax. I still had no idea what was happening, but at least my people did not appear to be under duress.

It only took a few minutes for Sergeant Demangel to find us in the cockpit. He immediately relaxed once he saw Black Francis and me. "Oh, thank god!" he gasped in relief. "Sorry, sir. We had no idea what was in those freighters. Albarn reported she lost track of you all at Razbauten, so we had no idea what was coming our way."

"Understood," I said, returning my gaze to the two fighters parked in front of us while listening to one more circling overhead. "Sergeant, what the hell is going on out there?"

Arnaud Demangel was generally a joyful person, but I had never seen him smile as wide as he did right then. "You wouldn't believe me if I told you, sir. I heard it all directly from the horse's mouth, and I can barely believe it myself."

●●-◆-◗-◆-●●

"Don't look at me like that, Eamon," Je'Sikka begged me. "I had no idea."

We were aboard the *Hornet*, seated on the bridge. With us were the flight officers of the other two Mar-Sitaaras, Melki, and a pair of Narman officials who did not do much talking. They were more interested in listening to what we had to say.

Warrant Officer Abwazni Tolchek, the pilot of the *Solar Wind*, spoke up to concur with his comrade. "She didn't," he assured me. "This was all Amella Henne."

I sighed. "Do you know she died aboard the *Serpent*?"

Tolchek nodded. "All too well. I watched it happen."

"So, how did she convince you to defect?"

"You know, even though the Mar-Sitaaras in the Kanarisian theater have all been commandeered by Section 615, they're owned by the fleet. Those are top-of-the-line warcraft, Lieutenant. They're sleek, sophisticated, and very expensive. Unlike our intelligence agencies, the Navy doesn't give plum assignments to people solely on the basis of their ideological purity. They're only going to give them to those smart enough to be able to handle them. Generally speaking, Mar-Sitaara pilots are intellectuals, not sycophantic psychopaths. We're not going to be impressed by finding out the government we're fighting for is running a chain of concentration camps. We're going to be appalled."

"Then how did two men like Lodai Nautik and Nord Veriilan end up behind the helm of one of those things?" I asked.

"Warrant Officer Veriilan was one hell of a pilot," said Qoalmun Nartyr, the commander of the ship that escorted us out of the Arad Valley. "The fact that he was also Samaari was probably why Takawa chose to keep him close. He was talented and fanatical. That's a perfect combination for a Section 615 aviator. Believe it or not, Lodai Nautik was stellar behind the controls also. That guy had his shit together before he started working with Intel. He didn't start falling apart until he ended up under Takawa's command."

"I've seen video of what that piece of shit was doing at Razbauten," Naktada told the pilots. "That man was evil."

Abwazni Tolchek nodded. "I heard. Henne told me all about it. Look, I'm no psychiatrist, but if I had to guess, Lodai never had a chance to back out of what he was doing. His mother is a fucking High Jurist of the Kyperion Court! His old man's a senator! For all he knew, his parents may have played a part in crafting the policy that led to what was happening in those camps. To admit the conditions in those mines were barbaric would be to admit his parents, people he idolized, were barbarians. I think he tried to convince himself those prisoners were the real monsters and that they deserved what we did to them. His descent into what he eventually became was probably hastened by all the booze he had to drink to twist his mind into rationalizing all that. The man never had a chance. He was raised to champion The Cause at all costs."

"I'm an Academy Marine," I told Tolchek. "*I* was raised to champion The Cause at all costs. From birth. You didn't see me brutalizing inmates at Saimsun. If I could cut through the bullshit, Nautik could have also."

"Trust me, Lieutenant," Nartyr told me. "I've been around a few Academy Marines. You're the exception. Not the rule."

After thinking about those I grew up with, I nodded. "Okay, I'll concede that point. So, how did Henne pull you into this?"

Tolchek leaned back in his seat. "She let us know we weren't alone. She was watching us, looking for people who were not on board with what was going on. Amella was pretty good at what she did. It didn't take her long to assemble a little network of Mar-Sitaara pilots who had had enough of the League and their bullshit. We didn't know who else was in on this, but she told us there were others who felt the same way we did. She told us if we stuck together and struck when the time was right, we could deliver one hell of a blow against the League for what they were doing. We just had to seize the opportunity. Henne told us that opportunity was today. So Qoal and I disembarked our Section Kommandos, lifted off, then slaughtered them from the air."

The pilot paused to shudder at what he had done before he continued. "Luckily, our objective was not very large. It was just a couple of Narman families. Still, we had to take them against their will. We couldn't convince them we were on their side until we showed them all the agents we blew up. It still took a lot of back and forth before they trusted us enough to bring us here. That's why we were a little late to your party."

Albarn breathed a big sigh of relief. "Well, I'm glad you made it eventually, Abe. When I first saw you, I thought we were doomed. It was beginning to look like I had bitten off more than I could chew with those Haiv fighters."

"It didn't look that way, Je'Sikka," Qoal said. "It *was* that way. What were you thinking out there? The Mar-Sitaaras are pretty goddamn deadly, but they're not invincible. Did you really think you could take on a dozen Haiv fighters by yourself?"

As I glanced at Albarn in anticipation of her answer, I saw her hands starting to shake. "I had a plan. I would duck under cover and have Owen lure them over me. When they passed, I was going to come up and take them from behind. I thought he could do it! Skaigard had a ninety-seven evasion rating on the simulator!"

Tolchek sighed. "The Haiv pilot who shot him down was callsign Voodoo. I trained against her during my Mar-Sitaara qualifications. She had an interception rating of ninety-nine. Damn near perfect. Don't beat yourself up over Owen, Je'Sikka. It was about the best strategy you could come up with given the situation. Had you been up against any other fighter jockey, you might have had a chance of pulling it off."

Looking toward the pilots, I asked, "Did anyone get her? Voodoo?"

Qoalmun shook his head. "Nope. Between the three of us, we blew fourteen

Haiv fighters out of the sky. She was among the three that bugged out and got away."

One of the Narman officials got up and walked to the window of the *Hornet* to look at the other two Mar-Sitaaras. "Those three aircraft took out fourteen others?"

Tolchek nodded. "Yes, sir."

The Narman walked to the other side of the craft and gazed at the two Warp Haugs. "Do you think those three fighters are enough to get those freighters past that dreadnought they've got in orbit?"

"Well, for starters," Qoalmun answered, "with all the ammunition we expended tonight, you've actually only got about one and a half Mar-Sitaara fighters. Second, even if we had a hundred of them, we're still not getting past the *Nebulean Phoenix*."

The Narman's question gave me a sinking feeling in the pit of my stomach. "Why do you want to get past the *Phoenix*?" I asked, even though I was pretty sure I already knew the answer.

"How many Marines were on that dreadnought when you first arrived on Kanaris?" the Narman asked me.

"Half a million."

"And how many are on it now?"

"With our latest resupply? Probably about four hundred thousand. We have about a fifth of our contingent on the ground concentrated around Narman's Pyke."

"So there are still about a half-million Marines in theater? Despite the fact we estimate we've killed close to one hundred and fifty thousand troops since this conflict started? We've been at this for a couple of years, Lieutenant. You still have the same number of troops you had when it began. We don't."

I turned to the alien among us, noticing that he was now wearing the same type of goggles that adorned the rest of his kind. "What about your people? Haven't you gotten word to the Morghul about what's happening here? Don't you have anyone coming to help?"

Melki sighed. "Yes. After we were crushed at the Satapadaya, we believed all had been lost. Facing certain death at the hands of the Marines, we had nothing to lose. We sent a distress signal to the Heyanaus Quadrant, the part of the galaxy we're from."

The alien sighed as his shoulders slumped. "Yes, Eamon Tauk. The Morghul are coming. They have a long, long, way to go to get here, but they will eventually find Kanaris. We would rather not be here when they arrive."

Chapter 6

The Council

When we decided to switch sides, I assumed my Marines and I would be integrated into a larger Narman force. I was shocked to learn my group almost had the numbers to absorb them instead.

"You destroyed us at the Satapadaya," Leila Hyfer spat at me shortly after arriving on our base with an entourage of both human and alien representatives. She was the most senior Narman officer to escape the carnage my Marines had wrought upon them during that pivotal battle, and she was still very bitter about it. Turning to Black Francis, she snarled, "We trusted you, you son-of-a-bitch! You betrayed us! I should have you shot as a fucking traitor!"

Black Francis hung his head at the accusation. "I don't know what to tell you, Leila." His voice was barely a whisper. "At the time, I was convinced I was doing the right thing. I thought we were confronting a far greater evil. Obviously, I was horribly mistaken."

Hyfer hauled off and slugged Francis in the jaw as tears started streaming out of her eyes. Several members of the Narman entourage rushed in to separate her from my platoon sergeant, but she landed several more blows before her companions could drag her away. Black Francis made no attempt to defend himself.

"Do you have any idea how many of my people you slaughtered, you miserable piece of shit?!?" the Narman officer wept. "Do you?!?"

"Do you know how many of my people you killed?" I asked Hyfer as I stepped into the space between her and my gunnery sergeant.

Leila's mouth twisted into a malicious grin. "I don't, but I'd love to hear all about it!"

"You murdered damn near every one of them," I told her. "You had your Quarakai rip most of us apart at the Pyke, even those trying to surrender to you. You gutted others. You cut them open and hung them from the trees outside the main gate to greet us as we arrived."

A fearsome-looking Morghul stepped into my personal space, trying to intimidate me. From the corner of my eye, I caught Melki inching forward to ensure his compatriot did me no harm. "It was I who gutted those fiends," the being confessed. He spoke my language flawlessly. "I only did to yours what you monsters did to mine."

"Easy, Kryndil," Melki told him, revealing the alien's name. I had heard of him before. Mazada Duum told me he was a sadistic beast who got his jollies from skinning Samaari prisoners alive. "Eamon Tauk saved my life. He saved many others, too."

Kryndil huffed. "You might owe him, Melki, but this shitstain has yet to earn any favors from me."

"We're at war," said a Narman woman as she stepped forward, separating herself from the rest of the Narman group. She looked like a civilian but carried herself with the bearing of someone used to being in charge. "There's no shortage of grievances to be had by any side of this conflict. They've done horrible things to us, and we've returned the favor every chance we got. That's the nature of war, comrades. Stand down, Kryndil. Yes, these Marines were our enemies, but now they've come to us intending to become allies."

"You think we can trust them?!?" the belligerent alien scoffed.

"Not really," the woman answered. "We're certainly not letting them anywhere near our home base. Considering the shape we're in right now, though, I don't think we have the luxury of passing on any potential alliances. We don't have to get along, Kryndil, but if we don't work together, it'll hasten the end of both our forces."

I felt a lump rise in my throat. The woman did not come right out and say it, but the implication was that the Narmans would be keeping us at arm's length. They were not going to fight us, but they were not exactly going to embrace us either. Not until we established a great deal of trust with them.

Turning her attention to me, the woman took two steps forward and extended her hand. "Hello, Eamon Tauk. My name is Talia Ghona. After you captured my father at the Satapadaya, I ended up in charge of the human contingent of rebel forces on Kanaris. I believe we need to talk."

Taking her hand and shaking it firmly, I answered, "I believe we do."

"What?!?" I gasped as I felt my knees go weak. I knew the Marines had seriously depleted Narman forces, but I had no idea just how few were left.

Black Francis was stunned as well. He turned to look at me as if to ask, *What the hell have we gotten ourselves into?!?*

Talia Ghona repeated herself. "You wiped us out, Tauk. Satapadaya bled us dry. We're left just shy of forty-three hundred troops to fight with. We're combat ineffective. All we can do at this point is defend our home base."

"And try to figure out a way to escape this planet," Melki added. "We need to get out of here before Morghul forces start showing up."

We were gathered in the troop compartment of the *Niberian Hornet*. The ship's cockpit was too small to accommodate us all comfortably, and it looked as if we would be there for a very long time. Our defection came suddenly. The Narmans were not prepared to take in a group our size, nor did they have the resources to support us. We had to work out how to tend to the sick and wounded, where we could shelter the civilians, and how we could transport everybody where they needed to go. Now that we knew how few Narman fighters there were, the rebels wanted to know exactly what we were bringing to their party. We had a lot to discuss.

"How many people do you have out here?" asked Bengin Meinhopf, the man in charge of Narman intelligence.

"About eight thousand," Dmitri Naktada answered. He had just completed a census of the prisoners we had liberated. "Only about a third of them are fit for combat, though. The rest are injured, wounded, sick, too old, too young, or clinically exhausted. Given time, we may be able to coax half of them to the battlefield."

"Do you have weapons for them?" asked Kryndil.

Black Francis scoffed. "With the equipment we took from Takawa's Marines, we can outfit about a hundred of the poor bastards. Maybe. That doesn't mean they know how to use any of this shit, though."

"We can train them," I told Francis. "And we have to come up with a way to equip them. Assuming we can do that, it'll put us up to...What?...eight thousand troops?"

"Seven thousand four hundred and twenty-five," Naktada told me. "Against a half million Marines. That's sixty-seven to one."

"Alright, I get it," I snapped. "We're a little outnumbered."

"Eamon, we're a lot outnumbered."

"Goddammit! I'm aware of that!" Turning back to the spy chief, I asked, "You know, when you launched that offensive along the Satapadaya Front using deserters you had embedded behind our lines, you damn near overran us. Do you think you could do that again?"

Meinhopf shook his head. "It's harder. The Marines are starting to back away from using convicts in combat zones, and those prisoners are the backbone of our infiltration network. The command considers them security risks now. Most inmate laborers are back at Narman's Pyke these days."

I nodded at the intelligence officer. "Which is something we might use to our advantage in the future."

"How?" asked Hyfer.

"I don't know," I admitted. "Not yet. I need time to think about it. Meinhopf, do you have any of those convicts on your side right now?"

The spy chief smirked at me. "Almost all of them. We got the ones that are still embarked on the mothership, too."

"No shit?" asked Naktada as he again started crunching numbers in his head. "Convict laborers are almost twenty percent of the Marine Expeditionary Force. If you got all the MEF's prisoners, that's 96,000 more fighters on our side."

"Not quite," Meinhopf said. "The latest contingent of replacement troops arrived on station two months ago. It's the Suma Corps. That's a hundred thousand fanatics. No convicts. No conscripts. Nobody forced into the Marines for political reeducation. Only tried and true patriots. They're one hundred percent volunteers and equipped with all that fancy shit you have. Word is that they're being cycled through Camp Vayipar now, and when they're finished, they'll take over the mines' perimeter security. We can't get anywhere near them, let alone infiltrate them. Anyway, with the Suma Corps on the mothership, we're down to about 77,000 convicts."

"That still drops the Marine numbers to 423,000 and boosts ours to about eighty-four. That means we're only outnumbered by about five to one now."

I wagged my finger at Naktada. "Keep doing that. Conventional military doctrine says that to launch a successful offensive, we need to outnumber the defenders by three to one."

"You're not going to do that with convicts," Meinhopf told me. "Like your liberated mining camp inmates, those prisoners are untrained and unarmed. Not to mention very poorly disciplined."

"Yeah, but we have them, and the Marines don't," I countered. As I looked over my people to solicit ideas, my eyes rested upon Haeli Deboara. I invited her to the meeting to give a voice to those we freed from the Blue Shirts. "I would think that we'd enjoy universal support from the camp inmates, also. Do you know how many prisoners there are in the Harnillium mines, Haeli?"

Still dressed in the ragged coveralls she wore when we pulled her out of Saim-sun, Deboara shook her head. "They kept us all isolated from one another. I have no idea."

"I do," Meinhopf said. "There are twenty-four Harnillium mines of various sizes on Kanaris. Just over seventy-five thousand prisoners are being held there."

I was impressed with the Narmans' intelligence chief. He had the answers we needed. "Let's assume that a third of them are in combat shape. That'd be...."

"Twenty-five thousand," Naktada said. "That makes us 109,000 strong and reduces the Marine advantage to four to one."

Kryndil sighed. "Okay. You've got 109,000 troops willing to fight. So what? A hundred thousand of them have no weapons or training!"

"I'll figure that out," I assured Kryndil. "Right now, we're just working numbers. Meinhopf, ten percent of the Space Marines are made up of people forced into the Corps for political reeducation. How successful are you at recruiting them?"

"Almost a hundred percent."

"That's forty-thousand more to us," Naktada said. "That makes it 2.6 to 1. And Kryndil, those Marines *are* armed and trained to fight."

"Conscripts?" I asked. "They're half the MEF."

Meinhopf agreed. "You're right. We're about fifty percent successful at recruiting them."

"That's one hundred thousand additional leathernecks in our pockets," Naktada announced. "That makes us almost even. 1.1 to 1."

I sighed. "But still a long way away from the three to one we'll need to seize the initiative."

Melki shook his head nervously. "Seizing the initiative is not going to help us, Eamon Tauk. We need to get out of here if we want to survive!"

I sighed again. "I understand, Melki, but we could steal the entire space fighter fleet, all the troop transports, and every freighter operating on Kanaris, and we still wouldn't be able to get off the ground. The *Nebulean Phoenix* will blow every one of us out of the sky before we can even reach orbit altitude. If we want off this planet, we have to seize control of the mothership! That's why we need to come up with a three-to-one advantage!"

"What if we destroy the Suma Corps?" Kryndil asked.

I turned to Naktada and shrugged my shoulders. "What if we did?"

Naktada shrugged back. "Then we'd outnumber the Marines by about sixty-four thousand troops. That's good, but not good enough. It still wouldn't be anywhere near the three-to-one advantage you're aiming for. It'd be more like 1.3 to 1."

The crowd momentarily fell silent while everyone tried to figure out a way to gather more troops. We stayed that way until Naktada looked at Kryndil and said, "Wait a minute. If we could destroy Suma Corps and another similar-sized unit without taking any casualties ourselves, we might be able to pull it off. We left several destroyed freighters at Saimsun and Razbauten. We could harvest the Nexilium-228 from the reactor engines. With all the Harnillium we have all over the place...."

"Forget about that," Melki said. "We can't make any Harnillium bombs."

"Why not?" asked Naktada. "It wouldn't take much to rig up a device that could vaporize an area five times the size of Narman's Pyke."

Kryndil took his blaster from its holster and held it up for Naktada to see. "Manufacturing a bomb like that is different than putting small amounts of Nexilium and Harnillium together in a chamber to make an energy beam like we do in this weapon. The more material you collect, the larger the reactive field will be. If those fields overlap, they begin to react with one another, which will set off an uncontrolled detonation."

"We could calculate the field size to determine how much space we need to maintain to...."

"No, you can't," Kryndil argued. "You have to be able to predict the fluctuations of the reactive zone, and unless you have Harnillium with a constant purity, you won't be able to do it. And we don't have the capability of refining our ore to the level required to make such a prediction."

"When the Morghul first landed on Kanaris," Melki added, "there were thirty thousand of us. We did not know if the empire was still on our tails, so the best and brightest minds we had decided to build a Harnillium bomb to thwart any attack our enemies may launch. Three weeks into this endeavor, an accident obliterated more than a third of us. We're not making any more Harnillium bombs."

Naktada swallowed hard. "Then what are we going to do?"

"A better job convincing the Marines that ours is the more noble cause," Black Francis said. "We need more than fifty percent of the conscripts. We need some of the enlistees as well. And officers."

Bengin Meinhopf shook his head. "It's not enough. No matter how just our cause is, we're going to struggle to reach out beyond those who are not already severely disillusioned with the Kyperion League. Even if most Marines know we're on the right side of history, they won't want to sign up to fight in an army they think has no chance of winning."

I nodded. "Meinhopf's right. Deep down inside, I was done with the League a couple of years ago. I didn't jump ship until I had nothing to lose."

"Then maybe we need to convince more officers that staying with the League will cost them dearly," Melki said.

"Yeah," I responded. "We need to get officers to our side. The benefit to that is officers come with more Marines. Not only the convicts, the conscripts, or the political undesirables. But the NCOs and professional warriors as well."

Meinhopf shook his head. "I can't have my convicts approaching officers and NCOs. They'll get burned."

I agreed. "They sure will. Convicts don't mingle with sergeants and lieutenants. They have no way to gauge if they're becoming disaffected or not."

"You wouldn't happen to have someone inside Narman's Pyke that would be able to feel out any of the higher ranks, would you?" asked the spy chief.

I gave him a nervous nod. "I might. I do have an asset behind the colony's walls. She'll have access to officers and NCOs, but I don't think I would trust her to try recruiting the higher-ranking personnel we need to turn. She's a technician, not a spymaster."

Meinhopf grinned at me. "We need her to surprise us, Tauk. I was never trained in espionage, either. Back before all the trouble broke at Narman's Pyke, I was a pipe-fitter."

"No shit?" I laughed. "How the hell did you end up becoming the spy chief for the Narman Rebellion?"

"Attrition," Meinhopf said. "I paid close attention to the missteps my predecessors made that got them killed and did what I could to avoid making the same errors myself."

Once our first round of discussions concluded, I walked outside, catching Naktada and Black Francis sharing a flask of Bera Sukka Brandy in the rain. "Hey!" I snapped as I snuck up on them from behind. "What the hell do you think you're doing?"

Instinctively, Francis tried to hide the flask behind his back. "I'm sorry, sir. I know you'd want me to have a clear head in there, but...."

"So, are you going to share it with me or not?"

Naktada and Francis grinned at each other in relief, then Francis handed me the liquor. I took a small sip, mainly as a show of camaraderie. I did not actually want a drink, but I still took comfort from the sting of the brandy as it burned its way down my throat. After I swallowed, I turned to Naktada and asked, "What do you think about what the Morghul said regarding the Harnillium bomb?"

Naktada smiled. "I think they're full of shit. I could store those two materials five kilometers apart from each other and still find a way to launch them together when I needed to. Just because the Mogs don't know what they're doing doesn't mean I don't."

I nodded a couple of times as my mind processed what our Tech War Specialist told me. The man was brilliant. I had complete faith in his abilities. After taking a moment to look around and make sure no one else was within earshot, I leaned in toward my men and said, "Once the Narmans are gone, I want you to get back to Razbauten and pull the Nexillium out of the freighter reactors."

Francis craned his head around to point his chin at the trio of Warp Haugs we had parked at our base's eastern perimeter. "What about those?" he asked me.

"Leave them," I said. "It'll stoke the Morghul's suspicions if those things suddenly turn up without any fuel. Besides, as long as they're there, we'll always know where to get our hands on some Nexillium if we need it."

Chapter 7

Epiphanies of Idiocy

When Agent Nala Biragor returned from surveying the damage at Razbauten, she marched right into the office of Section 615's field commander against the protests of his assistant. It did not appear that she was disturbing anything important, not that she would have cared if she was. "That wasn't a mine!" she snapped at her supervisor. "That place was a goddamn concentration camp!"

Major Izo Kuusip did not appreciate Biragor's intrusion. He liked her tone even less. "The inmates of Razbauten were working off the debt they owed to the League. That facility was manned by proven enemies of the state, Agent Biragor."

"There were children in that place, sir!"

Kuusip squinted disapprovingly at his subordinate. "Children can throw grenades, set off explosions, and fire a pistol just as effectively as an adult. You, of all people, should know that."

Without thinking, Biragor placed her hand over her belly, upon which lay a gruesome reminder of a previous tour of duty on Terrakand. "Yes, sir, they can. They're also far more receptive to being rehabilitated."

The commandant's glare intensified. "Are you accusing the League of some sort of moral shortcoming?"

Biragor ground her teeth. "No, sir. A strategic one. Several, actually."

Commandant Kuusip did not look even remotely interested in Biragor's assessment. "You have expertise in labor camp administration, Nala? I thought your specialty was identifying Narman turncoats lurking amongst our gallant Marines.

Of course, I may be mistaken, considering how thousands of enemy infiltrators went undetected along the Satapadaya Front until they fragged their officers and damn near handed us our asses."

Biragor let the major's insult go unchecked. She was on record predicting how much discontent there had been among the infantry. It was Biragor's former supervisor who decided her findings did not politically align with Samaari dogma and chose not to forward them up the chain of command. That was why she was still there, and he was not. "Sometimes a fresh set of eyes are needed to point out the obvious, sir."

"Indeed," the major conceded. "Then, by all means, go on."

"For starters," Biragor told him, "most of those mines depend on Blue Shirts for their security...."

"Of course they do," Kuusip interrupted. "There are few people more ideologically equipped for that kind of work. Most are too soft for it."

"The Blue Shirts may be emotionally suited for driving an involuntary labor force to meet such ambitious production objectives, major, but intellectually speaking, they have some shortcomings."

Kuusip's eyes narrowed. "Are you saying they're feeble?" Being Samaari himself, the major loathed the stereotype that portrayed his people as incompetent and arrogant. He was even more maddened that one of his underlings was arrogant enough to propagate it right to his face.

"I'm not calling them stupid, sir. They're..." Biragor paused as she struggled to come up with a less offensive term than *sadists*. "I'm calling them overconfident. They believe so strongly in their superiority that they tend to underestimate those they're trying to keep under control."

"That's a ridiculously broad generalization."

"Is it?" Biragor asked. "Then why did they only assign one hundred guards to oversee two thousand inmates at Saimsun, one hundred and fifty over six thousand at Razbauten, or seventy-five over...."

"Okay, Agent Biragor, I...."

"They didn't even have enough ammo on them to...."

"*Okay*, Agent Biragor! I get your point. I'll have the Tahnebaht people review their staffing levels. Is that it?"

"Hardly. Samaari Blue Shirts may be…" Biragor paused again to pick words that would not inflame the major's delicate sensibilities. After a sigh of frustration, she finally said, "…patriotic enough for driving inmates like they do, but regular Marines, particularly conscripts, are not. Nor are the people inhabiting the planets those conscripts are typically harvested from. If word of this gets out…."

"It could teach ungrateful scum their fate if they decide to bite the hand that feeds them." Kuusip looked as if he was beginning to lose interest in their conversation.

"Or it may spark unrest that could be fanned clear across the League. That is something we can't afford right now with the specter of a Morghul conflict bearing down on us."

"Exactly," Kuusip said. "We're facing an existential threat if the aliens discover where we are, Agent Biragor. To survive, we need Harnillium to produce the weapons that put us on an equal footing with these beings and the time to develop them. We must also eradicate our internal threats to challenge the Morghul with a united front. These mines help us accomplish all those goals."

"If word of what is going on in those camps gets out, sir, our front will be anything but united. We won't just be trying to stamp out insurrections on Portuna and Terrakand. We'll be putting down rebellions on Maxaroan, Dabrishat, Wardaan…."

"Then don't let that information get out, Agent Biragor," Kuusip snarled.

"Sir, the Narmans just liberated thousands of inmates from those camps! I can guarantee you that genie is already out of the bottle!"

"Then you must push it back inside," Kuusip growled.

All Biragor could do for a couple of moments was stare at the major, blink, and wonder how the man kept from drooling on himself. Eventually, she asked, "How the hell do you expect me to do that?"

Kuusip shrugged. "That's your problem. Not mine."

"How's that my problem?!? I'm in charge of countering Narman recruitment efforts!"

"It's your problem because I'm making you the agent in charge of misinformation suppression also. Effective immediately."

"Sir, I can't undo something that has already happened!"

"Not with that attitude you can't."

"I can't with any attitude!" Biragor snapped. "Neither can you! Look, major, we have to get ahead of this! We need to bring those camps into the light! Blame the abuses on rogue elements of the Tahnebaht Conglomerate! Stop the atrocities and...."

"Blame?!?" Kuusip gasped. "Blame?!? If you want to blame someone for something, blame the traitorous inmates for the heinous acts they committed to land themselves in those mines! You seriously want to blame the Tahnabaht Conglomerate?!? That's ridiculous!"

"Sir! I...."

"That's enough, Agent Biragor," the major sighed dismissively. "You've wasted enough of my time today."

"But, sir!"

"Did you not hear me, Agent Biragor? That's enough! You're excused!"

The major was right. Any more discussion of the topic would have been a waste of time at that point. Hers, in particular. Unable to fathom Kuusip's arrogance, willful ignorance, and just plain stupidity, she turned on her heel and marched out the door without rendering any of the usual exit formalities.

Once she was back in the hallway and safely out of sight of Kuusip's assistant, Biragor's knees buckled, forcing her to lean against the wall for support. Her head was reeling, and she caught herself on the verge of hyperventilating as a devastating realization swept over her.

With people like Major Kuusip in charge, the League stands absolutely no chance of winning this war.

When I was finally released from my meeting with the Narmans and their Morghul allies, I was spent. I had not slept in days. I had also discovered that the force I had just defected to was on the verge of defeat, and our only hope for survival was to somehow seize control of one of the most powerful spaceships in the galaxy. Despite my desperate need for rest, I left the *Niberian Hornet* to walk around for a little while in an attempt to clear my head.

I wanted to be alone, but our haven was full of thousands of newly liberated inmates trying to get used to doing things without being told. Those who could walk were wandering aimlessly all over the grounds everywhere I looked. I was half tempted to stroll into the rainforest to find some solitude, but I did not feel up to the task of taking on a random soroquid all by myself.

"So, do you feel as doomed as I do right now?" asked Black Francis, catching up to me from my blind side.

I sighed. "Yeah, they aren't projecting a lot of confidence, are they?"

"Nope."

As the two of us stood there, Leila Hyfer walked by, staring down Black Francis as she passed.

"You knew her when you went to the other side at the Satapadaya Front, didn't you?" I asked my gunnery sergeant.

Francis nodded. "I did. I served beside her before they moved us out of the lower trenches. We got along really well."

"It must be weird to see someone like her after betraying them like you did. My god, look at her eyes. She must really hate your guts."

"She does," Black Francis agreed. "It's pretty obvious. And for some strange reason, it's also kind of hot. I'm going to go talk to her. I'll catch up with you later, sir."

"Hey, Francis!" I called out to my platoon sergeant before he got away. "I don't think I'm an officer anymore! Stop calling me 'sir!' Call me Eamon!"

●●‑◈‑●‑◈‑●●

I found Akkam Lumuk where he usually did the most good. He was with the medics, trying to help lift the spirits of their patients. Waiting until he was transitioning between bedsides, I slapped him on the back to ask how he was.

"I'm all right, I guess," he told me. "I'd still rather be back on Gorsu Qat, takin' care of my mama. You think I'll ever get back there, sir?"

I wanted to tell Lumuk he would, but I knew the odds were against him. "I sure hope so. By the way, I'm no longer an officer. You can stop calling me 'sir.'"

"Yessir."

"My name's Eamon. You can call me that."

"Okay...Eamon...sir..." Lumuk looked very uncomfortable. "Do I have to call you Eamon, sir?"

Shaking my head, I said, "You've earned the right to call me whatever you want. Can I get you anything, Akkam?"

The giant shook his head.

"Well, if I can, you come get me. Okay?"

"Okay, sir."

As I was walking away from the triage area, I glanced down and spotted Daino Deboara lying on a cot, buried beneath a blanket. I knelt beside the broken man and patted him on the shoulder. "How are you doing?"

Daino recoiled at my touch, showing the tears streaming down his face as he looked up at me. "I...I...I killed my boys. How do you think I'm doing?"

"I have no idea, sir. I can't even begin to imagine what you're going through."

"If the Blue Shirts had gotten ahold of them again...." Daino flexed his fingers open and closed, wincing at the pain flaring up in his knuckles. "I didn't have the strength to keep running with them both in my arms. My joints...my joints...they all feel like they're full of sharp little rocks. My knees, my shoulders, my elbows...I ain't got nothin' left in them anymore! I'm weak!"

"Shhh. Settle down, Daino. You're not weak. You broke yourself trying to keep your boys alive...."

"And they're both dead, anyways! I should've gone with them!" Daino moaned. "Someone should've killed me, too! I ain't no fuckin' good out here! Not like this!"

As luck would have it, Haeli Deboara approached us just as her husband was on the verge of finally breaking down. Having heard what he had said, she rushed to his side and wrapped her arms around his neck, convulsing into sobs on top of him. "Daino! Daino! Stop it! You're not weak! I know what you did! I saw it every day! The things you put yourself through to keep us going...it was superhuman! You can't give up! You can't leave me here! It's going to get better! You'll see! I promise!"

Knowing Haeli and her husband needed time alone, I stood up and walked away, only to run into Akkam Lumuk again. "Is that her husband?" the behemoth asked.

I nodded.

"Is he gonna be okay?"

I shook my head. "He's a broken man, Akkam. Unless he can convince himself that he has something to live for, I don't think he's going to make it."

On my way back to the *Niberian Hornet*, I passed a small corral that, judging by the smell of it, had probably once been used to hold ubatis. It now contained our prisoners, forced to sit in the sludge with their hands bound behind their backs. Supai Takawa and Deena Vulk were tied to fence posts on opposite sides of the pen and gagged to prevent them from communicating with each other. They were being guarded by two of my First Squad Marines, Rikkal Tando and Zarba Asosi. "Where are the pilots?" I asked the latter.

"Considering that we wouldn't be here without them, we decided to allow them to stay locked in their staterooms instead of spending the night sleeping in ubati shit."

"Are they under guard?"

Asosi nodded. "They got two apiece."

"Two? How come you have twice as many Marines watching them as you do these people? You think they're that high of an escape risk?"

Asosi shook his head. "They ain't escaping, sir. Where the hell would they go? They'd be 'pede bait out there on their own. No, the extra guards are for their own protection. Sergeant Korman doesn't want any of the Razbauten inmates getting their hands on them."

I sighed. Had I not been so exhausted, I was sure I would have thought of that. "It's a good thing that at least Korman's got the presence of mind to account for that kind of shit. Yeah, we're not done with those guys yet. We'll probably need them to get us out of here at some point."

As I spoke with the guard, I could feel Agent Takawa's eyes boring into me from behind. After taking my leave from Asosi, I marched over to the prisoner and untied the cloth covering his mouth. "You got something you want to say to me, Supai?"

Takawa spat in my face and laughed. "Do you think you're going to get away with this, Tauk? Do you have any idea how many Narmans there are right now?" Craning his neck back to try to point his chin at Deena Vulk, he said, "Go ahead and ask her! They got no more than six thousand people left. Not fighters, Tauk. *People.* You think that's enough to resist us?"

"Maybe we don't have to resist you," I told Takawa. "Maybe we just have to hold out long enough for the rest of the Morghul to get here to do our heavy lifting."

"You'd better hope we get to you before the Morghul do. From what we've been told, the aliens from the empire consider their Kanarisian brethren traitors. If they're headed this way, it ain't to help them. It's to wipe the fuckers out. Think of them as a million doped-out Kryndils, chomping at the bit to sink their teeth into human flesh."

I nodded toward a group of former inmates. "I doubt the Morghul could be any worse than you."

Takawa sneered at the freed miners. "Fuck those traitors. They had it coming."

Sticking the gag back into Takawa's mouth, I told him, "So do you."

Takawa's words were still ringing in my ears when I climbed back aboard the *Niberian Hornet.* I was greeted by Dmitri Naktada, who was reading technical documents on the engineering console, and Black Francis, who was sporting a new black eye. Grinning at my platoon sergeant, I asked, "So, how'd it go with Hyfer?"

My platoon sergeant smiled back at me and pointed at his shiner. "I think she likes me!"

"Where have you been?" asked Naktada.

"Walking around. Trying to process what I've done."

"Any regrets?" he asked.

I let out an exhausted sigh and collapsed into the *Hornet's* co-pilot chair, reminding myself that Owen Skaigard would never need it again. "For myself?

No. I was marked for death. Had I not done what I'd done, I'd have been killed in the Arad Valley. For you guys, though? Yeah, I'm beginning to think you'd have had better odds if I'd not dragged you all into this. I'm having difficulty figuring out how this will end up as anything other than a big old suicide mission."

Black Francis took a seat in the captain's chair. "Takawa was leading us into a Killbilly ambush, sir. With the way those psychopaths are armed, even knowing they were there would probably not have saved us. Do you think those bastards would've spared us after all that trouble you had with Buffy, Lumuk, and Wooster Mikkaine?"

I shrugged.

"They most certainly wouldn't have. They're afraid of us, sir," Naktada said.

"Of a single platoon? That sounds a bit far-fetched."

"Does it?" asked Black Francis as he waved his hand toward the *Hornet's* bay window. "All I have to do is look outside to see the bastards were smart to fear us! A few days ago, we set out on a mission with less than a hundred people. When it was all over, we were thousands! Look, the Marines are stronger than we are. Much stronger! But that's all they know! Their entire war plan is predicated on overwhelming force. Lieutenant...."

"Call me Eamon, Francis."

"Eamon, think about this for a minute! They've got all the Marines, all the aircraft, all the artillery, and all the resources. But who do they have calling all the shots?"

The lightbulb suddenly went off in my head. "The Samaaris," I mumbled.

Black Francis pointed his index finger at me. "Exactly. They have businessmen pretending to be military masterminds. In other words, they have all the fucking idiots."

●●◄●►●●

Chapter 8

ELIA

When we defected to the Narmans, there were eleven members of my platoon we could not trust enough to include in our plans. They were all good people but had strong familial ties to their home planets. We did not think they could abandon their loved ones to fight an entity that likely still retained the fierce allegiance of their folk. Even so, once given the choice to join us or return to their kin, four decided to follow us into the Narman fold.

The prudent thing to do would have been to kill the rest. Had we executed our loyalists, however, we would no longer have been able to claim any moral superiority over the League. Since that was the argument we used to convince our Marines to take up arms against their former friends and comrades, we set seven of our platoon free in the Arad Valley and allowed them to find their way back to Marine forces.

The League did not treat them kindly upon their return.

The Killbillies that initially plucked them from the grass plains of the Arad Valley did not believe they were still Marines in good standing. They thought them to be turncoats that became separated from the rest of their treasonous platoon.

Tai Himoar, formerly one of my First Squad riflemen, was the first to regret not joining the Narmans with the rest of us. Of the four male Marines we released, he looked the weakest. The Killbillies set upon him the moment they had him in custody. They spent hours pulling out that poor man's fingernails, piercing his eyes with needles, and amputating random appendages. Through all that, Himoar's story never changed. It was, after all, the truth. Eventually, the inquisitors castrated their victim to soften up the other male captives, then let their ubatis eat him alive.

While the surviving men wailed and did everything they could to convince their captors they were not traitors, the Killbillies turned their attention to Elia Gyanis and Idris Jatmika, spending the night doing to them what Qilkorians typically did to females unfortunate enough to fall into their custody. Because of the special reverence their religion afforded to the Samaari nation, they spared Silma Hauken. They left her tied up beside them and made her watch as they ravaged her platoon sisters.

Fortunately for Arno Magger, Kobura Sunaipa, and Timit Gloav, a small squad of Section 615 Kommandos arrived at the Killbilly camp the following morning, taking control of the prisoners before they could meet the same fate as PFC Himoar. Though they restrained themselves from abusing the rescued Marines in the same manner as the Qilkorians had, the Kommandos still treated them as hostile prisoners. They were returned to Narman's Pyke and confined in Section 615's interrogation center. During their third night there, Timit Gloav hanged himself in his cell.

For eight straight days, Section inquisitors questioned the Marines continuously. The prisoners barely slept, were not fed, and were only provided water as a reward for divulging information their captors deemed sufficiently valuable. Though the Section agents spared them the sexual barbarism they experienced at the hands of the Qilkorians, the prisoners were still subjected to regular bouts of violence, much of which was quite savage.

Eventually, Idris Jatmika broke and confessed to being a mole. "It's me!" she screamed at her interrogators as she collapsed onto the cement floor of her cell. "I'm the one you're looking for! Tauk sent me here to spy on you from the inside! To commit acts of sabotage! To kill our commanders! Hang me if you have to! Just stop this bullshit! STOP IT!"

Agent Wahtstoan grinned at finally breaking one of his subjects. Turning to his supervisor, he said, "See, I told you these fuckers were rebels!"

Nala Biragor rolled her eyes and knelt beside the captive. The humid air caused a constant stream of condensation to flow down off of the cool cement walls, combining with the mold on the ground to cover the floor with a coal-colored sludge half a centimeter thick. Biragor's gloved hand turned black the instant it made contact with the deck. "Lance Corporal Jatmika," Nala said in a calm but authoritative voice, "what were you sent here to sabotage?"

"What?" the Marine sobbed.

"What were you sent here to sabotage?"

"Anything I can! Whatever I can get to!"

Biragor sighed. "I need specifics, Jatmika. Were you to go after the power grid?"

"Sure!"

"What about our armory?"

"Yes!" Jatmika cried. "That too!"

"Did they want you to...?"

"They wanted me to destroy whatever I could get my hands on!" Jatmika wailed. "Everything! Whatever you say they wanted me to do! I'll confess to whatever you say!"

Biragor lifted her hand from the cell floor and used her index finger to pull a wayward strand of hair from her prisoner's eyes, leaving behind a glistening black smear in its wake. "I don't believe you, dear."

Jatmika began to descend into hysterics. "What do you mean?!? I'm confessing!"

"No," Biragor said. "You're telling us what we want to hear. You were one of Tauk's machine gunners, not a sapper. You weren't trained to blow up things. Do you know what I think you are?"

At this point, Jatmika was sobbing too hard to answer. All she could do was shake her head.

"I think you're a patriot, Jatmika. A hero." Craning her head toward the only entrance to the space they occupied, Biragor shouted, "Guards!"

As two field Kommandos opened the door and stepped into Jatmika's cell, Biragor ordered them to take their prisoner to the showers, issue her a new uniform, and return her equipment to her.

"What?!?" Agent Wahtstoan protested. "Are you serious?!? She fucking confessed!"

"All six of them tell consistent stories, Blaiq. They had no idea about the defection until they found themselves locked in their seats aboard Albarn's Mar-Sitaara. Tauk gave them the choice to join the Narmans or return to the Marines. They all gave us the exact names of the troops who decided to stay with Tauk after the operation started. We tore apart their equipment and found nothing incriminating, no secret communications gear, no software viruses, nothing. These are our people, Wahtstoan."

"Are they?" Wahtstoan asked as he watched the Kommandos drag Jatmika from the cell. "You think they're still on our side after everything we put them through? After what the Qilkorians did to them?"

Biragor slowly shook her head in disgust. "I don't know. I would certainly consider them something of a security risk now. We'll give them a choice to stay with us if they want or be discharged for combat fatigue."

Agent Wahtstoan blinked in disbelief. "You're letting them go home?"

Biragor nodded. "As long as they sign a non-disclosure form stating that everything they've seen on this planet is subject to Tier One Security Classification and that revealing any of it will result in the immediate execution of a Termination Warrant. In case that's not enough, let Jatmika and the other ladies know that if they fuck me on this, I'll hire the same Killbillies that molested them to carry it out. They're to reveal nothing about what happened to them here."

Elia Gyanis and Idris Jatmika had been inseparable almost since Gunny Brumit assembled my platoon for me a couple of years before. When Jatmika saw what the inquisitors had done to her friend, she lost her composure and launched herself at Gyanis, wrapping her arms around the armorer's neck. "Those sons-of-bitches!" Jatmika wailed. "They're going to fucking pay for this!"

Despite the pummeling her face had taken, Elia smiled in her friend's embrace, revealing a couple of her broken teeth. "Don't," Gyanis told her friend. "We're free now. It's over. Don't give anyone any reason to hurt us again."

"We should've went with Tauk!" Jatmika said as she pulled back to look at her comrade. Elia Gyanis's left eye was swollen shut and colored multiple shades of black and purple. Her jaw had been cracked, her lips were puffy, and several handfuls of long dark brown hair had been ripped from the sides of her head. Without thinking, Idris reached out and ran her thumb across a deep cut that ran vertically across the Marine's left cheek. "That's going to leave a scar."

Gyanis shook her head as she stroked the dreadlocks piled up atop Jamika's crown. "They're going to fix me. Agent Biragor said that the League made a horrible mistake and they'll make everything right again. She said she's going to ensure that when the surgeons are done with me, I'm going to look just like new! Didn't they offer to do the same thing to you?"

Jatmika bristled at Elia's optimism. She always thought her friend was a bit too trusting for her own good. "I ain't letting those fuckers anywhere near me with a knife. I told them they could take their help and shove it up their ass."

Elia used her broken fingers to take her friend's face in her hands. "You need to stop, Idris! You're becoming what they suspected you were!"

Jatmika placed her hands atop Gyanis's. "We enlisted, Elia. We volunteered for this shit. We did our duty. We killed for these people. My god! Even after what we saw them doing at those mining camps, we stood by the League! And how did they repay us? They raped us. They imprisoned us. They beat us, accused us of being traitors, and tortured us! I'm not letting them get away with that!"

"*They* wouldn't have done any of that to us if Tauk hadn't set us up, Idris."

Jatmika winced, recoiling from her friend. "What?"

Elia felt awful playing that act to the woman she considered her closest friend, but her life depended upon everyone believing she was a true loyalist. 'Everyone' included Jatmika. Even if Idris was fully vested against the League now, Gyanis knew her friend lacked the self-control necessary to maintain their cover. Jatmika could be dangerously impulsive. And frighteningly violent. The woman was a product of some of the most vicious battles ever fought on Kanaris. She was no sadist, but Idris Jatmika was a true killer.

"That son-of-a-bitch knew where the death squads were," Elia told her friend, genuinely trying to steer her loyalties back toward the League. Gyanis knew Jatmika would lash out and get herself killed if she could not. She needed Idris to focus her rage on their former platoon leader to save her life. "The lieutenant couldn't kill us himself without losing the goodwill of the platoon, so he set us down in the Arad Valley and marched us right into a trap in the hopes that the

Killbillies would do his dirty work for him."

Unable to process what Gyanis was telling her, Jatmika pushed herself away from her confidante and stumbled to her feet. Before she could respond, the door to the interrogation center's out-processing lobby opened again, admitting Silma Hauken.

Like Jatmika and Gyanis, Hauken was outfitted in a dark green Marine uniform so new that there were no insignia patches affixed to it yet. That was where the similarities ended, though. Hauken had not been molested by the Killbillies in the Arad Valley. It did not appear that she had been maltreated by the inquisitors, either. She was a bit thinner, her cheeks had been drawn gaunt by dehydration, and the bags under her eyes showed she had not gotten much sleep, but otherwise, she appeared no worse for wear.

"Oh no!" Hauken gasped in genuine shock as she looked at Jatmika. Idris's bruises shone brightly, even through her ebony skin, advertising the mistreatment she had been subjected to. One of the stitches on her head had also opened up, and traces of fresh blood began seeping into the parts between the woman's dreadlocks. The Samaari Marine rushed forward to hug the machine gunner. "Idris! I'm so sorry!"

Before Hauken could put her hands on her, Jatmika planted both palms into the Samaari woman's chest and shoved her onto her backside. "Get the fuck away from me!"

As Hauken lay stunned upon the ground, Gyanis jumped up to grab her friend and ensure she did not do the lance corporal any more harm. Jatmika had never had a very high opinion of the Samaari spotter, but now she was seething with unchecked hatred toward the young woman. Gyanis knew what Jatmika was capable of when her blood was up. She was afraid that the machine gunner could kill Hauken right there in the out-processing lobby. "Idris! What the hell's the matter with you?!?"

"What's the matter with me?!?" Jatmika yelled. "What's the matter with you?!? She did this shit to us!"

"No, she didn't!" Gyanis yelled back. "She got captured, too!"

"Oh, nooo!" Idris insisted. "She didn't go through half of what we did! Did that bitch have to take on a train of a half-dozen dirty-ass Killbillies?!? No, she fucking didn't! Did she get smacked around by a steady succession of Section 615 inquisitors?!? Look at her! Of course, she didn't! Why didn't she?!? Huh?!?"

Idris Jatmika broke free of Gyanis's grip and took a few menacing steps toward Hauken. "Why was that, Silma?!? What did you do to earn all this special treatment?!? You tell them who you were? Who your daddy was? What kind of connections your goddamn grandparents had?!? You fucking Samaaris! It was your people that did all this shit to us!"

"That's enough!" snapped a sergeant as he led two other guards into the lobby. The three of them were carrying the women's field gear. After dumping out the bag of equipment on the lobby floor, the sergeant marched over to Jatmika and grabbed her by the collar, nearly lifting her off her feet. "Talk like that's going to land your ass right back in the dungeon, bitch!"

"Don't!" Hauken shouted as she jumped to her feet and grabbed the Kommando's arm. "Please! She's not well! That shouldn't be any surprise considering what she's been through!"

The sergeant hardly looked phased by Hauken's pleas, but he let Jatmika go anyway. He then nodded to his subordinates, signaling them to dump out the bags they were carrying. "Take an inventory of your gear, ladies. Ensure everything's there and make an official report of anything that may no longer be in working order so it can be replaced. Do it expeditiously. We're closing down the lobby in forty-five minutes."

"Wait!" Hauken called out before the Kommandos could get away. "Where's Arno Magger and Kobura Sunaipa?"

"In the hospital," the sergeant spat. "They won't be joining you."

Idris Jatmika did not bother to check her gear. She immediately set to throwing it all back inside the bag it was brought to her in.

"What are you doing?" Gyanis asked her.

"Getting the fuck out of here. I'm getting out of the Corps. I'm getting off of this rock. I'm going home and...."

Having not learned her lesson the first time, Hauken reached out to touch Jatmika's shoulder. "Idris...."

Spotting her combat dagger lying in the pile of junk at her feet, Jatmika picked it up and pressed the tip of the blade against the bottom of Hauken's throat. "I swear, Silma! If you EVER try to lay those Sammy rat fingers on me again, I will fucking gut you! DO YOU UNDERSTAND ME?!?"

Elia wanted to intervene on Silma's behalf, but froze in place. She feared that if she spooked the enraged woman, Hauken would bleed for it. Gyanis stood utterly still, forcing herself to cope with the realization that her best friend was truly lost.

Holding her hands up in surrender, Hauken nodded as tears welled up in her eyes. The Samaari woman stayed that way until Jatmika packed up her equipment and stormed out the door. Only then did Silma let her arms fall to her sides. Turning toward Elia, she said, "I'm sorry. I didn't mean to...."

"You don't have to apologize for not suffering as much as we did, Silma."

Stifling a sob, Hauken asked, "Then why is Idris blaming me for all this shit?"

"She's not blaming you," Elia answered. "She's blaming the League. Since the League is run by Samaaris and you happen to hail from Samaar Ghun, she's lumping you in with them."

"That's not fair," Hauken argued, her voice cracking. "We're not monsters, Elia."

"I know," Gyanis lied.

The Samaari took a moment to gaze out the door Jatmika had recently shoved her way through. "You think if I gave her some time she'd...?"

"Stay away from her, Silma," Elia warned. "I've known Idris a long time. She was not in good shape before all this happened, and now I'm pretty sure they broke her way beyond the point where she could be put back together. She's going to hurt someone. In fact, she's probably going to hurt a lot of people. If you don't stay away from her, you're going to be one of them."

Unable to respond to that, Hauken shifted her attention to the equipment the guards dumped at her feet. Picking up her dismantled armor, she tossed it back down upon the deck, using it as an excuse to finally unleash her tears. "They tore it all apart! Ruined it!"

Gyanis nodded. "It's okay. The Marines will replace everything the inquisitors destroyed."

"It's not okay!" Hauken snapped back. "My comm codes were in here! My correspondence history! All the messages I ever got from Draiq!"

Elia sighed as she inspected her own armor. Hauken interpreted it as a sigh of sympathy, but it was actually a sigh of relief. The war had taken a heavy toll on everyone on Kanaris, even on Section 615's tech specialists. The varsity team had largely been wiped out, and the third stringers the spooks were now using missed the chip Gyanis had added to her armor. She was still in business. Now, she only needed a way to discreetly disseminate the data it contained. Much to her relief, the solution to that problem might have presented itself with their dismantled armor.

Elia Gyanis was never particularly close to Silma Hauken, but she knew the Samaari once had a fiancée named Draiq Warmaqt. He was killed during the operation to pacify the Nimnaya Valley. "I'm sorry, Silma," Gyanis said to her comrade. "There was more in your data system than messages, wasn't there?"

Hauken nodded. "All our pictures...."

Elia smiled sympathetically, seizing the opportunity. "Give it to me. I'm sure I can put it all back together."

"And recover my data?" Hauken asked. "You can do that?"

"I'm an armorer who spent years working with Dmitri Naktada," Elia assured her. "After that, there isn't a whole lot that I can't do."

Chapter 9

The Proposition

The stolen freighters offered our liberated inmates protection from the elements, but conditions inside were cramped, claustrophobic, and unsanitary. Packing thousands of malnourished, exhausted, and physically compromised people into such tight quarters within an incredibly humid environment created the perfect breeding ground for disease. To discourage the outbreak of an epidemic that we lacked the resources to mitigate, we encouraged those well enough to walk to spend as little time as possible indoors. The climate on Kanaris was far from comfortable, but wandering aimlessly in the rain felt much better than drowning in your own blood while fighting a bout of hemorrhagic fever.

Knowing Daino Deboara would likely not survive a mild case of diarrhea let alone something like that, I donated my tent and cot to Haeli. Black Francis added his bed to the deal so neither would be forced to sleep on the ground. Both of us had been living on the *Hornet* anyway.

At first, I worried the other prisoners might resent the Deboaras' special treatment, but it seemed to make sense to them. Those who fled Saimsun knew Haeli as the woman who led the uprising against the Blue Shirts. The people rescued from Razbauten saw her as their savior, the one who convinced us to risk our lives to attack a camp about which we knew next to nothing. Word spread that I was reluctant to commit my platoon to a mission without a plan, but had been bullied into it by an emaciated woman who barely looked old enough to attend high school. The liberated inmates considered Haeli Deboara a hero. And their leader. They came to her with their issues and concerns, not me. The overwhelming majority of them believed she had earned the tent in spades.

Daino Deboara suspected their shelter had been earned in other ways, though. He knew about our night together in Saimsun and believed my gesture was predicated upon the hope of future trysts with his wife. "What the hell do you want?" he growled at me as I arrived at their door uninvited after we got things wrapped up with the Morghul.

"Daino!" Haeli snapped at him. "Eamon's the one who put this roof over our heads! Show a little gratitude!"

"For raping my wife?!? Fuck him!"

I could see the color rushing into Haeli's face, part out of anger and part out of embarrassment. "Shush! He didn't rape me!"

That was not the right thing to tell her husband. Not that there was anything Haeli could have said that would have eased his anxiety. Daino slowly lifted his arms to cover his eyes with his hands and moaned, "I fucking knew it! You wanted him, didn't you?"

"Goddammit, Daino! Stop it! We both did what we had to in order to survive! When are you going to understand that?!?" Indignantly jumping from her seat to lead me outside, she snapped, "You weren't the only one who made sacrifices, Daino! We all did!"

"Wait!" Daino shouted as his wife dragged me toward the door. "Where do you think you're going?!? Don't leave me here, Haeli! Don't you dare go away with that son-of-a-bitch!" Daino tried to get off his cot to chase after us, but his knees gave way the moment he put weight on them. He fell back crashing into his bed and started to wail.

Haeli buried her head in her hands as soon as we emerged into the rain outside. "I'm sorry, Eamon. He's not well. It's killing him to be this way." She paused to lift her face from her palms and cast a teary gaze back at the tent. "It's killing me, too."

Haeli looked vulnerable. Truth be told, though, she always had. Haeli Deboara was short, not even coming up to my collarbones. She had been out of Saimsun for over two weeks but was still significantly undernourished. Between her stature and thin frame, a casual observer could have easily mistaken her for an awkward teenager. It was not until you looked into her haunting blue eyes that you realized this was a woman who had tasted the blood of her enemies, and her invalid husband was the only thing that kept her from ravenously prowling for more. I sensed her to be a waif in the larval stages of becoming one formidable warrior. It was why I was there.

Turning to face me, Haeli said, "I've tried to make him understand why we needed to do what we did, Eamon, but he's having none of it. He thinks you want something from me."

I let out a long sigh. "Well, he's right, Haeli. I do."

Deboara winced and recoiled, stepping backward to put more distance between us. Realizing I had been misunderstood, I reached out and touched her shoulder. "Not that, Haeli. I'm sorry. I know that sounded wrong. What I want from you is your experience."

"In what?" Haeli asked, looking relieved.

"In being a prisoner. You led the uprising in Saimsun. You know how those prisoners think, how to reach them. You were in the meeting we had with the Morghul. If we're going to get the hell out of here, I need troops — a lot of them. There are 75,000 inmates working the Harnillium mines on Kanaris. We need to get them out of those camps."

Haeli's eyes narrowed at me. "So you can use them as cannon fodder?"

I shrugged. "That's not the way I would've phrased it, but yeah, we need them to fight. If they don't, they won't stand a chance at surviving this place. Neither will we."

As Haeli went to respond, she was interrupted by her husband pleading with her to come back inside. He sounded as if he was in agony, and she looked very anxious to see if he was okay.

Trying to divert Haeli's attention back to me, I told her, "I'm putting together a unit to infiltrate the camps. It's going to be made up of former prisoners who can pass as inmates, organize the captives, and collect the intelligence we need to support them from the outside. When we're ready, you'd have the miners rise up from within while we attack from beyond the perimeter. Ideally, we'd like to do multiple camps at a time, taking as many out as possible before the Blue Shirts can change tactics and force us to recalibrate."

"HAELI!" screamed Daino. "HAELIIIII!!!"

Once her husband's voice died down, I added, "I want you to lead it. We're going to train the shit out of you before you go, so it won't be easy, but you could be the difference in helping us get out of this place."

"HAELIIII!"

Deboara shook her head. "I...I...I don't know, Eamon. I don't know if I can. When we were in that mine, Daino saved us. He did the work of three men to make sure our quotas got met and we didn't end up incinerated as dead weight. I owe it to him to return the favor. He needs me, Eamon."

"He needs you to help get us out of here. Haeli, that's the best way you have to save that man's life."

"Maybe, but..."

"There is no 'but.' We have to keep hitting the Marines, keeping them off balance. If we let up and let them figure out how few we are, they're going to come at us in force. If they strike before we're ready for them, it's all over."

"I understand that, but Daino...."

"HAELIIIIIII!!!"

I watched a grimace wash across Haeli's face, and, for a brief instant, saw an expression of rage directed toward her husband. "I need time to think about it."

"We don't have time," I informed her.

"HAELI! I NEED YOU!"

"I have to go," Haeli said as she turned to walk back inside.

I grabbed her arm and tried another tack. "Do you remember when we pulled you out of the jungle? Nila Chisek asked you why you didn't die with your babies."

"Yeah," Haeli spat as she struggled to escape my grip. "I remember that fucking cunt!"

"Do you remember what you told her?"

Haeli struggled harder. "Let me go!"

"You told her that if you had died with your babies, there'd be no one left to avenge them."

With her free arm, Haeli slapped me across the face. I let go of her while she was still pulling against me, causing her to stumble backward. When she regained her balance, she pointed her index finger at me and snarled, "Fuck you, Tauk!"

"Haeli, I'm handing you the opportunity to make good on that promise."

"HAELLLLLLIIIII!!!"

"I'll make good on that promise, Tauk! That I can goddamn guarantee! But I'm going to do it when I'm fucking ready! It's going to happen on my terms! Not yours! Now, I have a man in there who fucking *destroyed* himself for us. I'm going back inside to care for him as he cared for me."

Haeli stormed away and stomped toward the door of her tent. Before she went inside, however, she paused to look back at me for a split second. It was then that I saw the last place she wanted to be was back inside that shelter. And I could see that she hated herself for feeling that way. Had it not been for her husband, she would have been begging me to unleash her against the Blue Shirts.

For a split second, I felt our cause might benefit by getting Daino Deboara out of the way, and became instantly disgusted with myself for even considering that as a viable option.

You'd better be careful, Tauk. If you don't pay attention, you just might end up becoming one of the monsters that you're trying to slay.

●●◄❖❁❖►●●

Chapter 10

ORAL HISTORY

When I returned to the *Niberian Hornet* that evening, I was surprised to find Melki and Bengin Meinhopf waiting for me. They were perched upon a pair of folding chairs under one of the Mar-Sitaara's wings, where the rain had a harder time soaking them. The *Hornet's* pilot was keeping them company.

"What are you doing here?" I asked the pair as I strolled up to Albarn's ship. "I thought you two went back to Xaramika." During our discussions, I learned that Xaramika was what the Morghul called their main settlement, though they were careful not to reveal any clues about where it may be located.

Meinhopf stood to greet me. "We covered a lot of ground, Tauk. Your openness and transparency helped us resolve a lot of big issues pretty damned fast. I think we'll all be stronger because of it."

"I'm glad you feel that way," I told them.

The spy chief nodded. "What you provided went a long way toward building a foundation of mutual trust between us."

"But the information really only flowed one way, Eamon Tauk," Melki added. I noted that he was not wearing the goggles the aliens usually wore. Apparently, they did not need them in the dark. "From you to us. If we're going to have a fruitful partnership, I feel it only fair to offer you something in return. Is there any information you think you need from us?"

As Je'Sikka Albarn motioned for one of her crew members to bring me a chair, I looked at the alien and said, "*Need* to know? At this point, not really. There are plenty of things I would *like* to know, however."

"Like what?" the alien elder asked.

"Like, what are you doing here?"

Meinhopf grinned. "I figured you would've asked where Xaramika is."

"I'm certainly curious about it, but right now, I don't think it's very important. Besides, you wouldn't tell me anyway. If you did, you'd be a fool."

Meinhopf smiled. "You're right."

Melki stood up from his seat and walked closer to where I stood. "To answer your question, we Morghul are hiding here. As you may have guessed, we are not from Kanaris. We're from the Heyanaus Quadrant, an expanse of the galaxy much closer to its center. Tragically, our race is one that often exceeds even yours in its brutality."

"Then why did you call them for help?" asked Je'Sikka Albarn.

"Because after we were annihilated at the Satapadaya Front, we had nothing left to lose," Melki told her. "The Marines already showed us what to expect if we fell into the League's hands...."

"What?" Albarn blurted out. "Are you telling me some of your people had already been taken prisoner by us?"

"Yes," Melki answered. "We got them back, though. What was left of them anyway."

"That was before your MEF arrived here," Meinhopf said. "When Narman Pyke's original security detachment first entered Morghul territory, there was a confrontation with an alien homestead. A Morghul family was captured by the Marines and transported back to Narman's Pyke, where they were experimented on. Cruelly. After we liberated the colony, we recovered their remains and the video of what had been done to them. To say what I watched was disturbing would not do it justice."

"As hard as it was for him to watch," Melki said, "It was devastating for Kryndil. The victims of that travesty were his daughter, her husband, and their children."

That explained a lot about Kryndil.

"You mentioned that you came here to hide," I said, trying to direct the conversation away from the outrage committed against Kryndil's family.

"Our ancestors were fleeing the Morghul Empire," Melki continued. "They were rebels."

"Really?" Je'Sikka asked. "They were freedom fighters, too?"

Melki grinned. "Hardly. The founders of our community just picked the wrong side in a contested succession, the wrong despot, so to speak. They fought to press their claim and lost. That's generally the way things happen in the Empire. When the dust settled, their choices were exile or death. They chose to flee, traveling as far as their damaged spacecraft would carry them, searching for an unexplored, habitable planet. Well, barely habitable in Kanaris's case."

Petty Officer Wadi Farad emerged from the ship and placed a chair beside me. As Melki and I both sat down, I asked, "They didn't like it here?"

"Do you?" Melki replied. "Kanaris was, and remains, a hard place to thrive on, especially without a means of resupply from one's native environment. The constant rain, the fauna, the microbes, and the natural calamities all took a toll on us. Thirty thousand Morghul landed on Kanaris, Eamon Tauk. Three generations later, four hundred of us remain. When you discovered this place, there were not nearly enough of us left to defend ourselves from you."

"Didn't you ever consider making contact and allying yourself with the colony?"

Melki laughed. "With humans? No, we were well aware of your nature."

"Our nature?" Albarn asked. "What did you know about our nature?"

"Quite a lot," Melki assured her. "In fact, I was told Daku Samadari backed the same person for emperor that our grandparents did."

Melki's tone suggested that Je'Sikka and I should have known who Daku Samadari was—the looks on our faces implied otherwise.

"You never heard of him either?" the Morghul elder asked. "The pirate king of the Heyanaus? He and his corsairs were human."

I shook my head. "Not ringing a bell."

"Ah. Whatever. Anyway, humankind has been known to the Morghul for centuries, ever since your species started traveling between the stars. Several of your lost vessels ended up in our domain. Others were captured by slavers and sold to us. Humans are rare in the Heyanaus but hardly unheard of. We knew what they were capable of, so we decided it was in our best interests to avoid interacting with Kyperion Marines."

Meinhopf continued the story. "We discovered the Morghul through the Quarakai. At the time, we thought they were just another animal. The Pyke's lead biologist, Dr. Briiz, had been studying them around our settlement and figured out they were pretty intelligent, though he still grossly underestimated just how smart they were. Wanting specimens to research but having no desire to antagonize the local population, Briiz had a platoon of Marines accompany him hundreds of kilometers away from Narman's Pyke on a safari. They found a troop of the creatures and started culling them. They expected the Quarakai to flee after being exposed to gunfire, as any other animal would, but instead, they attacked."

Melki leaned forward toward me. "You were at Narman's Pyke when the Quarakai assaulted the advance party, weren't you?"

I nodded.

"How many Marines were there?"

"About three hundred. A third of those were unarmed, though. They were defeated mutineers."

Melki grinned. "And how did two hundred fully equipped Marines fare against several hundred Quarakai that day?"

"Poorly," I told him.

"So did Briiz's hunting party," Melki revealed. "And there were only about eighty of them."

"Dr. Briiz himself was saved by his own laziness," Meinhopf added. "Instead of marching with the grunts, he was piloted around on a two-person hovercraft. Had he not been on that, he'd have been slaughtered as well. Those two were the only survivors."

Melki nodded. "It just so happens that the troop of Quarakai they attacked was familiar to us. They came to the Morghul asking for help, but we were not willing to enter a war we were ill-equipped to win. Instead, we offered the Quarakai refuge within our sanctuary, but those are beings that evolved in trees. They were not suited for underground living."

The Morghul live underground? I thought to myself. *No wonder they were so hard to find.*

"This caused something of a rift in Morghul society," Melki said. "Most of us wanted to retreat into our sanctuary at Xaramika. Others, mainly those who had close contact with the Quarakai, wanted to help them. They armed themselves with the few weapons we still had in working order and offered to fight alongside them if the Marines came back."

I could see a sadness rising in those bright red eyes of Melki's. "When your warriors returned, they came in great numbers. There were far more of them than the Quarakai could deal with. Dr. Briiz got many, many, Quarakai specimens that day. And they stumbled across that homestead of Kryndil's kin."

Meinhopf nodded. "Yeah, what Briiz did to those he captured twisted Kryndil's mind up into knots that we're probably never going to untangle. That's pretty evident by what he did to those airborne troops you found hanging from the trees."

I saw Melki cringe. "In war, finding things to fuel your nightmares is never hard. The memories of that night will probably stoke mine forever."

"You were there?" I asked.

Melki nodded.

"And you didn't try to stop it?"

The alien looked indignant. "Why would I? I came to those Marines with an offer of peace. In return, they tried to kill us in our sleep. I regret the agony Kryndil inflicted on them, but with hundreds of Marines converging on Narman's Pyke, we had no choice but to kill those troops."

"To be clear," Meinhopf told me. "It's not like the Marines ever showed us any mercy. Have we been brutal? Absolutely. But we've behaved to a standard that the Samaaris set. Also, unlike the Marines, we've made a good-faith effort to break this cycle of savagery. We removed Kryndil from field operations and made every attempt to be as humane as possible while defending ourselves."

"I've heard stories to the contrary," I told Meinhopf.

"We offer those we capture the chance to join us," the spy countered, trying to defend himself. "All the convicts we've caught have accepted this offer. So have more than ninety-five percent of Marine conscripts."

Ninety-five percent?!? That's one way to increase our recruitment among the enlistees, NCOs, and officers. Capture them. "What do you do to those who don't join you?"

"The same thing you do to those of us you capture," Melki said matter-of-fact-ly. "We kill them. Only we do it much more humanely. Except for the Samaaris. We have to feed Kryndil something, so we give them to him."

As much as I disliked those from the Guild planets, it seemed wrong to single people out for torture based upon the world from which they hailed. "Isn't that genocide?"

Melki waved his hands at the groups of haggard camp survivors milling about all around us. "Isn't that?"

It most certainly was. With Melki's point made, I sighed once more. "So, how did Narman rebels and the Morghul end up allies?"

Meinhopf took that question. "Once they were convinced the Marines were up to no good, the Morghul removed the weaponry from the ship that brought them here three generations ago and set it up in the area they knew the Samaaris would return to. On their third excursion into Morghul territory, the Marines got attacked by our Quarakai and a few Morghul mounted on naypetos. After a brief skirmish, the Morghul retreated. The Marines pursued them and marched right into the ambush the aliens had set. They were obliterated by an array of plasma blasters, losing three-fourths of their forces and all their aircraft."

The Narman paused to smile. "After that, there was practically no one left at Narman's Pyke to keep us under control. We rose up against the Pyke's security contingent and the Quarakai they had just started training to augment their numbers. We butchered the bastards and have been friends and allies with the Morghul ever since."

Meinhopf clasped his hands together and rested his arms on his knees. "The Morghul have taught us a lot, Tauk. I'm aware of things that few people, much less the Marine rank and file, know. In particular, I know what I'm fighting for. For the past couple of years, humans and Morghul have done very well together at war, considering the circumstances. I bet we can do even better at peace. They've enlightened us about the immense swatches of our galaxy we've not even begun to discover. To be honest, it doesn't sound like a happy place. I'm fighting to change that. I'm willing to risk my life to create a new dynamic where the different beings of the cosmos can live and work together for the mutual benefit of all."

"Here on Kanaris?" I asked.

Melki shook his head. "Anywhere but here. Caught between the League on one side and the Morghul Empire on the other, Kanaris will be laid to waste before long. It's a doomed world. If we're going to have a chance at a better life, or life at all, we need to get as far away from this cursed place as fast as we can. I hope we can trust you to help us achieve that aim."

Looking Melki right in the eye, I said. "Trust me? Several days ago, you watched me slaughter a platoon of some of the most incorrigible sadists I've ever known to spare your people the horror of falling into their hands. I brought them where you told us to. I not only handed you a highly valuable Section 615 asset, I exposed a mole that he was running in your organization."

"Deena Vulk?" asked Meinhopf.

I nodded. "Deena Vulk."

Meinhopf sighed. "The jury's still out on her. We can't be sure if you've exposed a spy or framed the woman who killed your girlfriend while trying to escape your custody. Having seen how the Marines treat prisoners, I wouldn't blame her a bit for slaughtering whoever she had to in order to get away from you people."

"Vulk didn't kill Jella Duverri to escape our custody. She did it to protect her cover. Jella and Vulk knew each other."

Meinhopf's eyes narrowed. "Prove it."

I grinned. "You didn't know that, did you?"

"I still don't."

"Then turn her over to Kryndil. Let him get to the bottom of it."

Meinhopf looked at me and laughed. "Kryndil?!? What do you think Kryndil could do to Deena Vulk? My god, you don't know a damned thing about her, do you?"

••–•–◉–•–••

Chapter 11

Painless

Meinhopf was right. I did not know a damn thing about Deena Vulk. She had been in my custody for days, but the woman was a complication I did not know how to deal with in the immediate aftermath of our defection to the Narmans. I had been harboring some pretty clear ideas of what I would do to Jella's killer if I ever got my hands on her. Now that I had the bitch, I feared that if I followed through with such dark fantasies, I might develop a taste for that flavor of cruelty. I had battles to conduct, and if I pursued them guided by my baser urges, the peace we achieved might end up indistinguishable from the war we waged to attain it.

After my conversation with Melki and Meinhopf, I spent the night wondering what I should do. Unable to come to a decision, I went back to the ubati pen, where our prisoners were kept, the first thing the following morning. I was surprised to find it virtually empty. The only two prisoners left were Supai Takawa and Deena Vulk. They were housed in a pair of narrow cages set up in the center of the corral.

The makeshift cells were barely long enough to lie down or stand up in. There was no cover over the prisoners, so the rain fell upon them unabated. That seemed to take a heavy toll on my former commander. Takawa sat forlornly in his cage, shivering and resting his head in his hands as he swayed to and fro. Vulk had both wrists cuffed to the sides of her enclosure but looked at me with a huge smile stretched across her mangled face. She seemed to be dealing with her situation far better than Supai Takawa was.

"Where the hell did all the prisoners go?" I asked Tormar Snae, the only person left standing guard.

"Sergeant Espiya and that rebel spook took possession of them." It appeared that Snae forgot that he was now a rebel, too. "They said we had reached an agreement to pool intelligence resources, so the Narmans are going to lead the interrogations with Espiya observing."

That was right. I remembered reaching a deal in theory but had not realized the details had been worked out so quickly. "Is Kryndil going to be involved with that?"

"That scary-looking Mog? I doubt it, sir, but that's above my pay grade. He wasn't around when Espiya emptied the pen, but Kamrak Qarsi told me that freaky fucker showed up during his watch and was *really* unthrilled once he discovered theSamaaris were spirited away from under his nose."

Pointing toward Takawa, Snae added, "I heard he's taken a particular shine to that guy, though."

Overhearing our conversation, the captive agent lifted his head. "Don't let that monster take me, Tauk! Please! I'm begging you!"

"Pussy," Vulk sneered at her former handler from a couple of meters away.

"Any idea why Espiya and Meinhopf left this pair behind?"

Snae shrugged. "My instructions are that you're the only one who can make a disposition on those two. The spooks know you've got a high level of interest in both of them."

I nodded. "That I do. Why is Vulk shackled to her cage?"

The sentry grinned. "She kept filling her waste bucket and launching the contents at the guards."

"There's no waste bucket in there now," I pointed out. Thinking that offering Vulk a small gesture of kindness might reduce her hostility level, I told the PFC to unshackle her.

"I'm not sure you want to do that, sir," Snae warned me. "She's a bitch to get back in chains."

"Just do it."

With a sigh of resignation, the sentry said, "Aye-aye, sir. Just don't blame me when she launches a deuce at your ass. She's freakishly accurate."

••-◄-●-◄-••

Supai Takawa was not the same man who defiantly spat in my face days before. He seemed to have found religion after learning of Kryndil's interest in him. Ever since, he had been consumed by the specter of having his skin peeled off by the Morghul executioner.

Takawa had seen people flayed alive before, and it made quite an impression on him. He found it to be a grotesque and horrifying experience to witness, and on the few occasions he woke up screaming in the middle of the night in a puddle of cold sweat, it was most likely dreams of people being skinned alive that did it to him. It was quite literally the stuff of his worst nightmares. As cruel and heartless as the field agent could be, not even he could stomach doing something so barbaric.

"Please, Tauk," Takawa begged as I approached his cage. His eyes bulged open, nervously darting from side to side as he spoke. Between the incessant rain pouring down upon his bare head for days on end and the fate he feared awaited him in some dank alien torture chamber, the man was going clinically insane. "P-p-please don't send me to Kryndil. Do you have any idea what that fiend is going to do to me?"

Without breaking my stride, I said, "I do. And I don't care." Though I had not decided what to do with that man yet, I was fascinated with his rapid descent into madness. I always thought he was made of tougher stuff.

The agent stood up and grabbed the bars of his cage with quaking hands, his fingers rhythmically squeezing and releasing the steel in a steady beat as he tried to plead his case. "You should care, Tauk! If you think you're so much better than the League, you wouldn't let this happen!"

"You want me to stop Kryndil?" I scoffed, letting him continue believing his fate lay in the aliens' hands instead of mine. "You want me to stop him like you stopped the Blue Shirts from tossing live children into that fire at Saimsun?"

That was not what Takawa wanted to hear. Releasing his grip on the bars of his cage, he took a step back away from me and began rubbing his ears so hard it was as if he were trying to scrub them right off. Attempting to stifle a sob, Takawa then bit his lip so hard he drew blood. "I'm sorry," the agent whimpered, earning a glare of contempt from Deena Vulk. "I'm so, so sorry. But I don't know what I could have possibly done to prevent it, though."

I stopped in my tracks, cursed, then turned around and marched back toward the agent's enclosure. "You could've done what I did! You could've done anything to stop it!"

"But there was only me!" Takawa cried as he threw himself against the side of his cell. Sticking his left arm out in a futile attempt to grab me, he stammered, "L-l-l-look, Tauk. You're a good man. Y-y-yeah, you are. I see that now."

Takawa paused as he released the bars with his right hand and slapped himself three times against the side of his head as if trying to get better reception. He then continued speaking as if nothing had happened. "Uh-huh. I do. I see you for what you are now. You're one of the good guys. I thought we were, I was, but we're not. Things are real clear to me these days. I know what we did, Tauk. I repent. FOR FUCK'S SAKE, I REPENT! Please have mercy on me! Just a little bit. Do what you want to me; just don't let them take my skin."

"I'm sorry, Takawa," I said, mimicking his earlier statement. "I'm so, so sorry. I don't know what I can possibly do to prevent it, though."

My stomach was in knots as I turned away from the agent. Despite my best efforts not to, I pitied him. He was right. Nobody deserved to be skinned alive. Not even him. Yet, I had no idea how to hold him accountable for what he had done. Shooting him in the back of the head seemed too merciful, yet I was loathe to do anything more to the man with my own hands.

As I approached Deena Vulk, I lashed out and slammed my forearm across the bars of her cell. "How about you, darling? You want me to arrange you a date with Kryndil, too?"

The disfigured monster before me stood up and smiled. As Vulk looked at me, all I could focus on was the dull red light of her artificial eye. It kept my attention from the sickening mess of charred flesh surrounding it. "You think I'm afraid of Kryndil, Tauk?"

"From what I heard, you should be. He might skin you alive if I give him the word."

Vulk scoffed and stood up as she started untying her shirt. "Oh? You think

Kryndil's taking orders from you, now? He doesn't even listen to the Council of Elders." As the fabric parted to reveal the skin of the prisoner's chest, I winced at all the scars the woman carried.

"You've been tortured before?" I asked.

The prisoner laughed. "Tortured? No, not really. Most of these are from childhood."

"You were abused?"

"Wrong again," Vulk laughed. "I did most of this to myself. When you first met me, half my face had just been burned off. Yet I managed to kill your girlfriend, a few Marines, and pump a couple of rounds into your sorry ass, too. I even had the presence of mind to slip a chip full of intel into the pocket of one of the corpses I made. You ever wonder how I managed that with such severe injuries?"

Recalling the morning I was shot, I remembered lying in the snow, unable to move, as Deena Vulk rifled through her captor's pockets. I thought she was going for his keys to free herself, but she must have slipped the chip she was talking about into that Marine's fatigues as well.

Son-of-a-bitch! I thought, forgetting the question Vulk had asked me. I was too busy remembering my view from the Sitaara transport as we were being evacuated. The Narmans killed several of us on Mount Toranad. As far as I knew, we left the bodies behind. Even Jella Duverii's corpse was abandoned on that mountain. The only corpse they recovered was that of the corporal whose pockets Vulk had rifled through. Takawa was sitting on it when we lifted off. I shot the agent a glare of pure rage.

That shit was orchestrated! Jella was murdered to obtain intelligence and give Deena Vulk street cred among the Narmans! That's probably how they got the plans for all the Morghul heavy weaponry!

"That bitch put a chip in that corporal's pocket on Toranad?!?" I growled at Takawa. "You fucking set us up! You know what? Fuck you people! Kryndil can have both your asses!" I was serious. I had been inclined toward mercy a couple of moments before, but I was now convinced that if there was anyone on Kanaris worthy of that Morghul maniac's attention, it was those two.

Vulk laughed in my face and again pointed out all the scars on her chest. "Answer me, Tauk! Any other person would have been paralyzed with agony had they been burned that bad. Yet, it hardly phased me! You know why?"

I shrugged. "I don't know. Adrenaline? Because you're some kind of cutter? You think that'll make you tough enough to face that monster?"

The prisoner smirked, oozing self-confidence. "I am tough. But I also have a condition known as Pain Asymbolia. Do you know what that is?"

I did not, but I took an educated guess. "You can't feel pain?"

Shaking her head, the prisoner said, "You're close. Not feeling any pain at all would be something called CIPA. I can feel it, but it's not anything unpleasant to me. It's just another stimuli. Kryndil knows all about it. He won't waste his energy on me."

"We'll see about that," I said as I started walking away. "You're going to die, Deena."

"TAUK!" Vulk screamed before I had taken a half dozen steps. When I swung around to face her, she held her hands up so I could see them. Without hesitation, she grabbed her left ring finger with her right hand and wrenched it back so hard I heard it snap. When she let go of it, Vulk showed us the jagged shard of bone sticking out of the skin below her knuckle.

Amused by the look of horror on Snae's face, not to mention the ones on mine and Takawa's, Vulk giggled as she worked to set the fracture back into place. "Rest assured, Lieutenant," she told me. "If the Morghul decide I'm their enemy, there's nothing they, Kryndil, or even you could do to make me suffer for my sins."

"Hell," she said as she sat down again, sinking into the muck of ubati shit at the bottom of her cage. "The power of all of you combined couldn't even hurt my feelings."

••-◄-●-◄-••

Chapter 12

METAMORPHOSIS

"**R**itza! Xi!"

Ritza Xi nearly leapt out of her skin when she turned to see who was shouting her name on the path between her barracks and the mess hall. Tired of people staring at what Sergeant Kyker and his buddies had done to her face during the Briggund Mutiny, Xi preferred to eat in the middle of the night when fewer Marines were around to gawk at her. She found the solitary walks back to her barracks both routine and comforting. The unexpected sound of someone calling to her through the rain, however, was neither. It was startling.

The voice sounded familiar, but the young woman it came from had a face almost completely covered in gauze. She looked like some sort of mummy from one of the ancient earthly civilizations. Eventually, from the whisps of long brown hair sticking out from the girl's bandages and the manner in which she moved, Xi put together which Marine from her past it might be.

"Sergeant Gyanis?"

Elia nodded as she closed the distance between them, holding her hand out to the former convict. "A mutual friend wanted me to find you."

Xi had a pretty good idea of who that friend would be. As she took Gyanis's hand and shook it, she was surprised to feel a small electronic device in the woman's palm. Xi gave her former platoon comrade a perplexed look. "You must trust me an awful lot to try passing me something this way."

Elia shook her head. "I barely know you. Tauk trusts you, though. He said he trusts you with his life."

Xi narrowed her eyes at Gyanis. "Well, right now, it appears he's trusting me with yours. What is this?"

"Video," Elia told her. "A lot of it. We're doing horrible stuff here, Xi. People need to know about it. Tauk wants you to make sure it gets out when you get back to the League."

Xi nodded, taking the device from Gyanis and casually slipping it into her pocket. "What happened to you?" she asked, lifting her chin at Elia's bandages.

The armorer sighed. "Tauk defected. He gave us a choice to go with him or return to the Marines. I came back. Unfortunately, we got intercepted by Killbillies who thought we were traitors who got separated from the rest of our unit."

Xi gasped, covering her mouth with her hand. She knew what the Qilkorians did to the females they captured. "Did they...?"

Elia nodded.

"I'm so sorry, Sergeant."

Shaking her head and clenching her eyes closed, Elia said, "Thanks. I'm sure it was nothing compared to what you've gone through. It only lasted a night. You were held at the Morale Center for...for...."

"...for a very long time," Xi answered, completing the technical sergeant's sentence. "Are you going to be okay?"

"Sure. I had surgery a few days ago to repair all the damage that was done. To be honest, the Section 615 inquisitors fucked up my face far worse than the Qilkorians did. To atone for their mistake, they fixed me up. When I take these bandages off, they said I'll be good as new."

Without thinking, Xi reached up to touch her own face. With her broken nose, shattered teeth, asymmetrical eyes, and the deep scars that ran across her cheeks and forehead, she thought herself hideous. "I wish the Marines would admit their mistake and fix me up, too."

"You're getting freed, Xi. Get fixed on the outside. You owe it to yourself. Xi, could you do one more thing for me? For us? To help us fuck these people?"

Ritza looked around nervously. "What?"

"You're staying at the holding barracks, right? Third floor?" Gyanis gulped nervously, secretly longing for Xi to refuse the favor. If she agreed to do it, there would be no going back. Gyanis would hate herself forever.

To the armorer's chagrin, Xi nodded.

"Go to the lavatory in the southwest corner. Third stall from the bulkhead. There's a tablet above the ceiling tile. The access code is on the back of that data stick I gave you. Take it to the fourth-floor lobby, open the device, and send the message at the top of the queue. After that, return the tablet where you found it. Can you do that tonight?"

"Sure," the former convict assured her, breaking Gyanis's heart. After a moment or two of staring into Elia's eyes, Xi asked, "How committed are you to this?"

Thinking about the chain of events that were about to be unleashed and the toll they were going to take, Elia's voice cracked as she answered. "I'm about as committed as you can get."

Xi nodded. "Considering that you're giving this video to me, I'm assuming you're staying here on Kanaris?"

"I am."

"Do you have anyone here in the Pyke helping you?"

Elia shook her head. "No. I'm all alone."

Xi frowned. "There's a Class Zero convict working in the Morale Center named Bina . She's on the same team you are and has a talent for figuring out who else is, too. Tell her I sent you. She'll ask if you have a message from me. Tell her, 'Zero Fury.'"

"Morale Center?" asked Gyanis. "She's a comfort woman?"

"I don't know any females being held in that building who aren't."

"Then how do I meet with her?"

Xi grinned. "Do you like girls?"

"Not that way."

"Well, you might have to get committed to your cause enough to start. Don't worry, though. From what I hear, if you need someone to change your mind about liking girls the way you might have to, she's the one to do it."

As an armorer, Elia Gyanis was an enlisted Marine, but her skill set was valuable enough to enjoy perks usually reserved for officers or senior NCOs. After getting reassigned to the MEF's depot-level repair facility at Narman's Pyke, instead of being billeted in the barracks, she was assigned a stateroom. Though her lodging was little more than a glorified closet, she still had the place all to herself, a rare luxury for a sergeant in the Kyperion League Space Corps. A few days after meeting with Ritza Xi, Gyanis returned home to discover an uninvited, though hardly unexpected, visitor.

"Idris!" Elia gasped as she turned on the light to find her friend sitting in the dark at the edge of her bed. "What are you doing here?!?"

"Hiding," Jatmika answered, a little startled as well. She was not expecting her friend's face to be completely covered in bandages. Correctly assuming they were from surgery, she refrained from asking about them.

"Hiding?!?" Gyanis exclaimed. "Here?!? If you have people searching for you, Idris, this is going to be the first place they fucking look!"

Jatmika nodded. "I know. I won't be here long, Elia. It's over. I just need some information and then I'll get the hell out of here."

"What's going on?!? What do you mean by, 'It's over?' What's the matter?"

"They came for me," Idris told her.

"Section 615?"

Idris scoffed. "Fuck no! They sent the MPs. Like those flatfoots would be any match for me."

I didn't think they would be. Not against a Recon machine gunner with rage issues.

Jatmika picked up a police battalion tablet and handed it to Gyanis. It still had fresh blood on it. "Someone reported me for subversion, Elia. I need to know who. Can you hack into this?"

"It's locked by law enforcement security protocols. I could hack it in my sleep." Elia reached for the cord to the diagnostic box on her belt, the armorer's equivalent to a rifleman's sidearm. She plugged it into the data port on the side of the stolen tablet and, with a dozen keystrokes, activated a breaching program to punch through the device's firewall.

As Elia's DB worked its magic, she looked up at Idris and asked, "What are you going to do?"

Jatmika let out a single sob. "It's over for me, Elia. I couldn't let them take me back to Section 615. If they did, I knew I'd never leave. They're definitely going to kill me after they find those cops' bodies. I'm a dead woman. All I can do now is take as many with me as I can. Starting with the fucker that reported me for subversion."

When the breaching program finished, the tablet screen suddenly lit up with the same picture Idris Jatmika had on her ID. "That saves us the trouble of searching for the warrant," Elia told her friend. Reading the report, Gyanis shook her head in shock and apprehension. "It's from your little outburst at the Interrogation Center when we were released. They've pegged you on suspicion of harboring anti-national sympathies and plotting the defamation of the League. Damn it, Idris! You fucking idiot!"

Jatmika bit her lip. "I don't have time for your outbursts, Elia. Look, there's a big difference between bitching about the government and actively undermining it. Whoever made that call obviously set me up. Who did it?"

Gyanis scrolled down to the bottom of the warrant. "Originator was anonymous, but...." Elia spent the next few minutes tracking the message's path through the distribution network to the router that sent the original file. From there, she checked the time stamp and the terminal number used to field the warrant, identifying the officer that put together the document. After managing that, Elia hacked the MP's email account and pulled up the last message read before the warrant was initiated. Then, all Gyanis had to do was look at the document's transmission code. "The originator of the complaint was Serial Number 67239283," Elia announced as she let out a long sigh and leaned back against the wall.

"Damn," Idris said, "that was quick."

"Like I said, these are law enforcement security protocols. I could do this shit in my sleep." *It also helps that I know exactly what I'm looking for.*

"Can you look it up?" Jatmika snapped impatiently. "The serial number?"

Elia shook her head and took a seat next to her friend on the cot. "I don't have to. I put her tablet back together a few days ago. That number's Silma Hauken's ID."

Despite her dark skin, the armorer could see the blood rushing into Jatmika's face. "I'm going to snap that bitch's neck, Elia. Then I'm going to take out the Killbillies who raped us. I saw them here. I know where they're staying."

Gyanis nodded silently, but Jatmika could see the gauze beneath the sergeant's eyes getting wet as it absorbed her tears. "I figured you would try to talk me out of this," the doomed woman said.

Elia shrugged. "If you killed those MPs, your only choices are to turn yourself in to meet a gruesome end at the hands of the inquisitors or go out in a blaze of glory. If I were you, I'd do the exact same thing. Give the Killbillies my regards."

Breaking down into sobs, Jatmika wrapped her arms around her friend and squeezed her hard. "I'm going to miss you, Elia."

"I'm going to miss you, too, Idris."

The young women embraced each other for a couple of long moments. When it was time for Idris to flee, however, she spun Gyanis around and twisted her forearm around Elia's neck. The armorer tried to struggle free, but she was a technician. She was not a combat Marine like Jatmika was. Like the MPs who fell victim to her earlier that night, Elia Gyanis was not even close to being a match for the recon gunner.

"Wh-wh-what are you doing?!?" Elia croaked, fighting for air.

"Shhhhh. Relax, sweetie. Don't resist. I'm just making sure you...."

Elia blacked out before hearing the rest of the sentence.

When Gyanis regained consciousness, she was bound and gagged on the deck of her tiny stateroom. She remained that way for several hours until a pair of Section 615 agents broke down her door and untied her.

Agent Nala Biragor arrived shortly afterward. "I assume Idris Jatmika did this to you?"

Elia nodded, as it hurt for her to talk.

"What did she want?" Biragor asked.

"She came to say goodbye," Elia answered in a raspy voice. Remembering what she found on the tablet, she added, "I saw blood on her. When I asked if she was okay, she started choking me."

Biragor stared at Gyanis for a moment before holding up a diagnostic box. "Do you recognize this?"

Instinctively, Elia reached for her belt. "It's my DB. Where did you get it?"

"From Jatmika's body."

Elia burst into tears, heaving with deep sobs. It was no act. Even though it was expected, Jatmika's loss was a devastating blow tripled by the indescribable remorse she felt over orchestrating her best friend's death. Gyanis was inconsolable. "What'd she do?" the armorer asked when she finally regained her composure.

"Well, first, she murdered three MPs sent to detain her under suspicion of violating the UCMJ's subversion articles. Once she finished with them, she went after a comrade of yours, Silma Hauken. She found a jagged piece of metal from some scrap bin somewhere and plunged it into the poor girl's throat while she was sleeping. She then broke the neck of the barracks security officer and stole his sidearm. She used that to ice some grunt bivouacking along the south wall and steal his M2117 rig. That was what she used to shoot up the Qilkorian quarters on the northeast side of the colony."

"Did she get the ones that raped us?"

Biragor shrugged. "I don't know. She was pretty indiscriminate. She got a lot of them before they finally got her." After examining Elia's expression for a few moments, Nala asked, "Does that disturb you?"

"That she might have missed some of the Killbillies that molested us? Yes, that disturbs me."

The Section 615 Agent nodded. "Fair enough." Holding up the diagnostic box they found on Jatmika's body, Biragor asked, "Why would Jatmika want this?"

Wiping the tears out of her eyes, Elia said, "What wouldn't she want with it? If she was looking for information, like where to find Hauken or hack into someone's armor, it's the perfect tool. The only problem is that she would have had no idea how to operate it."

"Are you sure?" Biragor asked. "I understand you two were close. You never showed her how to do anything on it?"

Gyanis shook her head. "She was my best friend, ma'am, but she was a machine gunner. Even if I tried to teach her how to operate it, it never would've stuck. Idris wasn't wired that way. Don't get me wrong; she was smart. Just not like that."

"Then how could she use this?" Biragor asked.

Elia broke down again. "She couldn't have! She must have had someone helping her!"

Gyanis could tell by the expression on Biragor's face that the agent smelled a rat. "Someone besides you?!? You expect me to believe she came here for your DB but didn't have you help her use it?"

The armorer glared at the field agent. "I guess you're going to believe what you want to believe, aren't you? All I can tell you is that she didn't. She was probably afraid that if she asked me, I would actually have helped her. Then we'd both be dead."

"Would you have, though? Helped her?" Biragor asked.

"Kill Hauken? No. Massacre Killbillies? Probably. Especially if they were the ones that fucking molested us."

It was a damning admission, especially to a Section 615 agent, but it smacked of the sort of brutal honesty that would have come from someone with nothing to hide. It might have been luck on Elia Gyanis's part, but her statement threw Biragor's instincts off. The agent still thought something stunk, but her gut told her the stench was coming from elsewhere. Time was crucial in that part of their investigation, and Biragor did not want to waste it barking up the wrong tree. After making arrangements to get Gyanis seen by the medical staff, she collected her subordinates and went searching for clues elsewhere.

Much to Elia's relief.

Idris undid some of the medical work that had been performed on Gyanis during the struggle to choke her out. That added another week of walking around Narman's Pyke with her head wrapped in gauze. When the doctors finally removed her bandages, though, Elia gasped in shock and surprise.

She was gorgeous. Her skin had been renewed to the point it was almost infant-like. Elia had a slightly darker hue than before, but her face was clear and flawless. They repaired her teeth, realigned her jaw, and put her nose back not the way it had been, but the way she had always wished it to be. They even thickened her eyelashes to the point where she would never need mascara ever again. Elia Gyanis was not as good as new as the doctors had promised. She was even better. The young woman was almost perfect.

And she hated it.

Elia kept her tears in check until she got back to her stateroom. Once by herself, however, she looked into the digital mirror and bawled.

It was not fair. Gyanis duped her best friend into a suicide mission so that Jatmika could become the silenced patsy for the next part of her operation. Despite her intent to soon follow Idris into oblivion, Elia hated that she could do something so vile and did not want to be that person anymore.

Surrendering to the first stage of a minor breakdown, she grabbed her battle dagger and started hacking away at the hair on the sides of her head. When she was done, she looked like she had been given a mohawk by an escapee from a lunatic asylum wielding a set of sheep shears. Elia spent the rest of the night sobbing and twisting what was left into long dreadlocks like Idris Jatmika wore.

The following day, Gyanis cleaned up the sides of her head with a proper razor and dyed her dreads bright crimson. She then spent the rest of the week fashioning a pair of high-tech goggles she could use to hide her piercing green eyes behind. After that, she braved her way into the tent city near the northwestern corner of Narman's Pyke, where the convict laborers were kept, to seek out mobsters from Zaimiraldo. They were famous for their intricate tattoos and, after paying a half month's salary to some junkie from Maxaroan as a finder's fee, found a true master that inked her up from her waist to her collarbone for another small fortune.

Once she ran through her savings on body art, the armorer stripped down to her bra and looked at herself in the mirror once more. The radical transition did not exactly make her happy, but it did make her look like someone other than Elia Gyanis.

And that would have to suffice for the moment.

Chapter 13

Scene of the Crime

Black Francis remembered the first time he ever saw a soroquid, the gargantuan centipedes of Kanaris. He had been in the Nimnaya Valley when one scurried onto the path in front of them and reared up nearly as tall as their point man. The leading Marine froze, and the attention of the entire squad zeroed in on the horror before them. That was when the other 'pedes overwhelmed them from behind.

It ended up a bloodbath. Four Marines were taken down right away, and the rest scattered into the jungle where they were picked off one by one. Nine fell victim to those demons that night before another squad came to Francis's rescue and set up a perimeter to fight them off. This happened long before the Killbillies arrived and set up the acclimatization course at Camp Vayipar.

Now, the soroquids were barely even a nuisance. Except for Dmitri Naktada. As a technician whose time in the field was not nearly as extensive as that of the other Marines, the armorer's exposure to them had been limited. So, when one of them scampered out upon the trail they were using just outside the ruins of Razbauten, towering over the leader of the column, Naktada lost his ever-loving mind.

"HOLY SWEET MOTHER OF FUCK!" Naktada screeched over the squad network. Fortunately, the Marines were in full battle dress. No matter how loud Naktada shrieked, or how unnaturally high an octave he hit, unless the terrors of Kanaris were issued the same battle helmets Francis's roughnecks were using, they would not have been able to hear a thing. "PEDE!" the armorer kept screaming.

"PEDE! PEDE! PEDE!"

No one else got very worked up about the creature. They had all been confronted by soroquids before and knew what to do without even thinking about it. The point Marine drew a bead on the lead animal, as did the pair of Marines flanking him. The rest of the column alternated aiming their weapons into the bush in the port or starboard directions. The four grunts bringing up the rear covered their flank. As the infantry's infrared array beamed into the underbrush, Naktada could see by hundreds of glowing eyes that the creatures had them surrounded. "MOTHERFUCKER!!!"

Black Francis was far more calm about the situation. When Naktada paused his stream of profanity long enough to draw in a breath of air, the mission's leader said, "Fire."

With the exception of Naktada's, the squad's plasma blasters went off nearly simultaneously. In barely a few seconds, a couple dozen giant centipedes had been killed and the rest were fleeing the scene in search of easier prey. Naktada was jumping up and down excitedly in the middle of the formation, frantically waving his arms about as if trying to shake off a host of fleas.

Black Francis could not keep himself from laughing. "You okay, Dimi?"

"No! I'm not okay!" Naktada shouted back, ripping a canister off his belt and holding it up to Francis's face. "I thought this can of ubati stink was supposed to keep shit like that the fuck away from us!"

"It is," Francis assured the armorer. "It probably just wore off. It's been raining pretty hard today."

"Wore off?!?" Naktada exclaimed as he sprayed the repellant in the air like room freshener. He then doused his head with it. "Wore off?!? No one ever told me this shit wears off! God-DAMN-it!" Dimitri rounded off the spectacle by pumping a couple blasts of ubati scent into each armpit, making the rest of the squad burst into laughter.

"You almost done?" Black Francis asked as Naktada began to settle down.

"Yeah, Gunny, I just hate bugs!" he said as he started marching down the trail again. "Especially ones a third longer than I am!"

Entering the destroyed mining camp, Naktada was fascinated by how quickly the jungle was reclaiming the site. "How long has it been since we razed this place?"

Black Francis replied, "A month? Six weeks?"

When the unit reached the spot where the prisoners slaughtered the Blue Shirts, Naktada saw the bones had all been scattered and picked clean. The scavengers had left little behind. Saplings were already sprouting from the cracks in the concrete foundations of the administrative office tents while kryptids and other small creatures hid in the decaying inmate living quarters. Larger things were lurking about as well. The armorer nearly stepped on a massive worm emerging from the saturated soil. It was thicker than Naktada's thigh.

"Whoa!" Sergeant Hermour said as she snapped a picture of it with her tablet. "I've never seen anything like this before! Look! It has gills!"

"It'd have to if it's going to survive in dirt this wet," Dmitri told her. "What are you going to do with the picture?"

"Upload it into the...." She was going to say the Alien Wildlife Classification Protocol but remembered she no longer had access to that system. That depressed her. Populating the AWCP database was one of the ways she enjoyed spending her downtime on Kanaris.

A little further up the trail, Black Francis tapped Naktada on the shoulder and pointed at the broken hull of a towering Warp Haug freighter emerging from the darkness. "There's your target."

The sight made Naktada shudder, remembering what had been lurking in the wreckage of *Wasp-Three* after they had crashed on Kanaris years before. He hoped there would be fewer things to worry about in that craft, considering they were thousands of kilometers from the ocean. At least this time, they did not have to clear it. They only had to inspect the engine room.

When they got a little closer, Francis pointed to a gaping hole near the freighter's stern. "Ain't that about where you gotta go?"

"That's precisely where I need to go," Naktada said in return, stricken a bit suspicious by how conveniently located the hull breach was.

"That must be where Albarn hit it. That should make things easy for us to get in there."

"Too easy," Naktada said as he picked up his pace. "Way too easy. That freighter's hull wasn't blown open. It was cut."

The armorer jogged to the wreck to confirm his suspicions, running up a mound of rocks and dirt someone had piled against the freighter to gain easier access to the breach. When he reached the opening, he shone his light into the starship. Whoever got to the Warp Haug first cut a corridor clear through to the reactor room.

Naktada let out a disappointed sigh and raised Black Francis on the commlink. "Looks like the Marines were on to us," he told the platoon sergeant. "We're not going to find any Nexilium here."

"You positive about that?" Francis asked. "Maybe we should go in and make sure?"

Naktada shook his head. "No. Not worth the risk. If I were them, I'd boo-by-trap the hell out of this thing to blow if anyone walked in there looking for reactor fuel."

"Really?" Francis asked. "Why?"

"Because you have to be pretty goddamn smart to get Nexilium out of an interstellar hyper-warp engine. The League'll know that anyone sent on an errand like this will most likely be the brains of the operation."

Qlaiv Sunda was the point Marine as the squad withdrew from the ruins at Razbauten. He had been one of Francis's Raiders and spent months patrolling No Man's Land along the Satapadaya Front. Not only was he used to using the cloaking camouflage technology the Marines adapted from the Morghul, he knew what to look for to keep it from being used against him. Had he not been the first person up the trail, that skirmish could have turned out far deadlier than it ended up being.

A warrior with Sunda's experience used his senses to seek out things that did not belong. That night, it was a ripple in the atmosphere that looked like heat shimmer, something that was wildly out of place in the rain during the middle of the night. Without thinking, Sunda turned sideways toward the anomaly to lower his profile and raised his rifle to fire if needed.

Sunda's adversary already had the squad's point man in his sights, however, and got off the first shot. The blaster beam hit Qlaiv on the chin and melted away a large chunk of his helmet's jaw guard, but aside from some singed facial hair and blisters on his lips, the lance corporal was still in action. He started firing wildly into the underbrush and ran further down the trail, zig-zagging and drawing the ambush's attention away from the rest of the squad.

Sunda's shots hit nothing, but they achieved what the Raider intended. They made the other side duck and gave a precious second back to the rest of his comrades to seek cover and prepare to fight. It was a second he did not afford himself. A burst of redirected blaster fire from the ambush's rear cut him down as he was diving for the tree line.

Black Francis conditioned his people to *always* scan their surroundings for features to take cover behind. They were used to the enemy popping up out of thin air and forcing them into a fight without warning. The Raiders also moved in ways that kept them from bunching up or leaving the entire unit exposed to any single vantage point. When Francis's troops saw incoming blaster beams bursting through the vegetation, they moved with a purpose, melting away toward safer places to return fire, except for Dmitri Naktada, who was *not* a combat Marine.

When the tree line erupted with a barrage of blaster fire, the rebel Marines knew they were grossly outnumbered. That single rifle squad was up against an opponent in platoon strength, meaning that for every one of my riflemen, there were four of their adversaries. Their instincts propelled them to get out of the way with great urgency. Naktada's instincts were much different. He froze in place, right out in the open, wrapped his arms around his helmet to protect his head, and lifted his right leg to cross it over his left to keep his genitals safe.

Not surprisingly, my Tech Warfare Specialist was hit almost instantly. He took a shot in his shoulder, which spun him around and sent him hurtling toward the ground, probably saving his life. The next three blasts were targeted to hit him center mass but instead blew apart his battle pack. A fourth grazed him in the derriere, burning a three-centimeter trough across both ass cheeks before he hit the mud.

At this point, Naktada finally knew that he needed to burn rubber and rejoin his comrades if he wanted to survive, but it was too late. The passive ultrasonic echolocation display on the armorer's visor showed dozens of enemy Marines emerging from the bush, charging his way.

Naktada lost his rifle when his pack got blown apart and destroyed the tether. Still, he reached for it anyway and revealed to one of the advancing riflemen that he was not yet dead. Without a weapon in his hand, he was utterly defenseless. As the enemy took aim at Naktada, my man made an insanely desperate gamble. Instead of going for his sidearm, he rolled away from his assailant and narrowly avoided getting himself shot again. He then flipped on his loudspeaker, activated his microphone, and shrieked, "PROTOTYPE P891 CIRCUIT! ALL SERIAL NUMBERS! LOCK!"

To everyone's surprise, the enemy's blaster fire came to a screeching halt.

Holy shit! Naktada thought to himself. *It fucking worked!*

Stunned and confused about what had just happened, the enemy Marines stood and looked at each other in disbelief. Naktada took advantage of the pause to find his rifle, take aim at the man who had nearly killed him, and blast the son-of-a-bitch right through the throat. The master armorer had disabled the voice control features in our weapons weeks before. Having experienced his very first combat kill, Naktada then leapt to his feet, laughed maniacally, and screamed, "PROTOTYPE EXO-ARMOR SYSTEM 444! ALL SERIAL NUMBERS! FULL SYSTEM SHUTDOWN!"

The enemy platoon was suddenly exposed as their camo tech de-energized. A couple panicked and tried to run back to the trees, but now burdened by twenty kilograms of dead weight, it looked as if they were moving in slow motion. The sight caused Naktada to laugh even harder. "PROTOTYPE P662 CIRCUIT! ALL SERIAL NUMBERS! LOCK!" That command disabled all the sidearms. The next took out their seibaras.

A pair of shots rang out from the opposite side of the battle zone, cutting down two enemy Marines and sending Black Francis into a tizzy. "Hold your fire!" He screamed at his troops. "Hold your fucking fire!"

My gunnery sergeant stormed up to Naktada, ripping off his helmet before putting his hand on the armorer's shoulder. "You alright?"

Lifting his visor, Dmitri said, "Not really, but I'm far better than I have any right to be." Taking a moment to look at his injured shoulder, he added, "I'm not bleeding."

"You're right," Francis said. "Looks like the blaster beam cauterizes the wound as it causes it."

"Man, it still hurts like a bitch!"

Francis grinned. "I bet it does."

Sergeant Hermour's eyes were wide in surprise as she approached Black Francis and looked over the scene before her. There were almost ninety Marines trapped in their armor. With nothing more than his voice, Dmitri Naktada had rendered the most advanced exo-system humankind had ever seen into a burden their adversaries could not escape. With their helmets stuck on and disconnected from power, they could not even communicate with each other. They were blind, deaf, and able to move only under great effort. "I don't fucking believe this."

Naktada shook his head. "I kind of do. No one from Peeli's platoon made it back to report what we did. The League has no idea what happened to those poor bastards. They never even found the bodies. They had no reason to suspect my test program was still embedded in the system software. And considering how they're rushing this shit into production...."

"Still," Black Francis giggled, "if you lose an entire platoon in your brand new state-of-the-art Marine battle system, you would think you would want to take a second look at your gear and make sure you don't have any issues."

The master armorer threw Francis a sideways glance. "That would delay production and cost the Tahnebaht Conglomerate money. They won't do something that drastic unless they have concrete evidence there's a problem."

"My god," Francis grinned. "They really do have all the fucking idiots."

"So," Sergeant Hermour chimed in. "What are we going to do with these people?"

Black Francis looked at the scores of captured Marines he now had on his hands, then at Naktada. The perma-grin the man had perpetually attached to his face instantly evaporated, betraying the gravity of the decision that had to be made. Turning to Naktada, he said, "You were a captain before all this. Not to mention, you're smarter than I am. What do you think we should do?"

The color drained out of Naktada's face as he held his good hand up in mock surrender. "Hey! Don't look at me. I was a technical officer, not a real one. In a combat operation, even Akkam Lumuk could've pulled rank on me. I was just sent here to figure out how to get Nexilium out of those freighters. You're the one in charge."

Francis gulped and looked back over his prisoners. "I was fucking afraid you'd say that." There were reasons Black Francis spent his time in the Marines making every effort he could to avoid getting promoted. Leadership meant making hard decisions. Hard decisions meant doing a lot of thinking and, by Francis's own admission, that was something he was not particularly good at.

As he looked at all the prisoners he now had to contend with, the burden of command weighed heavier on his shoulders than it ever had before. Black Francis knew that making the wrong decision could cost us all dearly, and even the right one could still haunt him for the rest of his life.

Chapter 14

THE COST OF VICTORY

B lack Francis marched up to First Lieutenant Viqtor Yaguun as Naktada finished activating the magnetic restraints on the last of the prisoners they had just captured. As he reached the Samaari officer, he took a moment to size the man up before saying, "I thought all you Suma Corps Marines were going through acclimatization training at Camp Vayipar."

"Vayipar ain't big enough to handle a hundred thousand Marines at once. We're Recon, so we got sent out to do something useful while we waited our turn."

"Lucky you," Francis told him.

The lieutenant nodded. "Yeah, lucky me."

When Naktada finished, he took a few steps back to inspect the prisoners. They were lined up in neat rows, three abreast, with their wrists magnetically shackled behind their backs. Each Marine carried their own gear, and all had their helmets removed so they could not communicate without their captors knowing about it. When the wounded armorer was satisfied the enemy platoon had been rendered defenseless, he limped up to the front of the formation and said, "They're good to go."

Francis nodded. "Alright, prisoners! We're moving you out! Forwaaaaard, MARCH!"

"Stand the fuck fast!" Yaguun yelled at his Marines. "You'll do no such thing!" The officer's troops craned their heads around to stare at their platoon leader, thinking he'd lost his mind.

"What did you say?" Black Francis asked as he stepped into the officer's personal space.

The lieutenant stared at him defiantly. "You heard me. I didn't stutter."

"It's over," Francis snapped at the man. "You took your shot at us. You lost."

"You cheated."

Francis laughed. "Cheated? We're at war, asshole. There ain't no rules to break out here. You can thank the League for setting that precedent."

Yaguun shook his head. "I certainly can't argue with you there."

"Then don't," Francis growled. "And get your ass moving down that trail."

The lieutenant shook his head. "How stupid do you think I am?"

"About as stupid as you can possibly be if you don't start doing what I fucking tell you to."

"Why?" the enemy officer asked. "So we can march our equipment to your rendezvous point before our execution? Give me a break, you piece of shit. I'm not interested in making any of this easy for you. If you want to ice us, you'll have to do it right here. We ain't walking to your gallows."

Sergeant Hermour heard the officer's diatribe and scoffed. "We ain't you, shitbird. We don't kill defenseless people in cold blood."

"Naktada," Francis sighed. "Power down the enemy's exo-armor except for the restraints."

"What?" Naktada asked. "What for?"

A couple of the prisoners made a break for it, prompting our armorer to act before he got an explanation. Activating his loudspeaker, he shouted, "PROTOTYPE EXO-ARMOR SYSTEM 444! ALL SERIAL NUMBERS! WITH RESTRAINT SYSTEM EXCEPTION, INITIATE FULL SYSTEM SHUTDOWN!" The escaping prisoners immediately fell on their faces once their armor de-energized.

Saeli Hermour's face dropped. "What are you doing, Gunny?"

The lieutenant smiled at her. "He can't risk leaving us alive, Sergeant. We know your secrets. We know how you took Peeli's platoon now. We know you can exploit a weakness in our system software. If this gets out, your little trick will be worthless."

"It was a trick we didn't even know we still had until a little while ago,"

Hermour told Francis. "It doesn't affect anything."

"It affects everything," Francis informed her. "It's a huge advantage we can't afford to just throw away."

"Wait! Wait!" Naktada pled. "How the hell are we going to get to that three-to-one ratio Tauk needs if we execute all of our prisoners?"

"Sergeant Hermour," Francis softly said as he turned to face the squad leader. "Leave me two of my Raiders. Take the rest back to the rendezvous and let Je'Sikka know the mine is secure. Tell her we need to bring the *Hornet* here."

"But Gunny...."

"Saeli, do it now. We don't know when the Marines might return to pick up their platoon."

Hermour looked sick to her stomach, but after spotting an uncharacteristic sadness in Gunny's eyes, she knew there would be no sense arguing with him. She dismissed herself with a nod and walked away to carry out Francis's instructions.

Naktada was not so easily persuaded. "Francis, give them a chance to...."

"This is Suma Corps, Dmitri," Francis interrupted. "We can't trust them. They'll do to us what we did to the Narmans at the Satapadaya. They have no choice."

"What do you mean they have no choice?!? They might...!"

Francis swung around and slapped the armorer in the center of his breastplate. "Dimi! Think about it for a second! These Marines know what's going on here! They know what's happening to the Portunese and the Terrakandians, and they know who's doing it to them! They can't join us! Because heaven help them if they lose!"

"What?!? If we win, we're going to do everything we can to build a better society!"

"No," Francis corrected him, "if you win, *you're* going to try to build a better society. After everything the Samaaris did to them in those camps, what do you think the Portunese will want to do to these pricks if the shoe suddenly lands on the other foot?"

"Th-th-they wouldn't...."

"Dimi, they already have!" Francis spat back. "You weren't on the ground at Razbauten! I was! I saw what the inmates did to the guards there! And you know what?!? I don't even fucking blame them for it! You saw what the Blue Shirts did to those poor people! Do you think you can judge them for their actions that night?"

"No! Of course not! That was different, though! These Marines haven't done anything like that!"

"Yet," Francis assured the armorer. "Yet. We both know what the Suma Corps' mission is down here, though."

Naktada raised his good arm and nervously ran his fingers through his soaked hair. As an intellectual, he knew Francis's argument was sound. All he could say was, "This isn't fucking right, Francis!"

"I know it ain't right. You're a smart man, Dimi. The smartest I've ever met. If you can use that big brain of yours to give me a logical, strategic reason that'll compel me not to do what I'm about to, I'm all ears, buddy."

All Naktada could do was stare at Francis for a long second. Finally, he cursed and stomped away. After swearing some more, he walked back. "I ain't got shit. Deep down, I know there really isn't much of a choice, but I guess I just don't want to burden my conscience by condoning what we have to do."

Francis turned back to the lieutenant and swallowed hard. There was no way out now. There would be no reprieve for the enemy Marines, nor for their executioner. Pulling his sidearm out, Francis pointed his weapon at the space between the officer's eyes. "I'm sorry, sir, but...."

"Whatever," the platoon leader snarled. "Just get it fucking over with."

Granting the officer his request, Francis squeezed the trigger, blasting a pulse of Harnillium energy through the lieutenant's skull and killing him instantly. He then approached the enemy unit's platoon sergeant, his opposite equivalent. Gunny Terso Jogen tried to spit at him, but his mouth was too dry. His last words were, "Fuck you, traitor."

Francis's next victim was much less defiant. "Wait, Gunny! Wait!" she pleaded. "You don't have to do this! I got a family! I...!" Francis's hands started to shake after killing that one.

Corporal Padi Frimen was one of Francis's Raiders. As the enemy Marines struggled to worm their way out of the killing zone, she pulled out her blaster and strolled toward them, intending to help her gunnery sergeant with the abhorrent task.

"What the hell do you think you're doing?" Francis asked her.

"They're trying to get away."

"They won't get far," Francis assured the corporal as he picked up the pace of the executions. "Just keep an eye on them. Start removing the armor and weapons from the ones I've already iced and stage it so it's ready to go when Je'Sikka gets here."

Because of the dark and the rain, Frimen could not see the tears running down the gunnery sergeant's face, but she could tell by his voice that they were there. "You don't have to do this alone," she told him.

Lowering his blaster, Francis turned to face the corporal. "Yeah, Padi, I do. This is the kind of shit that'll follow us to our graves. I'm not going to put something like this on my troops."

While Frimen left to start stripping corpses, Naktada pulled his blaster and took her place.

"Come on, Dimi. Put that thing away," Francis told the armorer.

Dmitri shook his head. "No way, man. We're in this together."

"Don't, Dimi. We both know you ain't no killer."

Naktada aimed his weapon and blew a hole through the head of a young Samaari private who was hysterically begging for his life. "I am now," he croaked.

●●◄●►●●

Chapter 15

THE GORAPARASILIM FACTOR

"What?!?" Haeli Deboara's jaw dropped wide open. It was the type of request she would have expected to hear from a Samaari Blue Shirt, not from Sergeant Terivenda Sotalain, my senior medic.

Teri glared impatiently at Haeli as she stood in the center of the tent that had been appropriated for council business. She was quite angered to have had to ask the question once, let alone repeatedly. She was already operating under a severe time deficit. "I've laid this out twice already. Do I really have to say it all again?"

"Uh...uh...I don't...I..." Haeli stammered as she mentally tried to piece together the facts Sotalain had presented.

Male patient. Ten years old. Parents deceased. Stabbed through cheeks by Blue Shirt during liberation. Infected by Kanarisian bacterium Goraparasilim, *which has destroyed optic and auditory nerves, leaving him both blind and deaf. Under a high regimen of locally derived natural antibiotic. Needs a prolonged super dose for an indefinite period of time to keep the infection from reaching brain. Treatment would exhaust limited resources and put other patients at risk of death from treatable injuries.*

"You're the tie-breaking vote, Ms. Deboara," the corpswoman said. "Do you need me to repeat myself?"

Haeli shook her head and looked at her fellow council members. She agreed to participate mainly to get away from her husband before he drove her insane.

She thought she would be deciding which bases the former prisoners would get farmed out to or how they would produce food for the liberated inmates. She had no inkling that her first petition would be to end a child's life.

"Haeli," pled one of her council cohorts, a middle-aged woman she knew from Saimsun. "We've lost so much life already. If we get them to hold out long enough, they can fix his sight and hearing." Haeli wondered how Kanni got on the council. Her heart was always in the right place, but the only thing she was ever really dependable about was making the wrong decision.

"If we deprive other patients of this medicine, they could end up in the same predicament as this boy," Sotalain snapped. She then turned her attention to one of the men who voted to save the boy but appeared to be wavering. "I'm not doing this for fun, sir! My goal is to save as many people as possible, not one against all odds! Make the right decision!"

For a second, the man looked like he might change his vote. He tried to say something but withdrew, refusing to look the medic in the eye.

"It'll be painless," Teri assured the council. "I've had to do it countless times on the battlefield. I know what I'm doing. Right now, that boy is trapped in an impenetrable silence that he is not accustomed to, alone, and in the dark. He's terrified. Keeping him alive in a fucking war zone is indescribably cruel!"

Even those who voted to ease the child's suffering were reluctant to champion their choice to the holdouts. That prompted one of the resisting women to say, "I'm sorry, sergeant, but I just can't be expected to tell a child we need to kill him."

"If you can't make tough decisions," Teri snapped, "then you shouldn't be entrusted with a position where you're expected to make them."

"The sergeant's right," Haeli said, finally breaking her silence. "Why the hell are we debating this? Here? Are you a doctor, Kanni?"

The woman from Saimsun shook her head.

"What about you?" she asked the man who was wavering. He shook his head, also. "Was anyone here ever a medical professional?"

None of the other six council members raised their hands.

Haeli sighed. "Then I think it's safe to say we're out of our depth. I would like to make a new motion to grant Sergeant Sotalain complete discretion over medical treatment, otherwise, we're going to be burdening her with our indecision every time one of these situations arises."

"I second the motion," quickly said one of the men who voted for euthanasia.

Before it could even get put up for a tally, the two women who wanted to continue the boy's treatment at all costs voted against it. The wavering man broke the stalemate by adding his vote to those agreeing with the medic.

With the issue settled, Sotalain stormed out of the tent to resume her duties. Haeli Deboara was hot on her heels. "Where do you think you're going?" asked my senior medic.

"With you."

"Why?"

"Because I made it possible for you to go ahead and do what you have to do. There is no way I'm letting that little boy pass away alone."

●●-●-●-●-●●

When Haeli Deboara walked back into her tent, her husband rolled over on his cot and let out an exasperated sigh. "It's about time! How long does it take to...?"

Haeli lost it, grabbing an empty ammo can that was within her reach and hurtling it right at Daino's head. He got his arms up in time to avoid a concussion, but the instant the man lowered them, his wife pounced upon his chest, knocking him to the ground as she smacked him about his head and shoulders with everything she had. "You miserable! Ungrateful! Selfish son-of-a-bitch! What the hell is the matter with you? You...! You...! You...! Aaaaaarrghh!"

"I'm crippled!" Daino cried back as Haeli rolled off of him. "Every move I make is torture, Haeli! I can't do anything for myself! I'm sorry! I'm sorry I wasted myself trying to take care of my...."

Unable to bear hearing it one more time, Haeli lashed out and back-handed her man across the jaw. "Don't you say it! Don't you DARE say it! Ever again! I know what you did, Daino! I know what you went through! You seem to keep forgetting what they did to me in that fucking place! Every fucking night! You think I enjoyed that?!? You think that was fun for me?!?"

"No, but...!"

Before Daino could go any further, Haeli let out a gut-wrenching wail that came from the depths of her soul. She then shoved her head between her knees and covered it with her arms as she heaved again and again and again.

Haeli was scaring her husband. He had never seen her like that. Not even during the worst days in Saimsun. Despite his agony, he reached out and put his hand on his wife's shoulder. "Honey...."

She violently slapped Daino's arm away. "DON'T YOU FUCKING TOUCH ME!"

Leaping to her feet, Haeli stepped away from her husband as a torrent of tears ran down her cheeks. "I held a boy today in my arms while they put him to sleep...."

"Put him to sleep?" Daino gasped. "You mean, like a dog?"

Haeli let out a primal scream and kicked her cot so hard it flipped an entire hundred and eighty degrees before it landed on the ground, causing her husband to scurry out of the way to avoid getting hit with it. "Yes, Daino! Like a fucking dog! He was blind and deaf and we didn't have the resources to care for him. Not without taking them away from people we knew we could save. He was so scared, Daino! And sad! But I held him because I was the one who got the council to let that happen."

Wracked with sobs, Haeli then said, "He smiled when I cradled him in my lap. He rubbed my face with one hand while Teri stuck the needle in his other and pumped that poison into him. Do you know what his last word was, Daino? Huh? You wanna take a guess?"

Mister Deboara shook his head emphatically. He did not want to hear anything more.

Haeli plopped down on the floor and buried her face in her hands. When she regained enough composure to speak again, she said, "His last word was 'mama.' And then he was gone."

The sounds wafting in from outside suggested a crowd was gathering around their tent. That was no surprise, considering how crowded their camp was and how little there was to do other than wander around. The realization she had an audience compelled Haeli to pull herself together. "I'm not doing the council again, Daino. Once was enough. I can't make any more decisions that might harm our own, even if it is for the greater good. I'm not cut out for it. I'm better suited for killing our enemies rather than our children."

For a split instant, her husband looked ready to say something, but the look on his wife's face made him reconsider. "I'm leaving to fight with Eamon Tauk, Daino. Whether or not I come back is up to you."

I looked at Black Francis and shook my head with regret. "I should have been there."

"The fuck you should have!" my gunny slurred as he leaned forward and nearly fell out of his bunk. "You're our leader, now. You're the guy who's supposed to have all the big ideas! The person who guides us into pulling this shit off! You need to learn to leave the nasty work to people like me, Eamon."

Francis was right. I needed to be the big-picture guy. It was hard to mentally make that transition, though. I felt guilty expecting others to do horrific things on my behalf without getting my own hands dirty. "If it's any consolation, it was the only decision you possibly could have made."

"I know it was," Francis told me. "And no, it isn't any consolation." My gunnery sergeant took another drink of brandy and tried to pass the bottle to Dmitri Naktada on the rack beside him. The armorer made no move to take it. He was passed out cold.

"This is going to save a lot of lives," I said. "Those eighty dead Marines mean thousands of living Portunese. It also buys us time to train the inmates. We don't have to go in before the Suma Corps anymore. In fact, now we have to wait for them to assume their posts in the mines."

Francis stared at me with a blank expression on his face. His mouth was slightly agape, and a bit of drool ran out of the corner of it. "I've killed a lot of people, Eamon," my gunny confessed as he wiped his chin with his arm. "It was always in the heat of battle, though. It was them or me. I never had to think about it much, you know?"

After pausing to take a drink from his bottle, he said, "Well, I sure got to think about it this time. I got to look each one of them in the eye before I blasted a hole right through their head. Capping the platoon leader and his gunny was easy.

They'd been around. They knew the score. The rest of them, though? They were just kids. Boys. Girls. Stupid fucking kids."

"You're only twenty-seven years old, Gunny. Those Marines weren't that much younger than you are."

"It ain't the years, Eamon. It's the experience. Those punks I shot didn't have a chance to learn a damn thing. They weren't like me. I've been places and seen some shit."

My gunny paused to cast a bleary-eyed gaze into the space between us. "Man, have I ever seen some shit. I feel like I'm fifty. I've been in battle almost nine years. For the most part, I'm okay with that. It's horrible stuff, but there's an adrenaline rush to it that I've gotten myself addicted to."

Francis took another long drink of booze. "Well, today, my man, I think I finally got over it. What I did in Razbauten wasn't war. It was murder. This shit ain't fun anymore."

I nodded and turned my gaze to the deck. "It's probably going to get worse before it gets better."

Francis knew that, but he did not need to hear it. He burst into sobs and buried his head in his hands. While he wept, I remembered what Gunny Malcolm said to me during the trek to Narman's Pyke.

Mark my words, Tauk. If you survive this shit here and go on to future missions, you'll eventually find yourself confronting people who maybe don't deserve it so much. And when that happens, after you've carried out your orders, then you'll be a proper killer. Not a ten-percenter, but a **killer.**

Seeing the pain Francis was in, I was sorry to realize that my gunny had made that leap.

"I got them all, Eamon," Francis said after he pulled himself together. "So, as long as we keep Vulk and Takawa in our possession, we don't have to worry about anyone getting back to Narman's Pyke and letting them know about the flaw in their new combat gear."

I shook my head and told him, "We only have to worry about Vulk now. Takawa's not talking."

"Huh? Why not?"

"He's dead."

Francis seemed to sober up a little. "No shit? What happened?"

"He committed suicide."

"How?" Naktada exclaimed. "He was in a cage! With a guard! How the hell did he manage to kill himself?!?"

"He bashed his head against the bars so hard he split his skull open and gave himself a brain bleed. It was pretty impressive by the sound of it. I would not have thought it physically possible. Vulk talked him into it. The guards said she spent days giving him lurid descriptions about what happens when Kryndil skins his Samaaris alive."

Francis blinked at me in disbelief. "Why did Vulk want him dead?"

I shrugged. "No reason in particular. Apparently, the bitch just got bored."

Chapter 16

Guests

When he woke up the following morning, Black Francis was no longer dwelling on the atrocity he had committed the day before. He was distracted by an epic hangover that had him struggling to stand up as Melki, Kryndil, and their human companions checked in with our perimeter guard before entering the grounds. "How do you think they get around?" my gunnery sergeant asked me.

"What?"

"The Morghul," Francis said, suppressing a gag as he leaned against the hull of the *Hornet* to steady himself. "How do you think they move from place to place? They're in the Arad Valley. Then they're at Xaramika. Then, our base. Then at wherever the fuck Kryndil hangs out at. How do you think they get to all these places? I've never seen an alien aircraft."

I had so much other stuff on my mind since we defected that I had not even thought about it. "Maybe they have a ship with cloaking tech that we haven't seen yet?"

"No, they don't," Je'Sikka said as she emerged from her ship and stepped beside us. "The jungle in this region is so thick that we're camped in literally the only place to land an aircraft within a hundred kilometers."

Before we could seriously debate the issue, our guests were upon us. In addition to the folks we were expecting, the Narman party brought along one we were not — a young boy we had never seen before.

"So," I said to our guests as I held my hand out to Melki. "To what do we owe the pleasure of this visit?"

The alien smiled as he adjusted his headgear to keep the sun off his face. Usually, the Morghul wore hooded cloaks and goggles when they went about their business outdoors. Both Kryndil and Melki came to us that time wearing large, circular helmets that made it appear as if they were adorned with black metallic mushroom caps atop their crowns. Their covers seemed big enough to protect the aliens from both the rain and solar rays. I sometimes swore that the Morghul acted like vampires with their aversion to exposing themselves to sunlight.

"We have set up another couple of bases to spread your people out," Melki informed me.

"Perfect!" Our current camp was rustic and severely overpopulated. Kryptids were always plentiful on Kanaris and kept us from going hungry, but there were so many people around we were starting to deplete the damned things. We had to venture further and further outside the perimeter to find food, which increased the danger of running into predators or crossing paths with an enemy patrol. Not to mention, having our entire population in one location made me a nervous wreck. If the Marines found us, we could all be wiped out with a single missile fired from the *Nebulean Phoenix*.

"Where are you sending them?" I asked the Morghul elder.

"Those you are training to liberate the camps, we will send to a place we call Ganamai. It's a large cavern with a small opening. If your pilot is skillful, you can still get one of your freighters in there, but just barely."

"Our freighter pilots are prisoners," I said. "I'm not sure how much I would trust them."

"I can do it," Je'Sikka said. "I can fly damn near anything. I'm kind of a prodigy that way."

"Have you flown them before?" I asked her.

"I sure have," Albarn said. "We had to evacuate a research station suffering a catastrophic structural failure on an asteroid in the Plaicieni Belt when I first joined the Fleet. We tried to do it in Wasp transports, but it was going way too slow. I suggested making one trip with a Warp Haug instead of ten with a Wasp. Since the hanger pod was destroyed, we would have had to fly it into a hole in the station's hub with a diameter only two meters wider than the ship. The freighter's usual pilot refused to do it. He said it was impossible."

"You proved him wrong?" asked Melki.

Albarn beamed with pride. "I sure did. I got in, loaded the entire population of the facility into the cargo hold, and got away without so much as scratching that Haug. That earned me my first Flying Cross and my very own Wasp to command."

"Your *first* Flying Cross?" asked the boy, who sounded very impressed. Like Je'Sikka, he had dark skin, black hair, and green eyes. They did not look close enough to be related, but I suspected he might also have been a product of her home planet of Niberia.

"I have four Flying Crosses," Albarn told him. "I got my last one right here on Kanaris."

"I was there for that one," I sighed, remembering how we crash-landed on the beach that day. "No offense, but I really hope I'm not around when she earns her fifth."

Getting back to business, I turned to the Morghul elder and asked, "What about the rest of our former inmates?"

"My understanding is that they need to recover, yes?"

I nodded.

"Well, they are not going to recover here. We're taking them in at Xaramika."

"You're letting us into Xaramika?" I asked.

Melki cast his eyes toward the ground in embarrassment. "Them. Not you, Eamon Tauk. Not your Raiders. Not yet."

I understood. The last time they trusted my people, we damned near destroyed them. "Melki, we've recently made a discovery that will significantly change our plans to liberate the mines. We might free a lot of prisoners in a very short amount of time. I need to figure out what to do with them."

"How many people are we talking about?" Melki asked.

"Damned near all of them."

Melki and Kryndil gasped. Meinhopf exclaimed, "That's 75,000 people!"

"It is."

Leila Hyfer shook her head in disbelief. "Impossible. How the hell do you think you're going to pull that off?"

I shook my head apologetically. "I can't tell you that. If we're going to be successful, we need complete operational security. Just like the location of Xaramika is crucial to your survival, this information is critical to ours."

Melki nodded in understanding. "Fair enough. Eamon, we're going to have to get creative. Xaramika might be able to take in twenty thousand." Turning to Kryndil, he asked, "What about your lair in Jamatta?"

"None," Kryndil barked. "I'm already infested with more humans than I can tolerate."

"Kryndil, you need fighters to help defend your lair."

"Fighters?!? The humans these people will end up with will be scrawny, weak little creatures without weapons! What are we supposed to do?!? Make them spears?"

"What if they were equipped with the same armor and weapons we have?" I asked the alien skin thief.

"Are you serious?" Kryndil asked.

"Dead serious," I assured him.

Kryndil stepped toward me. "Equipped and ready to fight?"

I shook my head. "Equipped. They'll need a lot of training. They might also need some time to get their strength back."

"Thirty thousand," Kryndil said. "I can take thirty thousand fighters."

"That leaves us with twenty-thousand we need to provide for," I told them.

"Take the fittest," Hyfer suggested. "Teach them how to live rough. Keep them on patrol to confront the Marines. Search and destroy."

Francis turned his bloodshot eyes upon the Narman officer. "That'll whittle down the number pretty quick."

Hyfer shrugged. "That's the nature of war. You think we're going to fight the League and not take any casualties? Besides, if you think you're going to have your fighting inmates equipped in all that new fancy gear, you should have quite the tactical advantage." There was a bitterness in Hyfer's voice hinting at her displeasure that our untrained recruits would end up better equipped than her proven veterans.

Grinning, I asked Albarn to open the aft doors of the *Niberian Hornet*. Turning to Hyfer, I pointed to one of my troops heading out on patrol in full combat gear. "You sound like you might be interested in a taste of that tech."

Hyfer scoffed. "You're goddamn right I am."

"Then follow me." We reached the back of the Mar-Sitaara just as the egress ramp lowered. Inside were more than eighty sets of new armor and Harnillium-based weaponry. Hyfer's jaw dropped open when she saw it all. So did those of the aliens. "We'll need some time to get it combat-ready, but after we're finished, it's all yours."

"Mine?" Hyfer gasped. "You're giving it to me?"

I shrugged. "We've got a platoon's worth of gear we captured from Mott Peeli's troops and we don't have anyone ready to use it yet. Black Francis suggested you could actually accomplish something with this stuff."

My gunnery sergeant shot me a look of surprise. He had not said that, but I figured giving him credit for the gesture might help thaw some of the ice between him and Hyfer after what happened at the Satapadaya.

It might have worked. Hyfer got very excited. She was practically salivating as she asked, "When do you think we could take possession of it?"

Before I could answer, I spotted Dmitri Naktada fall out of the *Hornet* in his underwear and roll down the starboard exit steps, still drunk from the night before. He then struggled to lift himself onto all fours before projectile vomiting into the mud in full view of our visitors.

Turning back to Leila Hyfer, I answered, "It might take a little while."

We were aboard the *Niberian Hornet*, seated around the table in the mission briefing room, when Bengin Meinhopf formally introduced the boy who was with them. Placing his hand on the young man's shoulder, he said, "This is Ovai Soldana. One of my most trusted operatives. He's our connection to Narman's Pyke."

I squinted at Soldana. "How old are you?"

"Fifteen, sir."

"And you're already a Narman field agent?"

The boy wagged his finger at me. "Yes. I am. And I'm a good one, too. Mostly because people like you underestimate me."

"Spying on Marines is a dangerous business," Black Francis said.

"I don't think there's anything but dangerous business on Kanaris these days," Ovai retorted.

"I can't argue with that," I agreed. "So, what brings you here to my camp?"

Meinhopf answered for him. "Have you made contact with your person inside the Pyke yet?"

I shook my head. "No. I've been a bit busy."

"I bet you have," Meinhopf told me. "And I bet that situation isn't going to change in the near future. You need someone to handle your source."

I looked at Soldana again. "And you're suggesting this brave young man? I'm not sure my person is going to trust their life with someone so...so...young."

"They will if you tell them to," Soldana said. "Make the introduction, sir. I'll handle the rest."

"And what are you going to have her do?" I asked. "My asset is good people. I won't have them getting absorbed into any risky missions on your behalf. My person is not expendable."

"None of my assets are expendable," Ovai assured me. "If we're going to reach that three-to-one ratio everyone's talking about, we need to keep all our people alive."

"Have you ever lost an asset?" Je'Sikka Albarn asked.

The boy nodded. "I have. And I take *every* loss very personally. I admit I'll likely lose more in the future, too. I can assure you, though, that none of my assets was ever lost because of something I did."

"You telling me you've never made a mistake?" Black Francis asked.

"I've made plenty of mistakes, just not with my assets. Look, sir, my objective is not very exciting or glamorous. It's simply to recruit Marines to our side. Because of the nature of our work, sometimes my contacts approached the wrong person and got turned in. Sometimes, Section 615 just got lucky. Other times, Marine counterintelligence was just better than we were."

It was an honest answer, but I still hedged. Elia Gyanis was an essential member of my team. I could not bring myself to put her life in the hands of a child. "I don't know, I...."

"He's the only one I got who can slip in and out of Narman's Pyke, Tauk," Meinhopf told me. "Unless you're going to be making regular trips yourself, you need to let Ovai work your asset. Make the introduction."

"You want me to go to Narman's Pyke with you?" I asked the young man.

Nodding, Soldana said, "I doubt I'll gain the trust of your asset if you don't."

"I've got a pretty famous face," I warned Ovai. "If I turn up in that place, people are going to know about it."

"Yeah," Black Francis said. "He's the guy who killed Gori Dravidas."

"Nobody sees me going into Narman's Pyke," Soldana bragged. "And nobody's going to see you. Once we make contact with your asset, I'll give them a device to transmit their intel to us. We can also relay our messages to them over the same circuit. We should never have to meet in person again. To get this set up, though, I need you to get me in contact with them."

I sighed. "How long have you been doing this?"

"More than a year."

"And how are you getting in?"

Soldana grinned. "There's a drainage pipe leading out of...."

I held up my hand, cutting the young man off. "Say no more. I know that route better than I would like to."

When our meeting concluded, Black Frances and I escorted the visitors back to the perimeter. As we approached the former ubati pen, I turned to Kryndil. "I have a gift for you, too," I told him. "If you're interested."

Unlike Melki, Kryndil was a creature of ill humor. "You have a gift for me?" he snarled. Unsaid, but implied in his tone was the sentiment, *What could you possibly have that I would want?*

Pointing my chin at the last prisoner I had in my camp, I asked, "You have any ideas what to do with her?"

The Morghul executioner stopped in his tracks and stared at Deena Vulk. "Yes. I have big plans for that woman."

"Then she's all yours," I told him.

Catching Kryndil and me staring at her, Vulk stood up, smiled, and waved our way with childlike enthusiasm. "Hello Kryndil darling! Have you missed me? Have you come to take me home?"

"Goddamn, that bitch is crazy," I remarked.

After giving me a single nod, the alien said, "You have no fucking idea."

Chapter 17

BINA

As a woman, Elia Gyanis had no reason to ever set foot inside a Marine Morale Center. If she wanted to take a lover, she was surrounded by young men who would enthusiastically give her anything she wanted. All she had to do was ask. Being blessed with good looks, she would not have had much trouble finding a female among her peers to pleasure her either, had she been so inclined. As she sat in the facility's lobby waiting for her date, Elia was grossly out of place, and it did not go unnoticed.

"What the hell are you doing here?" a heavily intoxicated comrade asked from the seat across from her.

Gyanis did her best to look aloof, but she blushed, and her hands started to shake. She tried to look the leatherneck in the eye but could not help herself from diverting her gaze. "The same thing you are."

"You telling me you can't find a date?" the rifleman laughed. "You'll be a welcome change from the ass pounding the guys here are used to taking."

"I'm not here for a man," Elia said as she tried to turn her attention elsewhere. The problem was that there was not much to look at. In the civilian world, skin palaces would be lavish and decadent. In the Corps, they were just another government building. Despite trying to provide the illusion of romance, the Morale Center lobby had all the charm of a hospital waiting room. There weren't even any pictures on the walls – just the scars one would expect to find in a room that regularly accommodated scores of young men full of testosterone, alcohol, and Post-Traumatic Stress Disorder.

After taking another long pull from a canteen full of mess deck hooch, the Marine huffed. "Ain't here for a man, eh? Maybe you just ain't had the right one yet."

Elia rolled her eyes. "How original. Let me guess. You think you're the right man?"

The Marine grinned. "You know it, baby."

"If you were the right man, you wouldn't be here paying for pussy, would you?"

The leatherneck's smile turned into a glare. "You think you're too good for me or something? If you were so hot, why are you here shelling out credits for a little trim?"

"Because I want an orgasm, not a relationship."

Before the Marine could retort, the sergeant working the desk called out, "Gyanis!"

Relieved by the reprieve, Elia stood up and exclaimed, "Here!"

The sergeant grinned, showing off a couple of broken teeth, trophies from a tussle he had with Barone Parsons months before. "I'm not taking attendance, sweetheart. Come to the desk, please."

When Elia got close enough for the sergeant to speak to her without yelling, he said, "Room 131. It'll be open."

Bina Dubarti smiled as Elia entered her room. Unlike the spartan décor of the Morale Center's lobby, the space in which Bina was forced to work was a little more homey. There were painted pictures of beautiful alien landscapes adorning the walls, colored sheets on the bed, and even a couple of houseplants on the nightstands. Bina herself was dressed in a floral printed robe, loosely hanging over lacey lingerie. She was gorgeous, with brown hair, flawless pink skin, and yellow eyes, a rare trait only found in people from Lanumoana.

"Well," Bina said as she laid eyes on her client. "This is quite a surprise. Ladies are rare in a Space Corps comfort station."

Elia shut the door and leaned against it, subconsciously keeping as much distance between herself and her host as possible. "Ritza Xi sent me."

Bina nodded. "That's quite a recommendation. Why don't you make yourself comfortable and come sit next to me."

Elia shook her head. "I'm not here for intimacy. I'm here to ask for your help."

Dubarti was having none of that. If Elia was reluctant to come to her, she would have to go to Elia. As she approached, the armorer tried to pull away. "No, Bina, don't. I'm not into girls that way."

The convict reached out and placed her hand behind Gyanis's neck, pulling her in close to kiss her. "I'm not either, but I don't have the choice of refusing who I sleep with."

The armorer tried to push her away. "Well, I do and...."

Bina shoved Elia up against the wall and forced their lips together. Sergeant Gyanis was raised in a moderately affluent family on Sumar Agadi, despite her red dreadlocks and tattoos. Though athletic, she was not tough. She was not a fighter. Bina Dubarti was. She grew up rough, running with the gangs of street urchins who ruled the alleys of Wardaan. Elia may have been a Recon Marine, but she could not match the aggression and hostility of a lifelong criminal like Bina Dubarti.

When Bina pulled her lips from Elia's, she put them close to her client's ear and whispered, "No, darling, if you want my help, you don't have any choice at all. The game you're trying to break into is unforgiving. You can't just tell people you're coming in here to have a go at a woman and expect them to take it at face value. You have to make them believe it. And if you want them to believe it, you'd better believe it yourself. You have to assume the role if you want to survive this. You can't pretend. You have to become what you need people to believe you are. Am I clear?"

Unable to speak, Elia nodded.

"Good," Bina said as she reached up and cupped Gyanis's breast in her hand. "Besides, if you walk out of here as fresh as you walked in, looking like we had nothing more than idle conversation, you're going to get both of us killed."

After Elia nodded again, Bina started unbuttoning the Marine's fatigues. "You're Elia, right?"

Finally regaining her voice, Sergeant Gyanis said, "Yes."

"Ritza stopped by before she left and told me to expect you. She described you quite differently, though. Brown hair, girl next door look. I was not expecting red dreads and all the ink."

"I've had a bit of a transformation," Elia said, stating the obvious.

"I'll say. What sparked it?"

Elia was not about to confess what she had done to Idris. Not to a convict she had just met. Still, thinking about what had happened to her friend caused Gyanis's lip to quiver and gave her credence when she said, "I spent some time in Killbilly custody."

Bina nodded as she pulled off Elia's shirt. She knew exactly what being in Killbilly custody meant for a woman. "Good."

Elia glowered at Dubarti in shock. "Good?!?"

"You've got an explanation for the sudden lifestyle change. The new look. Your sudden interest in loving women. Trauma doesn't really change who we're attracted to, but it does make people do unpredictable things. You got hurt, it messed you up, and you decided to make some radical changes. Now, you're engaging in a little experimentation. Maybe this thing we're doing will stick. Maybe it won't. You've given yourself some wiggle room, Elia."

Wiggling was exactly what Gyanis was doing as Bina started undoing Elia's pants. "Relax. I'm not a Killbilly. I'm not going to hurt you. Now, honey, what are you trying to accomplish by coming to me? What are your goals?"

"Recruitment," Elia gasped as Bina sucked one of her nipples into her mouth and slipped a hand into her panties. "We need to pull disaffected Marines under our umbrella and keep them under control until we have enough to launch an effective attack against the League."

Bina released Elia's breast long enough to ask, "Didn't you try that before?"

"Yes," Elia whimpered. She could feel herself getting wet and found it embarrassing.

Dubarti had been working Marine morale centers for a long time. She knew what she was doing and could sense the sergeant's discomfort. "It's okay, honey. Your body is doing what it was designed to do. Now, why do the Narmans think recruiting deserters will have different results than it did last time?"

"They didn't go far enough back. All they did was recruit the Marines at the front. This time, we want to hit the bastards all the way back to the mothership if we can. We also want them under a single command."

"Under Eamon Tauk?" Bina asked.

"Xi told you about him?"

"Her and others," the comfort woman said as she removed the last of Elia's clothing and led her to the bed. As she finished undressing herself, Bina said, "Tauk killed Gori Dravidas. Having him go over to the other side was a big deal. A lot of the Marines are thinking if someone like him is jumping ship, things must really be turning up rotten around here. Others have been posted in those mining camps the Tahnebaht Conglomerate has been running out in the jungle. They're terrified of Tauk attacking them while they're out there. They're also pretty disgusted by what they've seen the Samaaris doing to the inmates."

As Bina crawled over Elia and began grinding her body against the sergeant's, she said, "There're going to be a lot of disgruntled Marines in Narman's Pyke as they start returning from their rotations in those camps. Most of them are conscripts that were not exactly enamored with the League to begin with, but now that the curtain has been pulled back, revealing the cruelty the Samaaris are capable of, the fuse is lit. Your challenge isn't finding recruits, Sarge. It's going to be keeping them from going off prematurely. Which, I can say from experience, many of them are already prone to doing."

In spite of herself, Elia laughed. "Your customers tell you stuff like this? What they saw in the camps?"

Bina was about to bury her face between Elia's legs but stopped to answer her question first. "You would be shocked how many men come in here just to lay beside me in their underwear and cry on my shoulder about what they've seen happen or have even been forced to do. Of course, others enjoy taking me rough, slapping me around a bit, and bragging about all the sick shit they've participated in. If you ever reach a point where you need targets instead of prospects, let me know. I'll give you those names."

"Can you think of anyone who would be willing to do more than cry about what's going on out there?"

"Sugar, some of these guys are already about to strike back. In fact, one of my regulars came to tell me goodbye yesterday. Him and his buddies are planning on icing the Killbillies they saw helping Blue Shirts brutalize inmates at the

Harnillium mine they were posted to. They don't expect to survive that fight."

Elia sat up in bed. "I need you to give me that name."

Bina placed her hand on Elia's belly and gently pushed her back down. "First, you're going to have to let me finish what I have in mind for you. Then, after I teach you how to do that same thing to me, I'll give you the names you need."

Elia winced and covered her face with her hands. "Are we going to have to do this every time we meet?"

Dubarti nodded as she kissed Elia tenderly on her inner thigh. "Yes. At least we are until you get used to it."

What Bina Dubarti did to Elia was nothing compared to the horrors the Killbillies had inflicted on her, but the sergeant still felt soiled and dirty when she returned home. Within ten minutes of walking through her door, Gyanis was naked once more, bawling in the shower. She was ashamed, humiliated, alone, and considering giving in to the thoughts of suicide that had frequently invaded her thoughts of late. She leaned against the wall and sobbed, wondering what she possibly could have done to earn what the Qilkorians and Bina had done to her.

Then Elia recalled how she betrayed Idris Jatmika and doubted she had suffered enough. She was confident she deserved everything she got and more.

As the scalding water flowed over her head, Elia wondered how long she would have to wait before joining her friend in oblivion. If they ever did meet again in whatever came after death, Gyanis wondered if Idris would understand why Elia did what she had. The sergeant had listened to Idris's dark fantasies while together in the bush. Gyanis knew the woman was damaged and ready to blow. Idris had spent years conditioning herself to hate the Narmans, so there was no way she could ever join them. Yet, after seeing the horrors of what was happening in Saimsun, she had quickly grown to hate the League, too. Then the Killbillies got hold of her.

Idris Jatmika was a goner. Had she made it off Kanaris, she would have destroyed herself and likely left scores of innocent bodies in her wake. Elia saw that coming long before the Killbillies got to them in the Arad Valley. By doing what she did, Elia ensured that Idris's death at least had a purpose.

While Elia tried to rationalize her betrayal in the steam, she heard her tablet go off with the special ringtone she reserved for her more clandestine activities. "Tauk!" she gasped as she ran from the shower to grab her device without even bothering to dry off.

Gyanis quickly discovered she was not being contacted by her former platoon leader. Instead, she was the recipient of a mass messaging string delivering video evidence of the atrocities Peeli's Marines and Samaari Blue Shirts were committing at the Tahnebaht Conglomerate's Kanarisian mining facilities.

Everyone at Narman's Pyke had heard the rumors. Now, not only did *they* know the truth, their comrades aboard the mothership awaiting their turn in the jungle knew it too.

And Elia Gyanis knew that Ritza Xi was traveling at warp speed through space, heading to a destination where she would not have to face the horrors of Kanaris. For a change, she would be the horror people feared to face .

Chapter 18

VINDICATION

When Major Kuusip saw Agent Biragor marching down the corridor toward the briefing room, he was so enraged he had to restrain himself from shooting her on the spot. "Where the fuck have you been?!?" he snarled at her.

"Trying to figure out where those videos came from," Nala snarled back as she passed him in the hall. She did not even slow her pace as she walked by.

"I've been trying to find you for three fucking days, Biragor!" Kuusip snapped as he jogged to keep up with her. "Why the hell haven't you checked in to tell me what you found?"

Nala shrugged. "You've never been interested in what I had to say before. I figured I'd do us both the favor of not wasting our time trying to brief you now."

That was the last straw for Kuusip. He grabbed his subordinate by the collar of her fatigues, spun her around, and slammed her up against the wall. "I'm your goddamn superior, Agent Biragor! You don't have the luxury of keeping me in the fucking dark! Do you have any idea who's meeting us in the briefing room?!? Commandant Taillur! That man wants answers about how those videos got out and spread throughout the whole Marine Expeditionary Force! They even made it to the fucking mothership! And if they get out into the civilian population...!"

While Kuusip had her by the collar, Biragor reached out and grabbed the major between the legs, wrapping her fingers around his testicles and giving them a brutal twist. Kuusip immediately let go of the field agent. Nala did not return the gesture.

"Trust me," Biragor growled. "Those videos are already in circulation back home. Let's get something straight. Number one, you may outrank me, but you most certainly are *not* my superior. You're a far cry from even being my equal. Number two, I gave you the opportunity to get ahead of this and you laughed me out of your office. This is your fuck up, not mine, and I don't appreciate you throwing me under the bus to...."

"I...I...I didn't throw you under the bus," Kuusip said as sweat beads formed along his hairline.

Nala had thick, black eyelashes that matched her brows and hair. The dark makeup she used made her blue eyes stand out, especially when they twinkled in amusement. "Really?" she purred to Kuusip. "You didn't tell Commandant Taillur that I was in charge of suppressing misinformation and this Narman propaganda campaign getting out was the result of my incompetence?"

As Major Kuusip tried to stammer out an answer, Commandant Taillur and his guards rounded the corner and marched toward them on his way to the briefing room. Protocol demanded both Kuusip and Biragor snap to attention and salute as their commander passed, but Nala made no attempt to uphold the ritual, and the major feared any movement on his part would result in instant emasculation. The commandant did not seem to mind the lapse in tradition, however.

"Agent Biragor," Taillur said as he passed, "please refrain from feeling up the major during working hours. Let him go and join us in the briefing room. We have things to discuss."

As bad as the pain was in Kuusip's groin, it paled in comparison to witnessing the familiarity Taillur displayed toward Biragor. Coupled with the commander's disinterest in him being assaulted in public, the major was forced to reckon with the fact that his subordinate had the Section 615 director's ear, and in return, he had her back.

That meant Izo Kuusip was standing on very thin ice.

After reviewing all the data she had collected over the past few days, Nala Biragor turned to the room full of general officers and intelligence directors to summarize the results.

"The evidence suggests that when Eamon Tauk sent his loyalists back to Narman's Pyke, it was not the act of mercy that it seemed on the surface. Among the returned Marines was Lance Corporal Idris Jatmika, one of Tauk's machine gunners. She impregnated the network with this Narman propaganda and delayed its distribution for several weeks, likely timing it to send once she was off Kanaris and in a position to flee the Corps before it went out. Fortunately, one of Jatmika's former comrades, another lance corporal named Silma Hauken, detected her suspicious activity and reported it to the Military Police."

Biragor sighed as the screen behind her lit up with the faces of three MPs recently killed in the line of duty. "When the authorities went to take Jatmika into custody, she resisted. She managed to remove the weapon from one of the officers and gun them all down before fleeing from the scene."

General Ivan Kuolaada, the commander of Alpha Corps asked, "How did one woman manage to overpower and disarm three experienced MPs?"

Nala turned toward the presentation device and ordered it to bring up the picture of a Marine from the planet of Praminat. Once her image filled the wall, Biragor said, "This is Nila Chisek. She is a master in the martial art of Qılıç Elai. This fighting style is specifically designed to allow a smaller, weaker combatant to take on much larger, stronger adversaries. It also emphasizes methods to disarm one's enemies and use their own weapons against them. Nila Chisek was Eamon Tauk's praetorian and spent a lot of time training the platoon's female Marines in this stuff. I suspect she taught it to their Class Zero convicts as well."

Without any further questions being offered, Nala continued with her summary. "After killing the MPs, Jatmika stole one of their tablets. She then made her way to the stateroom of a Marine armorer friend, one Elia Gyanis, who she choked out to steal her diagnostic box. From there, her trail goes cold, and we have a couple hour blackout. We believe she used the box to hack...."

"Whoa! Wait a second, Agent Biragor," called out a military intelligence colonel. "Idris Jatmika was a machine gunner, not a technician. It takes a great deal of expertise to use an armorer's DB. Hell, she'd have to hack that before she could even hack the tablet, and those boxes possess far more sophisticated security protocols than police equipment does!"

"You have to remember that Dmitri Naktada was among the defectors who went to the Narmans with Tauk," Biragor replied. "We found a simple four-digit override code that cracked the device wide open that he probably slipped onto it without Gyanis's knowledge. This would have been well within the range of Jatmika's abilities."

"How do you know Gyanis didn't put the program there herself?"

Biragor shrugged. "It's possible. As you know, colonel, much of intelligence work is done with your gut. During my interview with Gyanis, she insisted that Jatmika must have had help, indicating she did not think her friend capable of working the DB. Based upon my fifteen years of interrogation experience, I assessed her to be sincere."

Moving on, Biragor said, "By hacking the MP tablet, Jatmika discovered what she was under suspicion of and who reported her. Knowing she was living on borrowed time, she set out to exact revenge against the Marine who turned her in and the Qilkorian death squad members who had recently abused her. She killed Silma Hauken and several squad men before being gunned down herself."

Biragor began pacing in front of her audience. "With Jatmika gone, we had no way of knowing these videos were in our network, duplicating themselves, until a few days ago, when they were broadcast throughout the Corps."

Commandant Taillur himself asked the next question. "Agent Biragor, what has been the reaction to this video among the rank and file?"

Major Kuusip, desperate to downplay the significance of the breach to the commandant, answered for her. "It's been surprisingly muted, sir. We expected riots, retaliatory attacks against the Qilkorians, and the grunts to frag a few Samaar i officers. There's been nothing of the sort, though. It's been quiet. I take that as a very good sign."

Nala Biragor looked at Kuusip as if he had just grown a second head. "Have you even watched the video, Major?" When her boss did not answer, she turned to the projector and commanded it to play the clip beginning at the one-minute mark. Pivoting to face her audience again, she held her hand up toward the screen. "Ladies and gentlemen, I give you Eamon Tauk."

"I know what you've seen is disturbing," I told them from the feed. The footage had been shot a few days before our defection. "Let me assure you that the longer you watch this video, the worse it gets. If you have any humanity left in you at all, you'll be tempted to lash out. You'll want to turn against the Samaari leadership and slaughter them wholesale. I don't blame you. In fact, I'm plotting their overthrow as we speak. I am begging you to stand fast, though. Any action you take now will be a futile and pointless waste of life on your part. You don't have the numbers or the organization to succeed. We're working to rectify that."

I paused to look at the camera. "I was raised to be a patriot, to fanatically support the League at all costs and carry out their mandates with blind and unquestioning obedience. After witnessing what I did in those camps, however, there is no way I can continue to do so with a clear conscience. Together, we can correct this horrible travesty underway on Kanaris. We can also reset the corrupt paradigm back home that encouraged these atrocities. We can bring about an order that benefits all League citizens, not just our Samaari overlords. For now, though, do nothing but wait. Whether in Narman's Pyke or on the battlefield, we're coming to collect you, and together, we *will* make this right."

"Computer, stop," Biragor commanded. When the video froze, she said, "The peace we're experiencing now is not a good thing. It's a sign our disaffected Marines are heeding the advice of an insurgent leader."

Nala could feel the tension in the room as the officers were hit with the realization that they all had targets on their backs and could be surrounded by thousands of potential assassins. Trying to relieve the strain, Kuusip laughed. "Come on, Biragor! Give me a break! Our Marines aren't rising up because they've been trained better than that and...."

"Major Kuusip, you already passed on the opportunity to mitigate this situation and failed to rise to the challenge. I don't really care what your opinion is on this now that...."

"Failed?!?" Kuusip scoffed. "Failed?!? Agent, you came to me with a cock-eyed plan to release this evidence ourselves and blame the Tahnebaht Conglomerate for the whole thing!" Still convinced of how ludicrous that suggestion was, he burst out laughing as he announced it. Many of the Samaaris in attendance laughed with him.

Commandant Taillur was no Samaari. Nor was he laughing. "I find it disheartening how many of you find such humor in a rare piece of sound advice. Had we heeded Agent Biragor's suggestion, we would have had a very damaging scandal on our hands. Now, we have a catastrophic one. Congratulations."

The room fell silent as all eyes shifted to Taillur. "I suggest that my Samaari colleagues extricate themselves from this mutual-admiration circle jerk they're all so fond of and start looking at the situation we're in with their blinders off. Our forces are seventy percent conscripts and convicts. They don't want to be here, and they certainly don't love their leadership." Glaring directly at Kuusip, he spat, "In fact, they hate your fucking guts."

Taillur stood up and rested his knuckles on the table before him. "Our Marine conscripts do not see those Portunese miners as enemies of the state. They see them as examples of what could happen to their own families on Gorsu Qat or Waardan if they don't roll over quietly and let the Samaaris take them in the ass. They have far more in common with those prisoners than with you officers that spent your childhoods on Samaar Ghun gorging yourselves on wine and caviar before forcing yourselves on the servant girls."

Pausing to look several of his colleagues directly in the eye, the commandant finally said, "Trivialize the gravity of this situation at your own risk, people. This threat could very well dwarf that of the Morghul menace bearing down on us at this very moment. Am I clear?"

Commandant Taillur was far from being the highest-ranking person in that briefing room, but there was no doubt he was the most dangerous. No one dared to contest his opinion.

Nala Biragor was the only one brave enough to speak after him. "Does anyone have any more questions?"

The agent's inquiry was met with awkward silence until Taillur took his seat and sighed. "Seriously? We're faced with the potential for a catastrophic mutiny, and no one has anything to ask one of the few people in this room who actually knows what she's talking about?"

Goaded by Taillur into asking Biragor something but unable to formulate an intelligent question, Major Kuusip raised his hand. "Do you have any idea who might be approaching the Narman sympathizers in our ranks to give them instructions?"

Though Biragor knew better than to trust the major with any names, she nodded and answered, "Actually, I do."

•• ◦ ● ◦ ••

Elia Gyanis was in the enlisted club when she spotted a heavily intoxicated corporal leave the building and stagger his way outside. Keeping a safe distance to prevent him from making her, she followed the man for a few blocks until he stumbled into a deserted alley to relieve himself. Under cover of darkness and the unrelenting Kanarisian rain, she was able to sneak up beside him just as he finished urinating on an overturned garbage bin.

"Corporal Freddi Yanuk?" she asked, causing the young man to nearly jump out of his skin.

"What?!?" the Marine gasped, still holding his junk in hand. "Who the hell are you?"

"I'm a friend of Bina Dubarti," Elia told him. "I'm glad I caught you before you tried taking on those fucking Killbillies."

"Killbillies?!?" Yanuk slurred. "I don't know what you're talking about!"

"Shhhh," Elia said, urging the corporal to keep his voice down. "It's okay. You were in Anga-Iskalei. They used Killbillies to patrol the perimeter there. I was at Saimsun. I know what you've been through."

"You were in Saimsun?"

Elia nodded.

"I heard everyone in Saimsun was killed. Or defected."

"Not everyone," Gyanis said. "I did neither."

"Then what are you doing here?!? In the Pyke?"

"Looking for you," Elia told him.

"Looking for me?" Yanuk asked. "For what?"

"I'm forming a network of like-minded people. Marines who are tired of committing unspeakable acts on behalf of the Samaaris. People who may be open to turning the tables on those little pricks and maybe giving the bastards a taste of their own medicine."

The Marine squinted, eyeing Gyanis suspiciously. "And Bina sent you to me?"

"Yes," Elia admitted. "But I'm not here on her behalf."

"Then, on whose behalf *are* you here?"

Elia Gyanis smiled. "Eamon Tauk."

Not long after her presentation, Commandant Taillur stepped into Biragor's office unannounced. Nala stood up to greet him, but he waved her back into her seat. "At ease, Agent. Relax. I wanted to speak to you before I returned to the mothership. You did good work on this. Too bad it was wasted on the buffoons who digest it. Like Major Kuusip."

When Biragor did not respond to Taillur's slight of her boss, the Commandant chuckled. "You don't want to pile on to that? Smart girl. It's okay; I've got a good enough idea of what you think of that imbecile. I don't need you to enunciate it."

"If you don't mind my asking, sir, why do you still have him in charge of this station if you've lost confidence in the man?"

"Because he's an idiot," Taillur responded. "And idiots can be useful. If I need someone to lead a high-risk operation that he may not return from, do you think I'd send someone I considered indispensable or someone I considered expendable?"

Nala smiled. "Expendable."

"Precisely. And not only will morons like Kuusip march blindly to their death, they'll consider it an honor."

"You don't think it's honorable to die for your cause?"

"I'd rather seek honor in making our enemies die for theirs."

"So do I, but sometimes I think our comrades are deadlier than our adversaries."

"I don't think that," Taillur growled. "I know it. Agent Biragor, with that in mind, I'm reorganizing the Section 615 Kanaris station. You'll no longer be reporting to Major Kuusip. Your responsibilities, which are identifying potential moles and deserters in our ranks, will remain the same. Right now, especially after that video got out, there is no more critical mission on this planet. We can't afford a repeat of the Satapadaya mutiny."

"Understood," Biragor said. "Are you relieving Kuusip of command?"

Taillur shook his head. "No. I'm just getting him out of your way and preventing him from keeping solid information from making it up the chain. I need him where he is, though. He's Samaari, so the upper brass trusts the information he feeds them. Having him in that position gives me the conduit I need to feed them what I want them to hear."

"Okay," Nala said. "I understand. Thank you, sir."

"No," Taillur said. "Thank *you*. I look forward to receiving your reports."

As the commandant turned to walk out the door, Nala asked, "Sir, are they going to do anything about those mines to make sure this never happens again?"

"What? Like close the camps, free the prisoners, and hold the people responsible for this travesty accountable?"

Nala nodded.

"Of course not, Birigor. In true Samaari fashion, they decided the best way to prevent videos like this from ever circulating again is to remove the cameras from the Marines' armor systems."

●●◆●◆●●

Chapter 19

REUNION

E lia's heart skipped a beat as the teenage convict grabbed her by the arm. She had been walking past Narman Pyke's sanitation complex, as the instructions she received told her to, when she was seized. At first, Elia thought she was being detained by Section 615, but then she saw how young the boy was who accosted her. Narman Pyke's counterintelligence apparatus had undoubtedly taken some heavy casualties of late, but she doubted they had been reduced to using children.

The boy led her toward the portable outhouse the Corps forced their laborers to use. As she tried to wrench herself from his grip, Elia snapped, "What the hell do you think you're doing?!?"

"Shhh!" Ovai Soldana hissed, trying to quiet her. "If you want to see Eamon Tauk, settle down!"

"You're here with Tauk?!?"

Soldana nodded, letting go of her arm. "If you want to see him, you'll go into that water closet and change into the set of coveralls I left in there. I added a shawl like the women use on Tyannik-8." After glancing at Elia's bright red dreadlocks, he added, "Thank god."

No one in their right mind wanted to work at Narman Pyke's waste management facility. It was for that reason that more than fifteen percent of the Corps' convict laborers were forced to. Despite toiling in the dark, with raw sewage, in an environment where some alien monstrosity might come out of nowhere and carry you off into the subterranean drainage network, it was not a bad gig for a prisoner. Because of the odor and creep factor of working underground on a planet like Kanaris, the Marines tended to stay where the light was. That meant the felons were left largely unsupervised, and Ovai Soldana's route into and out of the colony was rarely guarded.

The convicts knew Ovai did not belong there, but they would certainly not tell anyone. As far as they were concerned, he was one of them. To avoid attracting attention to him, they ignored the Narman operative for the most part, only addressing him to relay information that would keep him out of trouble. Soldana learned early on that prisoners made great accomplices.

Once Elia Gyanis was suitably disguised, Ovai walked her right past the disinterested guards and down twenty flights of stairs. When they reached the depths of the complex, the pair marched nearly half a kilometer to the rainwater discharge pipe, undid the access hatch, and found what was left of her former squad, Dmitri Naktada, and me waiting for her. Unable to contain her excitement, Elia let out a squeal of delight and leapt into Sergeant Hermour's arms. Bawling onto the squad leader's shoulder, Elia cried, "Oh my god, have I missed you!"

After a round of back slaps and comments about Gyanis's new look, I had the squad set a perimeter so we could talk.

"God, sir! I was beginning to think I would never see any of you again!"

I nodded, "Truth be told, we've had a couple of close scrapes. We very nearly didn't make it back to see you."

Elia nodded in understanding. "I almost didn't make it, either. We were apprehended by Killbillies not long after Albarn set us free."

All the joy of seeing Gyanis again drained out of me, replaced by the realization of what she had probably gone through while in Qilkorian custody. Shaking my head, I buried my face in my hands. "Oh, Elia. I'm so sorry."

The armorer reached out and put her hand on my shoulder. "It's okay, Tauk. They'll get what's coming to them."

"What about Jatmika and Hauken?"

Gyanis's eyes immediately welled up. "They're gone. Tai Himoar, too. Please don't ask what happened. I still can't talk about it."

"I understand. Look, Elia, we know the video got out. That was excellent work. Now, we need to capitalize on it. We were a little unclear on what we were going to do when we parted ways, but now our endgame has come into better focus. We can't stay on Kanaris. We're going to escape. To do that, we need to take the mothership."

Gyanis's jaw dropped open. "Are you fucking serious?!?"

I nodded. "Ovai has been recruiting turncoats in the Pyke for quite some time now. He's got nearly all the convicts. I'm working on freeing the camp inmates and arming any of them still capable of combat. I need you to work on collecting rank-and-file Marines for our cause."

For someone so young, Ovai Soldana was very business-like. He always got right to the point. "I work with a woman in the Morale Center. Her name is Bina Dubarti."

"I'm a bit ahead of you," Elia told him. "I know Bina. I'm sorry, but I don't know you. You never gave me your name."

"No, I didn't," Ovai told her. "Nor am I going to. If Section 615 gets my name, they could look me up on the old colonial database. I'd rather remain off their radar."

"Then what do I call you?"

"You don't," Soldana said, handing her a small transmitting chip. "Put that in your tablet. Use it to record the names of anyone you've recruited. Use those you've recruited to recruit more and exponentially...."

"Exponentially increase the pool of potential mutineers. I'm way ahead of you. Six weeks ago, right after our video dropped, Bina Dubarti turned me onto a client plotting to slaughter a group of Killbillies they knew from Anga-Iskalei. A week later, I had fifteen names on my roster. The week after that, thirty-one. Then seventy-five. And so on. Right now, I'm sitting on more than a company of Marines ready to start taking their frustrations out on the Samaaris. Bina's been helping me...."

Soldana shook his head in befuddlement. "Wait, how did you know about Bina Dubarti?"

Elia looked at me when she answered. "Ritza Xi turned me on to her."

I nodded and turned toward Soldana. "That makes sense. Xi was forced to work in the Morale Center for a while." Shifting my attention back to Elia, I said, "We need to win over the forces in Narman's Pyke. We need to get people onto the *Phoenix* and recruit there. We have to pull people onto our side until we outnumber the loyalists 3-to-1."

Gyanis gasped as she did the math in her head. "That's impossible! You need 375,000 mutineers to do that! You'll never get there!"

"We will if we get good at selectively eliminating those that aren't on our side," Naktada told her. "We've got to grow our forces and kill theirs. It's going to get bloody, Elia."

My mole nodded. "How many do we have now?"

Soldana shook his head. "We can't tell you that, either. I'm sorry, Elia, but you know better than any of us how dangerous your situation is. If you get caught, we can't afford that information falling into enemy hands. The data flow can only go one way."

Elia looked very uncomfortable. "And what happens if Section 615 gets their hands on you?"

Ovai shrugged. "Not much. All the names we have go into a database that I have no interest in reading. Even if I did, there's no way I could remember thousands of names."

"That's not what I meant," Elia said. "Who contacts me?"

"We'll find someone," Soldana assured her. "We'll come up with a code word that...."

Elia pointed her finger at me. "No, he and I will come up with a code word. If the Marines get their hands on you, they'll get it out of you. They're good at that."

Ovai nodded. "Fair enough."

Stepping up to Elia, I put my lips to her ear. "The password for any legitimate message I send you will be 'CUPID.' The name of my ubati. If I am being tortured and have to give up a code, I'll give them 'BRUMIT,' as in our old gunny sergeant. Understand?"

"Yes."

"Okay," Soldana said as Elia and I pulled away from each other. "Are we good now?"

Gyanis nodded. "We're good. Information only flows one way. Got it."

Soldana never noticed, but I saw Naktada grin so wide that he had to turn away from Ovai to conceal it.

When our meeting with Elia was over, and Ovai was gone escorting her back to the surface, I turned to Naktada and asked, "What were you smiling about?"

Dmitri laughed. "About the one-way flow of information? I had to keep myself from cracking up because telling Elia she can't have access to our data was not an instruction. It was a challenge."

"You think she's going to hack it?"

"I know she is. Gyanis is a hacker, and hackers gonna hack."

"You didn't try to stop her?"

Naktada looked at me as if that was the stupidest question he had ever heard. "Of course I'm not. I want her to crack that bitch."

"Why?"

"Because we can't fix that database's weaknesses if we don't know what they are."

Hacking the Narman database was slow going. Because of the Harnillium interference, Elia Gyanis had no direct connection to it. She did, however, have the path her information traveled once downloaded by Ovai Soldana. Using that, she created several programs to follow her submission data into the Narman ether to copy the roster and send the duplicate back to her. She sent more than a dozen files with every transmission, yet it still took a month and a half for one to work.

Once Elia was successful, she sent a message to Dmitri Naktada to inform him of what she had done, detailing how she did it and urging him to fix the weakness. She then went to work hacking the database itself. That took another three weeks, but once she was in, she arranged for her copy to get updated every time she submitted new information to the Narmans.

"There are only 7,427 in the entire Narman army?!?" Elia gasped after finally analyzing what was in her stolen file. *Even with Tauk's people?!? What the hell were we thinking?!?*

She started to do the math just like Naktada did.

7427 against 500,000 Marines. That's 67 to 1.

She probed the database a little deeper, finding the register of convicts they could count on.

74,832 unarmed, undisciplined convicts. Plus 7427 Narmans. That'd make it against 425,168 Marines — five to one, for whatever that's worth.

Shaking her head, Elia uploaded the eight hundred and eighty-eight names she had recently collected from her various contacts among the expeditionary force.

83,147 against 424,280. It didn't even move the goddamn needle.

"We're so fucked," Elia moaned to herself.

Chapter 20

THE XUN

My former praetorian, Nila Chisek, was a petite woman, but it did not matter. She was from Praminat, a mostly desert planet that developed the martial art of Qılıç Elai.

Qılıç Elai was an insanely effective fighting style that allowed someone of Chisek's stature to defeat an adversary many times her size. As our camp infiltrators would largely be without weapons during their mission, Nila was the one who schooled them in hand-to-hand combat.

To prove the effectiveness of the technique to the recruits, Chisek showed up to their first day of training in her underwear, a pair of black, form-fitting shorts and a matching sports bra. I had never thought of Chisek romantically in any way, but I had to admit that watching her walk through the rain in that attire was something of a turn-on. I had never known her to accentuate her looks, but she was a beautiful woman with an amazing body. To keep things from turning awkward, I had to keep my eyes glued on the unfortunate man on whom Nila would demonstrate her skills.

In stark contrast to the Qılıç Elai master, Norbu Maatik was a big man. He was half a head taller than I was and a solid wall of muscle. Unlike Chisek, he was not brought to the ring in his skivvies. He wore the uniform we had captured him in when we liberated Razbauten. He was also equipped with the gear the mining camps' Blue Shirts would possess. That included an M72 battle rifle, an M88 sidearm, a twenty-centimeter-long war dagger, and a whip. At Nila's insistence, the firearms were fully loaded and had a round in the chamber. To ensure Maatik did not try to reach for his weapons and attempt an escape before Chisek's lesson started, my four squad leaders had their blasters out and pointed at his head. If he so much as sneezed without permission, his brains would have been vaporized in the blink of an eye.

"Qılıç Elai was developed long ago," Chisek told a rapt audience. "It came to be on Praminat during a long period of civil unrest when the dictator Kötü Kalem forbade the general population from possessing weapons of any kind. Qılıç Elai is the martial art of the disadvantaged. It allows an unarmed warrior to defeat an armed one. It allows a short person to vanquish one who is tall. It allows the weak to dominate the strong. This fighting style emphasizes strength, speed, agility, and, most importantly, precision. It takes years to learn enough Qılıç Elai to stand your ground against a master...."

Chisek paused to turn around and flash a smug grin at the beast of a Blue Shirt standing behind her. "...but by learning just a few critical techniques, I can make you more than a match for any of these pathetic Samaaris."

Norbu Maatik grinned as he stared lustily at Nila. "This 'pathetic Samaari' is going to fucking blow a hole through your head and rape your corpse in front of all your wharf rat friends," he snarled.

Still smiling, Nila turned back to her platoon of students. "Some of you may recognize this monster. Some of you might have been victims of his. Just so you know, once this fight starts, it's just me and him. Nobody is allowed to intervene. Not Tauk, not his squad leaders, not even you. If that bastard wins this fight, he gets to do whatever he wants to me and then walk out of here with everything on him right now. Plus, we give him an ubati to keep the 'pedes away."

Among the sixty volunteers in front of her, Chisek saw a wave of apprehension wash over a young woman's face. Guessing she might have had a personal connection to Maatik, Nila walked over to her and said, "Don't worry. He's not going to win. In fact, when it's all over, he's going to be so defenseless, I'll even let you finish him off. Would you like that?"

The woman smiled. "I'd like that very much."

Strolling back out to the front of the formation, Chisek said, "The first rule of Qılıç Elai is *never* underestimate your opponent. You must know in your soul that the person you are up against is better than you are in every way. To defeat them takes perfection on your part. Any miscalculation can, and probably will, result in your death."

Waving her hand toward the former guard, Nila told them, "No matter how good a fighter I am, there's always someone better than me out there. That said, there are no bare-knuckle brawlers more over-confident than our Samaari enemies, and I made this offer to Maatik to demonstrate just how big of an advantage to you your opponent's overconfidence can be. I would never have cut this sort of deal with anyone other than a Blue Shirt."

Nila paused to turn a steely gaze upon her students. "The purpose of this demonstration is to shatter the myth of Samaari invincibility and show you just how horribly inept they really are. The Blue Shirts might have had absolute power over you in the camps, but when faced with someone who knows how to defend themselves, they really aren't much of an adversary. Not even one as big and scary as Norbu Maatik."

Chisek let out a sigh. "There might have been a time when Samaaris were worthy of respect, but not in living memory. They're merchants, not soldiers. They've been raised to believe they've been born into some sort of master race, and anyone raised outside of the Guild planets is an inferior human being. It's laughable, but they really think that shit. Fortunately for us, their grossly misguided sense of superiority is a considerable weakness." Nila paused to stroll within reach of her opponent. "In a fight for one's life, overconfidence is almost always a terminal affliction. Do not be afraid to use theirs against them."

"Are you ready?" Sergeant Hermour asked Chisek.

Nila nodded. "Go."

The four squad leaders lowered their blasters and stepped back. As soon as the sergeants' sights were off him, Maatik drew his pistol. As he raised his sidearm to send a bullet into the space between Chisek's eyes, it looked as if she just effortlessly yanked it from his hand and shot him with it. In reality, however, she spun it out of the Blue Shirt's grip so fast that it snapped the man's index finger against the trigger, causing it to go off. The weapon was pointed back at the Samaari when it discharged, sending the bullet ripping through the Blue Shirt's elbow. The wounded man screamed and fell to the ground with his right arm completely immobilized. Chisek was left standing above him with her adversary's gun in her hand and pointed at his head.

"In a real combat situation," Nila said as her pupils gaped at her in disbelief, "you would just finish this prick off with a single shot between his eyes and go on to take out any other threats within range. That's what Qılıç Elai is all about. Disarming your enemy and turning their advantage into yours. Now, what to do with that weapon after you've gained control of it is something the sergeants will teach you after I'm done."

Chisek took two steps to her right and handed the pistol to Sergeant Demangel. Returning to the Blue Shirt, she ordered him to get up.

Maatik shook his head as he kept his eyes clenched closed in agony. "I can't!" he cried. "My arm won't work! It's mangled! You win!"

Nila laughed and turned back to her class, "You see this? Look at how much heart these poor pieces of shit have! Note how quickly they fold and give up! They're only nasty when they have superior firepower or strength in numbers. Once you level the playing field, they ain't shit." Turning back to the Blue Shirt, Chisek screamed, "GET UP!"

"I can't!" the Samaari wailed.

"You're still three times my size and armed with a rifle, a blade, and a whip! Get up and fight!"

Maatik kept sobbing. "You fucked up my shooting arm! I can't do anything!"

"Remember that," I chimed in to tell the students. "We're going to train you to shoot with both hands just in case you end up this way. Sergeants, lift this sad sack of shit to his feet."

Once Maatik was again standing under his own power, Chisek glowered at him. "Go for your rifle."

"I told you, I can't...."

"Look, asshole! I'm coming over there to take that knife of yours and slice your tiny little prick off if you don't...."

Before Nila could finish her sentence, Maatik awkwardly tried to draw his weapon with his left hand. In a flash, Chisek leapt at the Samaari and took him down into the mud. During the ensuing struggle, the combatants rolled over each other three times. When they stopped, the Qılıç Elai master had the prisoner's sling wrapped around his neck, choking him out. Maatik was on top of her, but

Nila had him under complete control. She was holding the rifle in place with one arm while the other poked out from beneath him near the Blue Shirt's empty holster.

"As you can see," she told her students, "Maatik's body is between me and any incoming bullets. Had there been a weapon in his holster, I'd be using that to return fire. Once the other threats have been neutralized, I can then unclip the rifle from the sling and...."

Demonstrating the method, Nila used her left hand to release the tether and roll Maatik to the right. She bounced to her feet in the opposite direction. When she stopped, she had the Samaari's rifle in one hand and his dagger in the other. As Maatik jumped up to distance himself from his assailant and gasp for air, Nila pointed the firearm at his head and said, "Bang." Terrified, Maatik froze in place, trying to hold in his sobs.

As the Samaari whimpered for his life, Chisek ignored him and continued her lesson. "In a real scenario, don't get cute like I am now. Kill him and use his weapon to murder his friends. Qılıç Elai is about efficiency."

Tossing the rifle to Blevin Korman, Chisek showed her dagger to her students. "It's also about precision. The human body needs to move in specific ways to defend itself. It can be prevented from doing so by severing critical tendons."

"Please don't," Maatik begged.

Displaying the same mercy the Samaari had shown his charges in Razbauten, Nila spun around in a set of graceful maneuvers that were more like ballet than brawling, and sliced Maatik across the back of his left elbow. The Blue Shirt howled in agony.

"That was his triceps tendon. Now he can't straighten his arm."

Daintily sticking the dagger's tip into a point near Maatik's shoulder, she said, "And that was the supraspinatus. That'll keep him from lifting the limb." After severing several more tendons in Maatik's knees and at the back of his feet, the Samaari was reduced to a defenseless, immovable blob, screaming hysterically while he writhed in the mud.

Her lesson concluded, Chisek walked over to the woman in formation she had spoken with earlier and held the knife out to her. "Would you like to finish him off?"

Noticing a kryptid crawling across the ground, the woman shook her head. "No, I'd rather watch the bugs get him."

Nila smiled. "I like the way you think." With a nod to my sergeants, Chisek had our squad leaders drag the Samaari out of the way so the kryptids could feast without being disturbed. Serenaded by the screams of a war criminal slowly being devoured alive, the Qılıç Elai master looked over the volunteers.

"Your unit needs a name," she told the troops. "Just by volunteering for this outfit, you're going to do something I don't even think I'm brave enough to do. You're walking into Hell itself, without weapons, to try to prevent people you don't know from enduring what you have already endured. If you're caught, you'll suffer in ways even worse than before. We need to call you something that reflects such rare courage. Any ideas?"

There was a moment of silence before someone in the back of the formation called out, "How about the Xun?"

I saw Haeli Deboara, who was standing at the front of the platoon, smile. "You like that?" Chisek asked.

Haeli nodded. "I do."

"What is a Xun?" I asked her.

"It's a beetle that's pretty common on Portuna. It's only about the size of my thumb but will attack you like crazy if it thinks you're threatening its nest. They don't have venom or stingers, just speed and persistence. Of course, they eventually get crushed, but by the time you get them, the nest has moved somewhere safe while you were distracted."

As Maatik screeched in the background, I nodded in approval. "Then the Xun you shall be."

Chapter 21
Tradecraft

Bina Dubarti knew Private Bogislay did not have much experience with women. He had oily brown hair, a fat face on an oddly thin body, crooked teeth, and a nose whose tip was bent so far skyward it gave his whole face a porcine appearance. Bina knew he was the kind of man who would fall hopelessly in love with the first woman he ever slept with, and as luck would have it, that turned out to be her.

Fortunately, Bogislay was an easy client. He was usually close to climax before he even got undressed, and he was finished within a minute of climbing on top of her. The private typically spent most of his allotted time telling her how beautiful she was. "I wish we could be together, just you and me, forever," he told her again that day.

Bina wrapped her arms around the private's head and squeezed it close to her bare breasts. "So do I, Terin," she cooed back. "I wish we could just run from this horrible place and go somewhere where it doesn't always rain. We could get away from everybody and spend all our time on some deserted beach making babies."

"Then why don't we?" the Marine asked.

Dubarti laughed as if it were the dumbest question she had ever heard. "Because I'm a prisoner, Terin," she said, explaining the obvious. "You think they'll just let me walk away from here with you?"

"I could sneak you out," the private naively answered. "I can save my money and pay some Killbillies to...."

"I'm not going anywhere with any Killbillies, Terin. They'd turn me out as soon as they got their hands on me and make me do even worse things than I'm forced to do here."

"Well, then, maybe I could pay...."

"Shhh," Bina said as she placed the tip of her index finger on the Marine's lips. "There's no paying anybody to do anything, Terin. As long as the League is in charge, I'll be stuck right here, doing what I'm doing. My only way out of this is by walking over the ashes of the Samaaris. If you truly loved me, you'd help take those monsters down."

Private Bogislay sighed. "I can't do anything by myself, Bina."

"Of course, you can't, my love! You'd have to sign up with others with the same desire!"

"But I don't know anybody like that."

Bina took the boy's chubby cheeks in her hands and gently tilted his head up so she could gaze upon his face. "I do."

Bogislay swallowed hard as Dubarti watched his eyes fill with fear. Before he could say anything, however, a robotic voice called his name from a small speaker mounted beside the bed. "Your session at Narman Pyke's Morale Center has expired. Gather all uniform items and proceed directly to the disinfectant station. Failure to evacuate the room within the allotted time will result in a thirty-day suspension from all Morale Center services."

Not wanting to risk losing his privileges, Terin Bogislay stood up and hurriedly gathered his belongings. Donning a robe just before he reached the doorway, he glanced up at the timer and saw he had fifteen seconds left. He used it to turn his head to Bina and say, "I love you."

"I love you, too," Dubarti lied. "Don't let me down, Terin."

"I won't," Bogislay said before he walked out the door, the crack in his voice betraying his lack of confidence.

Bina Dubarti was still cleaning herself up when her next client entered the room. "Was that the one you told me about?" asked Elia Gyanis as she started removing her clothes.

"The private?" Bina asked. "With the freckles? Yeah, that's him. Kind of pathetic, isn't he?"

The armorer shrugged. "Love has a way of making men step up to the occasion.

Who knows? He might surprise us."

Dubarti ripped the soiled sheets off her bed and replaced them with a fresh set. "Or he could get himself captured and give us all up before the interrogation even gets started."

Gyanis sighed as she slipped out of her underwear and crawled into bed. "Maybe, but right now, we need everyone we can get. If we pump the right kind of information into him, he could do us a favor by breaking under questioning."

Bina laid down beside Gyanis and placed her hand atop one of her client's breasts. "I got confirmation a few days ago that they've determined the labor camps are too vulnerable. Instead of sending platoons of Marines to take over perimeter security, all Harnillium mining facilities are going to be guarded by company-sized units. They'll be using regular Marines until the Suma Corps start graduating the acclimatization course and can relieve them."

Gyanis gasped at the stupidity of the Samaaris. *More regular Marines? Can the Samaaris not think of a faster way to turn their own troops against them? I guess you can never learn from your mistakes if you've deluded yourselves into believing you're incapable of making any.*

"How are the Marines that have already done tours at the mines?" Elia asked.

"About as you'd expect," Bina told her. "It's still an early development, so we've only had contact with a few units that have been out long enough to rotate back. Based on what the other girls have told me, the Samaaris react to it like it's business as usual. Sick fucks. The rest seem pretty disturbed by the whole thing."

"Any patterns we can exploit?"

Bina nodded as her hand moved south across Elia's belly. "Yeah, maybe. There're children in those places, which affects people in a very primal way. Seeing the little ones going through stuff like that rattles the male Marines, but it *really* seems to fuck the women up. They're safer to approach. Of course, once we win the girls over to our cause, they have ways of getting the men to follow suit. Regardless, I got some names of people who seem safe to approach."

"Who?"

"Too many for you to remember. You're staying in Building 425, right?"

Shocked that Bina was aware of where she lived, Elia grabbed the woman's hand and pulled it away from her crotch. "How did you know that?"

"The Morale Center is cleaned by convicts. So are your quarters. You want to tap into a ready-made network of people who loathe the League? You got it! No one's better placed to do what you want than all the prisoners who perform the manual labor around here. Keep in mind, though, we're working for *our* interests, not yours. We're a lot more vulnerable than you are, Sarge. We need to know who we're dealing with even more than you do. So, yes, we checked you out. And lucky for you, you appear legit."

Gyanis swallowed uncomfortably. "What would have happened had I not?"

Bina flashed a menacing grin. "We may be more vulnerable than you, Elia, but that also means we have a lot less to lose. There's no shortage of people among us that are tired of all this shit and ready to end it all. It's not hard to persuade them to take someone like you with them when they go. You understand that?"

Elia nodded.

"Okay. All communication from now on will be done by dead drop. You'll find the list of names I just told you about on a chip in a used ration can beneath the dispensary machine in the women's bathroom on the third floor. In it will also be the location of the next drop. If you have any questions or information you want to get to me, you put it in that location three days before your pick-up date. Clear?"

"Clear," Elia answered. With her eyes betraying her suspicions, Gyanis said, "I thought you ended up here for being a part of a criminal drug smuggling enterprise. What exactly did you do for them?"

Dubarti smiled. "I ran their intelligence operations. Now, darling, there's one more thing we need to go over. We already have a network. To identify ourselves as part of it, we have a code word. If someone approaches you claiming to speak for me, you ask for the password. You understand?"

"Yes," Elia said, wondering if she was bringing Bina's network into hers or if Bina was sucking her into theirs. She suspected it might have been a little bit of both. "What's the signal we're supposed to use?"

Bina cast her eyes over Elia's unique hairstyle. "Red Dread."

"And a false code in case you have to give it up under duress?"

Bina smiled. "Smart. How about 'Narman Glory?'"

Gyanis nodded. "That'll do. So, I don't have to come here anymore?"

"Start reducing your frequency to keep up appearances. Ask for different girls. After a few months, give it up completely. It'll look like you had your trauma, went through a little phase, then got over it."

Four days later, Elia Gyanis found the empty ration container exactly where Bina said it would be. When she saw the list of names, her knees nearly buckled. She was expecting a dozen or so. Instead, there were almost five hundred, primarily airmen ferrying Marines to the camps. She could scarcely imagine how many they could turn from the Marines once company-sized units began cycling back from the mines.

This isn't a network, Elia thought to herself. *It's the beginning of a goddamn revolution.*

Per Ovai Soldana's instructions, Gyanis uploaded the names into the Narman database, then updated her count.

Still five-to-one. It barely moved the needle. Shit.

"Honey trap?" Agent Nala Biragor asked.

Sergeant Waldo Hoaris nodded his head. He had walked into the Section 615 HQ in Narman's Pyke and asked to speak to someone in counterintelligence. Since Biragor was on duty, she drew the interview. "That's what I said. Honey trap. The pathetic little prick fell for one of the whores at the Morale Center, and I think she's got him involved with those Narman sympathizers."

"And how do you know this?"

"Word is he's been feeling out my troops about their views on what we're doing here on Kanaris, and doing it poorly. Eventually, he tried laying his line on a patriot, who came and told me."

Pulling out her tablet, Biragor asked, "And who would this 'patriot' be?"

Hoaris squinted at her suspiciously. "I don't think I should out my source."

Biragor squinted right back at the sergeant. "You're not the spymaster here, Hoaris. I am. I need to make sure this person is being truthful with you and not just trying to get someone in trouble. If I act on a false sympathizer network, I could inadvertently warn off a real one."

"I promised him I wouldn't divulge his name to anyone."

The agent gave Hoaris a cold, expressionless stare. "I'm in the business of extracting information from people, Sergeant. Now, you can give me the name I want here in my office, or I can have you hauled down into the basement where we can do it the hard way."

The Marine swallowed uncomfortably. "Lance Corporal Kado Farma."

"Thank you," Biragor said as she noted the name on her tablet and hoped Hoaris never fell into enemy hands with critical information. He gave Farma up way too easily.

"You know," she told the Marine, "I don't think there are many Narman sympathizers around here anymore. People don't typically run out to join a losing side and all indications are that, militarily speaking, the Narmans are no longer a viable fighting force." That was the official company line she was required to push, though in the aftermath of the atrocity videos that just went out, she doubted it to be true.

Hoaris almost laughed in her face. "The Narmans never were a viable fighting force if you ask me. Not until they got our own people to turn on us. The bastards rose up along our entire line at the Satapadaya Front and damned near wiped us out."

"The rumors that the Narmans nearly overtook us at the Satapadaya front are highly exaggerated. Yes, it was a tough battle, but the enemy was never in any real danger of...."

Hoaris sighed and leaned back in the seat opposite Biragor's desk. "You can save that line of shit for the NFGs, ma'am. I was there. Marines in my own platoon, people I considered dear friends and comrades, tried to kill me during that battle. They'd gone over to the other side right under my fucking nose and damned near cost us everything. Ever since, I've been keeping eyes on my troops, Agent Biragor. I'll be damned if I'm going to let that ever happen to me again."

The field agent sat silent, staring at the sergeant for a moment before she pulled out her tablet. "Okay. What's this Marine's name again? The one you think is recruiting for the Narmans?"

"Private Terin Bogislay."

As Hoaris spelled out the Marine's name, Biragor typed it into the agency's database. When she finished, a picture of a brown-haired, freckled, pudgy-faced young man was splashed across her screen. He looked precisely like the kind of person who would have been a prime candidate to be snared in a honey trap had she been trying to turn him.

"So, what are we going to do about him?" Hoaris asked.

Biragor shrugged. "Keep an eye on him — a very close eye. Pay attention to who he's talking to. Do what you can to buddy up to the guy and drop hints of being disillusioned with our mission here on Kanaris. See if he'll try to pull you into the fold."

"And if he does?"

"You come to me," Biragor told him. "And only me. After what went down at Saimsun and Razbauten, we have to assume the Narmans have sympathizers in Section 615 also."

Chapter 22

RABAAT'S BANE

Nila Chisek was with me when we plucked Haeli Deboara from the jungle. When she heard that the escaping prisoners killed their children to save them from the cruelties they would have been subjected to had they fallen back into the hands of the Samaaris, Chisek was appalled. In the heat of the moment, she basically accused Haeli of infanticide and suggested she should have died with them.

Once removed from the chaos of the situation, Chisek began to understand the hopeless predicament the Deboaras found themselves in. She came to terms with the fact that what they did was an act of mercy, not murder. Outwardly, Haeli said she bore Chisek no ill will about what she said when her blood was up. Watching the tenacity with which Haili went after Nila during her Qılıç Elai training, it was evident that the Saimsun survivor still had some hard feelings about the comment.

When I arrived at the training ring, Haeli Deboara was lying in the mud, having just been brutally thrown to the ground by Chisek. Even though that must have been the fourth or fifth time she had been put down, Haeli jumped to her feet and, while still trying to use what Nila had taught her, charged in a futile attempt to give the Qılıç Elai master a taste of her own medicine.

After watching this transpire another half dozen times, I interrupted the lesson. "You're going to hurt her," I told Nila after taking her aside.

Chisek shrugged. "If I don't put her on the ground, she's going to hurt me."

After letting out a little sigh, I said, "She led the uprising in Saimsun. That was enough for me to pick her as a platoon leader by default. I need a no-bullshit assessment from you, though. Is she the right fit for the job?"

"Absolutely," Nila answered without hesitation. "Deboara's tenacious. She doesn't give up. That woman will let me toss her around all day for the opportunity to get lucky and bust me in my chops just once. When she's not in the ring with me, though, she pays very close attention and attacks every lesson with rigor and enthusiasm. She's mastered disarming techniques for rifle, handgun, and dagger...."

"In a few weeks? That seems like an awfully short amount of time to master anything."

"Sir," Nila told me, "these people practice amongst each other long after my lessons are over. I have to force them to sleep and recover from their injuries. These Xun are *motivated*. They want to start launching missions tomorrow but know we're not going to unleash them before they're ready. So, they're trying to get ready as soon as possible."

"How are they on marksmanship?"

Nila shook her head. "Well, we don't have the ammo to give them the range time it'd take to get them on par with the Marines they'll be facing. They're certainly not marksmen, but they're good enough at close range to get the job done. I do have my eye on a couple of naturals, though. With some extra time on the range, they could do some real damage. You know, sir, maybe we should equip them with blasters. Then ammo wouldn't be a problem."

I shook my head. "If one of them sneaks a blaster inside those camps and gets caught, the Samaaris will know they're getting infiltrated."

Nila nodded in understanding. "That's kind of scary, sending them in without weapons."

"It is scary," I told her. "Terrifying. That's why it's critical you get them trained in disarming those guards."

"Aye-aye, sir."

"So," I started, getting back to the reason I was interrupting Chisek's training. "Haeli Deboara's a good choice for platoon leader?"

Chisek nodded. "No doubt, sir."

Nodding back, I said, "Good. Tell her to come find me when you're done with her for the day. I want her to see something."

Kaito Rabaat was a repulsive human being. He possessed tiny brown eyes that were nearly swallowed up by his fleshy face. Long, soiled wisps of red hair hung loosely from his mangy scalp, failing to hide the dry, acne-riddled skin flaking off his forehead. Despite his relatively young age, he also had prominent jowls that flapped loosely below his jawline. His freakishly small nose wreaked havoc upon the proportions of his face and forced him to wheeze for air between a set of perpetually open lips.

Too lazy to adhere to any regular hygiene regimen, Rabaat's mouth was packed with rotting teeth, from which emanated a stench that could have gagged our ubatis. Still, Jilli Ventunius, a liberated inmate from Razbauten, kissed him full on the mouth, using tongue and all. When she finished, she looked Haeli Deboara right in the eye and hissed, "Don't you dare hurt him anymore!"

We were in a Morghul camp carved into the living rock of a mountain a few dozen kilometers from where my base was located. It was one of Kryndil's facilities where Hariana Espiya, my intelligence sergeant, and Bengin Meinhopf, her Narman counterpart, interrogated the prisoners we had captured in Razbauten. Haeli Deboara, Dmitri Naktada, and Furloq, a Morghul inquisitor, were with the prisoner and Ventunius in a sterile, bright, white room. Rabaat was stripped naked and lashed to a pair of steel beams, crossed to form a gigantic "X" against the back wall. It looked as if the Morghul were prepping him for an imminent s kinning.

Black Francis, Meinhopf, and I were just outside the door, in the tunneled-out hallway of bare rock, watching the interrogation on a large monitor mounted next to the entrance. At one point, Meinhopf had to turn up the volume so we could hear what was being said over the screams of men driven mad by sensory deprivation. It sounded as if they were locked much deeper within the bowels of the facility.

After Jilli Ventunius finished kissing the troll shackled to the cross-beams, I thought Haeli was going to get sick. She turned away from the spectacle and took a couple of deep breaths before spinning back around to face the couple again. "Jilli," she begged the former prisoner, "you can't be serious. He wasn't protecting you. He was abusing you. You don't have to do this."

Ventunius was young. She looked no older than eighteen. Unlike most other inmates we liberated from Razbauten, she appeared healthy and well-fed. "Kaito kept me out of the mines!" she shouted at Haeli. "He kept me fed! He protected me! I'd have died if it weren't for him! Or I'd have been...have been...."

Haeli did not need Jilli to finish the sentence. She knew what the young girl meant. Haeli knew it because what Ventunius feared was what Haeli endured at Saimsun. To let the girl know she understood, she gave her a single nod.

Turning toward Naktada, Jilli sobbed, "He saved me! I'm only here because of him!" Facing the Morghul inquisitor, she then spat, "You can't let those monsters take his skin!"

Haeli had seen young women like Jilli Ventunius before. They had lost every possession they had ever owned. Then the Samaaris took from them everyone they had ever loved. Then, practically everyone they had ever known. When the girls were left with absolutely nothing, the cretins responsible for all that loss would swoop in and claim them, twisting these children's shattered minds into seeing them as saviors rather than tormentors.

"Don't let them take his skin!" Jilli shrieked again.

Dmitri Naktada ignored her and addressed the prisoner directly. "There you are, Rabaat. We brought her to you. You promised us something in return."

I watched the Samaari mining engineer look longingly at Jilli and smile. "You did bring her to me. Thank you." I could tell by the tears in Rabaat's eyes that the man genuinely loved the young girl so passionately defending him. That did not surprise me at all. He was a hideous-looking creature who was probably not often the object of a woman's affection.

"And?" Naktada asked.

"You have to let us go," Rabaat said. "You have to let the two of us get away from here. To flee and start over."

Naktada shook his head. "Not going to happen. Even if we did, you wouldn't make it five kilometers through the jungle on your own. Your only hope is to stay here and join us."

Rabaat looked shocked. "Join you?!? Go against the League? I can't possibly...."

Dmitri turned to walk out the door. Before he left, he told Furloq, "Go ahead and do what you gotta do. Skin 'em both for all I care."

"No!" shouted Rabaat. "You can't do that to her! She's one of you!"

"He's right!" yelled Haeli. "What's the matter with you?!? That poor woman's sick! You would be too, if you'd been through half of what she has! She's not a fucking Samaari!"

"It appears she is now," Naktada said, nodding to Furloq to get moving.

As the Morghul inquisitor pulled a blade from his cloak and stepped toward the prisoner, Rabaat shrieked, "WAIT! WAIT! WAIT ONE MINUTE, GODDAMN IT! DON'T HURT HER! If I talk, you'll let us join you?!? Me and her both?!?"

Naktada paused and turned around. "That was the deal. If you help us get into those mines, we'll keep you alive. When our mission is complete, we'll turn you loose. You can go back to Samaar Ghun if you can figure out a way to get there."

"And Jilli can come with me?" the prisoner sniveled.

Dmitri shrugged. "That's up to her."

The engineer looked over at the young woman to his left. She nodded at him to let him know she would follow him anywhere. Hanging his head in resignation, Rabaat said, "Your best way in is to find the ventilation shafts. They're not guarded because you can't get through them without being chopped to pieces by the fans."

"Then how do we get through them?" asked Naktada.

"They get signals from sensors in the mine that monitor oxygen levels and the presence of toxic gases. The fans spin one way to push fresh air into the shafts and another if they need to pull carbon dioxide out. We once had a sensor malfunction that kept transmitting push and pull signals simultaneously. This caused one of the fans to seize as it kept trying to figure out which way it was supposed to go. Instead of spinning, the fan blades just kept vibrating back and forth. We didn't know it was bad until some big-ass six-legged lizard fell out of the roof one night."

"You know the frequencies these things work on?"

Rabaat nodded. "I do."

Sensing that Naktada and Rabaat had some technical things to work out, Haeli reached out to Ventunius to talk to her away from the Samaari engineer. "Why don't you come with me, Jilli? You don't need to listen to this. Let's get you somewhere more comfortable."

Naktada interrupted his questioning to address the two women. "She can go, Haeli. But you need to stay."

"Me?" Haeli asked. "Why?"

"Because as a platoon leader, you're going to be the one directing troops to find these ventilation shafts. You need to listen to what he has to say and get all your questions answered before you leave. We're going to be here for a couple days."

When Jilli Ventunius exited the interrogation room, she double-checked to make sure the door was shut behind her before wiping the tears from her eyes. After lifting her face from her sleeve, she looked up at Bengin Meinhopf and asked, "How long do you think it'll be before I get to kill that disgusting son-of-a-bitch?"

Meinhopf shrugged. "We have to finish liberating the mines first. After that, he's all yours."

When we landed back at base camp, I saw Daino Deboara waiting for his wife at our landing pad. Once Je'Sikka had us securely on the ground, I stepped out of the *Hornet* to let him know Haeli would be gone for a little while. Before I could open my mouth, however, Daino screamed out, "WHAT THE HELL DID YOU DO WITH MY WIFE?!?" I could tell by his slur that the man was quite drunk.

"She'll be away for a couple of days. We have a prisoner that she's...."

"YOU MOTHERFUCKER!" Daino shrieked, attracting an audience. "There's plenty of single women all over the place here! Girls who've lost their husbands! With all of them around, why the hell do you insist on trying to sleep with mine?!?"

My expression hardened. "I've got a fucking war to run, Daino. The last thing on my mind right now is trying to get laid. If you...."

"You lying piece of shit!" Daino cried, clumsily limping through the mud to close the gap between us while pointing his finger at my face. "You raped her! You raped her at Saimsun!"

Ignoring the crowd gathering around us, I kept my attention focused on Haeli's husband. "I did no such thing." I did not raise my voice but said it loud enough for those closest to me to hear."

"YOU DID TOO!" Daino yelled. "THE BLUE SHIRTS DRAGGED HER TO YOUR TENT AND...."

"I did not rape your wife!" I snapped back at him while marching his way. When we got close enough, I lowered my voice to a level only he could hear. "And if you don't stop making a public spectacle accusing me of it, we're going to have big problems here, Daino."

"What bigger problem could I have? I lost my home! My parents! My boys! The use of my hands and feet! And now I'm losing my wife to her goddamn fucking rapist!"

"For the last time, I did not...!"

"You did!" Daino spat.

"I did not!" I shot back, finally losing my temper. "But you know who did?!? Scores of Samaari Blue Shirts, you miserable piece of shit! And what did you do about it?!? Not a fucking thing! And now you want to publically accuse me, the only one who didn't force himself onto your wife, of that atrocity?!?"

"You son-of-a-bitch," Daino cursed as he weakly balled up his right fist. He swung at me as hard as he could, but with the shape he was in, I was effortlessly able to step out of his way. The man missed me and the momentum threw him off balance, sending him falling to the ground. The impact caused bolts of excruciating pain to tear through his limbs, overwhelming him with agony so intense, he could not even scream out. All he could do was lie twisted in the mud with his mouth open as he exhaled.

For public consumption, I called out for a medic. I then knelt beside him. From the sidelines, it looked like I was trying to help the man. In reality, though, I put my lips close to his ear and whispered, "I don't bear you any ill will, Daino. In fact, I admire what you sacrificed for those you loved. Despite all that, however, if you ever try to undermine my reputation and compromise my ability to command again, you'll leave me no choice but to fucking end you. Is that clear?"

••-•◦•-◉-•◦•-••

Chapter 23

The Encounter

Sleep was hard to come by for Section 615 agents in a war zone. Before Nala Biragor turned in for the night, she programmed her communications array to block all calls except those from high-priority sources. The watch commander's calls would still go through. So would those of Commandant Taillur, Narman Pyke's governing staff, and the Marine Expeditionary Force's Duty Officer. Those were pretty powerful people, so the fact that she had somehow put a lowly sergeant from the Epsilon Mobile Infantry Brigade in that same company caught her off guard.

"Who is this again?" Nala groggily asked as she checked the time. It was three in the morning.

"Sergeant Waldo Hoaris," the voice on the other end of the line answered.

The name sounded familiar, but in Biragor's sleep-deprived state, she was having difficulty connecting where she should know it from. "Yeah...umm..."

"I came to you a few weeks ago because I suspected one of my Marines was recruiting for the Narmans."

"Yes!" Nala exclaimed. It was starting to come back to her who the man on the other end of the transmission was. "You're Bogislay's squad leader!"

"Yeah, that's me."

"Alright! What's going on, Sergeant?"

"I caught the little prick sneaking out of the barracks tonight. He's meeting with his contacts."

Nala shot up from her cot in a panic. "Shit! Are you sure? How do you know this?"

"Because I'm watching them right now."

"Where are you?" Biragor asked as she grabbed her fatigue trousers and started threading her feet through the leg holes.

"I'm at the southeast corner of the Tahnebaht operations building with my back towards the launch pads. I'm looking into the alley between it and what I think is the waste processing facility. I'm sending you a link to my homing beacon."

Biragor's tablet pinged when she got the signal. Lifting it up, the agent looked over the map and saw they were close — barely two blocks from her room. "Stay put! I'm coming! I'll be there in less than three minutes!"

Nala turned off the comm link, threw on a black t-shirt, and slipped her feet into her boots without bothering to lace them. She then bolted for the door, dropping her sidearm into her pocket as she left.

••◂•▸◉◂•▸••

Private Terin Bogislay was very nervous. "Did you get what I gave to you?"

Elia Gyanis nodded. "I did, but it's very detailed."

"That's a problem? What's the matter? Don't you understand it?"

"No, I understand it just fine. It's just...just...I don't know how the hell a private would have access to intelligence this comprehensive."

"I have a source," Bogislay said.

"I need to know who that is," Elia told him. "I have to make sure it's legit before I pass it on."

Bogislay shook his head. "I'm sorry. I'm afraid I can't tell you that. My source was very adamant that I keep her identity to myself."

Elia grinned. "So, your source is a woman?"

The private grimaced. "I didn't say that...!"

"Actually," Gyanis retorted, "you kind of did."

Bogislay's nerves became even more unsettled. He started fidgeting. "Please, don't play games with me."

Elia took a step into Bogislay's personal space. "I don't have time for games,

Private. Frankly, I don't see you having the stomach for them. Not these kinds, anyway. Look, I plan on keeping you right where you're at. I would only go to her if something happened to you."

"Nothing's going to happen to me."

Gyanis laughed. "Terin, we're at war! Something can happen to any one of us at any time!"

"You can say that again," Sergeant Hoaris said as he stepped into the alley from the south side, pointing his rifle at them.

Both Gyanis and Bogislay instinctively hunched over to lower their profile before bolting for the north exit. Unfortunately, they found their escape route blocked by Nala Biragor. "Not so fast," the Section 615 agent told them. "Get on your knees and lock your fingers behind your head.

Gyanis thought about going for her sidearm and trying to take out Sergeant Hoaris, but his weapon was pointed right at her. She was an armorer. A technician. She was not a warrior. She did not have the speed, reflexes, or the quick-draw accuracy to kill the man before he killed her. After a split second of hesitation, she did as the agent ordered.

While the sergeant held the rebels in his sights, Agent Biragor slipped her pistol into the waistband of her fatigues, then used her left hand to grip Terin Bogislay's interlocked fingers together. With her right, she reached into the Marine's holster and withdrew his sidearm. Turning toward the other suspect, she said, "Hello, Elia. It's nice to see you again. Did he give up his source to you yet?"

"You know her?" Hoaris asked in surprise.

Answering the sergeant, Biragor said, "Yeah. We've met."

Gyanis stared at the counter-intelligence operative in disbelief, desperately wanting to ask Biragor, "You know Bogislay?!?" Wisely, she kept her question to herself.

Sighing impatiently at the armorer's lack of response, Biragor repeated her question. "Did the private give up his source to you?"

"No," Elia answered as she shook her head.

"That's strange," the agent said as she raised the Marine's pistol and shot Hoaris in the throat. As the dying sergeant collapsed limply onto the ground, she added, "Bogislay gave you up with nearly no effort at all."

Before Gyanis could respond, Biragor wrenched the private away from her and then kicked him in the gut, sending him stumbling backward while putting some distance between the two of them. As the Marine came to a stop, the agent drew her own weapon and put another round between Bogislay's eyes. She then turned to Gyanis and pointed at the private's body.

"He tried to convince you to join the Narmans," Biragor told Gyanis. "But you came to me. I had you meet Bogislay here, but Sergeant Hoaris ambushed you, thinking you were both Narman moles. Bogislay killed Hoaris; I killed Bogislay. Understood?"

Gyanis nodded meekly. "What do you want to do with me?"

Biragor grinned. "Well, I'm going to start by teaching you that if you have to meet with one of your contacts, don't do it in a confined space with only two ways out."

An hour later, Gyanis was in a safehouse that Agent Biragor had set up off Section 615's books. The two women were seated at a small table, facing one another, when Nala said, "I'm in charge of stopping Narman recruitment. That gave me some unique insight on how broad dissatisfaction with the League is amongst the troops stationed on Kanaris."

Elia nodded but said nothing. Intelligence work was rife with double and triple crosses. She was playing her cards close to the chest until she figured out what to make of Nala Biragor.

"Because I naturally have to confer with my counterparts doing similar work in other theaters of operation," Biragor continued, "I also have a pretty good idea of what the temperature of the populace is in other parts of the League's jurisdiction."

"And that is?" Gyanis asked.

"It's hot, Elia. Red hot. When news of us making contact with the Morghul hit the networks, people came together to confront what they believed to be an existential threat. By now, though, our citizens are catching hints of what a meat grinder this place is. 100,000 Marines have died on Kanaris over the past couple of years. Fifty thousand more have defected to the Narmans only to find themselves on the wrong end of our weaponry. That makes 150,000 humans that arrived as Marines but departed as corpses. And that's just combat. Seventy thousand have fallen to Kanarisian diseases, accidents, and wildlife encounters. Another 200k were wounded in action. Fifty thousand of those had to be discharged. They went home and started telling folks what's going on here. And now that the video you released is out there, people are talking about the camps. Outside the Guild worlds, the League is now regarded as a far more immediate danger than the Morghul are."

"You think I was behind the video?" Gyanis asked.

Biragor laughed. "Elia, I knew you were up to something the minute that shit with Jatmika went down. Technically, that was brilliant. You're really good at all the widget stuff. The spy shit, on the other hand, you pretty much suck at. It wasn't very hard to track you down."

"So," Elia said, "you got me, and you're not going to kill me?"

Biragor sighed and took a sip of her coffee. "You know, you can't hide more than 400,000 casualties. People started getting a sense that a journey to Kanaris was a one-way ticket, so they stopped joining the Space Corps. Since the League is convinced the Morghul will start showing up here in force, they've gotten a little heavy-handed with their conscription drives. They're sweeping up people by the millions on the non-Guild planets, yet leaving the Samaari populace largely alone. That's not going unnoticed, and it's breeding a lot of hostility. You know, the Morghul are probably coming to destroy us, but the data I'm seeing suggests we might implode upon ourselves before the aliens even get their shot."

"So, you want to help divide the League and help the Morghul take it over?" Elia asked. That did not make any sense.

Biragor shook her head. "The Morghul are going to take it over no matter what I do. The League is run by Samaaris. They are without equal when it comes to turning profits and they've bought their way out of every predicament they've ever put themselves into. The Morghul have no use for Samaari money, though. The Samaaris have no choice but to fight, and they don't have the acumen or the stomach for it. They don't know that yet, though. After subjecting themselves to years of propaganda, they've come to believe their own bullshit. They're preparing for a battle they think they can't lose. The bastards are in for a rude awakening."

Gyanis looked the agent in the eye. "Okay, then. All is lost. The Morghul are going to take us over and subject humankind to unspeakable horrors. What do you expect to accomplish by helping us?"

"Biragor leaned back in her seat. "When Takawa was captured, I got his files. Even the ones on Deena Vulk. I know what the Narmans are trying to do."

"And that is?" Elia asked.

"They want to escape Kanaris," the agent answered. "And I want to go with you."

"And where do you think we could possibly go?"

Biragor grinned. "Anywhere but here. Gyanis, things are going to get very bad. The worst thing about it is there won't be anywhere to run to. If we're defeated here and have to flee back to the Kyperion Quadrant with our tails between our legs, all we'll be doing is leading the foxes to the henhouse."

"It sounds hopeless," Gyanis said. "Unless you've got a better idea in mind."

The Section 615 agent shrugged. "I agree with these Kanarisian Morghul. Our best option is to escape."

Biragor took another drink from her cup. "You know, before coming to Kanaris, I was assigned to spy on the Ghuldari. I led the interrogations of prisoners we captured on Sivma-11. One of my more interesting subjects was a Ghoul that used to be one of their Deep Space Rangers. He'd just finished a long-range survey far beyond the borders of their quadrant. He'd discovered several Near Earth Environment worlds that would be far off the radar of both the League and the Ghuldari. Especially considering that I got to them before the Ghuldari did. As far as the Ghouls know, that expedition is lost in space."

"What does the League think of these places?"

Biragor shrugged. "Nothing at all. To get to them, they'd have to cross the entire length of Ghuldari territory, then an empty void even larger than that. It'd take us years to get there ourselves. We'd need to go under suspended animation."

"Suspended animation?" Gyanis gasped. "We don't have a ship capable of putting all our people on ice!"

"Actually, we do," the agent grinned, going along with Elia's game. Nala knew the Narmans were making a play for the mothership and was certain Gyanis knew it, too. "We've got one orbiting this planet a couple hundred kilometers above our heads."

"And you think we could capture it?"

Biragor leaned closer to Gyanis. "I know we can. We only need to pull half the Phoenix's crew to our side. From what I've seen so far, I think we're already well on our way there."

"You think half is enough?" Elia asked. "Wouldn't that make the outcome something of a coin toss?"

Nala shook her head. "Their half will be led by Samaaris commanding Marines gullible enough to believe all the fairy tales they're being fed. Our side will be directed by pragmatists leading troops who believe in their cause. Once we get our people in place, the fuckers won't stand a chance."

Elia Gyanis stared at Biragor for a long moment, sizing her up. She believed the intelligence agent was on the level, but Gyanis knew the League's spooks were trained to manipulate people's emotions. Gyanis had little doubt that Biragor could make her feel any way she wanted her to feel. Still, Elia had no choice but to trust her. "You know, I'll have to identify you to Eamon Tauk as my source."

Biragor nodded. "I know. You can give my name to him, Black Francis, and Captain Naktada. No one else."

The agent paused to pull a memory chip from her pocket and set it on the table. As she pushed it toward Gyanis, she added, "Give them that also. My job is to identify those Marines who may have a soft spot for the Narman cause. On this chip is a list of people who are prime candidates for recruitment. Obviously, you people already have the convicts and the Marines conscripted for political reeducation. This device has the names of conscripts whose families have fallen victim to the League. Those with grudges against League officials. People with relatives that got sent to the camps. Officers with nasty little secrets who would rather switch sides than have their dirty laundry made public. I've got officers in there, Elia. NCOs. Even a few Samaaris."

Gyanis looked at the chip, then back at Agent Biragor. "How many are on there?"

"Thirty-eight thousand," Biragor answered without batting an eye.

Elia did the math in her head. *That brings us up to 121,647, and the Marines down to 386,280. That cuts their advantage down to three to one. We're still far from our goal, but it moved the needle. If it checks out.*

Pointing at the chip, Elia asked, "How do I know if that's good information?"

Biragor shrugged. "You don't. But as a goodwill gesture, I'm giving you an entire Marine company. That information Bogislay gave you is legit. It came from me. Just proceed as instructed. You got some good people among them."

Elia glanced up at Biragor again. "Why are you coming to me with this? Isn't there someone else better at this espionage stuff who you could trust more?"

Nala shook her head. "Not really. You're smart, Elia. So is Tauk. And Naktada might be the most intelligent person on the entire planet. Of all the forces at play on Kanaris, I think your group has the most potential to pull off its mission. I'd much rather place my life in Tauk's hands than the Samaaris'. In fact, I believe I just have."

There was a moment or two of awkward silence as Gyanis tried to process what was happening. To break it, Elia asked, "So, what now?"

Biragor grinned. "I teach you spycraft. I'm going to show you how to organize your network and how to keep compromised units insulated from each other so that if one goes down, it doesn't take the rest of us with them. How to communicate through the chain without them knowing who commands them, and how to instruct them to pass information up to you. I'm going to teach you how to avoid getting caught in case the bastards wise up and assign someone other than me to catch you."

Elia leaned back in her seat and sighed.

"Is something wrong?" Biragor asked.

Gyanis shook her head. "No, it's just an awful lot to process."

The agent nodded. "It is. You have to look on the bright side, though."

"And that is?"

Nala gave off another smile. "You don't have to get naked with Bina Dubarti anymore, Red Dread."

Elia's jaw fell open. "You know about Bina?"

Biragor nodded. "Yeah. She works for me. Don't tell her that, though. She doesn't know it yet."

•●⬤●•

Chapter 24

CROSSING THE LINE

"**A**re you sure this isn't a trap, sir?" Dina Tiago asked me. We were in ambush position, deep into the Arad Valley, getting poured on while waiting for a Marine patrol to approach us from the east.

"It's never safe to be sure about anything," I advised her. "Especially something like this. This is going to be the first test of our intel network's reliability. I got the details on this patrol right from Gyanis."

"And where did she get it?"

"From the platoon leader leading the mission."

"I got 'em," said Sergeant Hermour from an observation post two kilometers ahead of us. "There's seventy-eight dogfaces marching your way. They're equipped with standard gear. Thirty-one of them are lit up green. Twelve are red. Thirty-five are yellow."

Naktada had developed a program that Elia Gyanis could distribute to her trusted armorers. Once installed in a platoon's shells, the software made their equipment emit a signal that, while invisible to them and their comrades, would cause them to glow with a colored aura when seen through our visors. Based upon Hermour's report, a dozen of Eglan's troops were League loyalists. The ones painted yellow were those the lieutenant deemed too risky to try to turn. He figured it safer if I was the one to see where their allegiances lay.

"You read that, team?" I asked over the platoon network. We got twelve red. I want to see nine of them KIA. I'd like the rest wounded severely enough so they can't return to battle."

"Nut shots," laughed a corporal from Third Squad, suggesting they aim for the enemy's genitals.

"Concentrate your fire on the yellows. Do your best only to wound them superficially if you have to at all. Don't fire at the greens! They're going to be shooting in your direction but aiming over your heads. Stay prone until the order to cease fire is given. Am I clear?"

"Clear!" my platoon answered back, almost in unison.

"Alright," I said. "And stay on your toes in case this thing isn't what we think it is. If I give the 'Code Seven' signal, kill every fucking one of them."

Fortunately, it never came to that. Eglan led his Marines right into our ambush as promised. We immediately opened fire, dropping most of his red troops and directing our blaster fire at the yellows. Thanks to our superior camouflage technology, the patrol could not identify what to fight back against. Many of them panicked, broke ranks, and fled the way they came, only to be intercepted by Sergeant Hermour's First Squad, who had followed them once they had cleared her observation post. The fighting was over in less than ten minutes, with Eglan announcing their surrender.

Once the hostilities were over, we rushed our prisoners further west to a mar-shaling area we had already prepared. There, we stripped them out of their armor and led them away individually for questioning. I handled Eglan personally. "You have something you want to say to me, Lieutenant?" I asked when we were comfortably out of earshot from the rest of the prisoners.

"Zero Fury," Eglan said to me.

I smiled at the man as I extended my mitt to him. "Welcome aboard."

Eglan smiled back, "I'm glad to meet you. You're the guy who killed Gori Dravidas?"

I nodded. "I am."

"Awesome. So, what happens now?"

"I need you to go back to Narman's Pyke," I told him.

The expression on Eglan's face dropped. "Are you kidding me?"

I shook my head. "I need someone who can identify those in the officer corps we can bring to our side."

"You want me to try to convince officers to commit treason?!? Are you trying to get me hung?!?"

"You will approach no one. We got people inside the Pyke to do that kind of stuff. We just want you to give us the names of those you think may be open to the suggestion. We also need dirt. There are officers who may not be willing to join us but might be persuaded to help by other means."

"Like by spying on the League?"

"Exactly," I answered. "We also need to form a shadow officer corps. I've received reports that Narman's Pyke is a tinderbox right now. If it goes off prematurely, you might take the Pyke, but you'll get destroyed by the troops still in orbit. We need people to keep things calm until the right moment."

"And when is the right moment going to be?"

"When we have enough people in place to take not only the Pyke, but the mothership, too."

Eglan nodded, understanding the importance and enormity of the mission I was handing him. "It's going to be risky."

"I'm fully aware of that," I told him. "Just so you know, those joining the Narmans today will face a force that outnumbers us by roughly three to one. You won't be any safer on our side of this conflict."

Tymar Hailo stuck his arm through the bars, reaching as far into the cell as he could. "Please, Ani," he pleaded. "Take my hand."

Anirae Labaat recoiled further into the darkness, shaking her head as tears ran down her face. "I don't want your hand, Ty. I want a knife. Or just a piece of sharp metal. Broken glass. Anything! I can't do this anymore! One of these days, it's going to be my turn under Kryndil's blade! I know it! I don't want to die that way!"

Being born Samaari came with many privileges, but no matter how prosperous a society was, they all had an underclass. Anirae never had any reason to feel special just because she was born on a Guild planet. In fact, she joined the Space Corps thinking she could thrive in a place where she could leverage her heritage to her advantage. She thought it would be far less challenging to stand out on a planet like Dabrishat as a rare Samaari among a horde of Dabrishati. It had to be easier than distinguishing oneself as a Samaari among a mob of other Samaaris.

But she was sorely mistaken. Anirae never experienced the advantages of being Samaari in the Corps, just the consequences. The only thing her ancestry ever earned her was the ire of her conscripted comrades and a dank cell deep in the bowels of Kryndil's Lair, where she waited for that monster to strip her of her skin.

Eventually, Hailo withdrew his arm and banged his fist against the bars of his lover's cage. "You're not going to die, Ani! I'm going to get you out of there! We're getting the hell out of this place!"

"How!?!" Ani cried. "We're in a fucking fortress! We're so far underground right now I don't even know how to find sunlight!"

Ty shook his head. "I can get us out of here, Ani. I've got a plan."

"What?" Ani gasped as she rolled onto all fours to crawl across the slime-covered floor to get closer to Ty. Lowering her voice, she asked, "You have a way out?"

Hailo nodded. "The turnkey's a Class Zero. A criminal. They never fucking change, Ani. They're always willing to bend the rules if they can get something out of it. During my last patrol, we made contact with a squad of Killbillies. I recovered two kilos of high-potency Demon Root from one of the bodies. I offered it to Baquir in exchange for two sets of fatigues and the opportunity to borrow his keys for an hour."

Tymar and Ani were a couple even before they landed on Kanaris. He did not defect to the Narmans because of ideology. He only switched sides after learning his girlfriend had been captured. Having heard the stories about what the Morghul did to the Samaaris that fell under their control, Ty crossed the line for the sole purpose of saving Ani from such a fate. As a conscript, he did not raise many eyebrows. Hailo kept his head low and never ceased looking for Anirae. It took eight months for them to be reunited, and he had no intention of losing her again.

"I got you a way out of that cell and a set of armor," Ty assured his girl, "I'm working on getting you out of the dungeon. Escaping Kryndil's Lair isn't the hard part, though. It's figuring out where to go after we leave. If we stay here, they'll eventually get around to killing you. If we go back to the Marines, they'll kill me.

I worked it out though, Ani. I got a way to go back to Narman's Pyke and look like a hero."

Now Ani reached through the bars to take her boyfriend's hand. "How are you going to do that?"

Ty smiled. "I'm going to bring them something they really want. I got information for them, Ani. I know where Kryndil's Lair is. I can lead them here. I also know that the Mogs live underground, in settlements that are all connected by a subterranean tunnel network. You know why you never see Morghul aircraft flying around Kanaris? It's because they travel in a goddamn freaky high-tech alien subway system! Ani, if the Marines capture Kryndil's Lair, they can get to all the rest of the settlements as well!"

Ani let out a single sob and tried not to get her hopes up. "You're a deserter, Ty. Do you think the Marines'll believe you?"

"They don't have to believe me. I'm going to bring them someone whose word they absolutely will trust."

"Who?"

Ty smiled even wider. "One of their spies. Deena Vulk. They got her locked in a sensory deprivation cell just down the corridor. Apparently, Kryndil can't physically hurt her, so he's trying to drive her mad."

For the first time in a very long while, Ani saw a faint glimmer of hope for her future. "When are you going to get us out of here?"

Ty let out a long sigh. "I got the jailor on my side, but I still need the dungeon guards to let us out. There's seven that we have to pass through to get topside. I have to figure out their price and how to get what they want to let us leave."

Ani immediately deflated. "That could take forever!"

"Don't think like that! You have to have faith in me! I'll work this shit out! I always do! I just need a little more time!"

Ani reached through the bars and grabbed her lover by the collar. "Ty, I don't think I have all that much time left!"

Chapter 25

To Anga-Iskalei

Black Francis was pretty cross when he glanced at me. "You shouldn't be here."

I let out a long sigh. We had been over this before. "I need to pick the platoon leaders for the Xun infiltrators. I can't do that hiding back at base camp."

"You should've delegated that shit to someone else, Eamon. You're our leader. You're running the whole show. You're supposed to be back at camp planning our way off this rock. If we lose you, who's going to carry us over the finish line?"

"The smartest man we got."

Francis scoffed. "Naktada? Don't get me wrong; I love the guy. The man's absolutely brilliant. His intelligence is focused on technical shit, though. He's the man I want inventing a better mousetrap, not leading our escape off this hell hole."

"Dmitri will always excel at whatever he sets his mind to. The man has a way of rising to the occasion."

"You should've seen how bad he freaked out at Razbauten when he got up close and personal with a soroquid for the very first time," Francis laughed. "Had you born witness to that, you might have second thoughts about his fitness to lead."

"If I'm not mistaken," I retorted, "had he not been there, that platoon of Suma Corps Marines might've wiped you all out."

Francis averted his eyes and stared at the ground. The memory of what he had been forced to do to the prisoners he took that night still stung. "There was no 'might' about it. Had Dimi not been there, we'd all have been goners."

Feeling a certain amount of smugness in hearing Francis admit he owed his life to Naktada, I leaned against the tree I was seated beside and put my head back. We were on our way to Anga-Iskalei, one of the largest mining camps the Samaaris had on Kanaris, to see if we could discover one of those ventilation shafts that Kaito Rabaat had told us about.

Our platoon was split evenly between seasoned Raiders and Xun infiltrators hand-picked as leadership candidates by Nila Chisek. We spent our first day riding toward the mine on naypetos, then corralled our animals under a light guard and made the rest of our way through the jungle without them. It took us three days to get to the base of Anga-Iskalei, and as we set up camp along the west slope at the edge of a large clearing, I was surprised by how much I missed Cupid. She was the ubati I had raised since watching her hatch from an egg at Camp Vayipar. I had been neglecting her since we defected and enjoyed watching her romp through the underbrush at my side. I could see she enjoyed being with me, too.

Luckily, our mission had been uneventful and quiet. That night was no different. The sky above us was uncharacteristically clear, and we enjoyed a comfortable night outdoors without rain for once. Both moons shone brightly above us and lit up the terrain almost as if it were day. After a while, I spotted the bioluminescent glow of sky jellies over the western tree line. I went to point them out to Black Francis but discovered he had fallen asleep the moment our little debate had ended.

Before long, the sky jellies were swarming over the canopy, filling the sky with a dazzling light show. I wanted to share it with someone, but I knew how precious sleep was to my troops. Then I heard Haeli Deboara startle herself awake. "Braison!" she called out. "Braison! Where are you?!?"

I jumped to Haeli's side to quiet her down. "Shhh! You were drea...."

"Braison!" Haeli called out once more. I could hear the panic rising in her voice. "Braison! Please...."

"Haeli...."

Realizing she had only been dreaming of her son, Haeli buried her face in her hands. "He was right there. He was right in fucking front of me! He was taking me to see Hauwi! God, I miss them! What the hell did we do to those poor babies?!?"

"What you had to do in order to save them from a horrific death," I assured her as I slipped my arm around her shoulders. "This may sound cold, Haeli, but you have to put this behind you right now. Fall apart all you want back at camp, but out here, your head needs to be on your mission. If you break down on patrol, you'll never be able to get back at the bastards who forced you to kill your boys. You'll end up letting them kill you instead."

Haeli grimaced but nodded in understanding. I could almost see her forcing her grief back down deep where it needed to be.

To help her, I pointed out the sky jellies. "Hey, take a look at those. They're beautiful, aren't they?"

I heard Haeli suck in a deep breath of air in surprise. "Oh my god! They are! And they always seem to show up when you need them most!"

And just like that, the memory of Haeli's dead son was suppressed until she knew it was safe to bring it out again. I was impressed. "You know, the first time I ever saw one of those things," I told her, "one of my dipshit Zeros tried to grab their tentacles and hold it like a balloon."

Haeli snickered. "Yeah, well, my dipshit husband did the same thing our first night in Saimsun. That was a horrible day. Braison and Hauwi were so terrified. Daino tried to distract them by doing what your guy did, not knowing they sting like a bitch. His hand swelled up twice its size, but he still swung one hell of a pick the next morning to keep from being culled. He used to be the toughest man I ever met."

I shrugged. "One day, maybe he'll be able to...."

"He'll never be the same," Haeli said. "Ever. The man I married died with my boys. What's left of him now is not even remotely who I remember him to be."

I was taken aback by the tone of her voice. "You sound like you hate him."

Haeli shook her head. "I can't hate him. He committed an unspeakable horror to spare me from having to do it. If I had been the one who covered my boys' mouths and noses and suffocated them with my own bare hands, well, I'd be the broken one unable to leave my tent back at base camp. He sacrificed his body for our children back in that mine. He sacrificed his soul so that I could keep mine. That poor man is in such agony, Eamon. He hates himself in ways I can't even comprehend. If I were half the person he was, I would put him out of his misery."

I could do it for her.

I was so shocked at the thought that entered my mind that I pulled my arm from around Haeli's shoulders. *What the fuck is the matter with me? Have I stooped that low?*

I remembered the night Haeli and I spent together in Saimsun. There was nothing romantic about it. Nothing at all. It was just an act performed for the benefit of the Blue Shirts who wanted to know what side I was really on. I had not been attracted to her that night, nor had she been attracted to me.

It was different now, though. Haeli was eating again and starting to fill out. The color was returning to her cheeks, and her hair was once more growing out and regaining its sheen. Joining the Xun had given her a purpose and ignited a spark that burned brightly behind those big blue eyes of hers. Every day, she looked less like a starving child and more like a woman. She was not as strikingly gorgeous as Jella Duverii had been, but she had an intensity to her that more than made up for it. That ferocity may have worried her husband, but it made me want to get to know her better.

Haeli mistook my pulling away as revulsion for suggesting that killing her husband would have been a mercy on the poor man. "I know. I'm a horrible person, aren't I? That guy gave everything he had for us, and now I think he'd be better off dead."

"No," I told her. "You're not a horrible person. Look, Haeli, we're all living in a pretty complicated situation right now. Daino's not the same person he was a year ago. Neither am I, for that matter. You aren't, either. This fight we're in forces us to change. We can't win it if we can't adapt. We're forced to make hard decisions, and that molds us into hard people. That's the nature of war. What you said about your husband isn't mean or ungrateful. It's just the cold truth, which is something we all have to face here. No one wants to say that Daino Deboara will not survive this war, Haeli, but anybody who's ever laid eyes on that man since we plucked him out of the jungle knows it."

Haeli hung her head and began to weep. "What am I going to do about him?"

"Well, we certainly aren't going to kill him." I think I directed that comment more at myself than at her. "You're going to have to make a choice, though. Do you want to spend your time here fighting for a chance at a new life or back with your husband in a futile attempt to cling to an old life that no longer exists?"

Looking at me with tear-filled eyes, Haeli said, "I can't leave Daino in the shape he's in."

I sighed. "Haeli, you already have. I'm pretty sure he knows that, but he probably isn't going to accept it until he hears it from you."

Haeli shook her head. "I can't. As messed up as he is, Daino's the only person left in my life. If I lose him, who will I have?"

Me. I tried to tell her that with my eyes. *I don't have anybody, either. We both have the same drive, the same mission. We're in sync and on the same trajectory to either freedom or death. Maybe if she knows I'll be there for her if she leaves Daino....*

I leaned in to kiss her.

Haeli pulled back and looked at me as if I had lost my mind. "No," she said as she scooted away from me. "No! You know, Eamon, I could kill Daino, but only because I love him enough to ease his pain. I could never betray him, though. Not like this."

Feeling like a total moron, I lowered my head in embarrassment. "I'm sorry, Haeli. Really. I don't know what got into me. I'm an idiot. Please forgive me. It'll never happen again."

Haeli's expression softened a little. "I'm sorry, too. I-I-I might have put out some mixed signals but...but...." After letting out a little sigh to get her thoughts together, she said, "Maybe in a different time and a different place, we might have a better chance, but not while I still have things to resolve with Daino. I-I-I...." Unable to say anything else, Haeli stood up and walked away in search of a new place to sleep.

Once she was gone, I glanced over at Black Francis, who was now wide awake and shaking his head at me. "What the hell's the matter with you, Tauk?"

Shaking my head back at him, I said, "I don't know. Obviously, I've got some issues I gotta work out."

••‹•›●‹•›••

Chapter 26

A Peek into the Abyss

I t took two days to find a ventilation shaft on the mountain overlooking Anga-Iskalei. It was expertly concealed. Whoever drilled it stopped about ten meters from breaking through the rock and changed direction, boring downward for the final twenty. That kept the opening hidden and prevented Kanaris's constant rain from pouring through it.

Upon discovering the opening, Black Francis and I looked at each other. "Does that thing remind you of the entrance to a soroquid nest or what?" he asked me.

"It certainly does," I said as I pulled out my flashlight and prepared to crawl inside.

Francis grabbed me by the back of my armor and tossed me aside. "What the hell do you think you're doing?"

"Taking a peek," I told him.

"Once again, Eamon: You. Are. Our. Leader. If you stick your head in there and something lops it off, no one will be left to make command decisions. It's your job to send someone else in there to...."

"I'll go," Haeli Deboara said as she stepped up to the hole in the rock. Without hesitation, all the other Xun fighters volunteered to go with her.

I was impressed. "You sure you all are ready for this?"

"We're going to have to lead people into one of those things soon enough," said a Portunese man I was also considering for a platoon leader slot. "I'd like to know what I'm in for before it comes to that."

Alright, then," I said as I passed Haeli the device Naktada made for us. "You know what to do?"

Haeli nodded. "Rappel down the pipe and activate the jammer to seize the fan. Crawl through the blades and take it to the end of the line. Then reconnoiter as far as I can without getting discovered."

Giving Haeli a grin, I told her, "You got it. Pick five and go. One stays behind at the other end of that tunnel and...."

"We stay within radio range of them so they can sound the alarm if something goes wrong."

Good girl. I certainly don't have to worry about you not paying attention, do I?

We set the Xun up like radio relay stations. As Haeli's team descended into the abyss, a half dozen of her comrades followed close behind, latching themselves to the rock walls at regular intervals to ensure radio communication went all the way to the surface. Our team really lucked out in that the shaft we found led to an area of the mine so remote that it took the recon squad two hours to discover where the inmate laborers were forced to work.

Ultimately, it was half a day for the entire team to return topside. When they emerged, we confirmed that we could immobilize the fans at will and knew precisely where everyone needed to go to blend in with the inmates. It was a very successful mission.

Our platoon seemed very pleased with itself, forcing Gunny to pull everyone together for a little talk. "Our job ain't over yet," he told our troops. "In fact, we just cleared the halfway mark. We still have to get back to our animals and return to our rendezvous point. I'll tell you right now that the return trip is the most dangerous part of any mission, particularly after you've pulled off a successful one. People tend to let their guard down. They think the hard part is over. Let me assure you that it ain't. Keep your eyes open and your guard up because this is where shit tends to go sideways. Understand?"

"Yes, Gunny," the Xun said in unison. Our Raiders said nothing at all. They had enough experience under their belt to know Francis was not talking to hear the sound of his own voice.

•●-●-◉-●-●●

Some things just can't be taught. Black Francis had spent the entire march coaching the Xun on what to look for when walking point. Anwar tracks. Tripwires. Heat shimmer where it doesn't belong. Other things are much more subtle and noticeable only after many hours in the bush. Some people are just naturals at detecting stuff out of place, though. They have the instinct to know when something is off-kilter. Haeli Deboara turned out to be one of those point-man prodigies.

We were on the tail end of our foot march back when Haeli stopped the line, moving toward the side of the trail and pointing her weapon ahead of her.

Crouching to lower his profile, Black Francis jogged to the front of the formation, making hardly a sound, only slowing as he approached our lead. "What do you got, Deboara?"

"A bad feeling, Gunny. I don't see anything, but something isn't right."

Francis stopped to survey his surroundings. First, he did a scan with his exo-armor's sensor array. When that came up empty, he muted his system audio so that no sound escaped his helmet, then lifted his visor shield. He spotted nothing out of the ordinary and only heard the falling rain. The odor, though....

Flipping his helmet visor back down, Francis powered his commlink up and said, "I can smell our ubatis."

"Is that a problem?" asked one of the Xun. "We're pretty close to where we left them."

"Quiet," I ordered as I turned up my audio array to pick up the sounds of the jungle around us. After a few moments of listening, I said, "I can't hear them."

"What the hell does that mean?!?" The voice belonged to another of our leadership candidates. The panic in her tone made me doubt whether she would still be one if we got back to base.

"Ubatis are not quiet creatures," Haeli told her comrade. "That's why we didn't take them to Anga-Iskalei. If you can smell them but not hear them, it means they're there, but not...."

"Quiet!" Francis snapped. "This isn't classwork, people! It's show time!

Sergeant Korman! You get your squad and sweep to the left. I want you to beeline south a half click, then turn west until you're parallel to our corral camp's right flank. That's where you're going to approach them from. Got it?"

"Aye-aye, Gunny!" Korman said as he collected his troops and melted away into the rainforest.

"Tiago!"

"Yes, Gunny!" Dina called out.

"Follow Korman! When he peels north, you keep going for another click before you do the same. I want you to set up a counter-ambush to smash anything that escapes and block any reinforcements that might be out there from reaching our camp. Go! Demangel!"

"Here!"

"Same as Korman, but heading north to attack their left flank! Hermour!"

"Yes, Gun...!"

KA-BOOM!

The explosion went off twenty-five meters ahead of Haeli Deboara, but when the fireball dissipated, she was no longer there. Neither was Black Francis.

"HAELI!" I screamed into the commlink. "FRANCIS!"

Before anyone could respond, another explosion ripped through our formation. Then another. After that, we were hit with an intense barrage of automatic gunfire from further up the trail.

My instinct was to charge forward and try to pinpoint the enemy positions, but I heard Francis's voice screaming from somewhere inside my head. *DON'T YOU FUCKING DARE! LEAD, TAUK! LEAD, GODDAMMIT! GET THE ATTENTION OF YOUR TROOPS AND TELL THEM HOW TO GET OUT OF THIS MESS!*

"Hermour!" I shouted into the commlink.

"Yes, sir!" Saeli screamed back.

"Find your grenadier and put a high explosive warhead on that rail gun at one o'clock!"

BRRRRRRRRRATATATATATA!

It was almost as if the rail gunner heard me give the order and turned his fire my way to shut me up. Flinging myself face-first into the mud, all I could do was cover my head with my hands and scream as loud as I could until the thunder died down. "Motherfucker!" I shrieked. "Hermour! Hurry up before...!"

BRRRRRRRRRRATATATATATABRRRRRRRRRRIP!

Rolling as fast as I could off the path and into the jungle, I just barely escaped getting cut in half by one gunner, only to find myself in the sights of another as soon as I came to a rest. He saw me at the exact instant I spotted him. As he raised his weapon to fire, I leapt to my feet and dove behind a large tree just as it erupted into a shower of wooden splinters. "THEY'RE KILLBILLIES!" I shouted to my platoon.

Finally able to grab my rifle, I fired from the right of the tree to catch the gunner's attention, then sprinted to take a shot at him from the left. The Qilkorian was wise to that trick, however, and when I emerged from my cover, I found him aiming right at me. He had me dead to rights, yet before he could squeeze the trigger, a burst of plasma fire caught him in the back of the head and put him down

.

Yes! I thought as I fell to my knees and tried not to soil myself. *We got a Raider in their perimeter!*

"HERMOUR!" I screamed into the commlink again. "WHERE THE FUCK IS MY...!"

Before I could finish my question, a rocket flew from our portion of the rainforest and struck the rail gunner's position. The explosion blew several trees apart at the base, causing them to topple over and come down atop our adversaries' position. It looked like a direct hit.

The key word there was "looked." Thinking that the rail gun was out of commission, a trio of Francis's Raiders broke cover to take over the nest. They were almost there when the Killbilly regained his senses and opened fire on the poor bastards, blowing them all apart.

BRRRRRRRRRRATATATATATA!

With that threat eliminated, the gunner went for other targets. BRRRRRRRRRRATATATA! BRRRRRRRRRRATATATATATA! BRRRRRRRRR...POP!"

The Raider inside the enemy perimeter finished off the nest.

Knowing her squad had taken casualties, I was about to call Hermour for a status report but stopped when I saw her emerge from cover and storm the position that had just been taken out. While Zarba Asosi and Private Datsol opened up on the left flank with their blasters, Rikkal Tando seized the rail gun and turned it onto the Qilkorians. I rushed up to join them.

As I ran to Hermour's position, I heard Sergeant Korman's voice pleading for help. "They got us pinned down over here! They're chewing us up! Somebody needs to put a rocket on that goddamn...!"

Phew! Phew! Phewphewphewphewphew! I could hear the firing in Korman's quadrant suddenly fall silent as our inside Raider took out the entire position that was keeping my people's noses in the dirt.

At this point, the Killbillies realized they had one of us behind the wire. More than half of them suddenly disengaged from the threat outside and directed their fire inward. "No!" I heard someone scream behind the lines. "What are you doing?!? The enemy's out there!"

Taking advantage of the disarray, I ordered my troops to advance. Those still mobile launched themselves at the ambush point and caused considerable damage. Sergeant Tiago's team actually punched through the enemy perimeter and caused half of our opponents to fall back in an unorganized retreat. Once they broke and fled, it was like shooting fish in a barrel.

With two of their three lines compromised, the remaining position did not stand a chance. Marines would have surrendered at that point. The Killbilles knew they stood good odds of earning a date with Kryndil if they got captured, so they fought to the last man.

When it was over, I grabbed Sergeant Korman as he limped by me. "You seen Black Francis?"

Korman shook his head. "No! Not since this all started!"

"Check the perimeter for him! Someone was inside, taking these fuckers out one at a time from behind! I think it was him!"

Korman shook his head. "It wasn't Francis! I caught that, too! I saw Killbillies on the west flank firing all over the place, trying to chase their target! Whoever the inside shooter was, they were short! Francis can't crouch that low and move fast enough to avoid getting hit! He would've stood his ground!"

"To the west?" I asked. After Korman nodded at me, I said, "Alright! I'll try to figure out where they were! You go find Francis!"

As I searched the area, I took a moment to examine the bodies of those who attacked us. They were not all Killbillies. There were several women among the dead, all of whom had an olive "0" stenciled on the shoulder of their armor crossed out with a red "X." As I began to realize who they were, I heard a distinctive "click" go off behind me. It was the sound of a Marine-issued M88 sidearm trying to fire against an empty chamber. "Hello, Tauk."

I spun around and found myself face-to-face with the man who brought me to Kanaris. He was sitting on the ground, pointing his weapon at my face. "Gunny Malcolm," I said as I snatched the pistol from his hand.

"Relax, you little prick," Malcolm laughed at me. "I knew it wasn't loaded. I used my last bullet on that bad-ass little bitch over there."

Turning to see who Malcolm was talking about, I spotted Haeli Deboara lying motionless in the mud about four meters behind me.

Chapter 27

GUNNY

Taking stock was painful. Of our eighty-person platoon, we had suffered seventeen killed in action, four Raiders and thirteen Xun. Miraculously, neither Black Francis nor Haeli Deboara were among the dead, though they certainly should have been. Haeli had been engulfed in the fireball of the first explosion, but her armor did its job. Her bell got rung when the blast lifted her off her feet and tossed her into the bush, but she was not seriously injured. Despite being disoriented and confused, she leapt to her feet and tried to sprint back to her platoon. Unfortunately, she could not get her bearings in the thick smoke and ran the wrong way.

Haeli was incredibly lucky. Her short stature, coupled with the low visibility in the immediate aftermath of the blasts, allowed her to slip through the space between a pair of Qilkorians while their attention was directed elsewhere. At first, the inexperienced Xun was terrified to find herself separated from her unit. Alone and surrounded by the enemy, she was resigned to the fact that sooner or later, she would be shot. Not willing to passively await her execution, however, Haeli decided to hit the bastards from behind and take as many down as she could before she met her fate.

That little woman probably cut down a half dozen enemy combatants before any of them realized she was there. As an added bonus, once her presence was known, half the Killbillies broke off the attack on us to try to get Haeli. Firing inside their own position sowed further confusion amongst the Qilkorians and negated every advantage they had over us, of which they had many. It was safe to say that had it not been for Haeli Deboara, that ambush could have wiped us out.

By the time Tiago broke through one of the Qilkorian flanks, Haeli was on her back heel. She was trying to hold off a trio of Malcolm's Zeros and doing poorly. We had been training the Xun at a very high tempo running up to that mission, but Haeli was no marksman. She was frightened and under considerable duress, causing her shots to fly wildly off target. She had to resort to grenades.

Haeli did not realize one of her assailants was so close. When she lobbed her first device, it bounced off a Zero's chest and flew right back at her. The explosion blew apart her arm and leg shields, then split apart her chest and back plates, letting shrapnel practically rip the flesh from her ribs. The Zero she was aiming for stepped in to finish her off, only to be cut down by one of Tiago's Raiders. Another grenade thrown by one of my people took out the other two Zeros and forced Gunny Malcolm out of his position without a rifle.

Malcolm did what he could with his sidearm but quickly exhausted his magazine. When he realized he was on his last bullet, he was preparing to shoot himself in the head when he spotted Haeli coming to her senses on the ground beside him. "Fucking cunt," he growled as he put his last round into the center of her chest.

Despite being in pieces, Haeli's armor still absorbed the shot. It flexed enough to crack a couple of ribs and knock the wind out of her, but the slug itself barely penetrated her skin.

Black Francis fared considerably worse. Like Haeli Deboara, he was launched into the jungle by the first explosion. Unlike Haeli's, Francis's armor did not do its job. The sharp end of a broken tree limb found its way perfectly between two of the gunny's armor plates and impaled him against the trunk. When Korman finally discovered him, Francis was still alive but losing a lot of blood. "If we don't get him back to the Hornet soon," warned Bledyn Marwhol, the Second Squad medic, "this man's going to be in some serious fucking trouble!"

Taking the corpsman at his word, I stomped back to where Korman was binding Malcolm's arms together. "What did you do to the animals in the corral camp?" I asked our prisoner.

"Wouldn't you like to fucking know," Malcolm laughed. Korman belted him across the jaw hard enough to nearly break it.

I pointed my finger at the sergeant. "Don't do that again, Blevin. I need him conscious."

"Aye-aye, sir."

"Let's try this again, Gunny. What did...?"

Malcolm spit a wad of bloody saliva into my eye. Knowing it would take a while to break Malcolm down, I forced myself to think. As I paced around the gunnery sergeant, I looked at the bodies littering the ambush site. Gunny's Zeros were fit. Like Malcolm, they could have marched clear across the planet to get to us. A couple of the Killbillies were significantly overweight. "You ain't telling me those fat fuckers walked here," I said to myself. "And they sure as shit ain't walking back."

"Sergeant!" I yelled to Korman, "Gather up what's left of your squad and go to the corral. These pricks would've had no choice but to kill the ubatis. They might've killed our naypetos, too, but I'm going to wager that they probably didn't kill theirs. If you can, get someone on one of those things and haul ass to t he *Hornet*! Tell Albarn we won't be able to get to her!"

After pausing to look at the medics attending to Haeli, Francis, and the rest of our wounded, I added, "She's going to have to come to us."

Korman returned by himself as I was helping the medics tend to our wounded. It turned out I was right. The Killbillies had taken the corral, killing the dozen people we left behind to care for our animals. The sergeant confirmed Cupid was among the dead, which affected me more than I thought it would. The naypetos were too valuable to slaughter, so they left them alive. I was slightly annoyed that Korman sent the rest of his squad to the *Hornet*. "That's going to leave us a little short-handed, Blevin."

Korman shrugged. "Strength in numbers, sir. If I only sent one or two and something happens to them, there won't be any help coming our way."

"You're right." Turning my attention to Lance Corporal Marwol, I said, "It's going to be damn near a day before they reach Albarn. Can you keep Black Francis alive that long?"

"I'll do everything I can, sir," the medic told me. "But I can't make any promises."

I nodded in understanding as I stood up. "I know you'll do your best."

After leaving Francis, I worked my way down the line of wounded, offering what little help I could, which was not much. I mostly doled out words of encouragement before moving to the next patient. When I got to Haeli Deboara and saw that she was awake, I took a seat beside her. As she tried to sit up to greet me, I insisted she lay back down. "Relax, Haeli. I'm not going to try to kiss you again."

Despite her pain, Haeli grinned. "You'd have better odds of success now. I can't exactly get away from you, can I?"

Gazing over Haeli's injuries, I said, "Man, you must really want that platoon leader slot, don't you?"

"You think I got it in the bag?"

"We have to see how you recover, but if Petty Officer Pariz can patch you up on the *Hornet,* I can safely say you're probably a shoo-in."

Haeli looked up at the sky with a big smile on her face. The woman was understandably very proud of herself and had every reason to be.

"You know, we don't have medals in this army we're part of now, but if we were in the Marines, I'd be putting you in for a Nova Cross, First Degree."

"I'm not sure what that is," Haeli said, "but it sounds prestigious."

"It certainly is. Had you not pulled off what you did, those Killbillies would've wiped us out."

Haeli looked a little embarrassed. "I didn't do it on purpose, Eamon. I got lucky."

"No," I corrected her. "You caught a break and ran with it. That's what warriors do. That's what a hero does. You got a lot of people that are very proud of you right now."

After letting out a long sigh, Haeli's expression soured. "What do you suppose Daino's going to make of this?"

"To be blunt, Haeli, I don't really care. And if he can't see how extraordinary you are at this combat stuff and how important you are to what we're trying to accomplish here, well then, you probably shouldn't care either."

••⟢ ◉ ⟣••

I found Gunny Malcolm sitting in the mud, tied to a tree with his arms magnet-ically shackled behind his back. Instead of blindfolding him, Sergeant Korman just moved the patch our captive wore over his empty eye socket to the peeper that still worked. Before I started speaking to the prisoner, I moved it back.

"You come to finish me off, Tauk?" Malcolm asked once he saw it was me that came to him. "You gonna get back at me for all that skin I stripped off your hide?"

I shook my head and replied, "No. You advised against pursuing vendettas after you flogged me. Remember?"

Malcolm laughed. "And you listened to me? You're going soft, Tauk."

When he finished snickering, Gunny fell silent as he pensively glanced about his surroundings. Once he got his bearings, he asked, "How's that woman I shot? She going to make it?"

It was my turn to laugh. "Who's going soft now? You feeling a little regret about shooting a defenseless soldier, Gunny?"

Squinting his one good eye at me, Malcolm growled, "I ain't regretting shit. We were in a fight, and I needed to make sure that woman didn't have any more surprises in her. We both had a job to do, and we both did what we had to. Me, you, her, we all play for high stakes in this game. Now that the battle's over and the outcome's decided, yeah, I'd like to know how she's doing. She earned my respect. If I had a few women like her and fewer of these death squad fuckers, we'd have had your ass."

I shook my head in disagreement. "No, you wouldn't. She made you. So did Black Francis. That's why we stopped before we marched into your kill zone."

Malcolm looked genuinely puzzled. "You made us? Really? Even through the Killbilly camouflage?"

I nodded.

"What gave us away?"

"Like I would ever tell you that. That's going to be one of our lessons learned. Not yours."

The gunnery sergeant sighed. "So, what's next here? You taking me back to camp? Interrogating me? Turning me over to that Kryndil shit-head?"

"None of that. In fact, I'm going to make you the offer we're making everyone we capture. Well, most everyone, anyway. Killbillies get shot on the spot. Those we can prove committed war crimes go to Kryndil. The rest we ask to join us."

"Join you?" Malcolm scoffed. "Have you lost your mind?"

Tired of standing, I sat in the mud alongside our prisoner and leaned against the tree. "I know you, Gunny. You don't have any genuine love for the League. We're doing things differently on this side. Join us and you won't have to worry about adding to those demons fighting it out behind that thick skull of yours. Ours is a righteous cause, Gunny. We both know the League's gone rotten."

"You know, Tauk, I may be a lot of things, but I ain't no traitor," Malcolm said without much conviction. It sounded like he wanted to join us, but something beyond his control, something even more powerful than the League, was keeping him from doing so.

"Come on, Gunny! For once, step up and fight for a cause you can be proud of!"

"I can't!"

"Bullshit! Why can't you?"

"Because I'm not a dirtbag turncoat!"

"No, you're a murderer!"

"Yeah, Tauk, I'm a fuckin' killer! Just like you!"

"You're a mindless sycophant incapable of doing anything unless the Marines tell you to do it!"

"That's right! I follow my orders!"

"You're a fanatic...!"

"And you think you aren't?!?"

"A psychopath...!"

"Let's see how well-adjusted you are after thirty years of continuous combat!"

"A fucking junkie!"

Malcolm did not have an answer for that one. He broke off eye contact and began scanning the mud around us.

My mouth fell open in shock. "Oh my god! That's it, isn't it? You can't join us because we don't have any Killbillies in our ranks. Without Killbillies, you can't get your hands on your dope, can you?"

Still unable to look me in the face, Gunny mumbled, "Yeah, well, we all have our faults, don't we?"

Suddenly uncomfortable being so close to the man, I stood up and took a couple of paces away from my captive. "You're not here fighting for a cause. You're not fighting for your comrades. Fuck, Gunny, you're not even out here fighting for a paycheck. You're fighting for your fix!"

Regaining his moxie, Malcolm finally turned his glare upon me. "You ain't seen half the shit I've seen, Tauk! You ain't done half of it, either! I fucking ruined myself for the goddamn Space Corps and how I deal with the horrors I've witnessed is my business! You're a long way off from earning the right to judge me, you sanctimonious little prick!"

I shook my head in disgust. "You're pathetic."

"So I'm pathetic! I never claimed otherwise! Look, you son-of-a-bitch, you go ahead and do to me whatever you think you have to do, but I ain't giving you any information, and I sure as fuck ain't joining your little-ass Narman pansy party! So, you can go ahead and shoot me if you want!"

All I could do was stare at Gunny in disbelief. "I'm not sure shooting you would be much of a punishment. Popping you in the head just might be doing you a favor."

"It just might!" Malcolm snapped back. "It'd save me from having to listen to all your goddamn preaching!"

●●⬛●⬛●●

Chapter 28

Fanning Flames

It took Korman's people eighteen hours to reach Je'Sikka Albarn and the *Niberian Hornet*. For them to get to us, it took only twenty-two minutes. After locating a nearby clearing in which to land, the pilot dispatched one of the hover transports to collect our dead and wounded. On board was Petty Officer Indira Pariz, the *Hornet's* flight medic, who immediately tended to Black Francis. "Oh boy," I heard her say to Bledyn Marwhol. "This isn't good. This boy's in bad shape."

Pariz did not wait for the rest of the patients to get loaded. She rushed to get Francis to the ship and promised to make a second trip back to pick up the rest. Our uninjured troops loaded the remainder of our captured naypetos with all the Killbilly gear we could find and made our way to the landing zone.

After everyone was aboard the *Hornet*, I walked over to Gunny Malcolm and pulled out the pistol I had tucked behind my belt. I removed the magazine from the handle and tossed it into the bush. I then dropped the weapon at Malcolm's feet. "By the time you find the ammo, we'll be long gone."

"You're seriously letting me go?" asked the shocked gunnery sergeant.

I nodded. "You ain't Samaari, you ain't a Killbilly, and as far as I know, you haven't brutalized inmates at any of the labor camps. You're free to go."

Malcolm shook his head. "Do you know my mission is to hunt you down, Tauk? To capture or kill you? My orders ain't going to change just because you threw me a break."

"Then you go ahead and do what you gotta do, Gunny." I pulled a canister off my web gear and tossed it on the ground next to Malcolm's weapon. "There's a can of ubati stink. It should keep the 'pedes off you."

"I thought I trained you better than this, Tauk. You have the advantage here. If you let people like me go, you're going to get yourself killed. I'm still coming after you! Do you understand that?"

"Yes," I said as I released Malcolm from his magnetic restraints.

The sergeant looked at me suspiciously. "Aren't you even wondering how I found you?"

I shrugged. "Of course I am. You're not going to tell me, though, and I don't have the time to beat it out of you." Reaching behind my back, I slid my hand into the bottom pouch of my ruck and retrieved a clear, vacuum-packed bag full of a fine, tan powder. It was Kan Qui Radix — Demon Root. I tossed the bag at Malcolm, but he made no attempt to catch it. It bounced off his chest and landed on the ground atop the pistol and ubati spray. "Have a nice life."

"Oh, we'll see each other again one day, Tauk! You can bank on it!"

As we lifted off from the LZ, I commandeered one of the bottom cameras and watched Gunny Malcolm for as long as I could. Before the egress doors could even close, he had taken a pinch of powder out of the bag and snorted it up his nose. He then laid back in the mud and watched us go with a big, stoned smile plastered across his face.

"You think he's going to make it back by himself?" asked Sergeant Korman, who was seated beside me.

"He will if he wants to," I assured the squad leader. "Though I'll concede he's just as likely to spend the next week in the throes of a KQR bender then blow his brains all over the jungle when he runs out of dope."

The scaffolds at Narman's Pyke could hang fourteen people at once. It was not nearly enough for General Ivan Kuolaada, who was trying to make a point. He filled those nooses three times, executing forty-two Marines for letting themselves be defeated by insurgent forces led by Leila Hyfer. On the fourth cycle, Kuolaada would only hang one man, the officer in charge of the doomed company.

Lieutenant Harol Raimus had to be carried to the gallows. It was not that he was afraid to die. It was just that the Section 615 inquisitors had crippled the man during their interrogation. To prevent him from uttering any subversive last words, they had also wired his shattered jaw shut.

"If anyone else out there thinks they can get captured, pledge allegiance to the enemy, and sneak back into Narman's Pyke, let this be an example to you!" General Kuolaada screamed at the hundreds of Marines assembled before him. He then waved his arm at Major Izo Kuusip, standing off to his left. "And for those of you who already snuck in, rest assured that we're fucking coming for you! Those treacherous swine you watched swing? THEY TALKED! Section 615 knows who you are, and they're coming for your pathetic asses!"

"Forty-three Marines turned traitor?!?" gasped a Marine standing somewhere in the crowd behind Elia Gyanis.

"No fucking way!" replied another. "They probably know there's a few among them, but they can't figure out who, so they're icing the whole lot of 'em just to be safe!"

A third cursed. "So they're going to start executing us for finding ourselves overmatched, outgunned, and led by some sorry Samaari primadonna that can't hold his own out in the bush?!?"

Tired of hearing his Marines chatter while they were supposed to be at attention, their squad leader growled, "Shut the fuck up! All those pricks confessed!"

"That don't mean shit, Sarge!" said one of his subordinates. "Those Section inquisitors can make anybody confess to anything! Look at that fucking lieutenant up there! What do you think they did to his poor ass to get him to talk?"

"Hey!" Gyanis heard another Marine pipe up. "You guys notice that they didn't hang any Samaari pricks up there?"

"Goddammit!" snapped the sergeant, making an effort to suppress the accent he inherited from a childhood spent on Samaar Ghun. "For the last time, shut the fuck up, or I'll have them hang *your* worthless little asses!"

The assembly was dismissed a few minutes after Lieutenant Raimus stopped twitching at the end of his rope. As Elia Gyanis shuffled toward the parade ground's perimeter, she studied the faces of her fellow Marines. The Samaaris and most of the senior NCOs looked satisfied and vindicated. The junior NCOs, the sergeants, and the corporals looked concerned. Like Gyanis, the rumblings of the rank-and-file had reached their ears, and what they heard concerned them.

The lesson General Kuolaada tried to deliver to his troops was, *Traitors will be dealt with brutally and without mercy. Your only alternative to absolute obedience is death.*

The message they received was, *Accepting Narman mercy will be punished with a prolonged period of torture followed by a public execution. If the enemy gets the upper hand on the field of battle, your only hope for survival is to join the rebels.*

When Elia returned to her room, she found Agent Biragor seated on her bed, dressed in a Marine private's uniform. "Well?"

"It was pretty disturbing," Elia answered. "Are you sure none of those were our people?"

Biragor shrugged. "That company just got here. Raimus was a popular officer whose patriotism was above reproach. His colleagues knew that, his friends knew that, and his immediate superiors knew it. They're all going to feel really vulnerable after what they witnessed today. They now know that Kuusip's going on a witch hunt. Careers will be ruined, good Marines will end up brutalized alongside the bad ones, and lives are going to be lost. This will help Eglan's efforts at recruiting the officer corps to our side."

Gyanis shook her head in disbelief. "I know they're the enemy, but my god. Those Marines were loyal to the League, Agent Biragor. They were framed and killed in cold blood. How do you sleep at night?"

Biragor leaned forward and rested her elbows on her knees. "I never met those people. Considering what you did to Idris Jatmika, I bet I'm sleeping better than you are."

Melki showed up at our base camp just before we arrived. He was standing at the foot of the egress door as it came down, but I had no time to talk to him. All I could say as I ran past was, "Black Francis has been hit! It's bad! We need supplies from the *Serpent*!"

When I returned to the *Hornet* with every medic left on base, Melki was missing but I was too busy to wonder where he had gone. He showed up less than an hour later with a half dozen alien doctors and a levitating stretcher. "Have them put Francis on here, Eamon! We have more coming for the others that are in critical condition!"

"Where are you taking him?"

Frustrated, Melki stepped forward and grabbed me by the collar of my armor. "What's more important to you, Tauk? Saving the life of your friend or finding out where I live?"

"Saving Francis," I gulped.

"Then put him on the stretcher!"

Haeli Deboara's injuries looked gruesome. Both of her eyes had been blackened, and her left cheek was deeply bruised. Her jaw was cracked, as were many of her ribs, especially where they attached to the sternum. She had various lacerations and burns where her armor had been blown away, but the big one was the gash on her side. It was going to take some work to get that one fixed.

With the painkillers and sedatives the medics had pumped into her, Haeli should have been passed out in a bunk. Instead, she somehow got to her feet, disconnected her vital sign monitors, and slipped through the chaos inside the *Hornet* without being challenged. On her way off the ship, she stopped by the cache of captured equipment, grabbed a Killbilly pistol, and walked off the airship, heading to the nearby tent she shared with her husband.

When Haeli entered their shelter, she saw her husband lying on his cot, drunk, red-eyed, and staring semi-catatonically at the ceiling. "Hello, Daino, I'm back."

Startled, Daino shot up from his bed. "Haeli?" he asked. "Is that you?"

Haeli's head was still swimming in narcotics. Stringing together a coherent sentence was difficult, but she fought through the fog to ask, "You didn't come to see if I was okay?"

Daino shrugged. "I'm having a bad day. My legs are killing me. They won't give me anything for the pain anymore, so I have to drink...."

"Oh, save me your bullshit, Daino!" Haeli sobbed. "I got launched into the air by an anti-personnel mine, shot three times, and had my side opened up by a goddamn grenade. I still managed to stumble here to check on you! And here you are, lying in bed, still drunk from the night before!"

Daino covered his eyes so his wife wouldn't see his tears. "I'm sorry I'm a cripple!"

Haeli sighed. "You are a cripple, Daino. I know you're all used up, but your real damage is in your mind. I keep hoping that you'll be able to overcome this stuff, but I'm not sure you can. I'm not even sure if you want to."

"I need help," Daino admitted. "I'm sitting here all day by myself, writhing in agony and staring at these bare walls while I listen to the rain that never fucking stops in this goddamn place! If only you'd stay with me...."

Haeli shook her head. "I tried that. I need a purpose, Daino."

"So do I!" Daino wept. "You were my purpose! And you left me to try to get yourself killed with that fucking Tauk! It's not fair! After everything I did for you and the boys!"

"You're right, Daino," Haeli answered. "It's not fair. You did nothing to deserve this. I can't sit here and wallow in grief with you, though. I have to get justice for our boys and do everything I can to make sure others don't meet their fate."

"And what am I supposed to do?!? Maybe you should just put me out of my misery!"

Haeli knew that that was what her husband would eventually say, and she was determined to show him that she would not be held hostage with the threat of suicide. Producing the weapon she had lifted from the *Hornet*, she threw it on the cot beside the father of her children.

"I could never hurt you, Daino. If you want to be put out of your misery, you'll have to do it yourself. I'm not going to sit here and watch you waste away, not while there are still Blue Shirts out there that need to be dealt with. I'm going to be staying with the Xun from now on. If you decide you want to support the path I've taken, you're going to have to reach out to me. This is the last time I'm coming to you."

Nodding at the weapon she gave her husband, she told him, "And if you can't live with that, well, you now have the option to die with it."

Three weeks after the command hung Lieutenant Raimus, Elia Gyanis was compiling the recruitment data and preparing it to be transmitted to Ovai Soldana. She had to recheck her numbers. Between the video of the Razbauten atrocities and the decision to hang a loyal platoon leader, they now had the names of nearly 170,000 Marines willing to switch sides once the signal was given. They were quickly approaching even odds.

Elia also learned that the Marines were losing their will to fight in the bush. Once they made contact with the Narmans, many units were fragging their officers and surrendering wholesale. In a couple of cases, the officers themselves gave the orders to kill their loyalists, falsely declared victory over the insurgents they encountered, and returned to Narman's Pyke under rebel command.

They were still a long way off from the three-to-one advantage needed to take the *Nebulean Phoenix*, but the gap was closing fast.

For the first time since Elia returned to Narman's Pyke, she felt that the Narmans had a real shot of pulling off their plans.

Chapter 29

WHISPERS OF THE MORGHUL

E ventually, the Morghul took Haeli Deboara away, too. When she returned a week later, I discovered my camp was basically sitting on the roof of a large Morghul settlement located a couple hundred meters below our feet. There was an entrance to the subterranean city nearby, but Haeli advised against looking for it when she returned to base.

"It's full of far more humans than Morghul," Haeli told me as we took shelter from the rain under the *Hornet's* wing. "Had you not practically destroyed the aliens at the Satapadaya Front, they'd have likely already brought you in. The Morghul leader, someone they call the Duvani, is still wary of you."

"The Duvani?" I asked. Despite fighting on the same side, I had minimal contact with the aliens since my defection. I regularly dealt with Melki, but besides him, the only other Morghul I ever interacted with was Kryndil, and I had only done that a handful of times. I knew very little about them. "Is he their king or something?"

Haeli shook her head. "From what I heard, he's actually a healer. And ancient. I've been told that he's nearing the end of his life and that someone else will have to become the Duvani soon. The general consensus is they're preparing Melki for the role."

"Did you see Francis in there?" I asked.

Haeli shook her head. "No, he was in really bad shape. Francis got shipped to the capitol. Xaramika."

•●-◦-◉-◦-●•

It took two months for Francis to recover from his injuries, but when Melki and Leila Hyfer returned him to base, he was good as new. Maybe even better than before he was wounded. He was back to his old self. The man had even shed the guilt he harbored about the massacre he committed in the ruins of Razbauten. "My god!" I exclaimed as I embraced my friend. "Look at you! It's like nothing ever even happened!"

"It was a close call," Melki told me. "He needed the attention of the Duvani himself."

"Are you ready for action?" I asked my second-in-command.

Francis turned to look lustily at Hyfer. "God, am I ever!"

Leila laughed and took Francis's hand. "Stop it. Get your head back in the game."

Realizing that Hyfer and Black Francis were now a couple, I let out a little laugh and shook my head, wondering how my gunny pulled that off. "How was Xaramika?"

Francis's eyes sparkled when I mentioned the place where he had been living for the past several weeks. "It's amazing, Eamon. Think about it for a second. The Morghul came here in a hyper-warp spacecraft a few hundred years ago. Tens of thousands of them. They live underground, even on their home planet, so the minute they landed, this super-advanced, space-age civilization started carving these cities out of the living rock. For centuries. They made homes, apartments, restaurants, government buildings, police stations, factories, offices, natural wonders, waterfalls – everything we would have in one of our cities. The only thing they don't have is sunlight."

"That gets taxing," Leila told me. "We humans need to get out of there every so often but have to do so without giving away our location."

Black Francis reached out and put his hand on my shoulder. "I saw how they get around, Eamon. Subway."

"Subway?"

My gunnery sergeant nodded. "They took all their interstellar travel technology and put it into building an immense underground transportation network. It glides around silently below our feet on magnetic rails, damn near at the speed of sound. The tunnels go all over the continent, completely out of sight. The entrances are so well camouflaged that you could be looking right at one and not even realize it was there. These people are amazing! I met their leader. The Duvani."

"Really?" I asked. "What's he like?"

"He's not a politician. He's an old doctor...."

"A healer," Melki interrupted. "There's a difference. Doctors treat their patients based on scientific deduction. What the Duvani does is...is...well...it's hard to explain. It's more akin to magic than medicine. The Duvani performs miracles."

A thought suddenly popped into my mind. "Haeli's husband is...."

"We have already examined Daino Deboara, Eamon," Melki told me. "Our resources are finite. We cannot waste them on someone who does not want to be helped."

"Are you saying Daino chooses to live like he does?" I asked.

Melki nodded. "The only thing he wants right now is to punish himself and his wife for what happened to their children. That man is a true tragedy, Eamon."

Having seen me try to kiss Haeli Deboara, Francis was uncomfortable discussing her husband. Attempting to change the subject, he asked, "How is everything going here, Eamon? How are our plans progressing?"

"Good, Francis. Good," I answered. "In fact, we're on the cusp of setting everything in motion." Turning to face Melki and Hyfer, I said, "I have to confess that the scope of what we're about to do has grown larger than what my forces can support. My people can take on the bulk of what needs to be done, but I'm afraid I have to come to the Narman army with my hat in hand. I need your help."

A few days later, I gathered all my key players together in the egress bay of the *Niberian Hornet*. My audience was Melki, Bengin Meinhopf, Talia Ghona, Leila

Hyfer, and Ovai Soldana. Supporting me were Je'Sikka Albarn, Dmitri Naktada, Haeli Deboara, and Black Francis. Displayed on the jumbo monitor mounted on the bay's forward bulkhead was a live video feed of Sergeant Korman. He was standing outside in the rain, outfitted and armed with the latest revision of the Marine combat kit we liberated from the platoon Francis ran into at Razbauten.

"Suma Corps has completed their training at Camp Vayipar," I told our visitors. "They are now on station, providing security to twenty-one labor camps. The Samaaris have put about half a brigade of those fanatics in each one. Our mission is to simultaneously liberate them all."

Bengin Meinhopf looked skeptical. "With all the deserters you've taken in lately, you've got what? Ten thousand troops total under your command? The Suma Corps is a hundred thousand strong. You said yourself you need a three-to-one advantage to launch a successful offensive. How do you expect to pull this off with the odds stacked ten-to-one against you?"

Grinning, I surrendered the floor to Dmitri Naktada. Before he reached center stage, he got on the comlink and requested that Korman start firing. With a blaster rifle in one hand and a pistol in the other, the sergeant began shooting rapid-fire plasma bursts into the rainforest.

"In the rush to equip the Marines with this new technology, the Tahnebaht corporation didn't notice the program I wrote to help me test our prototypes faster. I can shut the whole system down with the sound of my voice."

To prove his point, Naktada grabbed a microphone and powered up the speakers on the Mar-Sitaara's exterior. When he called out for Korman's gear to deactivate, both weapons stopped firing, and the sergeant's shoulders slumped under the weight of his gear. To show how defenseless he now was, Corporal Dori walked up to the man and pushed him over onto his side with three fingers.

Hyfer's jaw nearly hit the floor. "The Samaaris can't possibly be that stupid."

"They can," Naktada assured her. "And they are. It's the only reason I'm standing here talking to you today."

"Are you expecting to fly to every camp and personally shut down the enemy's gear?" asked Governor Ghona.

"I offered," Naktada answered, "but Tauk won't let me. He thinks I'm too valuable." Turning back to the microphone, my tech specialist turned Korman's gear back on and asked him to resume firing. Dmitri then reached into his pocket and pulled out a little black electronic device about the size of his thumb. "Each infiltration squad will be equipped with two of these. It's a silent transmitter that beams my voice to every Suma Corps combat kit. Once they press the button, the signal will hit the enemy's gear, where it will be demodulated and received. The equipment will react just like I was there."

"Seriously?" asked Ovai Soldana. "That shit works?"

Naktada pressed the button and again, Korman's weapons stopped firing while his exo-systems shut down. Dori also stepped in and pushed him over once more, though that time, it was just for fun.

Taking the stage again, I said, "We've identified a ventilation shaft for each of the mines that we can use to infiltrate. Two weeks before our operation, we'll send a twenty-person team of former inmates into each camp to make contact with the prisoners and start training them to resist."

"Is two weeks enough?" asked Hyfer.

"I did it in less time at Saimsun," Haeli answered. "We took Razbauten without training them at all."

"On D-Day," I continued, "the team lead will activate Naktada's device at shift change, when virtually every Marine on site is in full gear. While the Suma Corps troops are trying to figure out what's going on, half the squad will lead the organized inmates against the Blue Shirts, seizing their weapons. Another five-person team will grab grenades from the Marines and use them to take out the armory before they can send off any distress flares. Other squads will seize control of the freighters and take the pilots hostage."

"Former inmates are going to be taking over freighters?" asked Meinhopf again. "A few months ago, they were miners. Now they're commandos? This seems a little far-fetched."

"Actually," I said to the intelligence chief, "that's almost exactly how it went down in Razbauten."

"And what if those pilots don't want to cooperate?" asked Hyfer.

"Then we use the pilots we captured at Razbauten," answered Je'Sikka Albarn. "They agreed to help us as long as we set them free after we escape this planet."

I nodded in agreement. "Once the Blue Shirts are neutralized, the Xun will direct the inmates to disarm the Marines and relieve them of their exo-armor systems, loading it onto the freighters they will be escaping aboard. Blue Shirts will be killed. Tahnebaht management will be captured. The Marines will be set free, sending the message that those opting to surrender instead of fighting the Narmans will be treated humanely."

Our guests took a moment to digest the information we had just given them. Eventually, Governor Ghona asked, "What do you need from us?"

"A destination," I told her. "A place where we can house up to seventy thousand people."

Meinhopf loosed a long whistle of disbelief. "You know, when you first told us about this, I didn't think you'd ever actually reach the 'go' stage."

Melki smiled at Bengin. "I never had any doubts. Luckily, we've been preparing for this. How many freighters will all these people be in, Eamon?"

I shrugged, "We might have to commandeer as many as forty."

The Morghul elder grinned even wider. He seemed to like the idea of getting his hands on so many starships. "I just might have the perfect place for you. When do you plan to launch this operation?"

"One month from today."

"Then we will prepare accordingly."

Ovai Soldana was the one keeping track of Narman efforts to bring deserters to their side. He was one of the few people outside the Narman command and myself who knew our true strength. "Based upon my math, when this is all over, the Marines will still have a two-to-one advantage over us."

I nodded. "You're right. The way we see it is that we're only about halfway through our goal of recruiting conscripts. We think many are reluctant to join us simply because they don't think we can succeed. If we pull this off, we'll have proof that we can win. I expect to double our draftee membership when this is all done."

Soldana did a couple more minor calculations. "Okay, that'll put us on par. Still a long way from the three-to-one ratio you're looking for to get us out of here."

I nodded again. "You're right. I believe when we're done liberating camps, we'll have gone about as far as we can go in recruiting our sleepers. To achieve our ratio after that, we have to selectively thin out our adversaries. We're going to have to get dirty and start killing large numbers of loyalist Marines."

Chapter 30

Seeking Salvation

D aino Deboara spent days inside his tent, oftentimes not even bothering to venture out to look for food. The only reason the man did not starve to death was that he was Haeli's husband, even if the two of them were not seeing much of each other those days. Daino often held the pistol Haeli had given him, caressing it as he tried to work up the courage to join his two young boys in oblivion.

He had finally reached the decision to end his life shortly before Black Francis returned to base, but held off until he could see Haeli one last time. Though Daino did not blame his wife for what he had had to do to their sons, he was enraged at how she discarded him once the two of them had escaped Samaari custody. Daino had grown to resent his bride, and once he resolved to kill himself, he wanted to be sure that she watched him do it. She needed to see what she had done to him.

Deboara had not faced Haeli since she returned from Anga-Iskalei and handed him a pistol. She had been in rough shape that day, having received several serious wounds in the battle with Gunny Malcolm's Killbillies. When Daino spotted her just outside the *Hornet* with the Narman entourage, however, he could not see any trace of her injuries: no bruises, no scars, not even a slight limp.

Even more shocking was the sight of Black Francis, who Daino had heard would probably die as he was being swept out of camp by the Morghul medics. A mere eight weeks later, he was back and playfully wrestling with Sergeant Korman after they were done meeting with the Narmans. Daino knew Korman was a formidable opponent in any fight, yet Francis effortlessly kicked the man's legs out from beneath him and took him to the ground with a speed Deboara did not think him capable even before being injured.

My god! Daino thought to himself. *The Morghul can fix damn near anyone.*

Lowering his head to look at his hands, Daino tried to make a fist, only to feel like his knuckles were full of broken glass. After wincing and releasing his grip, he glanced up and caught sight of his wife speaking with the Narmans. As he watched her interact with the contingent from Xaramika, he felt the loathing he harbored for his spouse begin to dissipate, only to be replaced by envy.

Haeli was surrounded by important people. She was talking to the head of Narman intelligence, Bengin Meinhopf, and one of their senior military officers, Leila Hyfer. They were asking her questions, and both of them looked very interested in the answers she gave. Most importantly, Daino noticed they were not talking to her as if she were a subordinate. They were speaking as equals. She had earned their respect, and Daino could see they seemed to know how much she was worth to their cause.

They realize her value. That's something I seem to have forgotten. Oh, man. What the hell have I done?

When Haeli started to walk away after her conversation with the Narmans, she was smiling. That came to an abrupt halt when she spotted her husband. The sight of him stopped her in her tracks and made her gasp. There was a time when they were inseparable and so attuned to each other that they were almost the same person. Now, they could not have been more opposite. Despite her short stature, Haeli stood tall, her straight spine advertising her confidence. She walked with a sense of casual authority. With her hair pulled back and the fatigues she now wore somehow pressed and immaculate, Haeli projected herself as a woman who was tightly put together. She knew her purpose and how to achieve her goals.

Daino was a tall man but did not look it. His knees were twisted and seemed ready to buckle at any moment. His shoulders were slumped and his back was bent, giving his appearance every indication that he was a very broken man. He had been wearing and sleeping in the same set of ragged coveralls for days without bothering to clean them. The man had barely combed, let alone cut, his hair since fleeing Saimsun. He was lost without his family and left alone without a clue about what he was supposed to do with himself. He had become a parasite in the camp, sucking out their meager resources without contributing anything in return.

When Haeli looked his way, Deboara half expected her to glare at him with revulsion at what he had become. Instead, her expression showed pity, disappointment, and shame that she could do nothing for him. Unable to help himself, Daino broke down and wept in the rain.

Haeli took several steps in his direction, but her husband ambled away, waving her off. Turning his back on her, he limped past his tent, strolling toward one of the camp's other Mar-Sitaaras, where he spotted Melki speaking with its pilot.

"Sir," he called out to the alien when he finished his conversation. He was sobbing openly. "Sir! I'm...I'm...I'm...."

"Daino Deboara," Melki interrupted. "I remember you. Are you alright?"

Daino shook his head as he tried to regain his composure. "I can't do this anymore. I...I...I saw what you've done to Black Francis and Haeli. Is there anything that can be done for me? Please. I want to fight alongside my wife. I want to get us out of here. I want to do my part."

Melki smiled and placed his hand on Daino's shoulder. "If there is something that pains me very much, it's that we don't have the resources to help everyone who needs it. There are so many people from Saimsun and Razbauten who are suffering so much and will take so long to heal. We can't help them all. I know you are a heavy weight around your wife's soul. I know that lifting it will make her even better at what she does in the field. If I bring you in and we help you, we need assurances that you will put this gift we are giving you to good use. Can you make that commitment, Daino Deboara?"

"Yes," Daino told Melki, making a promise that fate would never allow him to keep.

●●⭤●⭤●●

A Marine infantry platoon comes with a lot of complicated equipment, gear that is typically far beyond the intellectual capacity of the average rifleman to maintain and repair. It is for that reason that every squad is assigned an armorer to keep the technology running. Without question, Marine techwar specialists are the brains of the operation, and the average armorer's intelligence quotient often exceeds that of the commanders they served.

The typical Marine volunteer was drawn into the Space Corps by patriotism. Armorers were attracted to the service by opportunity. They got a highly technical education and years of field experience, allowing them to command a high salary once they returned to the civilian sector. As a rule, they were not prone to blind fanaticism and detested serving under inept Samaari officers promoted by connections rather than ability. Having often spent their formative years being bullied by stronger peers, they tended to be repelled by the wanton sadism the Samaaris directed at people they considered troublesome.

In other words, armorers were prime targets for Narman recruitment. Being one herself, Elia Gyanis knew what made them tick and how to approach them. These were the people she recruited personally and had a considerable track record of success with. Sergeant Erbert Laumyn was one of her first converts and someone with whom she had shared a long history. After slipping a data stick into his diagnostic box, she took his tablet and pulled up an obscure program buried deep inside the DOS of his troubleshooting software.

"You list the members of your platoon there," she informed her collaborator, showing him the screen as the two sat side by side on her cot. "Beside each operating system serial, you enter a value based upon how susceptible you think they are to being turned. If you know they are already on our side, assign them a '1.' If you think they might be open to switching allegiances but have not confirmed it, they get a '2.' If they're Samaari, they automatically get a '3.' Senior NCOs and officers also get a '3' unless they've been turned and are confirmed to be on our side. The same goes for unabashed loyalists who are too risky to approach."

"Okay," Laumyn said as he took his tablet back. "And what is this supposed to do?"

Elia stood up and retrieved a helmet from her foot locker. Handing it to Laumyn, she said, "Put this on and look outside."

Erbert did as he was told. After dropping the visor, he peered through Elia's window at the parade ground. There were several companies out there practicing drill, and Laumyn watched a few of them marching around with their Marines outlined in an aura of red, yellow, and green. "Holy hell," he gasped.

"The red ones have basically been sentenced to death. If they make contact with the enemy out in the field, the Narmans have been instructed to show them no mercy. They are not to leave the battlefield alive. Yellows will be given the opportunity to join us. If they refuse, they'll be returned to base unharmed but unarmed. The greens are to be left alone as long as they're firing over our heads as promised."

Elia grabbed her tablet and punched in a code that transmitted directly to Lauman's helmet. The message, PYKE STRIKE, flashed across the inside of the armorer's visor, invisible to anyone but him. "What does that mean?"

"Kill everyone glowing crimson. Unfortunately, in this situation, any officers or NCOs in yellow will revert to red when this signal goes out. This will only be transmitted if you are locked in an active battle with Narman forces. If you see it, slaughter the loyalists, frag your officers and NCOs, then put your hands up." Gyanis sent out a different code. ENDGAME.

"And that?"

"It's our final mission. Take over your squad. After that, your platoon. Then your company. Join forces with the other greens and march your way up the chain of command until you've secured your area of operations, be it Narman's Pyke or one of the field bases."

Elia removed the helmet from Laumyn's head, deactivating the aura program. "Keep in mind, you won't be able to see those colors unless we activate the software, and even then, only the greens will have access to those markers. So, if you're out in the bush and those colors suddenly pop up, be forewarned you're about to come under fire. Hit the deck and aim for the treetops. If opposing forces can't get the upper hand without taking excessive casualties or inflicting them on our infiltrators, we'll call 'PYKE STRIKE,' and you'll help us get the reds. Then surrender. Understand?"

Laumyn nodded. "I understand. So, when do you think we'll finally get to ENDGAME?"

Gyanis shrugged. "The only thing I can say for sure is, 'before we're ready for it.' I'm certain it'll come as a big surprise when it eventually arrives, no matter how long it takes."

⚫⚫◂⬤▸ ⬤ ◂⬤▸⚫⚫

Chapter 31

One Minute to Midnight

On the day before our Xun were to leave to infiltrate their assigned camps, I had the troops assemble in front of the *Niberian Hornet* to address them one last time. They were no longer dressed in their training uniforms. They wore the same tattered coveralls they were rescued in. I watched several of them weep as they put those rags back on, and I must admit, witnessing that choked me up, too.

"Everyone of you survived unspeakable horrors suffered at the hands of the Samaaris," I told them with glassy eyes. "And yet here you are, preparing to slip back into the belly of that beast and endure all of those atrocities once more to ensure no one will ever again have to suffer as you have in the mines of Kanaris."

A crowd had already gathered around the Xun before I started speaking, but the longer I talked, the larger it grew. I caught myself taking long pauses to allow more spectators to hear me sing our infiltrators their praises.

"You know, back in the Kyperion League, they like to extoll the bravery of the Marines, building up the courage of the men and women prepared to lay down their lives for the benefit of others. Let me tell you something. I've led plenty of young Marines into combat, and I can assure you that while some are indeed freakishly fearless, most are just ignorant. They have no idea what they have gotten themselves into and are in for quite a surprise once they are exposed to enemy fire for the very first time. If the vast majority of them could go back and un-enlist within the first five minutes of combat, I'm pretty sure our battlefields would be very sparsely populated places."

As I started pacing in the rain, I sighed. "Look. There's no other way to say this. Some of you are not coming back. This should be no surprise, considering we've been telling it to you since the day you volunteered. You don't need us to point this out, however, because you've been in those camps already. You know what awaits you when you reach your objective. There is nobody in the galaxy who realizes more than you how arbitrary death can be in those Samaari hell holes. No one more than you can attest to how random Blue Shirt cruelty can be. Yet, you're going back anyway."

I stepped up onto an ammo crate to get a better look at my troops and shook my head at them in disbelief. "I mean, what the fuck is the matter with you people?!?"

The Xun did me the honor of laughing at my little joke. "Though I know some of you will fall victim to the Blue Shirts, I want you all to fight like hell to prove me wrong. We don't have very many infiltrators and trust me, we need every last one of you if we're going to continue our fight against the League. Also, keep in mind that none of you die alone out there. For every one of you that falls, dozens of imprisoned men, women, and children will be deprived of your protection. That's an unfair burden to place on your shoulders, I know. It's the truth, though. If enough of you get killed in action...."

I paused to wave my arm at the crowd gathered around our formation. "...then we'll eventually join you in oblivion. Our success is dependent upon yours. We're low on resources and even lower on options. There is no Plan B. If you fail, we're goners."

Stepping off my platform, I continued marching up and down the formation. "I don't think you're going to fail, though." Pointing to Dmitri Naktada, who was watching us from the top of the *Hornet's* deployment ramp, I said, "You've got a damn good plan, concocted by the smartest man on this fucking god-forsaken planet! And you wouldn't know it by looking at you, but you've got the technological edge! You're facing an enemy that, despite overwhelming evidence to the contrary, thinks it's elite, intelligent, and unstoppable! Each of those mining facilities is staffed with thousands of Suma Corps Marines charged with thwarting attacks by people who look like me! They're never even going to know you're there until it's too late!"

As I passed Nila Chisek, I grabbed her around the wrist and held her hand up in the air. "Remember your training! Remember what this woman taught you! Do NOT fight fair! I can assure you that your enemy will not! When it comes time to grab a rifle, pair off against someone you know you can take! Use his weapon to blow the brains out of one you can't! Remember the order of operations! First, infiltrate the freighters! Then destroy the armory! Disable the Marines! Disarm the Blue Shirts and put them down immediately to show the inmates you're winning and ensure the leathernecks realize you mean business!"

Pounding my fist into my palm for emphasis, I reminded the Xun to keep the inmates from becoming a mob. I told them to use the captives to strip the Marines of their weapons and armor, then direct them to transport anything of value, food, ammunition, ordinance, and prisoners, into the freighters.

"Remember your purpose in those camps! Make no action that does not advance the successful completion of your mission! You will be tempted to exact revenge upon the monsters that tormented you in Saimsun and Razbauten! I know I certainly would! Do! Not! Give! In! To! It! You do NOT have the luxury of time! Sooner or later, Narman's Pyke will become aware of what is going on and they WILL respond! You best not be there when reinforcements arrive! Get in! Do what you have to do and get the fuck out! DO YOU UNDERSTAND ME?!?"

"YES, SIR!" screamed the Xun.

I stepped back and looked at our infiltrators. They looked weak. They looked starving. They looked brutalized, defeated, and pitiful. Just like they were supposed to. I knew better than to count my chickens before they hatched, but at that moment, the feeling in my stomach was that we were going to pull this off.

As Black Francis emerged from the *Hornet*, casually strolling past Dmitri Naktada, I asked, "You got anything for our troops, Gunny?"

"I sure do," Francis assured me as he placed his thumb and index finger in his mouth and loosed an ear-splitting whistle. At his signal, dozens of Raiders pushed through the crowd with their arms full of canteens. "Drinks are on me!"

As my former Marines passed around the containers of hooch, I walked up beside my number two. "We can't seem to get our hands on enough food or ammunition, yet we never seem to run out of booze. How is that?"

Francis grinned. "We're in a rainforest with ample fruit and prolific amounts of alien microbes. Shit ferments out here in no time. We also got a couple hundred broken people desperate to forget the trauma that was done to them. Of course, they're going to figure out ways to stay inebriated. They've got nothing better to do."

As a rule, the Xun were by themselves. The camps had taken everyone they ever had away from them, so they signed up to fight because they had so little to lose. There were a few exceptions, though, and as the infiltrators broke formation to partake in one of Black Francis's drinks, a handful of loved ones rushed into the ranks to hold their warriors one last time.

Haeli Deboara was one of the few who had somebody at camp, yet no one came to bid her goodbye. She was painfully aware of the problems she and Daino had, but she found it difficult to believe that after all the history they shared, he could not be bothered to see her off. She could not comprehend that she meant so little to him, especially considering that despite their issues, he still meant something to her.

Aware that they could be parting ways forever the following morning, Haeli pushed through the mob to get to Daino's tent. She had no intention of fawning over him, but she wanted the man to know she wished him well. She wanted him to know she was leaving to help others, not harm him.

Whatever feelings Haeli wished to convey that night would forever be left unsaid, though. When she finally returned to her abode, she found it deserted. Daino Deboara was gone, and something in her gut was telling her that they had already enjoyed the final conversation the two of them would ever have.

As the *Niberian Hornet* lifted off the launch pad, I turned to Black Francis and said, "We should be on that craft, Gunny."

My second-in-command glowered at me. "You need to quit being so selfish, Tauk. Stop resisting your role. The troops in that bird are your responsibility, but only part of it. We're all depending on you to get us out of here."

"I feel like a coward staying back and leading from the rear."

"Get over it. Those people are risking a lot more than uncomfortable feelings where they're headed. You owe it to them to see this thing through."

"STOP!" screamed a voice from the perimeter. It came from a man shoving through the crowd of onlookers to get to the landing pad. He startled our guards, who raised their weapons and ordered him to the ground. Dangerously ignoring their instructions, he cried, "PLEASE! CALL THEM BACK! MY WIFE IS ON THAT THING!"

"Holy hell," I gasped to Black Francis. "That's Daino fucking Deboara!"

The last time I had seen Daino, the man could hardly move. Now, he was sprinting into the clearing at a speed far beyond what the guards could keep up with. Frustrated, one of the sentries pointed his rifle at Haeli's husband and screamed, "For the last time! Stop, or I'll shoot!"

"Hold your fire!" I ordered as I ran forward to intercept the trespasser. "Hold your fire!"

When Black Francis and I met Daino in the center of the LZ, the Hornet was already high above us and rendered invisible by its cloaking shield. As it disappeared, Daino collapsed on the ground and buried his face in his hands. "Goddammit!" he bellowed. "I just found out this morning they were leaving! You won't believe what I had to do to get here! I only wanted to see her before she left! I wanted to show her I was ready to help! I'm better now!"

Despite his own experience with Morghul medicine, Francis could hardly believe his eyes. "The last time I saw you, you were crawling out of your tent on all fours to shit in the rain. And now you're doing hundred-meter sprints like a twenty-year-old? Did the Duvani do that to you?"

Throwing his head back to look at Francis, he wept, "Yeah, man! The Duvani put me all back together! He healed my body and put my mind right! I wanted to show Haeli I was back! That I understand what she's doing and want to be at her side helping her! I don't want her going out there thinking I'm still a waste of skin!"

Francis and I reached down and pulled Daino to his feet. "She doesn't think that of you," I let him know.

"Bullshit!" Daino snapped. "I've wasted so much time wallowing in what happened to us that I couldn't do anything about it! I'm such a loser!" Pausing to wipe his eyes and look at me, he said, "I understand what she sees in you."

"Oh, for fuck's sake!" I yelled at him. "For the last time, I'm not having an affair with your wife! You know what? I got a confession to make. On our way to Anga-Iskalei, I acted on a serious lapse in judgment...."

"Oh man...." Black Francis groaned.

"...and I...."

"Don't say it, Eamon."

"...I made a pass at Haeli."

"And you said it anyway, didn't you?"

Daino blinked in disbelief at my admission. "You did? What'd you do? You grab her or something?"

I sighed. "I tried to kiss her."

"And how did she react?"

"She shut that shit down and got as far away from me as possible."

Daino grinned. "She did, huh?"

"She did," Francis told him. "I saw the whole thing. It was so pathetic that I'm standing here dying of second-hand embarrassment just thinking about it."

"Hey, Daino, I'm not proud of it at all. I'm very sor...."

Haeli's husband cranked his arm back and slugged me across the mouth hard enough to knock me to the ground. Immediately, a half dozen Raiders again drew beads on Deboara in my defense. Black Francis had to throw himself into their line of fire to keep them from making Haeli a widow. Waving his hands in the air, Gunny shouted, "Don't shoot! Don't shoot! Everything's alright! Lower your weapons!"

Once we were all out of the sentries' sights, Daino looked down at me and said, "Apology accepted." Then he walked away with a humongous smile plastered across his face.

As Francis helped me up, he said, "I saw that punch coming from light years away. I know you did, too. With all your training, you could have easily ducked or jumped back out of range."

Nodding as I tried to rub the pain out of my jaw, I said, "Yeah, I could've."

"Then why didn't you?" asked my gunnery sergeant.

"Because I kind of had that coming."

Chapter 32
CONTACT

Three weeks after Kotal Xirsi arrived in Anga-Iskalei, his wife disappeared into thin air. The man was exhausted and had been chipping away at a rock wall in a near state of catatonia. He was working on auto-pilot, and in his trance-like state, he did not notice she was missing until their shift ended. His daughter never saw what happened to her either. Not until Xirsi started screaming her name in panic did one of the other prisoners approach him and tell him to keep his voice down. "They took her," the woman told him.

"Took her?!?" gasped Kotal. "Who?!?"

The inmate subtlely pointed her chin at four guards leaning against the shaft wall, laughing amongst themselves as they passed around a flask of spirits. "Those four."

"Where did they take her? What did they want with her?" Kotal's voice was trembling in fear.

The woman glared at him as if he had gone daft. "What do you think they wanted from her?"

As Kotal's apprehension morphed into rage, he turned towards the Blue Shirts. The prisoner stopped him by grabbing his arm. "Don't be a fool. There's nothing you can do for her now. She's gone. They'll take your little girl next if you step out of line."

Kotal turned his gaze onto Gardi, his twelve-year-old daughter. Tears were streaming down her cheeks as she fought to grieve silently lest she attract the Blue Shirts' attention. She knew what the stakes were. He did, too. If Kotal followed his instincts, he knew the bastards would eventually get him under control and keep him alive long enough to watch what they did to his only remaining child.

As a father, Kotal had never felt so impotent. Every week, those four savages plucked a female out of the miners, dragged her back into some dark recess, had their fun with her, and returned without their victim ever being seen again. Not only did they act with impunity, but what they did was encouraged by their superiors. They thought it essential to remind the prisoners how powerless they were. It was one of the methods the Blue Shirts employed to keep their workers compliant.

Four months after losing his wife, Kotal's darkest nightmare came true. A Blue Shirt corporal grabbed the inmate and cursed him for working too slowly. To make him an example to the rest of the prisoners, the gang boss had him tied to the lashing post and flogged a dozen times. When he was returned to work, his shirt shredded and bloodied, Gardi was gone.

The inmate he grabbed to ask where his daughter was just happened to be the same woman who had broken the news about his wife. She would not answer his question this time. She could not even look him in the face.

Kotal Xirsi crouched low to run beneath the crowd of wretched inmates swinging their tools. Knowing where the Blue Shirts took their victims, the despondent father sprinted for the foursome's preferred killing chamber.

Before he reached the darkness, the enraged inmate armed himself with a pair of pickaxes and charged for the quartet of lights he saw in the distance. He knew they were mounted on the guards' headgear, and as he watched them bouncing frantically about before him, Kotal could only imagine what they were doing to his daughter. Then one of them stopped moving and dropped to the ground. Then another fell still. When the last two collapsed, the miner stopped running and approached more cautiously. Before he could determine what was happening, the Blue Shirts' lights went out one by one.

"Gardi!" Kotal hoarsely called out into the blackness, trying to find the fine line between getting his daughter's attention and not alerting more of the guards that he was back there. When no one answered, the man raised his weapons to defend himself, only to have them ripped out of his hands from opposite directions. Someone else took him from behind, slipping one arm around his neck to bring him down while using the other to clasp his mouth shut to keep him from calling out. "Quiet!" an assailant whispered in his ear. "The girl's okay."

"The...the...the Blue Shirts! What happened to the Blue Shirts!"

"They're dead."

"You killed them?!?" Kotal gasped. "Oh, man! Oh, shit! When they find those pricks' bodies, the bastards are going to slaughter us all! Every fucking one of us!"

"Not if they find them buried under a cave-in."

"You know how to do that?!?"

The man released Kotal's neck and said, "Of course we do. It wasn't all that long ago that we were where you are. We're Portunese, like you."

"Portunese?!?" Kotal exclaimed. "How the...? What the...? Who the hell are you?!?"

Haeli Deboara turned on her flashlight and pointed it under her chin to give her face a theatrically eerie look. "We're the Xun. We're going to get you out of this hole."

"You've come to rescue us?"

Haeli shook her head. "There isn't enough of us to do that. You're going to rescue yourselves. We're just here to show you how."

It began as a typical patrol, in orbit high above the surface of Kanaris. Fleet Lieutenant Eigun Bolga was at the yoke of his Haiv fighter with an angry grey planet below him and the *Nebulean Phoenix* above. Behind him were his two escorts; in front, nothing but a dazzling array of distant constellations. Bolga loved flying in the tranquility of space. It was the only place he ever felt truly at peace.

Bolga was in his zone, hovering in a Nirvana-esque state of semi-consciousness, when nearly every alarm in his cockpit went off at once as the profile of another vessel filled his entire field of view. It was not that the craft before him was that big. It was that it was that close.

"BOLGA! BOLGA!" screamed his starboard wingman. "PULL UP! PULL UP! YOU'RE GOING TO...!"

The lieutenant did not need the advice. He had already wrenched the yoke back as far as it would go. Thankfully, whoever was piloting the other craft took an equally aggressive evasive action in the opposite direction. Had they not, the two vehicles would have certainly collided.

As Bolga spun his Hiav fighter out of danger, he caught his port wingman cussing out the intruding spacecraft. "Did you not file a goddamn flight plan, you fucking idiot!" he screamed at the offender. "You can only come out of warp in sector Four-Alpha- Fifty-Seven! We'll have your fucking license for this, you...!"

The pilot's tirade was cut off by an equally excited stream of vindictives launched from the other vessel, only delivered in a language never spoken by human lips. Despite having no idea what was being said, the transmission caused Bolga's heart to skip a beat. "Oh my god," he gasped over the patrol circuit. "It's alien. IT'S ALIENS! MOTHER ONE! MOTHER ONE! THIS IS HAIV FORTY-FOUR! WE GOT ALIENS IN SECTOR! WHAT IS YOUR DIREC-TIVE!"

The watch commander did not even hesitate. The rules of engagement were clear. "Take it out, Haiv-44," she said calmly. "All active patrols redirect to sector seven and assist. General Alarm is activated; prepare for inbound friendlies. All theater resources are directed to intercept and destroy alien bogey."

In the blink of an eye, two dozen Kyperion missiles were locking onto the tres-passing vessel. It responded by diving toward Kanaris's atmosphere and deploying a shiny metal sphere in its wake. When the fleet's rockets entered the device's kill zone, the ball burst apart in a blinding flash of light that sent millions of shrapnel pieces hurtling through the combat zone, shredding missiles and Haiv fighters alike. Bolga lost both of his wingmen to the expanding cloud of metal shards.

Turning his Haiv fighter to lock onto the Morghil spacecraft, Bolga descended upon a steeper trajectory than his target. In the void, neither vessel could claim any maneuverability advantage. Once they entered Kanaris's atmosphere, however, Bolga's smaller Haiv fighter could benefit from less air drag. He had no clue what the Morghul ship had under the hood, but he hoped he could at least keep pace.

Bolga would never find out whether he could have or not. He might have been hot on the aliens' tail, but a slew of missiles launched from the *Phoenix* were gaining on them, too. To defend itself, the alien craft deployed another coun-termeasure that Bolga overshot. This one went off within Kanaris's atmosphere, behind him, and the shockwave not only destroyed the pursuing Haiv, but also propelled what was left of it into one of the intruding vessel's wings, crediting the pilot from Kaoshar as the first human ever to down a Morghul spacecraft.

As the Morghul ship spun in a fiery spiral toward the Kanarisian surface, it launched several escape pods from its hull before it exploded. Most landed in the planet's Hot Zone. Their occupants likely survived the landing, only to succumb to the countless hazards that could befall a solitary being in the two lower thermal zones.

A trio of them landed in the region of Navataena, just far enough away from the subterranean Morghul settlement of Xaramika that no one there ever saw them land.

On the other hand, one of Section 615's Killbilly patrols in the Arad Valley had witnessed it all.

Chapter 33

The Saint

Raqeda Duzid looked at Haeli as if she had lost her mind. "You want us to organize a rebellion in two weeks?!?"

"I do," Haeli answered. They were gathered inside one of the shacks that quartered the inmates sentenced to mine Harnillium at Anga-Iskalei. "I organized the uprising at Saimsun in less than half that time. We liberated Razbauten without preparing anybody at all."

Kotal Xirsi, the man whose daughter the Xun had saved, shook his head as he talked to Duzid. "Two weeks is an eternity in this fucking place, Raqqi. Think about it. How many people die here every day? Every week?"

Haeli craned to look at all the faces crammed into that little hut. Many were very emaciated, with gaunt cheeks and dull eyes sunken deep into their faces. There were a half dozen of them she would bet against making it seven days, let alone double that.

Aza Boani agreed with Xirsi. "I think it's going to be a challenge to keep these people hidden for two weeks. That corporal who flogged Kotal today doesn't buy the story about his buddies dying because the ceiling collapsed on top of them. He thinks something stinks, and he's snooping around all over the place, trying to get to the bottom of it. Sooner or later, he's going to stumble upon the Xun."

"Or your daughter, Kotal," added Moda Boani, Aza's wife.

"Corporal Peniista's a fucking idiot," Xirsi told Haeli.

"True," said Mevari Muqadas. "But he's tenacious. The man's going to be wandering all over the place, sticking his nose in every corner of that mine until he gets distracted by something else. You need to be careful about him."

Haeli nodded in agreement. "We're careful about everybody in Anga-Iskalei. Trust me, we know how deep we are inside enemy territory. We're making sure we don't stay in one place too long."

"So, how is this going to work?" asked Kotal.

"By introductions," Haeli told him. "I have nineteen people who need teams. We need to form two units to blow the armory before they can shoot off a warning rocket. We need four groups of about thirty each to take over the freighters. Four squads of the same size will take out the Blue Shirts. The rest need to direct the prisoners to disarm the Marines and confiscate their weapons and armor. We also need to train you. I'm going to show ten of you how to rip a rifle out of a Samaari sadist's arms and use it to kill him and his buddies. That ten is going to teach ten more. And so on, and so on."

The people around Haeli nodded. "You think this will work?" asked Moda Boani.

Looking her right in the eye, Haeli said, "I know it will. We have the numbers. Sister, we outnumber those Blue Shirts by about forty to one."

"But the Marines...."

"The Marines will be a non-entity."

"How can you be so sure of that?" asked Raqeda Duzid.

"Because we've done this before," Haeli told them with complete confidence. "Look, I won't tell you this isn't dangerous. It is. This mission is going to get some of you killed. Maybe even a lot of you. Let me assure you, though, not attacking the Samaaris will eventually kill you all."

Haeli paused to look each of her inmates in the eye. "Let me give you some advice. Get it through your heads that this thing is happening in fourteen days. Not all of us are going to reap the benefits of the sacrifice we are going to make. Whatever happens, though, whether we live to breathe free or die trying, this hell will be over for us."

Mevari Muqadas grinned and leaned in toward Haeli. "I can't wait to do this. Those Blue Shirts took everything I ever had to live for. I personally don't even care if I escape with you. Right now, the only thing I want is to make those bitches pay for what they did to us."

••–•–●–•–••

The Samaaris kept the prisoner shacks elevated on a short set of stilts. If the floor of the hut made direct contact with the ground, the guards would not be able to see if any inmates were trying to tunnel out from beneath their shelters. That was the space Haeli Deboara slipped into to hide while the guards rousted the prisoners out of bed.

While crouched beneath the inmate quarters, Haeli watched the Blue Shirts chase their victims out into the rain, where they did a head count. A working party of other prisoners entered the dwelling immediately after it was cleared to retrieve the body of a man who had expired during the night. From her vantage point, the Xun leader could see he was not the only Portunese to die in his sleep.

Once everyone was accounted for, the Blue Shirts screamed at their charges to get through the chow line. As the mob of inmates ran past her hiding spot, Haeli rolled out from beneath the hut and joined the crowd. It was raining hard enough that the mud she was covered in swiftly washed away to the point where she only appeared soiled in mine dust, just like the rest of the prisoners.

As soon as Haeli reached the food line, a Suma Corps Marine returning from night patrol grabbed her by the arm, dragging her away from the food. Turning to a Blue Shirt sergeant, he said, "I'm taking this one for a little while."

The sergeant slapped the Marine's wrist to break his grip on the infiltrator. "No, you're not. That one's going to work. You can have her when she's done her time in the hole."

"Fuck that!" the Marine snarled. "I'll be going back on perimeter guard by then!"

"Tough shit. You know the rules. Grab one of the bitches getting off. They'll be up here in a couple of minutes." As soon as he finished talking to the Marine, the Blue Shirt turned around and back-handed Haeli across the mouth. "What the fuck are you lookin' at! Get your ass in that mine!"

Wobbling a bit from the Samaari's blow, Haeli took a few steps toward the chow line, further enraging the Blue Shirt. He threw out his foot and kicked her in the kidneys, sending her flying into the food carts hard enough to knock one over. "I didn't say you could eat, bitch! I told you to get to work!"

Nodding rapidly, Haeli leapt to her feet and jogged toward the mine's entrance. As she approached, the other shift was leaving. A dozen Marines were waiting for them, picking out prisoners to entertain themselves with before their next watch began. Eight or nine women were dragged away before they could get anything to eat. So were a couple of young men. And at least one small boy. After watching that, Haeli was seriously reconsidering her orders to leave the Marines alive when they left.

As Haeli reached the mine, she watched a trio of guards drag a battered man to the surface. "You seriously thought you would get away with laying your little rat hands on a Blue Shirt, you miserable little fuck?!?"

"H-h-he w-w-was killing m-m-me...." the poor man stammered.

"Yeah!" shouted one of the guards. "He was! And now we are!"

"HEY!" the third Blue Shirt screamed at the inmates as they passed. "LOOK OVER THIS WAY! EVERY ONE OF YOU! ALL EYES ON ME!"

Once the Samaari was sure he was the center of attention, he pulled out a seibara borrowed from the Marine security staff and deployed the blade. "THIS IS WHAT YOU GET WHEN YOU STRIKE A BLUE SHIRT!" The guard then swung the weapon and sliced off one of the prisoner's arms. As the miner screamed in agony, his tormentor took off the other. The energy field radiating off the device's rod cauterized the wound as it passed through the inmate's flesh and bone. The man would not be bleeding out. Not even after the savages took each of his legs.

"That's enough gawking!" shouted another guard as one of his comrades unsheathed his dagger to remove the amputee's genitals.

Pulling out his bullwhip, another foreman cracked it across the back of a young girl to Heali's left. "It's starting time! Get in that hole and get to work!"

Haeli trudged down the shaft with the rest of the inmates, working her way into position to slip away unnoticed, which was precisely what she did when she reached the side corridor her comrades were camping in.

Once separated from the crowd, the Xun infiltrator allowed herself to breathe a sigh of relief. She was thankful that Black Francis and I had listened to her before we formed the infiltration squads. Originally, we had planned on sending at least one Raider, a former Marine, into the mines with each unit. Haeli argued that they would never fit in and were incapable of acting normal in such a cruel environment.

She was right. What went on in those mines far exceeded the horrors of combat. The only people hard enough to endure that level of savagery were those who had spent enough time there for it to be normal.

People like Haeli Deboara.

It was Nila Chisek's signature move. That was all the inmates had to learn. Grab the M72 by the barrel with the left hand and the stock with the right. Push the muzzle into your adversary's chest while pulling the butt toward you. Bend your knees to guide your victim over your shoulder. When the guard is in the proper position, push off the ground to lift him off his feet and flip him over your back as you twist the tether release. As the Blue Shirt hits the ground, switch the weapon's safety off, choose your next target, aim, and fire.

Obviously, it was easier said than done, but a motivated student could master it in a few days, and Anga-Iskalei had no shortage of motivated students. And the Xun brought twenty complete M72 rigs with which the inmates could practice.

For the first week the Xun were there, all they did was train inmates in that technique. Twenty candidates at a time were smuggled into the instruction area. The recruits' fellow prisoners would work extra hard to make sure the trainees' Harnillium quotas were met. When one of the prisoners mastered the technique, they would rejoin the miners while another candidate was sent to learn Chisek's method. The Xun worked around the clock, and within seven days, they had seventy insurgents they were confident could take a Samaari's weapon away.

The second week was instructing the different squads on their missions. At shift change, there were usually four freighters on station. The off-going shift would have to be on board before anything could happen. Only when they were in place could those tasked with blowing the armory get on with their jobs, using the grenades that Haeli had given them. That would be the signal to disable the Marines and charge the Blue Shirts.

Three days before the operation was to launch, the Xun were training their teams how to get the armor off an immobilized Marine. As always, the pupils staggered in, breaking away from the main workforce only when it was safe. For ten days, this went off without a hitch. On the eleventh, Corporal Peniista, the nosey Blue Shirt who was unconvinced his colleagues had died in an accident, finally picked the right shaft to go poking around in. Or the wrong one, depending on one's perspective.

Peniista did not get the drop on the Xun. On the contrary, the Xun made him long before he made them, and the insurgents retreated deeper into the shaft as he advanced. If needed, they could have backtracked all the way to the ventilation shaft and gotten themselves to the surface without being detected. The problem was that not all the recruits were with the group yet.

Unaware that Peniista was between him and the Xun, Mevari Muqadas slipped into the shaft and jogged right at the guard. The corporal waited until Mevari was about to run into him before he flipped on his flashlight and asked, "What the fuck do you think you're doing?"

At first, Muqadas froze. Then, he turned and ran. Peniista took off after him, screaming, "Stop! Stop, you son-of-a-bitch! Stop, or I'll shoot!"

Heeding Peniista's orders, Muqadas slid to a halt and put his hands behind his head. "Where the hell am I going to run to, anyway?" the inmate panted to no one in particular.

Peniista was out of breath when he caught up to his prisoner. Grinning wide, he said, "I asked you a question, you little prick! What were you doing back here?"

"Get fucked."

"Oh, you think you're a brave one, eh?" Peniista reached for his radio. "We'll see how brave you are once...."

Spinning around to face the guard, Muqadas grabbed Peniista's M72 by the barrel with the left hand and the stock with the right. He then perfectly executed the Qılıç Elai he had learned from the Xun. In an instant, the Blue Shirt was on his back, and Mevari Muqadas was standing above him with an assault rifle in his hands.

Fortunately, Muqadas did not shoot the cretin. Instead, he used the rifle to bludgeon the man, shattering his jaw and cracking his skull. Then, inexplicably,

Muqadas paused his attack to let Peniista crawl away toward the main shaft.

"What are you doing?!?" Kotal Xirsi snapped when he caught up to his friend.

"Salvaging our mission," Muqadas snapped back. "Get the rest of the recruits up here! Get ready to slip into the mine and sneak back to your sectors! I'll keep the Blue Shirts distracted. Tell the Xun to stay out of sight!"

"You're not gonna...."

Muqadas punched Xirsi in the shoulder to shut him up. "Like I said before, I don't have anything left to live for, but for you people, I'll happily die. Just don't let me do it in vain, Kotal. Make it mean something. Fuck these bastards right in their goddamn asses! Got it?"

The prisoner waited until Peniista was nearly at the main shaft when he charged, loosing a cry of unbridled rage that grabbed everybody's attention as he pounced upon his victim. "You motherfucker!" he screamed as he throttled the Blue Shirt in the face. "You piece of shit! I'm not your goddamn woman!" Muqadas then hit Peniista with a blow that put his lights out.

A couple of guards set upon the prisoner and began to throttle the crazed inmate to get him off their comrade. In response, Muqadas wrapped his arms around the limp Samaari and buried his teeth into the man's throat. When the Blue Shirts finally pried the inmate off Peniista, Mevari took a large chunk of his victim's jugular vein with him.

As Muqadas predicted, virtually every guard in that swath of mine set upon him before dragging him away. Once they were gone, the Xun's recruits fled back to their assigned sectors and got back to work, serenaded by the screams of their comrade bouncing off the rock walls surrounding them.

At the end of their shift, the miners passed what was left of Muqadas's corpse as they exited the shaft. All four of his limbs had been sliced off, as were his genitals. His face was so twisted by the agony he suffered that he was not even remotely recognizable.

"Who was that?" asked one of the inmates not privy to witnessing the event.

Without looking at the man, Kotal Xirsi answered, "A saint."

Chapter 34

The Rising Xun

It was shift change at Anga-Iskalei, and Haeli Deboara stood at the edge of the inmate camp, nervously watching the freighters. The entire base was enveloped in a torrential downpour; the thick clouds made the early morning hours nearly as dark as night, and the air was so saturated with humidity that it was as if the Warp Haugs were shrouded in fog. They were hard to see. A lot harder to see than Haeli, apparently.

"Hey!" called out a passing Blue Shirt. "What the hell are you doing over there? You're supposed to be going into the mine!"

Haeli ignored him and was rewarded with the sight of one of her Xun waving a flashlight from a distant cockpit window. She could not tell which, so she would have to count signals. That was one.

"Hey!" the Blue Shirt shouted again. "I'm talking to you, bitch! Get over here, now!"

Haeli spotted the second signal, much further away than the first.

"If I have to come up there and drag your ass to work, you're going to be sorry!"

The leader of the imminent insurrection stayed put even though nothing happened.

"This is your last fucking warning!"

Finally, Haeli saw the third light. "Come on," she whispered to herself. "Just one more...."

"Goddammit!" the Samaari snarled as he started marching her way. "I'm going to break every bone in your lazy-ass, fucking body you...."

The fourth signal was sent as the guard was almost upon her. Still ignoring the Blue Shirt, Haeli spun around and nodded at the window of a nearby shack. Seconds later, a half dozen inmates led by Jaq Otash exited the dwelling and started making their way to a platform just outside the armory.

"Look, you fucking whore!" growled the Blue Shirt as he reached out and grabbed Haeli by the hair. An instant later, he was on his back with an inmate in control of his weapon. Before he could scream for help, Haeli stomped her foot down upon the Samaari's throat and crushed his larynx. After her victim was rendered silent, Haeli used her other leg to roll the Samaari onto his stomach and stomp him again to snap his neck. Not wanting anything to go to waste, she unbuckled the dead man's web gear and slipped it onto her shoulders, giving her access to his pistol and extra ammunition. She then took aim at an unsuspecting Blue Shirt near the parade of Portunese being herded toward the mine, holding her fire until a bit of hell started breaking loose.

She did not have to wait long. Her grenadiers' timing was nearly perfect. After the vast majority of the night shift miners were out of the main shaft, but before the oncoming crew had reached it, two grenades thrown by Otash's team landed on the platform where the facility's distress flare was staged. When they went off, they blew the tail off the rocket and ignited its propellant, sending it corkscrewing through the Marine berthing hangers. When it exploded, it incinerated dozens of leathernecks as they were turning in to their racks and wiped out the contingent's command staff. It was an amazing stroke of luck.

When Haeli's target turned around to see the commotion, she pumped a bullet through his heart. Before he hit the ground, she identified another target and killed him, too. She took out a third, a fourth, and a fifth before she ran to another position.

From the Blue Shirts' perspective, things escalated very quickly. They did not have time to process what was happening, let alone try to control it. As soon as they turned to see the explosion, they were being dropped by disciplined rifle fire from one direction. From the other, they were being rushed by the prisoners. Some of the inmates had them disarmed and neutralized so efficiently that it almost seemed like magic. Other prisoners who had not been trained by Haeli's Xun came at them with pick axes.

The insurgents could not get to all the Blue Shirts in time. A couple dozen of them managed to get their weapons up and mow down scores of inmates during the first minutes of the operation. They were so insanely outnumbered that most were quickly overwhelmed while trying to reload. Others were shot by the Xun once they were armed and in a position to return fire. Many were killed as they desperately screamed into their radios for the Marines to save them, completely unaware that the leathernecks were trapped in their armor and could not even save themselves.

In mere minutes, nearly two hundred Blue Shirts were massacred by the people they had tormented. A few managed to escape into the bush. A few more ran into the mine to avoid the inmates' rage.

Not everything went exactly to plan. The off-duty Marines, the ones who survived the rocket explosion, were not wearing exo-armor. While their comrades on patrol were frozen in place, scores inside the camp had full mobility. They grabbed their plasma blasters, rushed to where the melee was thickest, and screamed out the loudest battle cry they could muster. For a fleeting moment, the violence paused while the inmates turned their attention to the troops taking aim at them. When the Suma Corps remnants squeezed their triggers, however, nothing happened.

Kotal Xirsi could not help but laugh at the looks on the Marines' faces when they realized the weapons they held were worthless. Most of his comrades did no such thing. They immediately opened fire and cut down the hapless defenders.

The inmates the Xun had trained performed admirably. Those who were not instructed by Haeli's people were something of a mess. They were not an insurgent army. They were a mob that Haeli struggled to get under control. Many swarmed the freighters, clamoring to get aboard, not realizing their mission was not yet done.

"This isn't over yet!" Haeli screamed at the crowd from a megaphone she liberated from the camp commandant's quarters. "If we don't arm ourselves, the Marines will just hunt us down after we leave! You need to get to the perimeter and strip the troops of their weapons and armor! Quickly! I can guarantee you that it is only a matter of time before the League is made aware of what's happened! You also need to leave the Marines alive so that...."

The prisoners' protests drowned out Haeli's pleas, so she cranked up the megaphone's volume as high as it would go. "WE DON'T HAVE TIME TO GIVE THOSE ANIMALS THE TREATMENT THEY DESERVE! THESE FREIGHTERS LEAVE IN LESS THAN AN HOUR! NO ONE GETS ABOARD EMPTY HANDED! WE HAVE TIME FOR TWO TRIPS BACK AND FORTH TO THE PERIMETER! GET OUT THERE AND BRING BACK AS MUCH AS YOU CAN CARRY!"

When the prisoners finally got the point and left to loot the leathernecks, Haeli turned to Lux Parranda, the leader of the teams that seized the freighters. "How many of these Warp Haugs can we fly out of here?"

"Two," Lux answered. "One pilot resisted and got himself killed by one of the inmates. Another just refuses to cooperate. He's a feisty little fuck. How many people have we got to transport?"

"Maybe seven thousand, give or take. You think we can fit them all into two freighters?"

Lux nodded. "It'll be tight, but I think we can...."

"Lux!" screamed one of his team members as he sprinted up to them. Haeli noticed he had blood on his knuckles. "We were interrogating the pilot who won't cooperate!"

Parranda glared at his man. "Who told you to do that?"

The inmate shook his head. "Yell at me later. The bastard said that Haiv fighters fly into the mine's radio range every morning to confirm everything is going okay. If they don't get the right signal, they're supposed to attack!"

"What's the signal?" Lux asked.

The prisoner pointed at the facility's control tower, which was now lying across the path to the mine and burning. "They were the ones that had it!"

Haeli and Lux exchanged panicked glances, then Haeli once again picked up her megaphone. "HURRY UP OUT THERE! THESE FREIGHTERS ARE NOW LEAVING IN FORTY MINUTES!

••◗◖•◗●◖•◗◖••

Chapter 35

SACRIFICE

Like everyone else in Narman's Pyke, Elia Gyanis was cut off by what was happening in the mines by Harnillium interference. She knew that the Narmans would make a move against the labor camps at some point, but she had no idea when. At least, she had no idea until she walked to work the morning it commenced.

Elia was used to seeing Haiv fighters lifting off from the Pyke's landing pads. The start of her shift coincided with the launching of the aircraft's daily missions to check the mines. Gyanis never had any idea what the fighters were doing, only that they did it at the same time every morning. On that day, four craft ascended into the air, then blew apart in a violent explosion the instant they cleared the colony's walls.

At first, Elia had no idea what had destroyed the ships. Then, a blast of plasma fire from a distant mountain breached the wall and took out the airfield's control tower. Several more seemed to come out of nowhere and laid waste to the colony's anti-air defenses. A few seconds later, she heard the distinctive sound of three Mar-Sitaara aircraft passing overhead, followed by more explosions as the hangars were destroyed. She never saw the squadron that attacked. They were obscured by Morghul cloaking technology, so, for all practical purposes, they were virtually invisible.

Unable to help herself, Gyanis stood fast for a moment to marvel at the destruction her comrades had wrought. Then the sirens went off and reminded her that she was in the line of fire. Coming to her senses, Elia sprinted for cover. As she ran, the insurgent Mar-Sitaaras made three more passes. One of the bombs hit close enough to lift the woman clear off her feet and send her sliding through the mud.

When Elia lifted her head, her ears were ringing, and her insides hurt, having been pummeled by the shockwave. Despite her aches, Gyanis was not seriously injured. That was more than she could say for Narman Pyke's air capabilities. They had all been reduced to rubble, as had the rocket pad they depended upon to summon help from the mothership.

As the Pyke's Marines slowly emerged from cover, visions of the horrors Elia had seen in Saimsun flashed through her mind, and she imagined thousands of those poor souls finally getting liberated from the cruelty of the Blue Shirts. All around her, troops began frantically running about, desperately trying to pull their comrades from what was once an airfield, screaming out for medics. Elia stayed still, however, sitting in the mud and admiring the carnage Je'Sikka Albarn had unleashed.

She had to make a special effort to keep herself from smiling. Elia could feel that what happened to Narman's Pyke was the first big step toward the end of their time on Kanaris.

One way or the other.

The first outsiders to detect something amiss in the mines was the crew of the *Cirilian Blowfish,* a Warp Haug freighter approaching the Dag Nazni facility. Dag Nazni was located near two gigantic waterfalls that fed an immense subterranean river. Forever shrouded in a perpetually hazy mist, visibility was never good when the *Blowfish* came to call. On the day of the camp's liberation, it was even worse due to all the smoke added to the equation.

The *Blowfish* was already making its descent when it first noticed the Tahnebaht corporation's administration offices were ablaze.

"Do you see that shit?!?" exclaimed the vessel's co-pilot.

Uveh Unger, the man behind the *Blowfish's* helm, nodded in disbelief. "My god! The prisoners have control of the mine! What the...what the...Where the hell are the Marines?!?"

Unger took control of an exterior camera below the cockpit and zoomed in on the pandemonium below. He spotted dozens of liberated inmates racing toward the grounded freighters on site. They all carried some sort of Space Corps equipment. Some were hauling exo-armor pieces. Others had weapons, ordnance, or ammunition. To the *Blowfish's* pilot, it was clear that Dag Nazni was not under League control.

"What the hell are we going to do?!?" asked Unger's co-pilot.

"Get the hell back to Narman's Pyke!" the captain answered as he wrenched back on the yoke, arresting the *Blowfish's* descent and propelling it skyward once again.

As the Warp Haug reversed course, the inmates below opened fire on it. That was a waste of ammunition. The *Blowfish's* hull was thick. Rounds from a standard M72 could not even scratch it. Once the freighter climbed above the cloud cover, they set course to their main base at the Pyke and headed east.

Despite the Harnillium interference, Unger's co-pilot grabbed the vessel's transmitter and tried to call for help.

"What the hell are you doing?" the pilot asked. "Our radio range is barely four kilometers on this planet."

"Maybe there're Haiv fighters nearby," the co-pilot said. "If we can raise one, maybe they can do something!"

"The odds of you connecting with someone out here are a million to one."

"They're fucking straight zero if we don't even try!" the co-pilot spat back. Speaking into his microphone again, he said, "Is there anybody out there? This is the XO of the *Cirilian Blowfish*! Does anybody copy?"

The co-pilot repeated himself a dozen times without a reply. On his thirteenth try, a woman's voice broke into his circuit. "Go ahead, *Cirilian Blowfish*. I read you."

As the co-pilot shot his boss a look of I-told-you-so, a Mar-Sitaara warship emerged from the clouds off their starboard side. "There's trouble at the Dag Nazni mine!" the man shouted into the transmitter. "The prisoners have taken over! The mine is no longer under League control!"

"I know," Je'Sikka Albarn answered as she blew the freighter out of the sky.

•• ‹•› ◉ ‹•› ••

I had no way of knowing any of this. The same Harnillium interference that pre-vented Narman's Pyke from realizing what was erupting all over the Kanarisian wilderness also kept me entirely in the dark. All I could do was pace around base camp. The troops left at my disposal were the backup team, the Rapid Response Force. If we got word that any of the rebellions ran into trouble, we had a Mar-Sitaara full of former Marines and a freighter the Narmans had sent us from Xaramika. The pilot looked familiar when he stepped out of the Warp Haug with Melki. "Do I know you?" I asked him.

The pilot nodded. "Yeah. We met once. You captured me in Razbauten."

It all came back to me. "That's right," I said suspiciously. "You flew us out of there. Aren't you supposed to be in a cell?"

"Abel Dorn is now married to one of the prisoners you saved from Saimsun," Melki informed me. "He's one of us now."

Dorn nodded. "I want to crush these sick bastards as much as you do. You have no idea what they did to my wife."

"Actually, I do," I assured the pilot. I still did not trust Dorn enough to be flying missions for us, but it was far too late to do anything about it at that point. Turning to Melki, I asked, "Has any information started coming in yet?"

Black Francis laughed. "The shit just started, Eamon. It's going to be a long time before we start hearing things."

Francis was right, and I knew it, but I hated him anyway for saying it out loud. "How the hell are you so calm?" I snapped.

My gunny reached into his pocket and pulled out his flask.

"You're fucking drinking during an operation?!?" I gasped.

Black Francis nodded. "Just a little to take the edge off. You want a nip?"

Letting out a sigh of disgust, I snatched the container out of Francis's hand. "Yeah."

•• ‹•› ◉ ‹•› ••

"We got everyone aboard?" Haeli asked Lux Parranda when she walked into the freighter's cockpit.

Kotal Xirsi was the one who answered. Like her, he was wearing Blue Shirt web gear full of ammo, grenades, and a pistol. "Yes, ma'am. Everyone's aboard, and the equipment's secured."

"How much did we get?"

Xirsi smiled. "Almost all of it."

"And the Marines?" she asked.

"What about them?"

"They were supposed to be left alive," Haeli reminded him.

Kotal nodded. "Most of them were. Bloodied, beaten to within an inch of their lives, and left out in the elements in nothing but their underwear, but alive."

Haeli sighed. "Xirsi...."

"Look," Kotal told her. "They resisted. After everything those monsters did to us, you have to expect our people wouldn't be very inclined to treat them nicely. They were looking for an excuse to fuck those Marines up, and those arrogant pricks were stupid enough to give them one."

Deboara did not have time to debate the merits of Xirsi's argument with him. What was done was done. Turning to the pilot, she handed him a small data stick. "Take us to these coordinates."

With a single nod, the pilot took the device and inserted it into the navigation console. He then shifted a couple of controls to lock all the vessel's hatches for lift-off. His last action was to reach over to his right and yank the pin out of one of the grenades dangling from Kotal Xirsi's web gear. "Fuck you," he snarled at Haeli. "Take yourself to those goddamn coordinates!"

Kotal looked at his chest in horror. There were seven or eight explosive devices attached to his webbing. He had no idea which one of them was about to go off. He then glanced up at Lux and Haeli, who were staring at him in shock and disbelief. "RUUUUUUN!" he screamed.

The Xun did not have to be told twice. Both of them dove for the exit. Sensing they were not going to make it, Kotal threw himself against the control panel to ensure his body was between his grenades and his comrades. When the device went off, it detonated the others and blew parts of Xirsi and the pilot all over the cockpit.

Haeli and Lux survived the explosion but were stunned and deafened by the blast. When Haeli regained her senses, tears began streaming down her face. It was not so much that she was trapped in a disabled Warp Haug that disturbed her so much. What shattered her heart was how little consolation it would be when she broke the news to Kotal's daughter that he died a hero on the precipice of winning both of them their freedom.

Chapter 36

Homecoming

S ancari Gul forced her way into the Warp Haug's cockpit and pulled her two comrades out of the smoke. Though the armor she wore into Anga-Iskalei was stored in the cargo bay, Gul was wearing her helmet to maintain radio contact with the Xun teams on the other ship. Flipping her visor up to be better heard, she cried, "Haeli! Haeli! Are you okay?!?"

"I think so!" Haeli coughed, trying to hear herself over the ringing in her ears.

"Hang tight! Jaq's bringing the other freighter down to get us!"

Haeli reached out and grabbed Gul by the collar. "No! Wave them off! Tell them to get their asses to the objective and send help! Tauk's got a rapid-reaction team ready to deploy if something like this happens! Go! Tell them now!"

While Gul relayed Haeli's instructions to their comrades on the other freighter, Deboara stumbled back into the cockpit to survey the damage. The vessel's controls were totally destroyed. A huge hole had been blown into the panel casing, shredding the electronics behind it and shorting it out with conductive debris and various body parts of Kotal Xirsi. Haeli took a moment to bang on the bay window, hoping it was compromised enough to be smashed out. Unfortunately, it was completely intact, denying her an easy escape route.

Looking to her right, Haeli saw two more Warp Haugs on the tarmac. She knew both were operational. They only needed a pilot who could fly one and a means of getting out of the craft they were trapped in. Then Haeli glanced to her left and realized things were about to get a little more complicated than that.

Haeli Deboara instructed the liberated inmates to leave Anga-Iskalei's Marines alive. Those were orders she had come to regret. The mine's perimeter guards were beginning to filter back into the camp, staggering and limping dazed out of the jungle like a mob of military zombies. They had been disarmed, abused, and humiliated. Many of them were dressed only in their underwear. What caught Haeli's attention was that some of them carried M72 assault rifles, suggesting that there might have been a source of weapons in the facility that the Xun had missed.

The firearms were not an immediate concern to Haeli. There were not many of them, and her people were protected by an exterior hull nearly a meter thick. It was impervious to small arms fire. What worried her much more was the uncertainty of what else she had overlooked.

It did not take long for her to determine the threat that escaped her attention. She was watching a group of underdressed Marines conversing among themselves when she spotted one of them pointing to a platform higher up the mountain. Lying lifeless upon it were a half dozen troops the Xun had taken out with concentrated rifle fire. Behind them, partially obscured by Kanaris's lush vegetation, was an anti-aircraft missile battery more than capable of blowing big holes in their shelter.

Or in any aircraft coming to rescue them.

The plan required the freighters full of liberated inmates to be flown deep into Kanaris's lowest Hot Zone, where they would be set down on the beach near an entrance to the Morgul's subterranean tunnel network. While the former captives were offloaded, technical teams of Narman and alien operators would storm the vessel and wipe out its navigation recorders. That was standard practice to ensure if the Marines ever got their hands on one of the rebel crafts, they could not track its movements to figure out where the access points to the Morghul underground were.

Once the technicians were done, the stolen vessels would be flown to the freighter graveyard, accompanied by the *Solar Wind* piloted by Abwazni Tolchek. Once the Warp Haug was disposed of, the Xun would embark upon Tolchek's Mar-Sitaara and be ferried back to our home base to stand by if needed to help another facility.

The first group to arrive was from the Mamjana camp, led by Kristal Urbi. Well, it was originally led by Urbi, anyway. Their twenty-person team was reduced to three people still fit for combat, and their commander was not one of the survivors. They were now led by a woman named Mina Fetig, who looked familiar but was someone I did not really know. She returned exhausted and demoralized.

Reaching out to shake her hand as soon as she descended the *Wind's* access deck, I swallowed hard when I saw them. "Welcome home. Is this all of you?"

Fetig nodded sadly. "Ours was a smaller mine. When the uprising started, we took out the Blue Shirts easily enough but ran into trouble trying to disarm the Marines. The inmates spread themselves out too thin, and some of the troops managed to get weapons away from our liberated prisoners. We still had the advantage, but we took a lot of casualties. When we finally regained the initiative, we didn't have enough people to spare the enemy troops the way you wanted. We had to kill them to safely get them out of their shells. Even that was too slow, though. We got all the weapons, but only about a quarter of the armor. I'm really sorry, sir."

I hung my head and placed my hand on Fetig's shoulder. "I'm sorry, too. Go get some rest."

When Fetig and her two companions were out of earshot, I turned to Black Francis and sighed. "That shit's on me. I should've had a better plan for the smaller mines."

Black Francis nodded. "You should've. So should I. So should've the dozen other people who helped us plan this. Don't dwell on it, Eamon. Learn from it."

The team from Kuul Gazu was the next to show up. They did a little better. They only lost half their squad and prisoners. They got all their equipment, though. Their problem was timing. One of their prisoners, faced with summary execution for some trivial offense on the day of liberation, disarmed and killed his Blue Shirt early. That set off the operation prematurely, when half the inmates were still underground. Luckily, the leader of Kuul Gazu's Xun still managed to take out the rocket platform before they could fire a distress flare, but it ended up being a suicide mission.

Xun operators from Cuupa Sidi and Foarmag arrived together. Cuupa Sidi's operation fell apart when all the Samaari pilots chose death over collaboration. The only thing that saved them was that one of their inmates had been a pilot before becoming a prisoner. He flew them home. Foarmag's liberation went like clockwork. All the Xun returned, and they lost less than two percent of their miners.

We got word that Wimaluk was a total loss. When Je'Sikka Albarn surveyed the site, she was fired on by the facility's anti-aircraft battery. It took all her skills to keep from being hit, allowing her to return fire and take out the platform. Her report stated that the Xun successfully liberated the prisoners, disarmed the Marines, and herded their charges onto three freighters. They were then shot out of the sky by anti-air missiles controlled by the tower they left intact. No one survived.

The next of the Xun to arrive was Jaq Otash from Anga-Iskalei. Skipping all formalities, he sprinted off the *Wind* with his team, grabbed me by the collar, and exclaimed, "Haeli's stuck on the ground! We have to get back and save her!"

Before I could give the order, Abel Dorn was sprinting to his Haug while my Raiders and every able-bodied Xun we had left ran to embark upon Qoalmun Nartyr's *Inferno*.

••-‹•›-●-‹•›-••

While we waited for the Anga-Iskalei rescue party to return, fifteen other units filtered into our base. Only two more had everything go more or less to plan. The rest were varying degrees of disaster.

The worst of them was Eghi-Poalsun. A large contingent of the mine's Marines were on a long-range patrol and were more than four kilometers from the camp when the Xun deactivated the leathernecks' exo-armor. Gilmar Kaji, the Xun entrusted with one of Naktada's transmitters, was killed in action and unable to put the remainder out of commission when they returned. The result was a dozen of our Xun and a few hundred poorly trained inmates engaging in a futile firefight with twice as many elite, battle-hardened Marines. When they failed to check in, all I could do was send Je'Sikka Albarn to give them as much air support as she could to buy them time.

After the last Xun unit checked in, I walked up to Black Francis, who was tallying the results reported by the incoming units. "How many of our Xun made it back?"

"One hundred and twelve."

My knees nearly buckled. We had sent four hundred and eighty. "How many prisoners did we save?"

Francis sighed. "Forty-eight thousand."

That time, I had to grab my gunny's shoulder to steady myself. "We were supposed to save seventy-five thousand. We lost almost thirty thousand people?!?"

Black Francis glared at me. "No. We saved nearly fifty thousand. We also destroyed the League's Harnillium mining operation. Completely. Right now, the Tahnebaht Corporation has ZERO extraction capability. Eamon, as painful as this is, your operation was a resounding success. You fucking did it."

As Francis tried to make his point, the *Niberian Hornet* cleared the canopy and descended into camp. Once it landed, Je'Sikka Albarn walked off with a glum look on her face. She had just returned from Eghi-Poalsun. "Well?" I asked.

Je'Sikka shook her head. "They were overrun. Everybody's gone. I took it out, though. I bombed the shit out of it. Marines and all."

Turning to Black Francis, I held out my hand. "You mind passing that flask of yours to me?"

Hours passed with no more news. The longer I waited, the faster I seemed to drink Black Francis's liquor. I passed out just before sundown, only to wake up and vomit a few hours later. While retching in the rain, I caught sight of Daino Deboara lurking about the landing pads' perimeter, anxiously awaiting word of his wife's fate. Having nothing to give him, I avoided making eye contact with the man and staggered back aboard the *Hornet*, making a mental note that he now looked in better shape than I was.

Je'Sikka Albarn offered to make a trip to Anga-Iskalei to see what was going on. I commanded her to stay put. One Mar-Sitaara might have been lost. I was not going to risk another. Abwazni Tolchek was not around to receive my orders, though. After waiting hours for Abel Dorn to arrive, and with no other inbound Warp Haugs expected, he decided to take the *Solar Wind* to the doomed facility. He landed at our base camp just before dawn.

"The *Inferno's* gone," Tolchek reported as he disembarked. "The wreckage is strewn clear across the camp."

It was news that took our breath away. Black Francis and I looked at each other in disbelief. Our Raiders were on the *Inferno*. My troops. The vast majority of the only people I even knew anymore. In one fell swoop, I lost pretty much everybody I had to command.

"And Dorn's freighter?" I croaked.

"On its side, blocking the mine's entrance, engulfed in flames. There were no signs of life except a few Marines. Now, there aren't even those."

Daino Deboara, seeing the dour expression on our faces, wormed his way through the small crowd gathered around us. "She...she...she's gone, isn't she?"

I cared for all the Xun, but Haeli was the only one I had a personal connection with. The news of her death hurt. I did not think I could answer Daino without my voice cracking, so I just nodded and handed him the flask I still had from Francis. He grabbed it from my hand as he tried to hold in the sobs. "I'm joining the Xun, Tauk," he told me as he stumbled backward a few steps. "Teach me what you can. I'm going to kill every Samaari motherfucker I ever lay eyes on from this point forward."

Fifty thousand forced labor inmates were safely underground, being cared for by our Narman and Morghul allies. The Harnillium mines, drained of prisoners and imploded by Mar-Sitaara bombing runs, had ceased to exist. Half of the elite Suma Corps had been wiped out. Though it was quickly replenished by new craft from the *Nebulean Phoenix*, for a little while, we had even destroyed the League's entire air wing. Our accomplishments exceeded all expectations.

Yet, so did our losses. The Xun was down to a quarter of its strength. My people fared even worse. Our rapid-reaction force was what remained of our Raiders. When the *Inferno* went down, almost all of the people we defected with were lost with it. All we had left were our command staff. Black Francis. Our intel sergeant, Hariana Espiya. Dmitri Naktada. Nila Chisek. Terivenda Sotalain, our senior medic. And Akkam Lumuk.

Akkam Lumuk, I thought to myself, watching the giant weep hysterically in the rain while he sat by himself in the mud. *Like me, that guy has been here from the beginning. How the hell did he survive this long? I guess all the effort I put into keeping him out of harm's way must have helped.*

Still drunk, I staggered over to the behemoth and offered him a sip from the bottle I held.

Pulling himself together a little, he said, "No, thank you, sir. I don't drink."

"Now would be a pretty good time to start," I told him.

Lumuk didn't answer. He just shook his head and buried his face in his hands again.

We could feel our losses. So many of us were missing that we did not even have the manpower to post watches. That was how Melki got in unchallenged. I was walking into the jungle to take a leak when I practically tripped over him.

After I got my heart rate back to normal, I spotted Abel Dorn behind him. And Lux Parranda. And....

"EAMON!" Haeli shrieked when she saw me. Bounding out of the rainforest, she leapt into my arms, wrapping her arms around my neck and pressing her lips against mine. When she finally pulled back, tears were streaming down her face. "Oh my god! I didn't think I would ever see you again! Or Black Francis! Or Nila! Or...!"

Stunned by disbelief, at first, all I could do was blink. "What the...how did...Oh my god! Haeli!" Finally convinced she was not some booze-borne hallucination of mine, I hugged her back. "What the hell happened out there?"

Suddenly cognizant of the people gathering around us, Haeli let me go to wipe her eyes. "The fucking pilot locked us all in the Warp Haug and sealed us inside. He then pulled the pin from a grenade one of the prisoners had on his chest and blew the cockpit. We left the Marines alive like you wanted us to, but the bastards were able to manually operate the anti-aircraft missile battery and started blowing holes in our ship! They got the Mar-Sitaara you sent to rescue us!"

"The sons-of-bitches got me, too," Dorn said. "They hit me in one of the aft thrusters. I thought I was a goner, so I steered toward that platform, figuring I'd take them out as I went down. I got the bastards. And, unbelievably, survived the crash."

Haeli reached over and hugged the pilot. "He saved our lives."

"After she saved mine," Dorn countered. "The Marines weren't too happy about me taking out that missile platform, so when I finally came to a stop, they were coming after my ass. Haeli was able to organize some of the surviving prisoners into a rescue party and attacked them from behind. Wiped the fuckers out."

"I wouldn't have been able to manage that had you not had their undivided attention," Haeli told him. "Those Suma Corps pricks killed a lot of prisoners, but we were able to get out of all those holes they punched in our hull. We then crawled into one of the remaining Warp Haugs and escaped!"

"Oh my god!" I gasped, grabbing Haeli's hand. "I got something to show you!"

Dragging Haeli through the crowd, we ran to the tent she shared with her husband. We were almost there when a flash went off inside, followed by a loud bang. In that brief instant of bright light, we caught the silhouette of Daino, sitting on his cot, holding a gun to his head.

"NOOOOOO!" Haeli shrieked as she pulled out of my grip and rushed inside the shelter. She screamed again when she saw what her husband had done to himself. Instantly realizing that Daino was far beyond help, she backed out of the tent and collapsed weeping into the mud. I was too stunned to comfort her. All I could do was stand there wondering why Daino Deboara would kill himself now, after the Morghul had put him back together and left him so excited to begin patching things up with his wife.

A video loop from one of the *Hornet's* surveillance cameras cleared up the mystery. I caught Daino Deboara on video as Haeli emerged from the tree line and called my name. Hearing his wife's voice, he spun around and ran to her, only to stop when he saw Haeli jump into my arms. I had to pause the tape at that point and zoom in on his face. His expression was heart-breaking, twisting into a blend of shock, grief, and resignation. As dozens of others rushed in to greet their comrades, Daino turned to push his way back to his shelter against the flow of traffic.

That man never realized that his wife kissed me out of exuberance, not passion. And by blowing his brains all over the wall of his tent, he ensured that he never would.

Chapter 37

AFTERMATH

Haeli Deboara was understandably despondent. We were in my stateroom aboard the *Niberian Hornet*, sitting beside each other on my bunk. Haeli bawled hysterically into the palms of her hands while I stared at the deck, trying to think of something comforting to say.

"That son-of-a-bitch!" Haeli cried. "That son-of-a-bitch! He waited for me to get back so that he could do it in front of me! He was hurting so horribly, and I knew it! I gave him that gun so he could have a quick way out when his pain became too much to bear! It wasn't because I wanted him dead, Eamon! It was because I couldn't stand watching him suffer so much! I figured he would do it when I was gone! Not reward me for saving thousands of inmates by splattering his brains all over our tent! Goddamn him, Eamon! God-DAMN him!"

My jaw dropped open. *Oh my god. She doesn't know he was better. She has no idea the Morghul cured him!*

I hung my head in shame at the part I played in Daino's suicide. I then turned my gaze toward Haeli and saw the fury in her eyes. Whatever love she ever had for Daino Deboara had morphed into pure hatred. Her husband did not deserve her rage, but neither did Haeli deserve to blame herself for Daino's death, which is what she would do if she ever learned that her kissing me was the trigger that led to it.

What do I do? I asked myself. *Do I tell her and break her heart, or do I let her believe her husband despised her enough to kill himself in her presence?*

As painful as it would be, I decided to tell her the truth. I turned to face her and said, "Haeli, Daino was...."

Haeli cut me off by pressing her hand over my mouth. "Don't!" she snapped. "I don't ever want to hear that son-of-a-bitch's name again! Ever!"

I grabbed her wrist and gently pulled her hand away. "But...."

This time, Haeli covered my mouth with her own, slipping her tongue between my teeth as she wrapped her free arm around my neck to pull me closer. She then wrested herself out of my grip, took my hand, and placed it on her breast.

"But...."

Shifting position to straddle my lap, Haeli leaned back and unbuttoned my shirt. "But nothing. Fuck him. The man who killed himself was not the man I married. He became something completely different. And you know what? So did I. I'm not the mousy little housewife I was on Portuna. I'm not the shell of a woman I was at Saimsun who let the Samaaris debase me in any way they wanted to so that I could keep my family alive. I'm a warrior now, Eamon. I've got a whole new purpose in life, a destiny that I fully intend to see through. I'm going to fight them tooth and nail until they are crystal clear on who the master race in this galaxy most certainly is not!"

I still wanted to tell her the truth, but she lifted her own shirt off and started sucking on my neck, moving her tongue southward along my chest.

You need to tell her, Eamon!

I know, I will. In a minute.

No, Eamon! Now! Before things go too far!

Haeli unbuttoned my fatigue trousers and slid them down my thighs.

I think things have already gone too far.

Don't be a dirtbag! Tell her, goddammit!

I wanted to. I really did. But I didn't. It was not even the promise of sex that had me keep the truth to myself. It was that we all still had a very dangerous road ahead of us. If Haeli was going to survive it, she needed the fury that burned inside her. She needed to be that warrior she now thought herself as. Not the woman who drove her crippled husband to kill himself.

I left Haeli asleep in my rack and walked to the briefing room to clear my head. A few days before, this was the heartbeat of our camp, typically filled with dozens of people. Now, it only held Melki, Je'Sikka Albarn, Black Francis, and Dmitri Naktada, who had just arrived from disabling the navigation recorders on the stolen freighters.

"How is she?" asked Black Francis.

"About how you'd expect," I answered, feeling like scum. Daino's body had probably not even reached room temperature, but I had already slept with his wife.

The men in the room did not notice anything in my tone, but I was certain Je'Sikka picked something up. She gave me a look as if to say, "Please don't tell me you already went and got your freak on with that poor guy's widow." I caught myself unable to look her in the eye as I walked over to the water station and poured myself a drink.

"Are you okay, Eamon?" Melki asked. "You took some heavy losses today."

"I did," I answered as I took a seat closer to the alien. "It's going to take some time to get back up to strength."

"That's not going to happen here," Melki told me. "You don't have the forces you need to keep this base secure anymore."

I nodded. Melki was right. "I guess I need to bring some of those miners we rescued back this way for training."

"Or you can come to us," Melki suggested.

"To Xaramika?"

The alien nodded. "You dealt the enemy a heavy blow yesterday, Eamon. A very heavy blow."

Naktada agreed. "The Suma Corps has been rendered combat ineffective. They're out of the equation. Do you know what our odds are now?"

I shook my head.

"Combined Narman and Morghul forces are about seventy-five hundred. We got seventy-seven thousand convicts behind the walls. Forty thousand political conscripts. Fifty thousand regular conscripts, whose numbers will probably skyrocket after news of our raids makes it out. And now, we have about forty-eight thousand inmate miners in our ranks and enough weaponry to outfit fifty thousand. Eamon, we have around two hundred and twenty thousand troops at our disposal. Statistically, we're damn near even with the League."

Melki smiled at me. "The Duvani wants to meet you, Eamon. All of you. He wants to bring you into the Narman fold and help us initiate the next phase of the operation. It's time to start reducing the number of loyalists among the Marines."

Narman's Pyke was still smoking when what was left of the Suma Corps marched across the tarmac to the parade grounds. A few of them were still in full combat gear. About half were wearing fatigues. The rest were in their underwear. They did not even have boots, so were forced to trudge through the wrecked airfield barefoot.

Once they were assembled in formation on the parade ground, General Kroaht looked at them in disgust. "So, this is what passes as elite these days?" the commander of the Marine Expeditionary Force sneered. "I hope you people are proud of yourselves. You got defeated by a wretched little mob of unarmed Portunese malcontents! They were starving! Emaciated! Broken! Yet you...you...you let them fuck you right up your tight little asses!"

The rest of the base's Marines began gathering around the humiliated Suma Corps as Kroaht continued addressing them. "How could you let yourselves be...?"

"We didn't let anyone do anything to us, General!" interrupted a lieutenant with a death wish. "We weren't defeated by the Portunese! We weren't even defeated by the Narmans! We were defeated by the goddamn Tahnebaht Conglomerate! Those fuckers equipped us in gear with a major security flaw that the enemy was able to exploit! They shut us down without firing a shot! Trapped us in our exo-armor! The Samaaris served us up to those bastards like sheep to the slaughter!"

General Viqaar was the Suma Corps commander. Incensed by the open defiance of a junior officer, he stormed to the edge of the stage and screamed, "You hold your fucking tongue, lieutenant, before I come down there and cut it out of your mouth!"

The lieutenant reached over and pulled a dagger from the belt of the gunnery sergeant standing next to him. "You want my tongue, Viqaar?!? Come down here and fucking get it!"

"Praetorians!" Viqaar shrieked at the dozen guards standing behind him. "Seize that Marine!"

Like the rest of Suma Corps, Viqaar's praetorians arrived on Kanaris with the latest exo-armor and plasma blaster technology. As they marched down the steps to carry out the general's orders, their equipment shut down, causing their joints to lock up and sending them all tumbling over each other until they came to rest in a pile on the muddy field. Elia Gyanis, who was watching the spectacle from the crowd, nearly laughed out loud as she let her deactivator fall from her hand onto the waterlogged turf. She then used her right foot to grind it into the mud, burying it forever.

A murmur of discontent began to rise from the crowd as they were confronted with irrefutable evidence that the lieutenant was speaking the truth. This caused General Viqaar to panic. Unlike his praetorians, Viqaar was not dressed in armor, but he did have a plasma pistol on his hip. He drew it, pointed it at his subordinate, and squeezed the trigger. Nothing happened.

The rumble of conversation from the rank and file turned to laughter as the Marines watched Viqaar's face turn red. That stopped when Section 615's Major Kuusip drew his M88 and killed the insubordinate officer for the general.

As Kuusip walked back to his position, Agent Biragor shook her head in disgust. "What the hell do you think you're doing?"

The major glared at her in return. "What does it look like? I made an example out of that son-of-a-bitch!"

"You didn't make that man an example, you simple little shit," Commandant Taillur growled. "You made him a martyr."

●●⬩⬤⬩●●

Chapter 38

Trek to Xaramika

There was a Morghul settlement and a tunnel close to our base. Most of the Xun were blindfolded and marched there. Once underground, the cover was removed from the humans' eyes, exposing them to the subterranean metropolis the aliens had spent centuries carving out of the rock. As our people marveled at their surroundings, the Narmans hurried them toward the shuttle by assuring them that Xaramika was even more impressive.

The rest of us were flown there by Je'Sikka Albarn. When the *Niberian Hornet* landed on a pad quite some distance from the entrance to Xaramika, we stepped off the egress ramp unarmed and without armor. The two dozen Morghul who greeted us on naypeto mounts were combat-ready. We were entirely at their mercy, and I was not at all comfortable with that. Mainly because they did not seem very comfortable with us, either.

The leader of our alien escort stepped forward and said something in their native language, a tongue I could not even begin to decipher. I shook my head at the officer and said, "I'm sorry. I don't understand."

"He's greeting you," Melki said, translating for us. "He's welcoming you to Xaramika, though very formally, indicating that he does not really mean it."

The officer frowned at Melki as if he did not appreciate the sentiment. That was odd as it implied the alien understood our language, though he made no effort to speak it. "Do they know what we're saying?"

Melki nodded. "You'll be able to understand them, too, after your surgery."

"Surgery?" I exclaimed. "Nobody said anything to us about any surgery!"

"Don't worry about it," Black Francis said. "You're going to be amazed by what it can do for you."

"It's a simple procedure," Melki assured me. "We're going to implant a cochlear translator into your ear canal. Once that's done, you'll be able to understand us, as well as virtually every other being known to the Morghul Empire."

"Every other being?" Naktada asked.

Melki grinned. "Yes, Dmitri. The Heyanaus is full of many different alien races. It's a shame you have yet only to meet ours. Well, besides Quarakai, there is one other species here, but you won't be able to realize it's not Morghul."

"Really?" Je'Sikka Albarn gasped. "How many other peoples are...?"

"Many," Melki said, cutting her off. "Look, we don't have time to go into this right now. Major Uvo needs to fix special goggles to you all, and we need to get going. It's twenty kilometers to the entrance to Xaramika."

"That's an awfully long walk to do blindfolded," I told Melki.

"They have naypetos for us to ride," Melki assured me. "Except for Akkam. I don't think our beasts can handle someone of his size. I'm afraid he will have to walk."

Lumuk did not like that idea. He looked at the aliens in sheer terror and energetically shook his head from side to side. "No! No!" he pleaded. "Don't leave me alone with them, sir! I don't know them! I can't understand them!"

"Settle down, Akkam," I told my giant. "I'll walk with you so you won't be alone. Will that be better?"

Lumuk nodded and nervously bit his lip. As I was putting him at ease, Melki grabbed two sets of goggles and slipped them onto Akkam and me. They were odd devices, obscuring our vision so we could not see more than three meters in any direction. It allowed us to walk but blinded us enough to prevent picking out landmarks to tell where we were going. "Is this really necessary?" I asked.

"Absolutely," Melki assured me. "You ever wonder why we Morghul are so hard to find? It's because we force those who know where Xaramika is to stay in Xaramika. Those allowed to leave have proven they are willing to forfeit their lives to protect the secret of its location."

"Really? How could you possibly prove something like that?"

Melki grinned at me. "That's something even more secret than Xaramika's location."

The hike to Xaramika was miserable. Without our exo-armor, Akkam and I had little protection from the elements. We were also at an even higher elevation than we were used to, so we were chilled by the combination of unrelenting rain and high winds.

Unable to communicate with our Morghul escorts, I had a long conversation with Akkam Lumuk instead. Despite having known him for years, I had never spoken with him much. The giant told me all about how much he missed his mother and how he longed to get back to her. He described his home world of Gorsu Qat in loving detail as only someone with crippling homesickness could. He also spoke about a childhood spent being tormented because of his size and gentle nature and his fear of never getting home again. Lumuk also let me know about one other thing that was weighing heavily on his mind.

"You're not going to leave me alone here, are you, sir?" the giant asked through chattering teeth.

"We may have to sometimes, Akkam. When we go on missions. It'll be okay, though. You'll be safe here."

"Safe?" Lumuk asked. "I've only ever felt safe with you, sir."

I laughed. "Seriously? You felt safe when the soroquids were preying on us in the Hot Zone? How about during the mutiny when our own Marines tried to kill us? When the Quarakai butchered what was left of us in Narman's Pyke?"

I could have gone on about how Akkam nearly had his brains blown out at Camp Vayipar, the assault on the Satapadaya, or the horrors we witnessed at Saimsun, but the lummox interrupted me. "I knew you and the people in our platoon would try to help me if I got into trouble. Everywhere else I'd been, I was always on my own."

"Akkam, you're...."

"Don't leave me here, sir!" Lumuk was begging me, his voice cracking. "I don't know anybody in this place! They're going to hate me like everyone always does!"

I stopped walking and grabbed the giant by the elbow. "You've spent weeks back at base caring for the inmates we freed from those camps, Akkam. You're a good man, not to mention a goddamn big one! Those people you helped are going to remember you. For once, you're going to be surrounded by people who love you. You're going to be alright."

"It doesn't feel that way, sir! It feels like we's in an awful lot of trouble right now!"

"We are," I confessed as one of the Morghul issued a set of terse orders to us. I had no idea what he said, but I assumed he was telling us to keep moving. As we started walking again, I said, "We're facing some long odds right now, Akkam."

"You got a plan, though, right?"

"I don't know if it's a good one, but yeah, I got a plan. At least the start to one." I paused to let out a long sigh. "Actually, I got a few ideas. I'm still working shit out. Right now, I'm concentrating on getting to that 3-to-1 ratio. Once we hit that, I'll better understand what to do next."

"Then we's gonna be all right," Lumuk said, letting a little smile stretch across his face.

"I wish I had half the confidence in myself as you have in me," I chuckled.

"Well, you ain't let me down yet, sir."

Maybe I hadn't, but Lumuk's comment made me remember everyone I had. Harlund Merik and the squad I left *Wasp-Three* with. Gunny Brumit. Barone Parsons. Sergeant Kal-Xati and so many more that never made it past the Satapadaya. Had I been a better leader, maybe they would all still be alive. I also thought of Captain Pustov and Gunny Malcolm. I doubted either harbored a very favorable opinion of me at the moment.

Oddly enough, as the two of us trudged through the rain toward Xaramika, I discovered that it did not matter what men like Pustov and Malcolm thought of me anymore.

It was only the opinion of people like Akkam Lumuk that I cared about.

●●-◆-●-◆-●●

Chapter 39

Hear No Evil

When I woke from surgery, the universe seemed to hold a little more clarity. I never thought I had problems with my hearing, but I noticed now I could detect the footsteps of bugs crawling across the cavern walls. The Morghul were also speaking to me in a language I could understand. That was difficult to get used to because now the sounds coming out of their mouths did not match how their lips were moving.

After letting us get used to our new hearing for a couple of hours, Melki arrived at the recovery room and gave us each a set of goggles, though he was no longer wearing his. "We evolved in caves, Eamon. We're adapted to underground living. We like it dark, far darker than is comfortable for you." To my surprise, the goggles made everything bright as day and could be set to each wearer's preferences.

Once my command staff and I were adequately equipped, the alien led us to a large meeting chamber quite some distance from the surgical facility. In the center of the room stood a long table. At the far end of it, seated upon a throne so high he could look down upon the rest of the council, sat an ancient Morghul so ravaged by age that he could barely move. Yet, once his eyes caught sight of Akkam Lumuk, his face lit up in a beaming smile that showed off the bare gums hidden behind his wrinkled lips. He looked as if he had been waiting to meet my giant his entire life.

The old Morghul's name was Saaxirad, and he was the Chief Elder, the Duvani. Despite how it looked, Saaxirad did not rule the others. He merely ran the meeting, dispensed advice when asked, and cast the tie-breaking vote if needed.

To hear Melki tell it, Saaxirad spent most of his time on the council fighting to stay awake. I was told the old alien's real passion was healing the sick.

On either side of the table sat five Morghul council members. At the very end of it, closest to where we were standing, was one human, Talia Ghona, and one of the immense glider Quarakai, a brute they called Kiimbana. All wore long grey robes, similar to those worn by the Morghul I had first encountered upon Mount Toranad when I was shot. As he was the most familiar to us, Melki introduced the council, beginning with those seated to Saaxirad's right.

"Dhola is the Elder responsible for Morghul affairs," Melki told us. Pointing to the empty seat beside her where he would usually sit, he then said, "As the Elder in charge of human affairs, I work very closely with her."

Walking toward us, Melki touched the shoulder of an alien with a brownish tint to his skin. "This is Tarsus. He is the elder in charge of technology. Beside him is Korbat, who is responsible for resources. Finally, at the end, is Talia Ghona, our human liaison. You already know her quite well."

Melki crossed over to the other side of the table and placed his hand atop the head of the Quarakai. At the time, that seemed very condescending, but I later learned that was how the native tree-dwelling Kanarisians showed respect toward one another. "You've probably met Kiimbana before, too, Eamon. He was among the Quarakai that attacked you when you first arrived at Narman's Pyke."

Kiimbana snorted. "I no think we meet. All Marines I see at Pyke no live." The Quarakai looked awkward in his robe. They did not typically wear clothes and found them ridiculous.

"I'm happy to have lived long enough to meet you again under better circumstances," I told the bruin.

"Next to Kiimbana," Melki continued, "is Heva, Elder of ecology. To her right is Qero, who is responsible for education. Then there is 'Voraq. She is our elder for justice. Finally, we have Lipsis, our elder responsible for intelligence."

"Thank you," I told Melki and the rest of the council of elders. "We're happy to be here and to finally join you...."

"Who you?" Kiimbana asked. The Quarakai were not much on formalities or small talk. Their language was primitive, as was their capacity to process long sentences. The more words we used to convey our point, the less they understood.

"I'm Eamon Tauk," I told the Quarakai. "I was a platoon leader for the Marines. Beside me is Black Francis...."

"He no look black!"

Francis grinned. "No, I don't."

"Then why you called Black?"

"It's not important, Kiimbana," Melki said, trying to keep the conversation on track. "What matters is that he is Eamon's second chief."

I nodded in agreement. Pointing to Je'Sikka, I said, "Warrant Officer Albarn is the pilot of our assault craft. Beside her is Dmitri Naktada, our techwar specialist...."

"You what?" asked Kiimbana.

"Our smart guy," I answered.

Assured that the Quarakai understood that, I went on to introduce my intel sergeant, praetorian, and senior medic. I then waved my hand towards my giant, who looked as out of place among us as Kiimbana. "Finally, this is Akkam Lumuk. A great warrior."

As dark as Lumuk's skin was, I could almost see him blush. "Naw, I ain't no warrior. I get scared kind of easy."

Saaxirad, the chief elder, smiled at Akkam's honesty. "You do?" he giggled. "That's okay. So do I, sometimes. Can you come closer to me? I can not see so well anymore. I want to get a better look at you."

Lumuk glanced at me as if to ask if that was a good idea. I nodded at him to go ahead. As Akkam approached the throne, Saaxirad's praetorians emerged from the shadows at the back of the room.

"It's okay, guards," the Chief Elder assured them. "He's a big man, but I sense he has a gentle soul. Isn't that right, Akkam?"

Lumuk nodded. "I don't want to hurt nobody, sir."

"Of course you don't," Saaxirad laughed. When Lumuk was close enough, the Morghul elder slowly reached out and wrapped his long fingers around the giant's forearm. "Oh, my. I sense such great sadness in you, Akkam Lumuk. So many have hurt you, haven't they?"

Lumuk grimaced as if he was reliving some of his most painful moments. "Yes, sir."

"But why?" Saaxirad asked. "You've never done anyone any harm. You've always sought to avoid violence, haven't you? You will scarcely raise a finger to help yourself, yet you will lunge into the face of danger to save someone else. Or even something else, as Azmet must have seemed to you."

Akkam looked confused. "Azmet?"

"My son," Melki told him. "When that Marine struck my child across the head with his rifle, you intervened. That little man almost killed you for it."

"Yeah, Duum," Lumuk said, remembering the day we defected. "I dunno why I did that. I killed Duum that day. And some other people." Akkam almost sounded ashamed.

"It's okay, Akkam," the Duvani told him. "It's who you are. It was a horrible thing you did, but you had no choice. Had you not, many good, decent beings would have died that day. And some very evil people would have survived to kill even more."

Lumuk hung his head. "I suppose, sir."

"What do you mean by 'suppose?' Can't you see what you have done?"

Akkam shrugged. "I have a hard time explaining a lot of things, sir. I'm not that smart."

Saaxirad sighed. "You're plenty smart, Akkam. You just see the universe in a way very different than what most beings do. You long for it to be how it should be instead of how it is. Oh, to see the cosmos through eyes like yours! Can you help me do that, Akkam? My time in this old, broken body is growing very short. Could you help me see things as you do before it's too late?"

There was an audible gasp among the Morghul gathered around the table. Dhola, the Elder for Morghul Affairs, cried, "But Saaxirad! You just met him! You can't possibly know enough about him to...."

"I know him plenty, Dhola!" the Chief Elder snapped. "It is not as if I have never done this before! For the times we are in, facing the dangers we are facing, this man could be the key to our survival!" The old Morghul slowly turned his head away from Dhola to face me. "At the very least, he can put our minds at ease about whether those standing before us can be trusted or not."

My people traded befuddled expressions with one another. We had no idea what was going on. It felt like Saaxirad had spent a long time putting together a highly complex puzzle, and the piece he needed to complete it had just fallen into his hands. Knowing Lumuk's limitations, this concerned me.

Moving closer to the table, I asked, "What do you want with Akkam, uh...uh...I'm sorry, I don't know the proper honorific to address you by."

The elder laughed. "We don't have honorifics, Eamon. You can call me Saaxirad. Simply Saaxirad. As for what I want with Akkam, that is between him and me."

I took another step forward, causing the guards to emerge once again from the shadows, poised to intercept me if I lunged for any of the Morghul. "Oh, please relax!" Saaxirad told his praetorians. "He's only concerned about the safety of his soldier!" Turning his attention back to me, he said, "I can assure you that I only want to help poor Akkam, Eamon Tauk. I will not hurt him, nor would I ever force him to do anything he does not want to do. My intentions are pure."

"Then why won't you tell me what you want with him?"

"I believe you call it 'operational security.' We have missions planned also, Eamon Tauk. It is important that as few people know our plans as possible."

"In other words, you still don't trust us."

The Duvani smiled again. "Oh, I do now, Eamon Tauk. I trust you completely. I made you trustworthy."

"Made me trustworthy?" I scoffed. "How the hell did you do that?"

As Saaxirad's face saddened, he motioned for one of the guards to activate the monitor on the wall behind me. As I turned around, I saw a video of a hysterical Samaari prisoner seated with his hands chained to the table in front of him. "PLEASE KRYNDIL!" the inmate shrieked. "PLEASE DON'T! I'M BEGGING YOU! DOOOOOON...!"

Suddenly, both sides of the Samaari's head exploded, launching his eyes from their sockets and spilling his brains out the two gaping holes where his ears had once been. The prisoner then slumped over and slid out of his chair until the chains were pulled taut against his wrists.

"Only we can remove those implants in your ears without them going off, Eamon Tauk," Saaxirad told me. Oddly, his voice contained no menace, only sympathy. "We can also set them off remotely; well, as remotely as we can set anything off on this planet. So, don't remove those implants. Don't get captured.

Don't betray us. Please know that we did not do this out of malice. We did it out of desperation and fear. Eamon Tauk, we want to trust you. We want you to succeed. We want you to accomplish everything you are trying to do. We just cannot afford to blindly put our fate in anyone else's hands right now without an insurance policy. No one would be more disappointed than me if we were forced to activate the charges in those translator implants."

After looking at the horrified faces of the people I had led into Xaramika, I turned back to Saaxirad. "Well," I said. "Off the top of my head, I can think of several people who would probably be more disappointed than you if you felt you had to pull the trigger on the shit you just put in our ears."

Saaxirad smiled. "Not true. Your troops are loyal, Eamon Tauk. They follow your lead. They would not be disappointed to see you killed. They'd likely die with you. The dead can not be disappointed." Turning back to Lumuk, the Duvani reached out and placed his hand atop Lumuk's bare head. "I can feel your fear. Your implants do not explode, Akkam. No matter what happens, you are safe."

"You know," I said to the Morghul Elder, "trust is supposed to work both ways."

"Indeed it does," Saaxirad agreed.

"Then, if you don't intend to harm Akkam, give him the choice right now to leave you. Let him go."

Saaxirad pulled his hand off Lumuk. "Fair enough. Akkam, I want you to know I can fix you."

"Fix me?" My giant looked confused. "I did not know I was broken."

The old Morghul nodded solemnly. "I can tell you were not born this way, my son. You were robbed of your potential. It happened long ago, probably when you were too young to remember. I can return it to you, Akkam. I can turn you back into the person you were born to be. Would you like that?"

Akkam shrugged. "You mean you can make it so I'm not stupid anymore? Or scared all the time?"

"I think I can. You're always making memories, Akkam. They enter your mind through your eyes, your ears, your nose, your skin. When you were hurt, it blocked the path that allows them to come back out again. You can free them sometimes, but it's very hard for you, isn't it? I can make it so that it becomes much, much easier."

Terivenda Sotalain, my senior medic, stepped forward. "You can tell all that by just touching his head?"

The Duvani cast his gaze upon her. "Yes, I can sense his brain waves. I've been doing this a very long time, Sergeant. A *very* long time."

"If you do that for him, what do you think he's going to do for you?" I asked once more.

"I will fix him no matter what," Saaxirad told me. "But I would very much like him to let me see through his eyes if he will let me."

"What does that even mean?!?" I snapped, growing frustrated with the Duvani's riddles.

"It's okay, sir," Akkam said to me, finally speaking for himself. "I trust him. I don't know how, but I can feel that he doesn't mean to cause me any harm. I'll be alright."

Saaxirad smiled wide. "Good! I'm glad, Akkam. You have nothing to fear from me." Turning his head to face me again, the Duvani then said, "With that settled, how about we get you some chairs so we can discuss how to kill more Space Corps Marines?"

Chapter 40

A Shift in Paradigm

A real bed. I had not slept in one in years, not since I was in the hospital recovering from the lashing I received from Gunny Malcolm when I came back to Kanaris. It was about the same for Haeli, who was lying beside me.

"God," she cooed as she threw her bare leg over my stomach. "I never thought I'd ever be so comfortable again."

"Or dry," I added. Morghul rooms had dehumidifiers, a luxury that I never realized I needed so much. Not having pruned fingertips felt blissfully strange.

"What did you think of the food?" Haeli asked.

"Strange, but delicious." After I had briefed the council on the software we used to distinguish friend from foe among enemy units, we were treated to a traditional Morghul meal. It consisted of a giant fungus they had brought to Kanaris from their home world that had the texture, flavor, and nutrients of rare beef. It was served with a spicy sauce whose base ingredient was a substance squirted from the abdomen of an alien insect when it needed to defend itself.

Rolling over onto her back, Haeli looked at the ceiling and sighed in contentment. "How long do you think we could live in a place like this?"

"Live?" I asked. "I think you could survive here a very long time. Living is a different story. Like the Quarakai, humans weren't meant to live underground. I don't think we could thrive here. It's too dark, too confined, and as good as that meal was, we need some sort of surface fruits or vegetables to keep us from dying of scurvy."

Haeli considered that momentarily before asking, "Eamon, if we get out of this mess, what's next? What will we do?"

I sighed. "You know, I was going to leave the Corps for the last woman I was with. We were going to get the hell out of here, find some NEE planet to settle down on, and make a bunch of babies. I still kind of like that idea."

Haeli frowned and scooted further away from me. "I tried to do that on Portuna. It didn't work out. You know what? Since we were deported, I've been beaten, raped, shot, and nearly blown up a few times. None of that even came close to the pain I felt losing my children, Eamon. I'm never getting married and having kids ever again."

"Then what are you going to do?" I asked her.

"Fight."

"You know, I've been trained to fight my entire life. Since I was a baby. I've been in combat for four years. I'm tired of it, Haeli. I've had enough."

"My war's just begun, Eamon. I'm not going to rest until I'm sure that the people responsible for what was done to us get what's coming to them."

"You know, right before I killed Gori Dravidas...."

Haeli lifted her head off the pillow. "You killed Gori Dravidas?!?"

I winced in surprise. "How did you not know that?"

"Because you never mentioned it to me until now. He was with the Marines who wiped out Kusan Plaat. That was my uncle's village. I was there when it happened. I was a child then but escaped with a couple of my cousins. I watched that monster line up a bunch of teenagers, one in front of the other, against the wall of their school building. He then shot them in front of their screaming parents to see how many he could kill with a single bullet. I recognized him after the news broke about all the stuff he did on Deraghun."

"Trust me, I'm not excusing what he did," I told Haeli. "But he eventually had a change of heart. He was the one who exposed the atrocities on Deraghun, so he was the one they blamed for it. Anyway, his last words were, 'There's more to life than killing.' I think he was right."

Haeli shrugged. "Maybe he was. It's hard to live much life when you constantly have to run away from being killed. Look, Eamon, in this little corner of the galaxy, there's predators and there's prey. I've spent my whole life as prey. Now that I'm a predator, I'm not going back."

The two of us eventually drifted off to sleep but were awakened a few hours later by the intercom system alarm. Between my lack of rest and unfamiliarity with the runes that made up the Morghul alphabet, I could not figure out how to answer the incoming call. I could only press buttons until the alarm stopped and a hologram appeared in the middle of the room showing Black Francis and Melki staring at me. Both of them had dour looks on their faces. I knew I was not about to get good news.

"Can't we even get one night of peace?" I snapped at the two of them. "What is it now?"

"It's Deena Vulk," Francis told me. "The bitch escaped Kryndil's Lair."

It took months to arrange, but eventually, the planets aligned, and all of Tymar Hailo's bribed guards were on duty at the same time. He secured three sets of fatigues and armor, weapons, and rations and positioned them in a rarely used passageway to the surface. Ty then unlocked his lover's cell and led her to the stashed gear to dress herself up. Once Anirae Labaat was safe, Ty went to spring Deena Vulk.

"Who the fuck are you?" Deena asked, squinting at the first light to pour into her cell in months.

"Someone who's going to get you out of here."

"Out of Kryndil's Lair?" Vulk scoffed. "Are you daft?"

"I've bribed the guards to...."

"Bribed the guards?" the prisoner asked suspiciously. "With what?"

"Demon Root."

"And why should...?"

"Look, lady, this offer has an expiration date measured in seconds. You want to come with me or would you rather stay here?"

Vulk looked about her surroundings and shrugged. "I guess I'll go. I've certainly got nothing to gain by hanging out in this place."

For someone locked in the dark for months, Deena Vulk was surprisingly agile. She marched with a limp and had trouble keeping up, but it was more a matter of her working the kinks out than any lingering disability. It was not long before she was moving faster than Anirae.

It took a couple of hours for them to navigate the back passageways and find a ladder leading outside. Ani looked at it with apprehension. "Ty, I don't think I can make it up there."

"Look, bitch," Deena mocked Labaat as she pushed past to start her ascent. "This is do or die time. You keeping up or giving up?"

Tymar sighed. "She's right, Ani. There's no other way. Either you get up that ladder, or we're finished."

It was thirteen stories to reach sunlight. Ani made it, but just barely. Once she found herself in open air, she collapsed in the mud and let the rain pour unobstructed onto her face as she gasped for oxygen.

"Where are the guards?" Vulk asked once Ty emerged from the hole in the ground.

"Paid to be patrolling somewhere else."

"With Demon Root? You paid Narman officers with dope? I find that hard to believe."

"We don't have money," Tymar reminded her. "Drugs are currency. They can be traded for something the officers do want."

Vulk shook her head. "Sounds like bullshit to me. But, hey, whatever. This is your show. Lead the way."

"I need a minute," Ani begged. "I need some rest."

"We don't have a minute," Ty told her. "I bought the two patrols working this shift. The units working the next weren't bribable. We have to go."

It was an arduous march. There were times when Ty had no choice but to carry Ani on his back to keep her going, much to Deena Vulk's dismay. By nightfall, however, they were safely beyond the range of the base's patrols and reached a point where Tymar had arranged to have a trio of naypetos left for them. The fugitives had a comfortable head start on any search party dispatched from Kryndil's Lair, and now that they had mounts to ride, they would only increase the distance between themselves and any posse coming their way.

But first, rest. As they set up camp, Ty laid Ani back against a tree and told her to close her eyes. "We don't have long," he said to his lover. "We have to get going again in a little while, but sleep while you can."

Once Ani was settled in, Ty turned to Vulk and said, "See? I told you we could do it. All things considered, I'd say that was pretty easy."

Vulk nodded at him. "It was easy, alright. Too easy. That's not raising any alarms for you?"

Tymar shook his head. "I paid a pretty high price to get us out of that place."

"I don't care what you spent, moron," Vulk told him. "The bastards working with Kryndil are fanatics. They're motivated by nothing more than their hatred toward the League and the Samaaris that run it. They don't give a fuck about money."

"What are you trying to say?" asked Tymar.

"We didn't escape Kryndil's Lair, you simple sack of shit! They practically threw us out!"

To call General Kroaht's living quarters aboard the *Nebulean Phoenix* a "stateroom" would be a gross understatement. It was an orbiting mansion equipped with dozens of robotic servants whose only reason to exist was to attend to the commander's every need. It was a vulgar display of power and privilege so obscene that Commandant Taillur loathed to visit it. He preferred it when Kroaht came to his quarters for their little trysts.

Taillur was not summoned to the general's room for intimacy this time. Kroaht called for him because he was on the verge of a nervous breakdown, and Taillur was the only person he could trust enough to vent to.

"I'm fucking finished!" the commander of the expeditionary force cried after he had dismissed the droids. "Harnillium production's dropped to zero! Tauk wiped out our Suma Corps! Icing that lieutenant in public has driven our conscripts into the enemy's arms in droves! Even Kuusip had to admit that, and he's the stupid prick that shot that whiney bitch! We aren't producing product, the

Narmans have driven us out of the jungle, and we can't trust our own troops enough to take it back! The only thing we nominally control anymore is the Arad Valley, and even there, we're taking more losses than we can sustain!"

Taillur knew the general wanted him to say everything would be okay, but the Section 615 commandant had never been a yes-man. "Have you sent these developments up to Kyper yet?"

Kroaht's hands were shaking. "Of course I have!"

"And?"

"They're dispatching the Mathusula Corps to replace Suma," Kroaht said. "They're also sending the *Admiral Phranqen* to our theater."

"Ouch." The dreadnought *Admiral Phranqen* and the 355th Marine Expeditionary Force attached to it was commanded by General Tyberius Sqaar, an old rival of Kroaht's. It was the League's way of adding insult to injury. Both men knew that Sqaar was not coming to reinforce Kroaht. He was coming to replace him. The general was right. He was "fucking finished."

"What am I going to do?" Kroaht asked, pleading with his lover to show him a way out.

"You need a win, Druze. A big win. You need to break the Narmans, figure out where the Morghul capitol is, and take it before the *Phranqen* gets here."

"What the hell do you think I've been trying to do for the past few years?!?" Kroaht shrieked.

"You've been trying to do it the League way," Taillur told him. "With Samaari officers using Samaari tactics. Do you know why there's a Marine Academy, General? It's because we needed to train a cadre of pragmatic officers who know how to fight and improvise using strategy and intelligence instead of ideology. Dump your Samaari officers, Druze. Turn your senior NCOs into junior officers and get to fucking work."

Kroaht shook his head. "I can't dump my Samaari officers, Nilton."

"Why the hell not?"

The general collapsed into his seat. "Because they're the only people I know who are definitely on my side."

Taillur reached over and grabbed the liquor decanter off a nearby table. He removed the top and took a long pull straight from the bottle. "If you're not willing to start sacking your Samaaris, your odds of survival would probably be better if you gave up and joined the Narmans."

Kroaht chuckled humorlessly. "If I didn't know that the bastards would have Kryndil skin me alive the moment they got their grubby little fingers on me, I might consider it."

•• ◦ ⬤ ◦ ••

Chapter 41

TURQS

One thing the Narmans had that we did not were ubatis. They still had a horde of the little beasts at their disposal, and the moment word went out that Deena Vulk went missing, the Morghul unleashed a swarm of them into the rainforest surrounding Kryndil's Lair.

Governor Ghona put Francis and me in charge of a freshly created platoon of former Marines and freshly trained Portunese from Saimsun and Razbauten. After our ride to the scene of the crime via the Morghul tunnel shuttle, we learned Kryndil's troops had tracked the fugitives to their first campsite, where they discovered Vulk and her consorts had left on naypetos.

"We're not going to catch up to them now," Kryndil admitted. "We need to get in front of them by air and intercept the shits." Catching me staring at him, the Morghul skinner asked, "You have something to say to me, Tauk?"

I shrugged and looked into Kryndil's blazing red eyes. "Your base is every bit the underground fortress that Xaramika is. How does Vulk simply walk out of here? Through all the security we went through to get into this place? Through all the Narman soldiers you have patrolling the forests above us? It sounds like an inside job to me."

"It was an inside job!" Kryndil snarled back. "She was released by one of our jailors! Trust me, Tauk, that miserable little bastard will get what's coming to him when I get my hands on him! Unlike Deena Vulk, Tymar Hailo and his girlfriend will be able to feel it when I rip the skin off their bodies!"

Melki was beside himself over Vulk's escape, even more upset about it than I was. "We can figure out how they fled later! Right now, we have to get to these people before the Marines do! We need Vulk and her co-conspirators back under our custody right now!"

"We'll get them, Melki," Kryndil said. "Relax."

"I won't relax!" Melki spat. "And neither will you until we catch those people! They know where your base is, you idiot! If she makes it back to Narman's Pyke, she'll lead the Marines right to your front door! And if the Marines take your lair, they can follow the tunnels right to Xaramika! We'll be finished!"

"I can assure you, Melki, the Marines will never take my Lair intact. I'll butcher every one of them that dares try!"

Our plan was to set up camp where we thought our odds best to cross paths with Deena Vulk. The *Hornet* would do regular runs to chart the course of the ubatis, following their trail to ensure we could intercept them. If the war hogs deviated from the predicted path we mapped out for our quarry, Albarn would buzz us so we could pull up stakes and shift location.

The spot we picked to camp on was a geographic wonder. If Vulk continued to flee east, she would run into a place where an ancient earthquake split a massive mountain in two. The western half had collapsed and dropped several hundred feet, leaving in its wake an impassible rock wall.

To go north to get around it would have meant an arduous climb uphill, even for the naypetos they were riding. Traveling south entailed a much easier journey toward lower elevations until they met a fissure in the cliffs that would allow them to pass and continue towards Marine lines. It was the perfect place to mount an ambush. We found this out the hard way by running into one while approaching it from the east.

Requiring stealth, we marched to our objective in full combat dress and without any animals. We were all but invisible to human eyes but stood no chance at all of getting within two kilometers of an enemy ubati without being detected. Half a click away from our destination, we were set upon by nearly a dozen enraged enemy war hogs.

The snout of an ubati could lead the beasts to within a few meters of us, but to finish off the attack, the creatures had to see what they needed to bury their teeth into. Our camo-tech saved us from the animals, but our blasters but gave our position away to the Killbillies. They opened up on us with an insane amount of firepower.

"SPREAD OUT!" I screamed over the commlink as I rushed for cover. All around me, tree trunks were being shredded as I bolted through clouds of wood splinters, looking for a place to hide. After narrowly avoiding being ripped to pieces by an automatic rail gun, I joined three other troops trying to find cover behind a rock barely big enough to shield two. Using my ultrasonic echolocation, I swept the field of fire and was relieved to see no one lying motionless in the killing zone. Still, our assailants continued to blast us with a rain of steel projectiles.

"They can't see us," I assured my troops. "That means they can't decipher any targets. Can anybody see anything?"

"I can!" answered Teki Tavono, one of my new squad leaders. "I got a pair of shooters on the north ridge...."

A pair of blaster shots burst out from somewhere behind my left flank. "Make that past tense," said Tavono's sniper, Zarbi Xud.

"Kasmi!" I called out to my nearest armorer. "I need a bird up there!"

"The drone's already in the air!" Sergeant Mora shouted back. Yelling at one of our grenadiers, he snapped, "Qalon! I got four targets painted atop the ridge redirecting mortars! I need you to hit 'em with an airburst! Tracing signal six-seventeen!"

"Roger that!" Lance Corporal Otasi replied as he assigned the drone's frequency to the warhead he was preparing to fire. Five seconds later, he launched a rocket from his position that stained the cliff summit red with a Killbilly mortar team before they fired a single shot.

"Keep that bird's eyes open, Kasmi!" Black Francis ordered as he charged uphill with five other troops. "What are we running into?"

"We got seven bogeys up there! They're coming right at you and getting ready to clear the..."

The first Killbilly to reach the ridge raised his Gatling rig and followed the smoke trail still wafting through the air from the rocket Qalon Otasi had just fired.

When he figured out where it originated, the Qilkorian squeezed the trigger and sent a couple hundred rounds to the position in the blink of an eye. Fortunately, our grenadier was long gone.

Even though Black Francis was no more than four meters from them, the Killbillies never knew he was there. Three of them died without ever figuring it out. The rest of them, realizing the futility of fighting an adversary they could not identify, dropped their weapons, fell to their knees, and threw their hands in the air to surrender.

"I'm sorry! I'm sorry!" one of them cried. "Don't kill me! You can have them back! We didn't hurt 'em! Well, not too bad anyway! One of 'em was already kind of hurt when we found 'em!"

With the battle over, I ran up alongside Black Francis. "They got Vulk? Already? Those prisoners couldn't possibly have gotten here by now."

Francis shook his head. "Not on a naypeto, they couldn't have. They'd have to be on a hovercraft."

I lifted my visor to show my face and deactivate my camouflage. The Killbilly winced in surprise. "You're human?!? I thought you were the fuckin' aliens!"

"Who do you have?" I asked the Killbilly.

"W-w-we got a couple of Mogs, man! We caught 'em out by Navataena! They fell from the goddamn sky!"

I grabbed the Killbilly by the hair and wrenched him to his feet. "Take me to them."

The Qilkorian led us about three hundred meters into the bush to where they had a pair of aliens tied to the base of a tree. They were not Morghul as the Killbilly suspected. These were creatures who more resembled Quarakai than our hosts back in Xaramika. The top of their heads were skull-like, with prominent brow ridges surrounding bright orange eyes that blinked from the bottom up. Below their eyes were a series of wrinkled bags followed by a primitive primate snout dominated by a pair of large nostrils. Their ears were about the size of ours but attached nearly perpendicular to their heads. Though they vaguely resembled earthly apes, they were covered by brown, reptilian skin and crowned with a mane of dreadlocked hair growing from a straight line down the center of their heads, leaving the sides bare.

Their clothing was also much different from what we had grown accustomed to on the Morghul. For starters, they did not wear goggles and seemed quite comfortable in the Kanarisian light. The beings were also adorned in jewelry. A lot of it. They had long, ornate earrings dangling from their lobes and layers of beaded necklaces around their collars. They were dressed in tunics and trousers instead of robes, with armored shoulder guards bearing runes similar to those in the room I was assigned back in the capital.

Turning to Black Francis, I sighed and pointed at the writing on their clothing. "Those are Morghul letters, Gunny, and that clothing looks awfully military to me. This is probably a recon party from the Empire. We might have just run out of time."

●●◄❖►◉◄❖►●●

The Narman war hogs lost Deena Vulk's scent well before our ambush. Odds were our fugitives caught wind of our fight with the Killbillies and decided to get to Narman's Pyke the hard way. Our ubatis followed their quarry to a wide, shallow stream, then lost them. We rejoined several other Narman platoons to branch out and cover a wider area, but to no avail. Eventually, we had to come to terms with the fact that Vulk had given us the slip. We returned to the *Niberian Hornet* with four Qilkorian prisoners and what appeared to be two liberated alien soldiers.

Thanks to our implants, we could understand the two aliens perfectly. Unfortunately, their translator devices lacked the software needed to understand us. When we turned them over to Melki in Xaramika, we had to let him do all the talking.

The elder gasped when he stepped into the *Hornet's* cockpit and saw them. "You're from the empire?"

The taller alien shook his head. "We're from the Riftiq." Melki would tell me later that the Riftiq was a region too remote to fall entirely under Empire control. They paid lip service to the capitol, periodically sent the central authority a monetary tribute, and took care never to criticize whoever occupied the throne. In return, the Morghul Crown left them to their own devices. The lax oversight led to the Riftiq becoming a haven for smugglers and organized crime.

Pointing at our visitors' uniforms, I asked, "Does the Riftiq have an army?"

To answer me, Melki spoke Kyperion. "We call these fighters Turqs. You would call them Rangers. They patrol the borders of the Riftiq, looking for threats. Being much closer to Kanaris than the nearest Empire base back in the Heyanaus Quadrant, they were the first to receive our distress signal."

Relieved to find they were not the tip of the Morghul spear, I asked, "Can they get us the hell out of here?"

Melki shook his head. "These are tough beings, but having the firepower to take on something like the *Nebulean Phoenix* would provoke the Empire into acting against them. They cannot take on the Marines any better than we can."

Turning back to the Turqs, Melki asked what their names were. "Arot," said the one that had been doing most of the talking.

"Xanu," said the other one. "Who are you? And how did you end up here?"

Melki shrugged. "I was born here. We're descendants of those with good reason to believe that the Riftiq was not far enough away to find safety from the throne."

"I understand," said Arot. "They tried to press a claim for Mal-Ghura?"

Melki nodded.

"How long ago?"

"Three generations."

Arot exhaled in surprise. "You are Nesiat's people? Those who fell under the spell of the Duvani?"

Melki nodded once more.

Arot shook his head. "Then this planet may not be far enough away from Mal-Ghura, either."

"What's Mal-Ghura?" I asked Melki.

"The seat of the Morghul Empire," the elder answered. "It's our home planet."

"If you were born here, wouldn't it make this place your home planet?" asked Arot.

Melki shook his head. "We merely exist here. My ancestors' ship landed on this planet with its last gasp of life. They tore it apart to build Xaramika. Ever since we have become fewer and fewer. We did not settle Kanaris; we were marooned on it. We've never thrived in this place, only wasted away. It would not surprise me if the next generation became our last."

Taking a seat opposite our pair of new arrivals, Melki asked, "What's it like back in the empire? Has anything changed since my forbearers left it?"

"Of course it's changed," Arot told him. "It has changed several times. Sometimes it's good; sometimes it's not."

"How is it now?"

Xanu shrugged. "Like always, the answer to that question depends on your perspective. There are many people who will thrive under any emperor and just as many who suffer. The only constant in Morghul society has always been conflict."

"The Duvani tried to stop that," Melki told them.

"And look where it got you," countered Arot.

The elder sighed. "We had peace here on Kanaris since the time we landed. We had plenty of other calamities, but war was not a plague we had to contend with until the humans showed up."

"Sorry about that," I said.

Ignoring me, Melki asked, "Is the army still running things?"

Arot nodded. "Yes, as frightening as that is. At least Hiruslar is keeping the Gharqat junkies away from the more developed areas of the realm."

"The army's still using Gharqat?"

"It's illegal," Xanu told him. "But it's still widespread. Unofficially, the military depends on it."

"What's Gharquat?" I asked.

"A narcotic used by our warriors," answered Melki. "It inverts our senses so that pain and discomfort are perceived as pleasurable, almost ecstatic, sensations. It also sends our metabolisms haywire, so we become stronger, faster, and...."

"Psychotic," Arot added. Even though he could not understand me, he figured out I could understand him. Based on Melki's mannerisms, he guessed what we were talking about. Looking me in the eye, he said, "When Morghul warriors are on that stuff, they're impossible to put down. They just keep coming and coming and coming and coming. The more hurt you give them, the more they want. They beg for it. When Gharqat is in the equation, an enlistment in the Morghul military is a one-way trip."

Melki agreed. "It is very addictive. Saaxirad believes it was Nesiat's position to forbid our soldiers from using Gharqat that cost him the support of the military, and hence, the throne of Mal-Ghura."

"Too bad Nesiat lost," Xanu said as he broke into a minor coughing spell. "Maybe they could have kept it out of the civilian population also."

"Civilians are using Gharqat?" gasped Melki. "For what?!?"

"They can work longer and harder," Arot said. "You can get five years of labor out of a Morghul in one, which is about all it takes for them to blow a circuit in their brain."

Thinking of Gunny Malcolm's addictions, I was less than surprised that the first intelligent alien species humanity ever met would also be grappling with a substance abuse crisis. It was proof that war could force anything into warping their minds to relieve the horrors of it.

Melki sighed as he looked at the two Turqs. "It has been a long time since we have had any contact with the empire. If they find us here, do you believe it will end as badly as we think it will?"

Xanu shook his head. "No, it will be even worse. They won't want the Duvani's disciples polluting their subjects with heretical ideas. After having been a prisoner of the humans, however...."

The Turq paused to turn his orange eyes toward me. "I would rather meet my end at the hands of the emperor's assassins than be played with by these hideous things."

•●-<●>-●-<●>-●•

Chapter 42

The Duvani

The Killbilly reached down and wrenched Deena Vulk from her dreams by the hair. "Got the bitch!"

Vulk did not scream out in pain or surprise. She let out a battle cry, then smashed her fist into the bruin's throat, causing him to drop her as he gasped for air. Deena hit the ground running but did not make it two steps before realizing she was surrounded by a ragged group of Qilkorian death squad men covered in varying degrees of filth. Interspersed among them was the occasional Class Zero female. They had better hygiene than their male comrades but looked far fouler in disposition. All of them had their weapons trained on the fugitive and looked ready to fire. "My god," Vulk said to them. "You might just be the biggest collection of ugly fuckers I have ever seen."

Gunny Malcolm laughed. "Ain't that the pot calling the kettle black." Stepping up to their captive, Malcolm took her by the chin to get a better look at her scarred face and robotic eye. "That doesn't look like our technology. That looks like alien shit."

"It is," Vulk said, making a dangerous admission considering whose company she was in. Pointing to the patch dominating Malcolm's face, she added, "Don't you even think about taking it. It's calibrated to my brain, not yours. It can't be reprogrammed. It dies with me."

"Does it now?" Malcolm grinned. "You know, you don't seem too disturbed about running into us."

Deena shrugged. "I'm not. In fact, I was hoping to find you."

"Me?" Gunny asked. "You know who I am?"

"No," Vulk answered. "But you're a Marine, aren't you? That's who I've been looking for."

Malcolm eyed his prisoner suspiciously. "Who are you?"

"Deena Vulk."

The Marine flinched. "Seriously? You're the bitch who killed Jella Duverii?"

Vulk nodded. "That was too bad. I always liked Jella. I had to keep my cover from getting blown, though. She knew I was Section 615."

"That was the girlfriend of one of my guys at the time. You almost killed him, too."

"I know."

Malcolm frowned. "He's looking for you, you know."

Deena shook her head. "Not anymore."

The gunnery sergeant raised an eyebrow. "You kill him?"

"Last I heard, he's still alive and causing us all sorts of trouble. No, Tauk had his chance to settle our score, but he punted. He decided to let Kryndil do it for him. If he's looking for me now, it's as part of the posse that's probably gaining on my tail."

"Now, why would there be a posse on your tail?"

Vulk looked Malcolm right in the eye so he knew she was telling the truth. "Because I just escaped from Kryndil's Lair, and now I know where it is."

Two weeks later, Nala Biragor was aboard the *Nebulean Phoenix*, addressing General Kroaht himself in the decadent stateroom Commandant Taillur hated so much. "Are you telling me Deena Vulk escaped Kryndil's Lair all by herself?" Kroaht asked.

"No, she was aided by a Marine deserter, Tymar Hailo, and a prisoner of war, Anirae Labaat."

"And where are they?" asked Commandant Taillur.

"According to Vulk, Labaat perished due to exhaustion. Hailo committed suicide shortly afterward. Gunny Malcolm found their remains, which corroborated her story."

"Did you verify cause of death?" Kroaht asked, betraying his lack of field experience on the surface of Kanaris.

"Malcolm found bones, General," Biragor informed him. "Soft tissue does not last long in the rainforest."

Kroaht descended into thought for a few moments. "Do you trust those coordinates she gave you?"

Biragor nodded. "I do. I also trust Vulk's assertion that their escape was far too easy. They marched right out of that facility without so much as seeing another Narman soldier. Malcolm verified that there were indeed Narmans scouring the jungle looking for something, but the bulk of them were way off course. All they were picking up were Killbilly death squads trying to collect bounties."

"What about her strength assessment?" Kroaht asked. "Do you believe there are only a few thousand enemy personnel guarding Kryndil's Lair?"

"That would be in line with our estimates of Narman force strength. Of course, those estimates were developed before they...." Nala caught herself before implying that the Portunese were liberated. The Samaaris preferred to consider them stolen. Biragor split the difference by saying, "...seized the laborers manning our Harnillium mines."

"So, Kryndil has a few thousand troops," Kroaht mused. "I have hundreds of thousands. I don't see how they can hold out against such overwhelming force."

"Sir," Biragor pled. "It's a trap. Vulk believes it. I believe it and...."

"That'll be all, Biragor," Taillur said, dismissing the agent. "As always, your work has been exemplary. Give Major Kuusip my regards when you get back home."

Once they were alone again, Kroaht turned to his intelligence chief. "What do you think?"

Taillur shrugged. "I think she's right. This has trap written all over it."

"But a few thousand against a few hundred thousand? Come on, Nilton! I don't care what kind of trap they have in mind. No one overcomes odds like that."

"Druze, think about this for a moment. Marines know how to fight on land. You know how to fight on water. You can fight in the air and the vacuum of space. The only place you don't know how to fight is underground. You've never done it before. No one has. We've never had to. If you do this, you'll be entering an alien environment where the enemy has all the advantages. I think Kryndil's dangling a juicy piece of bait before your eyes and daring you to take a bite."

Kroaht sighed and leaned back into his plush couch. He then ordered a drink from one of his mechanical servants. After he downed a glass of liquor and demanded one more, he turned to Taillur and said, "You're probably right. All of you. This is a battle better fought by engineers than riflemen. That would take time, though — a lot of it. I don't have time, Nilton. What I have is General Sqaar speeding this way to send me back to Kyper in chains. If I'm going to escape this quagmire whole, I need to win this fucking war."

"What if Kryndil hands you your ass?"

The general shrugged. "Then he hands me my ass. I'm no worse off than I am right now. I'm still the commander of a failed mission to Kanaris. What do I really have to lose?"

It was a rhetorical question, but Taillur answered it silently. *The lives of a few hundred thousand Marines. That's all.*

•●•◆•●•◆•●•

Saaxirad tried to soothe Akkam Lumuk. With great effort, he pulled one of his old, gnarled hands out from beneath the sheet that covered him and rested it upon the giant's bare head. "It must have been painful."

With tears streaming down his face, Lumuk nodded. "All I ever wanted was to take care of my momma. I ain't ever wanted to hurt nobody. Nobody at all! But everybody's always wanting to hurt me! All the time!"

"I know, Akkam. I know." Saaxirad's voice was weak and gravelly. He was fading fast now, and the things he had always taken for granted, like eating, drinking, talking, and breathing, were so much more difficult. "The universe...is...is...it is such a cruel place. Those aspiring to power always seem to strive to validate their strength by preying...upon the gentle."

Melki hovered over the chief elder on the other side of the bed, looking down upon the Duvani with great concern. "You need to rest, Saaxirad. This can wait."

The old alien slowly shook his head. "No, my son, I don't think it can. Saaxirad's time is near." Letting his hand fall back to his side, the Morghul turned to Lumuk and said, "That's enough about the Marines, Akkam. Tell me about your parents. What did your father do?"

Lumuk shook his head. "For a livin'? I don't rightfully know, sir. I remember him, but not well. He was a mean man. One of the meanest. He would always come home and beat my momma."

"Did he beat you, too?"

"Just once," Lumuk told the alien. "When he decided I was big enough, he hit me so hard I went flying halfway across the house. To hear folks tell it, before my old man could slug me again, my momma beaned him upside the head with a wrench so heavy she could barely lift it. She didn't quit wailing on him until he stopped moving."

"Did she kill him?"

Lumuk shrugged. "I heard he was alive, but he may's well been dead. I ain't ever seen him again after that."

"You...you...you said, 'to hear people tell it.' You didn't see your mother attack him yourself?"

"No, sir," Lumuk answered. "That man walloped me so hard I went to sleep for a month. And when I woke up...well...it's kind of hard to explain. Everything was different. I couldn't remember things that I should've known. I didn't talk the same as I used to. Stuff looked strange, sounded strange, smelled strange. And I was scared, sir! I was scared all the time!"

Melki cast a sympathetic gaze down upon the poor farmer from Gorsu Qat. He had thought Lumuk earned the scars all over his head in combat. After hearing the story of the man's childhood, he now suspected they were left behind by the surgeons who saved little Akkam's life.

Saaxirad let out a long, sad sigh. "Whatever became of your mother?"

The tears started pouring out of Lumuk's eyes again. "I don't know, sir. I ain't seen her since they took me away from Gorsu Qat. Last I saw her, she was spittin' mad at the harvest brokers tryin' to underbid us for our crop of wirsa fruit. Momma said she wasn't sellin' to anyone at them prices, and she got everyone else to refuse business with those misers, too! I thought they were goin' to do somethin' to her, but they always seemed to mind their manners when they see me. Once they got me outta the way, though, ain't no tellin' what's gonna happen to her."

As Akkam sobbed, Saaxirad placed his hand atop the giant's head once more. "I'm so sorry, son."

"I ain't ever going to see her again, am I?"

Saaxirad drew in a deep breath before answering. "I am not going to lie, Akkam. We will probably all meet our demise here on Kanaris. There is very little chance we will ever get off this planet. That said, a little chance is still a chance. What would you be willing to do to get out of here, Akkam? What would you do to see your mother again?"

Lumuk lifted his head and wiped his eyes. "I'd do anything, sir."

Saaxirad smiled. "Anything?"

The giant nodded. "Anything. What do you want me to do?"

"I want to heal you, Akkam."

"Heal me? You can fix me?"

"Oh, yes," the elder cooed. "Your father broke you, Akkam. With a single blow, he created an entirely different person. A being unable to live up to his full potential. I can't turn you into what you were before you were hurt, but I can transform you into someone who can exceed all human capabilities. I can make you see things with clarity. Gift you back the intelligence you were born with, maybe even more."

Saaxirad let go of the giant's head and wrapped his long, arthritic fingers as far as he could around the giant's bicep. "Giving you the intellect to match the raw, unbridled power with which you were endowed could create an almost unstoppable being, my son. We would make you a force to be reckoned with."

Unable to contain himself, Lumuk reached out and grasped at Saaxirad's robes. "You can do that?"

"He can," Melki told the giant. "Saaxirad has given me a very important job to do. I am to lead the Morghul after he is gone. If we do this, you'll become my protector. The entity unto which I will entrust my very life. Do you think you're up to a task like that?"

"How are you going to fix me?" Lumuk asked. "Will it hurt?"

Melki smiled. "Oh no. Of course not." The Morghul elder walked over to

Lumuk and guided the giant to his feet. "All you have to do is lie down next to Saaxirad on the other side of the bed."

Lumuk eyed Melki suspiciously. "He ain't going to try to...you know...touch me like I'm a girl or anything, is he?"

Melki nearly choked trying to suppress a laugh. "No, Akkam. Trust me, Saaxirad's body has aged far too much to be subject to those sorts of urges anymore. All you need to do is lie there..."

As Lumuk stretched himself out upon the massive mattress, Melki wiped his hand across the giant's face, pushing his eyelids closed. "Relax, Akkam. Relax. Take in a deep breath. Hold it in your lungs...then slowly let it out through your nose, paying close attention to the sensation of it passing through your nostrils."

The alien watched Lumuk's massive chest rise and fall several times before saying, "Good, Akkam. Good. Now relax all the muscles in your toes. Take in another deep breath. Then another...good...now, relax your feet. Now, your calves. Good. Take in another deep breath. Hold it. Now, let it out through your nose again."

Melki talked Akkam through relaxing his thighs. Then his torso. Then his fingers, arms, and shoulders. By the time the alien was done with the bruin, Lumuk was in a state of rest so deep it was akin to being hypnotized. "How are you feeling, Akkam?"

"Good," the giant responded in a voice that was barely more than a whisper.

"Excellent," Melki cooed. "Akkam, before we go any further, I have to ask you one last time: Are you doing this willingly?"

Lumuk felt amazing. He was more at peace than he had ever been in his entire life. "Yessss," he purred. "I want to do it."

"Okay," Melki said as he reached into his pocket and pulled out a capsule. "Take in one more deep breath."

As Lumuk inhaled, the alien broke open the little canister and held it up in front of the giant's mouth. "Good. One more breath, extra deep..."

Lumuk did what the alien told him to, and fumes from Melki's capsule flooded the giant's lungs. His reverie was instantly broken, and he shot up out of bed, throwing his arm out and grabbing the alien by the throat. "What was that?!? What did you do to..."

Before he could finish his sentence, Lumuk's eyes rolled back into his head as his body went limp. After he collapsed back onto the mattress, Melki pulled out a couple more capsules and repeated the process to ensure he would stay unconscious.

"Is it done?" Saaxirad groaned.

"I hope so," Melki answered. "He is a big man. If he comes to, this could end badly."

"Then we...then we...we better get this over with," the dying elder gasped. "Lock the door."

Chapter 43

A FORCED HAND

I never did figure out how to use the intercom in my room at Xaramika. Every time the alarm sounded to let me know I was being called, all I could do was press buttons until the hologram showed up in the center of the room. This time, it was Melki summoning me.

"Eamon, we've had to call an emergency council meeting. I have sent Akkam Lumuk to collect you and Haeli."

"Haeli?" I asked.

"Yes," Melki answered. "The liberated inmates now make up the majority of our population. She is the closest thing to a leader they have. Well, both she and you. There's enough room at the table for both of you."

No sooner did Melki sign off when the buzzer sounded at our room's entrance. When the panel slid open, Akkam Lumuk stepped through it, smiling from ear to ear. Before I could even greet him, he wrapped his massive arms around me and lifted me off my feet, nearly crushing me in an exuberant bear hug. "He fixed me, sir! He fixed me!"

I said nothing in return. The man was squeezing me so hard I could barely breathe, let alone talk.

"Akkam, I think you're hurting him," Haeli said as she stepped into view, fastening the last few clasps on her tunic. With no mines left to liberate, the Xun had traded in their ragged coveralls for proper uniforms.

"Sorry, sir!" Lumuk said as he dropped me to my feet.

"It's okay!" I gasped, looking up at the giant. Physically, Lumuk looked the same as he always had. It only took one look into his eyes to see he was someone else entirely, though. He was happy, confident, and spoke effortlessly without constantly pausing to pick the right words out of that muddled mind of his. Yet his fundamental nature remained the same. He was still empathetic, protective, and eager to please. "My god, Akkam, what did they do to you?"

"I don't know exactly," he answered. "I was asleep for it but...but...well, we need to get to the council meeting. Melki will fill you in on the rest."

When Akkam Lumuk showed us into the Council Chamber, he led us to our seats and disappeared into the darkness behind the Duvani's throne, where the praetorians stood. A few minutes later, Kryndil walked in with Lipsis, the Morghul Elder in charge of intelligence, and his Narman counterpart, Bengin Meinhopf.

Once they were all seated, a bell went off, summoning everyone to rise for the Duvani. This time, there was no Saaxirad. It was Melki who entered the hall. Stepping into the space between the throne and the table, Melki nodded sadly at the council and said, "We knew the time was near, but it has finally arrived. Saaxirad is no more."

The humans gathered around the table gasped in shock and grief. The Morghul, however, applauded. "All hail Melki! May he reign long!"

Bengin was standing beside me. I turned to him and asked, "I take it the Morghul don't mourn?"

Meinhopf shrugged. "Per their beliefs, the Duvani doesn't really die. He gets instantly reincarnated into the body of his chosen successor. In their eyes, Saaxirad is now Melki, and Melki is now Saaxirad. They're one and the same."

"Thank you, everyone! Thank you!" Melki said. "It's great to be able to once again move under my own power! Please be seated. We have much to discuss, and time is short. Just so you know, Saaxirad expired during the process of healing Akkam Lumuk. Truth be told, he would likely have died that night, anyway, but Saaxirad was a healer, and he wanted to cure Lumuk before he transitioned. As you all know, Melki is *not* a healer, so it will take me quite some time to tune this body to wield that magic. Saaxirad's last case was a success, though, and Akkam

Lumuk is now our newest praetorian. In fact, he is my main praetorian. I hope to have him at my side for many, many years."

Once the council had descended upon their chairs, Melki let out a long sigh. "Bengin Meinhopf, would you please tell the Council what you told me this morning?"

With a nod to Melki, Meinhopf leaned forward to rest his arms on the table. "Our sources in Narman's Pyke have confirmed that Deena Vulk is now in Marine hands."

All at once, the Morghul council members turned to glower at Kryndil. Unrepentant and full of defiant rage, Kryndil glared right back at them. "Spare me your scorn," he growled.

"If you had just executed Vulk when you received her, we would not be in this situation," Voraq, the Justice Elder, spat. "But no, you let your sadism put us all at risk."

"That's enough," Melki said, trying to deny Kryndil the opportunity to respond and get himself into even more trouble. "What's done, is done. We can't undo it. We just have to deal with it. Bengin, please go on."

"The Marines now have the coordinates of Kryndil's Lair," Meinhopf continued. "They also know that if they take that, there's a tunnel that can lead them all the way to Xaramika."

"Oh no!" exclaimed Dhola, the Elder responsible for Morghul affairs. "We need to evacuate that entire facility and fill the tunnels."

"I'll do no such thing!" snapped Kryndil. "Let them come! We're ready for them!"

"You're not ready for those kinds of numbers, Kryndil," Melki said. "You need to evacuate your lair and reposition to Xaramika."

"I already told you I will do no such thing!"

"I am not asking you to do this, Kryndil! I am telling you to...."

"Or what?" Kryndil asked as he stood up, making Akkam Lumuk emerge from the shadows to intercept him if he approached Melki. "What are you going to do if I refuse your commands? Are you going to fight me and the Marines at the same time?"

"I will not shed Morghul blood," Melki told his errant subject. "Not at this late hour when I need every ally I can get."

"Then you worry about Xaramika, and let me take care of my lair!" With that, Kryndil stormed out of the room.

Once he was gone, Dhola turned to Melki and said, "We can still fill the tunnel. We just need to start from our end. We'll seal the sick monster off!"

"No," I said. "Wait a minute. If Kryndil insists on fighting the Marines, let him. We can use that battle as a filter to ice the Loyalists and save the troops we have on our side. This could be what we need to reach our ratio! With the Suma Corps gone...."

"The Suma Corps will not be gone for long," Meinhopf said. "Well, they will, but they're soon to be replaced by the Mathusala Corps, who're expected to be in theater within a matter of days. Word is that they will not be equipped in the same armor as you are, Tauk. Not until they figure out how you immobilized it."

I stopped and looked at Meinhopf. "That could be a problem."

"It *is* a probem, Tauk," Meinhopf told me. "And it's not even our biggest."

"There's more?" I asked.

Meinhopf answered. "Much more. General Kroaht is being replaced. The entire 247th MEF is being relieved and swapped out with the 355th. That's a half million fresh troops arriving without convicts. We'll have no one on the inside. No one on the mothership. We'll be starting from scratch." Bengin turned to face Melki. "We're too weak to begin at square one again."

It was Melki's turn to deliver more bad news. "As many of you know, a Turq reconnaissance party was shot down over Kanaris. A couple of their survivors are in our custody. They received our distress signal. That means the Empire has it, also. The Turqs, being who they are, are grateful to us for saving them from the Qilkorians. Their customs compel them to remain in our service until their debt to us is repaid."

"How many of them do we have?" asked Lipsis. "I was told they are some of the greatest warriors in the Heyanaus."

"We have two," I told the Morghul intelligence chief.

Lipsis shook his head. "That's not going to do us much good."

"Not really," Melki agreed. "The best they can do is help us with information, which they have. They told us Morghul forces are inbound and expected to arrive within the next few months. They have a much further way to travel than the humans do."

Governor Ghona leaned back in her seat, put her hands behind her head, and tried to sum up our situation scientifically. "We're fucked."

"Wait a second," I said as I stood up and started to pace. "Kroaht's getting relieved. His replacement is on his way here. If Kroaht wants to avoid being sent home in disgrace, and trust me, he does, he's going to need to act fast. I'll wager that he'll throw everything he's got at Kryndil's Lair with little planning and a lot of desperation. He'll turn that place into a goddamn slaughterfest!" Wagging my finger in the air, I said, "We might be able to turn this to our advantage."

"I admire your optimism," Governor Ghona said mockingly. "No matter how misplaced it may be."

"If we can spare our moles, cull the loyalists, have our people in orbit seize the mothership, and pull it all off before the 355th MEF or, heaven forbid, the Morghul get here, we can get off this rock!"

"Do you seriously think we can do that?" asked Melki.

"No," I answered. "But if we don't try, we're all going to die in this god-forsaken place.

Chapter 44

The Big Bang

After Melki's briefing, I needed to do some thinking. Actually, I needed someone smarter than me to do my thinking for me. I needed Dmitri Naktada. When I arrived at his chamber and rang the bell, however, no one answered. Nor would he pick up when I tried to raise him on the commlink. Nor had anyone else heard from him since before the council meeting. It was nearly a week before I caught him, and when we finally met, he was packing.

"Where are you going?" I asked as I watched the man throw all manner of gadgetry in his bag.

Naktada was all smiles. "I'm sorry, Eamon, I can't tell you that."

"What? We're keeping secrets from each other now? Dimi, I don't think I've ever held anything back from you."

Still smiling, Naktada said, "Well, you need to start. Big things are happening. I hear your responsibility now is to formulate a way to take over the *Nebulean Phoenix*."

I nodded. "It is. There's a lot of moving parts to it, though. I can really use your help."

Naktada shook his head. "You don't need it as much as the guys who are about to be facing a couple hundred thousand screaming Marines."

I gasped. "You're going to Kryndil's Lair?!?"

"I didn't say that. Only that the side that's going to be fighting on Kanaris needs me to do something they are not at all equipped to pull off. But I am. Look, you already have the best person to help you with what you have to do. Elia Gyanis.

She's good, Eamon."

"On a tactical level?" I asked.

"No," Naktada answered. "But neither am I. Look, she's the one you need to relay your orders to our people on the *Phoenix*. She's the one with all the names...."

"I thought that was Soldana."

"Bitch, please," Naktada laughed. "She hacked his shit in a month. She also made it virtually unhackable to anybody but her. Elia's one of the elite, Eamon. Don't be afraid to lean on her. Tell her what needs to be done, and let her do it."

Nodding in resignation, I said, "Okay, I'll track down Soldana and get the roster for the people we have on the mothership."

"Go to Meinhopf. Soldana's not here."

"Really?" I asked. "Where the hell is he?"

Ovai Soldana plugged his programming module into the platoon leader's helmet and injected the new program into it. "You see anything different now?"

Lieutenant Dering looked at the members of his platoon. "Yeah, everyone has a green tint to them."

"Yep. Those are the people you don't want to shoot. Our friendlies in the enemy units will look the same way." When Soldana finished with Dering, he walked through the mud to get to the platoon sergeant. The rain had stopped a few hours before, and the patrol was being treated to a rare night of clear skies in the Kanarisian jungle.

As he worked, Ovai addressed the Narman fighters gathered around him. "If the troops are highlighted in red, blow them away. Leave none alive. Yellow means nobody's sure where they stand. If they're shooting at you, I guess you should go ahead and shoot back."

Soldana reached his hand out and pointed his open palm toward a Narman corporal a few paces away from him. Her sidearm flew out of her holster and spun through the air until it ended up in his grip. "If you ever get into that fancy new exo-armor system, you can also disarm them like that until they clear up whose side they're on."

A few of the troops laughed. "Wow! The new armor can do that?" asked the fighter who had just lost her pistol.

Ovai nodded. "Yeah. Naktada rigged this one up for me a few weeks ago. I haven't had to disarm anybody with it yet, but I was able to pull the chair out from beneath a major back at the Pyke a few days ago while he was getting ready to sit in it. That was pretty funny."

"I don't think you should be playing around with that shit when you're in enemy territory, Soldana," the gunny sergeant said as his shell was being updated. "That's no time for childish pranks. It's a good way to blow your cover."

"It's also a great way to steal a colonel's tablet while he's distracted by the spectacle the major was making of himself," Soldana shot back.

The troops laughed again, making Soldana feel good about himself. He always felt sorry for the folks on long patrols. It was miserable duty.

"Hey, you're the spy kid, aren't you?" asked a squad leader.

"Yep. That's what people say."

"You aren't tech support, so why are you out here doing this?"

Soldana shrugged. "I was coming out here anyway to warn you about what you're up against and let you know to be vigilant. I got confirmation that the Marines are headed this way in force — fifty thousand of them. After we took down some of their planes at the Pyke, they won't risk an air assault."

"You sure about that?" asked a private looking up into the sky above them. When Ovai followed his line of sight, he spotted several dozen fireballs that appeared to be entering the atmosphere. With a long sigh, Ovai pulled his device from the shell he was working on and threw it over his shoulder in frustration.

"Motherfucker!" the platoon leader spat as he pulled a flare gun from his belt and fired a purple beacon into the sky toward Kryndil's Lair.

"You fired the wrong color!" shouted a rifleman who seemed to be in denial. "That's the signal to get underground!" The gravity of their situation seemed to sink in when the grunt spotted other purple flares ascending above the tree line. "Oh. Fuck."

"Why the hell are you all standing there?!?" cried another grunt as she started jogging into the bush. "Run!"

A few of the troops followed her. Ovai decided not to. He sat in the mud, leaned against a tree, and marveled at the beauty of Gaiomedi, Kanaris's giant ringed moon. The lieutenant sat down beside him. "You think this was the way you were going to go out?"

"No, but I can't say I'm surprised," Soldana answered. Then he was vaporized.

When Haeli, Black Francis, Keila Hyfer, and I got topside at Xaramika, the mushroom clouds were still rising above the distant horizon. That was impressive, considering we were near the summit of a fairly sizable mountain, making the horizon much more distant.

Haeli covered her mouth in horror. "Oh no! Is there any way they could have survived that?"

Black Francis and I looked at Leila. "Kryndil's Lair is deep underground," she told us. "Much like Xaramika. It's highly unlikely those bombs compromised the settlement, but the lush jungle surrounding it? The one that protects it from being discovered? Yeah, it's been reduced to dust. For a couple hundred kilometers around that, the rainforest will just be the blackened husks of charred trees. Even if they had the coordinates, it could've taken the Marines years to find the entrance to that base. If there's half a brain among them, I'm betting they can figure it out in a matter of days. A week tops."

"You've been there?" Francis asked. "To Kryndil's Lair?"

Leila nodded. "Many times."

"Do you think they can get inside?"

Leila shrugged. "It depends upon how much they're willing to sacrifice."

"Kroaht's back is up against the wall," I told her. "I'm betting that he'll be ready to sacrifice everything."

Hanging her head, Leila shrugged her shoulders. "Then they'll eventually get in."

Nuclear fire was still raging above Kryndil's Lair when I descended back into the catacombs of the Morghul capitol and sought out Bengin Meinhopf for a current roster of our infiltrators. With Suma Corps gone, we only had four corps of regular infantry in theater. My background as an Academy officer allowed me to predict the order of battle. Alpha Corps would go in first, while Beta Corps would wait in reserve at Narman's Pyke. Gamma and Delta would be standing by on the mothership.

"Alpha Corps is the one knocking on Kryndil's door right now," I told Meinhopf as I poured over the numbers on one of the secure monitors in the Intelligence Control Center. "That's a hundred thousand Marines. How many do we have resisting them?"

Kryndil's got around two hundred Morghul and two thousand Narmans. We reinforced him with every liberated camp inmate willing to wield a blaster and physically able to do so. That was an impressive eight thousand people. The enemy still has plenty more than the three-to-one ratio you say they need to take us."

Pouring over the Alpha Corps roster, I said, "Not so fast. We got 11,567 political conscripts embedded among them. And my god! After we sacked those mines, Elia's recruitment efforts went into hyperdrive! We have 38,777 of those assaulting Kryndil on our side. Bengin, it's not ten thousand of us against a hundred thousand of them. It's more like sixty thousand of ours against forty thousand of theirs! We're going to fucking smoke them!"

Meinhopf shook his head. "They wiped out our anti-air. They have complete control of the skies. It's not quite that easy."

I frowned, realizing that Meinhopf had a point. "Then Kryndil's got to draw the enemy underground, where air superiority would be mitigated."

Again, Meinhopf disagreed with me. "If we give those pricks access to our front door, what's to stop them from launching a couple more nukes right down our throat?"

"The tunnel to Xaramika," I told him. "If they nuke Kryndil's Lair, they lose their path to the jackpot."

"That's a dangerous assumption."

"That's a fact," I countered. "Remember, I was raised on this shit."

Dismissing the numbers on the Marines standing by in Narman's Pyke, I pulled up our data on Gamma and Delta Corps, who were still in orbit aboard the *Nebulean Phoenix*. I could not help but smile. "Those units still have convicts attached to them. 38,401 of them. 56,854 conscripts. That's 95,255 against 104,775."

"That's not three to one," Bengin informed me. "The Loyalists still outnumber us."

"Barely," I replied. "Also, three-to-one is what you need to breach fortifications. Our ninety-five thousand infiltrators are already inside. Plus, we have the element of surprise. With the right plan, this is entirely feasible. But we've got to move! We need to have control of that ship before the Mathusula Corps gets here!"

Meinhopf sighed, deflating until he let himself fall into an empty seat. "I thought your numbers sounded off. Mathusula Corps arrived on station two days ago."

I closed my eyes and hung my head. "Goddammit. We need a fucking break, Ben. We gotta figure out a way to neutralize the Mathusula Corps."

Chapter 45

KRYNDIL'S LAIR

Two weeks into the battle for Kryndil's Lair, Elia Gyanis was sitting in Narman Pyke's enlisted club, listening to a group of fearful Marines discuss the rumors filtering in from the front lines. A highly inebriated PFC was desperately seeking something to pin his hopes on. "I heard they finally got inside," he told his drinking companions. "Maybe they'll wrap this up before we have to go in."

"They got in, all right," said a young sergeant, intent on finishing an entire bottle of mess hall hooch by himself. "An entire division of us. Twenty thousand leathernecks ran screaming into that hole on the side of the mountain. You know how many got out?"

No one said a word, forcing the sergeant to answer his own question. "Not a single fuckin' one of them."

"Bullshit," said a staff sergeant at the bar. "Who told you that?"

"No one," the Marine said as he swallowed another pull from his bottle of booze. "I was there."

"In the hole?" asked another grunt.

"If I went inside, I would've died with everyone else. I was the division forensic specialist. I sent the drones in to find out what happened."

"And what did you see?"

"Bodies," the intel sergeant said. "Well, parts of them, anyway. All over the place. It's a fucking massacre out there."

"You're Alpha Corps?" the staff sergeant asked. "What the hell are you doing here? Why ain't you back at the front?"

After another drink, the Alpha Corps sergeant said, "Someone had to present the video to Corps staff."

"I heard Alpha Corps is almost combat ineffective," said a female corporal. "I heard they're about to put us on standby orders."

"I'm pretty sure they are," slurred a drunken private. "I overheard Lieutenant Garfuun at the call center begging his mommy to pull some strings and get him off of Kanaris now."

Several Marines groaned in unison. "That sounds about right," moaned one of them. "Fucking Samaaris," spat another.

Gyanis had heard enough to sleep happy that night. She made eye contact with the intel sergeant and smiled, knowing he was on her side. A pie-eyed Samaari, who most certainly was not, stood up and offered to walk her home. "I'll be all right," she said, declining his offer.

"But it can be pretty dangerous out there these days," he told her.

"You're right," she said. "For you. It's been hard on Samaaris lately, hasn't it? One or two of you people seem to be turning up dead every night in Narman's Pyke. Maybe you should be asking people to walk *you* home after dark."

Elia strolled back to her barracks without incident. When she got to her room, she opened up her tablet and accessed the MEF's casualty reports, a system the armorer had hacked about the same time she broke into the Narman database. Setting her search window for the past seven days, she discovered that, indeed, Alpha Corps had lost their entire Second Division three days prior. 19,680 troops were listed as Code 44. Killed in action. She downloaded the names and cross-referenced them with the Narman database listing active combatants. She got 10,287 matches.

That meant more than ten thousand of their people were spirited out of Kryndil's Lair and sent to Xaramika. The League believed them dead, but in reality, they were lying low in the Narman army, waiting for their chance to strike back at the commanders who would have had them slaughtered. That was far better than the 6,888 infiltrators she had recorded for Second Division before the battle started. The Narmans were stronger now than they were when the brawl began.

Still, that did not present the complete picture of the fight over Kryndil's Lair.

The same system that sent casualty reports up to the mothership also contained action reports. Though the Marines were losing people, they had resources. They possessed many things that the Narmans did not, so even though they were hemorrhaging people, Alpha Corps was slowly gaining ground.

In fact, a report filed earlier that day claimed the topmost level of Kryndil's Lair was now in League hands.

••–◄–●–◄–••

LCPL Timo Haim was shaking as he stormed through the hole in the mountain. It cost three hundred lives to take the short tunnel leading to the first layer of the facility, and the bodies were still there. There was no time to clean them out. If the Marines were going to continue their advance, no matter how slow and bloody it may be, they had to keep feeding the machine. They had to keep pumping the condemned deeper and deeper into the bowels of Kryndil's Lair.

The tunnel was slow going. There was no solid ground to get a footing on. Haim had no choice but to trample over the putrid remains of his comrades, slipping in the pulverized flesh and blood that slickened the dead. He could feel the bones breaking as they trampled over the corpses, and the uneven ground constantly tripped them up. It probably would have been faster to crawl through that mess, but none of them wanted to be so close to the dead.

When Haim emerged from the pipe, he ended up face-to-face with something that made him shriek out loud. It was the body of a Morghul defender, its mouth wrenched open, frozen in the scream it was bellowing as it died, its red eyes gone black. The being's torso had been split wide open, spilling out a pile of unrecognizable organs that the young Marine could not even begin to identify. He was at once both horrified and mesmerized by the spectacle. He had never seen an alien before.

"Hey, you!" shouted a nearby Marine sentry with orders to kill anyone running the wrong way. "Move your ass! You trying to make shit easier for the Mogs by giving them a stationary target?"

Shaking his head, Haim jogged forward to catch up with the rest of his squad. "Kill your lights!" someone ahead of him screamed.

"No!" answered another. "They live underground! They're used to the darkness!"

"Son-of-a-bitch!"Haim shouted over the squad's commlink. "Lights on or lights off?!? Doesn't anyone know our goddamned enemy?!?"

"We don't know shit!" growled Corporal Puter. "But I've only seen one alien body in this mess! The rest have all been human!"

Puter said something else, but he was drowned out by the crackling sounds of the internal Geiger counter going off inside Haim's headphones. "You guys hearing that?" the young Marine asked. "Keep your shells intact! It's hot in here!"

"Of course it is!" shouted Sergeant Raili. "There's hundreds of us tracking nuclear dust into this place from the outside! I guess the command figures that if we can't shoot 'em, will kill 'em all with radiation pois...!"

Raili was cut off when a blast of plasma fire cut through the smoke and struck him in the helmet, sending a shower of sparks flying through the air. The bolt of energy melted a fist-sized hole in the man's headgear, vaporized his brains, and severed his arm when it blew out from his jaw. The sergeant's legs immediately gave out and he keeled over sideways, coming to a rest among the other bodies that lined the path to the fighting ahead.

"MEDIC!" screamed one of the riflemen.

"Leave him!" shouted Corporal Puter, who, with Sergeant Raili's death, had just received an instant promotion. "He's gone! Keep moving unless you want to join him!"

The squad bolted down what passed for a city block in Kryndil's subterranean refuge. On either side of them rose ornately sculptured walls depicting Morghul icons, scenes of triumphant moments, and starscapes of different worlds holding revered places in alien culture. The settlement was carved to accommodate thousands of beings. After a few hundred years of population decline, however, it was largely abandoned until its creators went to war with the humans.

"It's beautiful," Haim gasped as he ran down the street.

"It's also honeycombed with windows and doorways that can hide a million Mog snipers," Puter replied. As if to prove the corporal's point, another plasma blast shot out from above, hitting their Samaari sapper square in the face.

By instinct, the Marines rushed to throw themselves against the wall that the fire came from and pointed their weapons upward. If the sniper wanted a second shot at them, they would have to lean out of their opening to take it, exposing his position. It was so smokey inside that the Marines could only see a story or two high.

"Where the hell did that come from?!?" cried Desma Binay, the squad's own sniper, as she scanned the heights for a target.

"It could've come from anywhere!" answered her spotter. "We can't see shit up there!"

"Keep moving!" barked Puter. "They're shooting and scooting! Let someone else be in their sights when they find another nest!"

Two blocks and another pair of dead Marines later, Haim's squad stumbled upon the company that found the ramp to the next level down. They were stopped from going any further by a wounded captain. His left hand had been blown off and his visor shattered, exposing him to high levels of radioactivity. By the time Haim met him, the man's face was swollen and blistered. It looked as if his skin could begin peeling away in droves at any moment. He was dying and he knew it. Still, he was determined to direct the assault as best he could.

"Where's your platoon leader!" the captain screamed at Puter.

The corporal shrugged. "He should've been here by now!"

The officer cursed as he scanned the troops for someone higher in rank. Finding nobody, he said, "I guess that makes you platoon leader!"

Puter's shoulders slumped. Getting effectively promoted from corporal to second lieutenant in the space of an hour did not bode well for how the mission was going.

"Look here, lad!" the captain screamed at Puter. "We're blowing them back! We're going to send a barrage of Spaz rockets to the next enemy stronghold! You're going to be right behind them! After the explosion, you run in there and secure their position! If you take it, you get to hold it! No more advancing for you! You'll be relatively safe!"

"And if we don't take it?!?" shrieked Puter.

"Then get as many of those motherfuckers as you can before they get you and I'll see you soon in the great hereafter! Whatever you do, don't run back this way! We're fighting just as many deserters as Narmans, so we can't tell friend from foe!

If you're going to die, die fighting the enemy! Not getting fragged by your fellow Marines!"

Seriously?!? Haim thought to himself. *Our own guys are going to kill us?!?* The lance corporal never had much love for the League, even before he learned what they were doing to the Portunese in the mining camps. He had a large family back on Orbewan, though, so he never seriously considered defecting because he could not bear the thought of never seeing his clan again. With an irradiated captain promising to slaughter him if the Narmans did not, the young man realized loyalty earned him nothing but death in the Kyperion League Space Corps. His only hope of ever seeing those he loved again was jumping ship. His only problem was he had no idea how.

The captain pointed down the tunnel he would soon be sending the Marines. "You're gonna lead your people about fifty meters down that pipe! There's a cross tunnel down there you're gonna slip into and secure. That'll give you a good head start! We're gonna fire our rockets right past you about three hundred meters further...."

The officer paused his instructions to get violently ill, another side effect of his radiation sickness. When he finished, he wiped his lips with his injured limb. "You stay put until that shit explodes downrange! Then you haul ass to catch up with it before the Narmans come to their senses and kill everything that moves! Got it?!?"

"Got it, sir!" Puter answered as more than a dozen grenadiers got into position in front of the tunnel.

Haim turned to the Marine beside him and said, "They better wait until we're out of the way before they unleash that shit."

"Third Platoon!" Puter screamed at the Marines gathering around the pipe. "Queue up and get ready to go!"

As the gaggle of leathernecks began to form up, Haim took a good look around. There were about sixty Marines there, yet Corporal Puter was the highest-ranking grunt among them. Haim thought that very odd and wondered how they lost all their senior NCOs but barely any ground-pounders. Before he could think about it too long, the captain screamed, "CHARGE!"

Haim half expected to be cut down the moment they started running, but he was shocked to encounter no hostile fire as they sprinted to the cross tunnel. They all got to cover effortlessly and crammed themselves into position. After that, there was nothing but silence. Haim was standing close to the corporal, so he asked, "Aren't you going to say any...."

The lance corporal was interrupted by a single missile flying past them in the wrong direction. It sailed unimpeded right through the tube and exploded amid the grenadiers preparing to unleash their own hellfire. This set off the Marines' personal ordnance and the munitions they had staged in preparation for the assault. The blast was horrendous, and the fireball resulting from it licked the crosstunnel where Haim was sheltered. Instinctively, he crouched down to lower his profile and closed his eyes until the racket died down. When he opened them, Puter was pointing a pistol in his face.

"This is a one-time offer, Timo," the corporal said matter-of-factly. "You can come with us and join the Narmans or walk back up that tunnel and take your chances trying to rejoin the Marines."

"They'll shoot me if I go back that way," Haim told him.

Puter shook his head. "That group's gone. It'll be the next one that'll probably cap your ass."

That was all the persuading Haim needed. "I'm going with you."

One frantic three-hundred-meter dash later, Haim was confronted by another Morghul alien, though this one was very much alive and clad in its own version of radiation-resistant armor. One of the other corporals was yelling at it. "You got 'em! You blew 'em all the fuck up! Come on! We can retake that position!"

The Narman officer standing beside the armored Mog shook his head. "We don't have the numbers to hold real estate down here! The best we can do is make the son-of-a-bitches bleed for every inch they take!" Turning his head to look at Haim, the officer shouted, "Keep moving, Yellow!"

"Yellow? Huh?" Haim asked.

Puter grabbed Haim's wrist, opened his forearm console, and typed in an alphanumeric code. For a second, the lance corporal's visor video went haywire. When it stabilized, everyone around him had a green aura around them. Except for Haim. His was yellow until Puter typed another code into his system. "We weren't sure about you," the corporal admitted. "We knew you were a good guy, but didn't know if you had it in you to defect."

Haim looked up at the tunnel where he had just come from. At the far end of it, he could still see the glow from the fires raging above. "Up until the moment they said they'd shoot me if we lost, I didn't think I did either."

As one of the Narman soldiers collected Haim's weapons, Roma Wayste, one of the platoon's armorers, walked up beside the lance corporal and patted his shoulder. "I'm glad you're coming with us, Timo. I had a feeling you would. You're good people."

Haim nodded but was in no mood to celebrate. "Aren't you worried about never seeing your family again?"

Wayste shrugged her shoulders. "We've got better odds seeing them on this side than on the other."

"You sure about that?" Haim asked apprehensively.

"I didn't say our odds were great, only that they're better than with the Marines."

"Alright, everybody!" yelled a Narman sergeant to the new arrivals. We're getting you out of here!" Pointing to a long stairway that wound itself deep into the darkness, the man said, "Take those steps all the way until they stop! There'll be a platform down there with people directing you to outgoing shuttles to Xaramika!"

"Shuttles?!?" gasped Haim.

"The Morghul have been here for a few hundred years," said a Narman private who was on the public commlink network. "From the looks of it, they spent most of that time with nothing better to do than carve their way all over the continent. The stuff they've done down here's amazing!"

A couple of kilometers deeper into the subterranean network, the defecting Marines and their Narman guides passed through a radiation decontamination station, beyond which they were allowed to remove their helmets. A kilometer later, they reached the platform just in time to watch a large shuttle pull into the station. When it stopped, a party of aliens stepped outside, pushing massive, levitating crates of equipment before them. They directed the boxes to the front of the transport and moved them further down the magnetic rails until they disappeared into the darkness. The last person off the tram was a tall, thin man with bright blonde hair.

"Oh my god!" gasped Roma Wayste. "That's Dmitri Naktada!"

"Who's that?" asked Haim.

"Among us armorers, a goddamned legend!"

●●◦●►◦●◦◄●◦●●

Chapter 46

THE SKINNER'S FATE

K ryndil's Lair was a sprawling subterranean fortress. Its entrances were challenging to find, and once they were, they were virtually impregnable. Deena Vulk had regularly visited the settlement before she was imprisoned there and knew everything there was to know about the complex. Without the intelligence she provided to the Marines, there would have been no way they would have been able to find the Morghuls' prison base, let alone breach it. Even with Vulk's information, however, the battle to take the facility proved deadly. It cost the League thirty-three Marine casualties for every Narman defender they put in a body bag.

The conflict's price tag was on glaring display to General Kroaht as he and his staff marched across the barren battle-scape to the captured labyrinth. The Marines had hit the area with virtually everything they had. What had once been lush Kanarisian rainforest was now a cratered wasteland covered in radioactive ash. And corpses. Now that the fighting had died down, the Marines had retrieved their dead. Their broken bodies were stacked a story high along the path they had beaten to Kryndil's Lair and, with no vegetation visible within eyeshot anymore, were the only source of shade from the rare appearance of the Kanarisian sun.

"Where is General Kuolaada?" Kroaht asked a young major walking up to greet him.

"He's dead, sir," the major answered. He sounded very weary. "General Kuolaada was killed in action."

Kroaht winced. "How?"

The major shrugged. "I don't know. I was fighting the Narmans when it happened."

"And the colonels?" asked one of Kroaht's henchmen.

"Sir, I can't say. All I know is that when we went into those caves, we flushed a bunch of Mogs out. They counter-attacked, destroyed all the command posts, and fled back underground through a passage we must have missed. By the time Captain Pustov got topside, he discovered the enemy had wiped out our entire command structure. He informed me I was the highest-ranking officer in our whole area of operations."

"You?" Kroaht gasped, obviously impressed. "You're the one that led our Marines to victory?"

The major pointed at the pile of bodies towering above them. "We took the objective, sir, but I don't know if I could call this a victory. If we win too many battles like this, we'll lose the goddamn war."

Kuolaada nodded solemnly. "How many Marines did we lose?"

"Just shy of eighty thousand, sir."

"We lost the entire corps?!?"

The major nodded. "Yes, sir."

"And how many enemy fighters did we take out?"

Casting his eyes toward the ground, the major said, "Six hundred, maybe."

Kroaht looked like he was about to faint. "We spent damn near an entire corps of Marines to put down a couple companies of rebels?!?"

The major shrugged. "A few companies. We took about five hundred Narman prisoners. And a few score of aliens."

"You've got Morghul prisoners?" the general asked, already forgetting about his losses.

"Our orders were to bring them in alive. That's what we did."

"And Kryndil?"

The major sighed. "We got him."

Oblivious that he was still standing in the shadow of the dead, Kroaht screamed out in celebration. His underlings did the same. The few enlisted troops to witness the celebration looked away in disgust.

When the officers settled down, the general said, "Get that monster up here!

Front and center! Colonel Ronin! Call our interrogators over to take that fucker into custody right away!"

Ronin hopped on the commlink without delay, summoning the Mar-Sitaara they had arrived on. "Gunny! Gather your Killbillies and march them up this way on the double! We got Kryndil!"

Still consumed by his exuberance, Kroaht slapped the major on the shoulder. "What's your name, son?"

"Pursair, sir," the major responded, not nearly as delighted as the general was. "Major Tomon Pursair."

"You ain't no major anymore, goddammit! You did some pretty incredible work here! You did a fucking general's job, son! I'd make you one if I could, but not even the Commander of Combined Forces can do that without Parliament's approval! The best I can do is make you a colonel! You ready for that?!? You think I can trust you with a brigade?"

Had he not just survived a grueling battle for Kryndil's lair, Pursair might have shown more appreciation for having just skipped a pay grade, but he was exhausted. The best he could manage was, "Thank you, sir. I'll do my best."

"Welcome to the Colonel's Club!" shouted one of Kuolaada's staff officers as he pummeled the former major with a celebratory back slap. Pursair glanced over his shoulder as his superiors applauded him. He offered an apologetic look at the few battered Marines he had left after the battle for Kryndil's Lair. The exhausted troops stared back at him with revulsion. It was not Pursair they were disgusted with; it was the general staff who seemed oblivious to the price their infantry had paid to gain the commanders their prize.

Ronin's Killbillies arrived on the scene about the same time as Kryndil, who was dragged before the general by a pair of hulking Section 615 commandos. The alien had been stripped naked and exposed to the radiation, though he seemed far more resistant to it than the humans were. His arms were bound behind his back at both the wrists and the elbows. He must have been in a great deal of pain, but he still smiled menacingly at his captors as he was thrown into the mud at the general's feet.

"So, you're the Kryndil everyone is so terrified of," the corps commander sneered at the prisoner.

"I am," Kryndil sneered back, addressing the general flawlessly in the man's own language. "And who the fuck are you?"

"General Kroaht."

Kryndil scoffed. "A general, huh? You know, a good general should inspire terror in his enemies. I find it hard to fear a coward who leads so far from the rear that his adversaries don't even know what he looks like.."

Kroaht squatted down to look his prisoner in the eye. "You should be terrified of me, considering I'm the man who's going to have you killed."

The Morghul laughed in Kroaht's face. "I bet I have you killed long before you kill me."

"That's a pretty bold statement coming from a man...ur...uh...thing, in your situation."

"Trust me, your predicament is far more dire than mine."

Kroaht laughed. "How do you figure that?"

The alien cast his gaze upon the pile of Marine bodies towering over them. "Look at all those lost souls. You have so many corpses. How many of ours do you think you killed? Fifty? A hundred? I'll tell you exactly how many you got. You shot just enough of my forces to allow the rest to escape. Now, while you're here basking in your 'victory,' my troops are taking their positions on the high ground, waiting for the perfect time to strike. You may have taken this base, General, but you'll never hold it."

The corps commander looked at Pursair. "Is that possible?"

The major shrugged. "Kryndil's Lair is massive, general. It's big enough to hold thousands of troops, but I can't say how much of it was actually occupied. We certainly didn't find any stores capable of supporting that many people."

"Did you look?" the general asked.

"We didn't have enough people left to explore the entire network, sir. So, no."

Kroaht ground his teeth together. "Then that's something we need to do before...."

"No, you don't," Pursair interrupted. "This was basically a prison camp. Considering these savages killed all the inmates before we could get to them, it's not even that anymore. This place has no military value, and all the intelligence here is stuff the Morghul have extracted from us – shit we already know. If you were to ask me, sir, I'd say bring in an engineering regiment and blow the whole tunnel network to smithereens, then retreat back to base and leave it alone."

The brigadier general standing to Kroaht's right said, "It doesn't matter how many troops that ugly fuck claims to have; we got multitudes more! I say let them attack! We can take them! If they come at us with everything they got, this could be our opportunity to do away with them once and for all and find the tunnel to Xaramika!"

"You don't have the troops you think you do, General," the major told him. "Most of our casualties were not Marines killed in battle. They deserted. Just like on the Satapadaya."

Turning to address Kroaht directly, Pursair said, "Look, sir, the Narmans and the Mogs knew they couldn't hold this place. I don't think they ever intended to. They used pinpoint sniper fire to selectively take out our officers, senior NCOs, and Samaaris...."

"How the hell could they tell who our Samaaris were when they're encapsulated in nuclear-grade exo-armor systems?" asked another brigadier general in Kroaht's entourage, a studious-looking woman named Marina Dara.

"I have no idea, ma'am," the major answered. Waving an arm at the wall of bodies, he added, "Your proof's in there, though. If you download the stats of our deceased, you'll find that Samaaris are disproportionately represented. I think snipers took out the officers and NCOs. There's a good possibility the Samaaris were butchered by their own comrades as they defected."

Kroaht squinted at the major. "How many Marines do you think went over to the enemy?"

"North of forty percent, sir."

"Oh, bullshit!" scoffed Brigadier Wysteria, another of Kroaht's staff officers. "There's no way the Narmans have that many sympathizers in our ranks! We need to get Beta Corps up here right now while we still have momentum! We need to take the tunnels and find our way to Xaramika!"

Showing an uncharacteristic amount of balls for a major, Pursair looked Wysteria right in the eye. "You do that, and you'll only weaken us and make them stronger. We can't send Beta in there until we know how compromised they are."

"What? Do you trust what's coming out of this Mog's mouth more than you trust us?" Wysteria snarled.

Saving Pursair from the temptation to truthfully answer the brigadier's question, the one-eyed gunnery sergeant who had just arrived to collect Kryndil laughed out loud.

"Do you find something humorous about all of this, Gunny Malcolm?" Wysteria snapped.

Konor Malcolm shook his head. "Sorry, sir. I was out of order."

"I'll say you were," the brigadier general snapped. "Get over here, collect your prisoner, and get the fuck out of my face before I have you busted to buck private!"

"Aye aye, sir," Malcolm said as he stepped forward to lift the prisoner out of the radioactive sludge they had him kneeling in.

"Wait a second," Kroaht said, grabbing Malcolm by the arm as he passed. "You've been kicking ass for the Corps a long time, Gunny. What do you think?"

"About what?"

"That Mog is daring us to bring more troops here. He says he'll counter-attack and wipe out the next corps like he did this one."

Malcolm laughed again. "That prick doesn't have any troops to take this place back, General," Malcolm told him. "Even if he did, why would he want to? It's been compromised. We know where it is. It's no longer any use to them."

"Exactly," Major Pursair said, earning himself another blistering glare from Wysteria.

"Sir," one of the staff colonels said, trying to get the general's attention. "We need to know what's down in those catacombs. We have to at least see if there's an escape path the Narmans could have fled down. We have to see if it leads to Xaramika."

Kroaht turned to face one of his quieter underlings. "What do you think, Brigadier Dara?"

"I don't like it," the junior general said. "I tend to agree with the major. It sounds like the prisoner is trying to goad you into doing what he wants. I think it unwise to do that. This place is worthless. We accomplished our mission. Declare victory, blow it up, and withdraw to Narman's Pyke."

Wysteria shook his head in disagreement. "I always thought you too timid for flag rank, Marina."

Gunny Malcolm sounded exasperated. "Even if there's a tunnel to Xaramika down there, you don't want any part of it. Once they draw us deep into that hole, they can bury us all alive by blowing the ceiling and collapsing the shaft." Pausing to point at Kryndil, he added, "If you want to get to Xaramika, that's the fucker that's going to show you how to get there. Look around you. You've wasted enough Marines trying to seize this place. Take your victory and go home."

"Goddammit, Malcolm!" Wysteria barked. "The general doesn't seek counsel from junkie gunnery sergeants! Collect your prisoners and get the fuck out of here!"

Kroaht sighed. "Settle down, Henri. You may be right, but so is Marina. We need to gather all the information we can about this complex, but we need to be careful about it."

Turning to one of the colonels, Kroaht said, "Get back to the Pyke and summon General Zener down here with the Mathusala Corps. I'm not willing to feed any more traitors into the Narmans' ranks. I want troops we can trust to sweep out the catacombs. Also, let General Ursala know that Bravo Corps will provide topside security to watch our flank. We need to ensure we can fight off anything that comes down from the high ground while Mathusala's beneath the surface. I want a show of overwhelming force to scare off any foolish notions the Narmans might harbor about launching some sort of counterattack!"

Pursair looked at the barren hills towering above them on all sides. "You want to muster almost two hundred thousand Marines right here in the bottom of a punch bowl?!?"

Not liking the major's tone, Kroaht said, "You sound exhausted, son. That's understandable, considering what you've been through. You and your Marines have earned some rest. Gather your troops and prisoners and follow Gunny Malcolm. There's a Wasp transport inbound that'll take you all back to the Pyke."

"But, sir! The forest has been blown away and burned! There's no cover down here! If the Narmans emerge on those hilltops, they'll take out fifty Marines for every rebel we get! They'll fucking...!"

Before Pursair could say anything else, Malcolm grabbed the major around the arm and led him away from the general. When they were out of earshot, the gunnery sergeant asked, "How long you been in the Corps, sir?"

"Eleven years."

"That's plenty long enough to know that once a Samaari officer has locked his mind onto doing something mind-numbingly stupid, there ain't nothing in this galaxy anyone can do to persuade him off of it."

"But he could be leading two entire Corps of Marines into a trap!" the major argued.

Gunny Malcolm nodded. "Yep, he very well could be. Lucky for us, we have the opportunity to get the fuck out of here before the enemy springs it."

Chapter 47

An Unwelcome Reunion

The news that they had captured Kryndil's Lair was not met with much celebration in Narman's Pyke. Beta Corps had been activated and deployed to the battle site even before Kroaht's staff could return to base. When Gamma Corps began landing in the Pyke to take over for Beta, they were stunned to find the colony practically deserted.

Elia Gyanis crossed paths with a platoon of Gamma Marines while walking home from work. "Where the hell is everybody?" asked a second lieutenant.

"Kryndil's Lair," Elia told him.

"All of them?" gasped the platoon leader. "Along with the Mathusala Corps? They're concentrating two hundred thousand Marines in one spot?" Hearing their lieutenant's outburst set off a rash of stunned murmuring among his troops.

"I'm sure the generals know what they're doing," Elia assured the officer.

"If the generals knew what they were doing, maybe we'd still have an Alpha Corps!" shouted a private who had overheard her.

"Shut it!" barked the lieutenant as he ordered his Marines to continue their march.

That night, Elia went back to the enlisted club. It was the best place she could go to get a feel for what was happening beyond the colony's walls. Gyanis sat at the bar, surrounded mainly by Gamma Corps sergeants since the junior troops were busy settling in. "One hundred thousand Marines," she heard one of them gripe. "Gone. They fucking iced an entire Corps to take that hole in the ground."

"And I hear they're now packing it full of two hundred thousand more!" lamented another. "You know, our enemy's job is to bury our sorry asses! By ordering us so far underground, Kroaht's doing half their job for them!"

"Fucking Samaaris," cursed a third. "I'm done letting those stupid mother-fuckers get my people killed! I've half a mind to start putting their ignorant asses in the dirt!"

Elia's goggles were equipped with the same technology the Narman battle visors had. With little more than a few blinks of an eye, she could activate the soft-ware that color-coded the troops based on their standing in the Narman database. As long as they had their tablets on them, which they always did, she could detect where their loyalties lay. After turning on the program, nearly everyone around her was shaded in red. The armorer felt herself smile. The subversive conversation she had been eavesdropping on was between true-blue League loyalists. Patriots. People who had dedicated their lives to fighting for the Kyperion Cause. If the League had lost that group, they had lost the war. Elia Gyanis could feel that the end was near. They were on the verge of victory.

As Elia peered deeper into the room, she caught sight of a table in the back accommodating a dozen or so Marines that were shaded in green. Among them was a freshly promoted colonel who had just returned from Kryndil's Lair.

Happy to see she had such a high-ranking officer on their side, Elia nodded at the colonel when he glanced up and caught her looking at him. Tomon Pursair smiled and nodded back.

••◄►●◄►••

When I walked into the council chamber, I found Melki sitting in his chair, looking very glum. Lumuk was standing behind him and did not appear very much happier. "How bad is it?" I asked.

"It's bad," the Duvani confessed. "It's very bad. The Marines have captured Kryndil. We had a plan, Eamon. A good plan. We were going to lure the enemy into the tunnel to Xaramika and blow it, killing thousands of the enemy and sealing the path to our capital. If they have Kryndil, that doesn't really matter."

"Do you think he'll talk?"

"Everybody has their breaking point, Eamon. Even Kryndil. He will hold out for a while. He may even hold out longer than that tunnel. Eventually, he will give them what they want, though."

"What are we going to do then? Evacuate?"

Melki scoffed. "And go where?"

"Another settlement?"

The Duvani shook his head. "The Marines will have the others before they get to Xaramika."

"Then blow the tunnel like you said," I told Melki.

The alien sighed. "Well, that's our other problem. We Morghul know how to build a tunnel, Eamon. We've been digging through rock our entire existence. It takes a lot to destroy one of our creations. We need a big bomb to do something like that."

"How big?" I asked.

"As big as you can imagine."

I swallowed uncomfortably. "A Harnillium bomb?"

Melki nodded. "We've been harvesting fuel from all those freighters you captured. Naktada has been helping us. We had everything set and ready to go, but Kryndil was the only one with the device to set it off. We needed to make sure no one else blew it prematurely."

"Oh, no," I gasped.

"Oh, yes," Melki groaned. "Right now, the Marines' Mathusala Corps is fighting to get into the tunnel. Naktada is trapped behind the battle, trying to rewire the device we've created to set it off manually. If he fails, the Marines will kill him. If he succeeds...."

"He'll kill himself," I said as I collapsed into one of the council chairs.

"Eamon," Melki called to me.

"What?" I answered, fighting to keep my eyes from welling up as I realized I was about to lose someone who had been on Kanaris with me from the very beginning.

"The Mathusala Corps is no longer on the *Phoenix*."

My eyes suddenly popped wide open. "We can seize it!"

Melki smiled sadly. "I think now is our time. You need to go to Narman's Pyke."

"Okay, I'll get Soldana to...."

"Soldana's dead," Melki said.

I felt my shoulders slump. "Fine. I'll have Je'Sikka Albarn fly me there. After we take over the Wasp transports, I'll have her ferry us right to the mothership."

"I'm going with you," Akkam Lumuk said.

I pointed to Melki. "You're supposed to be protecting him."

"I am," Lumuk told me. "If we don't gain control of the *Phoenix*, we lose, and the Duvani dies. I'll do much more good there than I can here."

"Ok, I'll..."

Before I could finish my sentence, Bengin Meinhopf ran into the room, panting and looking like he was trying to decide whether to celebrate or cry. "He did it!"

"Who?" I asked.

"Naktada! He just turned night into fucking day out there!"

Elia Gyanis was outside when a new sun suddenly appeared on the horizon in the direction of Kryndil's Lair. She had seen what happened to the sky when the *Phoenix's* nukes went off, and it was nothing like this. It looked like the distant tree line itself was on fire. Though she was confident that she was witnessing death on an epic scale, she could not help but stare at it with her mouth agape. Then the shockwave hit, nearly splitting her eardrums and shattering windows all over the colony despite the explosion being hundreds of kilometers away.

When Elia got back to her feet, she sprinted to her barracks while doing the math in her head. *Alpha Corps gave us thirty-eight thousand new troops. Gamma is on station, and after what I heard at the club, I bet we can get sixty thousand of them when we're finished. Beta Corps is gone. Mathusala Corps is gone. That means here on Kanaris we have two hundred thousand troops against forty thousand loyalists. That means we outnumber them by...*

The armorer's train of thought drifted as she did the calculations.

...FIVE TO FUCKING ONE!

When Elia got to her barracks, she bounded up the stairs, taking the steps three at a time until she got to her floor. She then ran into her room, slammed the door behind her, and pulled out her special tablet.

"Come on, Tauk," she pleaded as she booted up her device. "Come on. Give me the signal. The *Phoenix* is up above us with only a hundred thousand Marines on it."

And more than half of them are ours.

The signal Elia was looking for was one I was not willing to give electronically. It was show time, and this operation was too important to leave to chance. I needed to command it myself. Piling my new platoon, including Akkam Lumuk and Haeli Deboara, into the *Niberian Hornet*, we took off and headed for the ledge leading to Narman Pyke's discharge pipe.

On the way there, we came within a hundred kilometers of Kryndil's Lair. Below us, the jungle was turning black, as if it were dying before our eyes. "What the hell...?"

"It's the radiation from the nukes," Lumuk told me. "I heard them talking about it to the Duvani. Life on Kanaris has no resistance to it. The fallout from the Lair is killing everything it touches: trees, animals, even the bugs. Kiimbana's lost all his clan now. He said he was going back home to join them in death. Our Quarakai are no more."

When we landed, I was relieved to see no water pouring out of Narman Pyke's discharge tube. We disembarked quickly and raced through the tunnel to contact Gyanis and set our uprising into motion. It was fifteen kilometers to the Pyke, and we cleared that distance in record time.

We slowed when we got beneath the colony. Turning to Akkam Lumuk, I said, "You remember this, big guy?"

Lumuk nodded. "This is where we went when we left Duum behind."

Since he had been helped by the Duvani, Lumuk seemed like a completely different person. Hearing him speak of Duum while sharing a common memory helped convince me he was still the same guy, but with a near-total personality inversion. It was all for the better, though. "You remember which way to go?"

Akkam nodded and directed an index finger a bit to our right. As he did so, a blast of automatic gunfire erupted from where he was pointing and knocked him off his feet. Then, all hell opened up on us from every direction, mowing down my troops in a lethal rain of gunfire. We never had a chance to shoot back. I threw myself on top of Haeli as I went down, making her the only one in my platoon who did not get hit. I ended up taking a round in my backside and another in my left shoulder. My battle pack took six.

When the firing stopped, the lights went on. Major Izo Kuusip was standing above me. Beside him was Gunny Malcolm, a half dozen Killbillies, and Deena Vulk.

"Aaaaw! Look at that! Tauk was trying to protect another ladyfriend of his!" Vulk taunted me as she rolled me off of my girl. Pulling a pistol off her belt, the red-eyed troll aimed it at Haeli's head and said, "I can't believe I get to kill another one of your little babes!"

"Put it away!" ordered Nala Biragor. I had not seen her since the Satapadaya Front, but I was relieved to remember that she was one of our most trusted sources of information. "We need to interrogate the survivors first! You can play with them later!"

"If you want to question me, you better get a medic over here!" I heard Black Francis say. "I'm losing a lot of blood!" He was leaning back against a stanchion, applying pressure to the wound in his leg.

As I was trying to make sense of what happened, Gunny Malcolm leaned down beside me. He had finally gotten rid of the patch that covered his missing eye socket and had a permanent cover surgically attached to his face. "After you vaporized Kryndil's Lair, I figured you'd come back here to seize Narman's Pyke. It's the only place you can commandeer the Wasp transports you need to bring you to the mothership. Did you forget that I knew about this place, too?"

"I'm actually kind of surprised you're alive, Gunny. I figured you'd overdose in the bush with all that Demon Root I gave you."

Malcolm smiled. "I ain't gonna lie. I threw myself one hell of a party out there. Eventually, I had to get back to work, though."

I nodded. "You sure did, didn't you? Congratulations on a successful mission. You must be pretty happy with yourself."

Gunny Malcolm shrugged. "It's just a job. My last job, actually. I'm retiring."

"To do what?"

"Other than dull my senses with Killbilly dope? I have no idea." Gunny Malcolm reached down and took my hand, shaking it softly. "I'm sorry my last mission had to be you. Good luck, Tauk."

As Gunny Malcolm turned away, he handed his rifle to one of the Section Kommandos and marched back into the darkness. His Killbillies followed him.

Chapter 48

AGONY

Years before, Gori Dravidas, the Butcher of Deraghun, gained the advantage during my blooding ceremony. He had me dead to rights, dagger in hand, ready to slit my throat. I was totally at his mercy and certain the remainder of my life was measured in seconds. Yet, I was not afraid. Not even a little bit. I was angry, frustrated, and full of hatred, utterly unconcerned about my imminent death.

This time was different. I was terrified. Like the other survivors of Malcolm's ambush, I was tied to a chair in one of the abandoned, windowless offices deep in the bowels of Narman Pyke's sanitation complex. A Section 615 Kommando stood guard outside our door while Deena Vulk was inside with me.

For the first moments of my interrogation, Vulk said nothing. She just stared at me while she occupied herself by twirling my dagger up into the air and catching it by the blade. She stopped when Akkam Lumuk started screaming. The offices were sealed with heavy iron doors, but Lumuk's cries easily penetrated the barrier. Letting a smile creep across her face, Deena asked, "Do you hear that, Tauk? Isn't that your big boy? I knew he was going to go first. I heard he's a real pansy."

Next to go were a couple of my Narman riflemen. We had not been together very long, and I was ashamed to realize that I had not learned their names before I got them killed. Black Francis broke next, causing Vulk to laugh as she started waving her fingers in the air like she was conducting an orchestra. She did not stop until Haeli joined in on the chorus. "Ahhh," sighed Vulk. "I was wondering when we'd hear the soprano. You know, it usually is the women who hold out the longest. Because of childbirth, we generally have a higher pain tolerance."

Deena grabbed a chair from behind the desk and slid it over directly in front of me. "How high is your pain tolerance, Tauk?"

I said nothing. I wanted to conserve my energy.

Vulk giggled at my silence. "Oh? You seriously think you'll be able to keep your mouth shut through this? Really? That's so cute."

Dropping the dagger so it stuck in the floor, the disfigured agent pulled several nylon straps from off the desktop and expertly bound my fingers to the arm of my chair so that only the tips were showing. She then picked up the dagger and stuck the point of the blade just beneath the nail. She had barely started and already hurt me enough for my eyes to clench closed. "You ready for this, Tauk?"

I shook my head. "No! No! Please! Don't! AAAAYYYEEEEEEIIIIII!!!!"

Vulk meticulously pushed the blade through the quick, slowly twisting the knife all the way through until it nearly reached the digit's first knuckle. I screamed harder and longer than I ever had before, to the point I nearly passed out from hyperventilating. Deena was an expert in inflicting agony, however, so she knew how to keep me conscious. She eased off just as she suspected I might be on the verge of blacking out.

"Shhhhh," she told me. "Breathe, Eamon. Breathe. I need you to stay with me."

"YOU FUCKING WHORE!" I screamed at her, shooting snot out of my nose. "I SHOULD'VE FUCKING KILLED YOU WHEN I HAD THE CHANCE!"

Vulk shrugged. "It wouldn't have made any difference. It'd just be somebody else in here doing this stuff to you. The one you really should've killed was Malcolm. Had it not been for him, nobody would've known about that little tunnel you were trying to sneak through."

"Yeah, I should've fucking...AAAAAAAUUUGHHHH!!!"

The agent twisted the blade to slice the nail away from the skin at its sides. That certainly hurt, but all things considered, it was the least painful of all the things Vulk was doing to me. What was really excruciating was when she went to work on the back of the nail.

When the nail finally popped off, it was something of a relief. The respite did not last long, though. Before I could catch my breath, Vulk took the blade's tip and began "tickling" the raw nerves running along the surface of the fleshy bed.

That was agony every bit as horrific as when she first started working on me. The pain never dulled.

"If you know what you're doing," Deena said to me, "you can work a single finger for hours. You just have to be careful not to sever any nerves."

As I shrieked and shrieked and shrieked, I wondered what they were doing to Akkam Lumuk. He was screaming so loud that he sometimes drowned me out. I only heard the others on the rare occasions when Akkam and I simultaneously paused to catch our breaths.

An eternity later, when Vulk was preparing to turn her attention to my third nail, I tried to buy a pause. "You...you...you...." I sobbed. "...you're supposed to ask questions during an interrogation."

Vulk laughed. "You think this is an interrogation? Honey, this is just my way of thanking you for turning me over to Kryndil. I'll leave the inquisitors a few toes and maybe your balls to work on...."

A commotion suddenly erupted in one of the other offices. It sounded like a brawl had broken out, and then I heard a woman try to scream for help before getting abruptly cut off. For several moments afterward, the cries of the prisoners were drowned out by guards pounding on a locked steel door, demanding to be let inside. Then, I heard the panel slide open just before a quick exchange of gunfire. Vulk pulled her pistol and aimed it at our office's only exit.

"Vulk!" called a woman from the hall outside. "Open up! It's Agent Biragor! I need help. It's over!"

Vulk pressed a code into the keypad near the entrance, allowing the door to retract into the wall and Biragor to stumble inside. Her mouth was split open, her left eye was already blackening and blood was pouring out of her nose. "The big guy...Lumuk...he...he...he broke one of the arms off his chair and attacked me. He killed a couple of guards. I got him, though. I...."

Vulk ran to look out into the hallway. While her back was to the Section 615 agent, Biragor lifted her pistol and shot Deena in the base of her spine, dropping her to the deck. Nala then stumbled toward the exit and threw herself against the wall to take aim down the passageway. "I tried to save him," Biragor told me. "but he attacked me first before I could explain. He killed his inquisitor and was about to finish me off when...when...I'm so sorry, Tauk. I shot him. I had no choice."

"You killed Lumuk?" I sobbed. "Goddammit! He never hurt anybody that...."

Biragor squeezed off a couple of rounds at a pair of guards rushing into the hall. She then killed Major Kuusip as he emerged from Black Francis's interrogation. "I'm working with Elia Gyanis. I'm on your side."

Grabbing the knife Vulk had dropped on the floor, Biragor cut one of my arms free before handing me the blade to slice through the rest of my restraints. "Get Black Francis. I'll get your girlfriend."

I had no idea where Black Francis was, so I walked into the first office I found with an open door. It was Lumuk's room. My giant was sprawled out on the floor in a pool of blood, his lifeless eyes staring at the ceiling. "Oh, Lumuk!" I sobbed. "I'm sorry!"

"Grieve later!" Biragor snapped as she typed in a master override code into the keypad outside the room Haeli was in. When it slid open, she blew away an inquisitor despite him lying in ambush for her. "You have to leave before reinforcements arrive!"

"I've got a couple of other...!"

"No! You don't!" Biragor's eyes were darting wildly about as she tried to focus. Lumuk had hurt her badly. "They're gone! They killed the other two."

"Then I've got to get to Elia!" I exclaimed. "I have to give her the orders to...."

"You can't!" Biragor screamed at me, her voice conveying her frustration. "You can't get past the guards all over the main level! The only chance you have is to haul ass back the way you came!"

"But...!"

"Am I not clear?!? You'll be captured if you try anything but escaping! If you have something to say to Elia, tell me and I'll relay it to her!"

"She'll only take directions from me!" I yelled.

"Then we're fucked! This is the end of the line, and we're all doomed!"

As I broke Black Francis free, two more guards came down the steps, only to be capped by Biragor. She was right. We were out of time. Running into the other office to free Haeli, I said, "We need to initiate the uprising here and on the mothership! Elia needs to embed the activation message on the uplink!"

Biragor's legs went wobbly, and she collapsed onto her backside. Her concussion was getting the better of her, and I could tell she was losing consciousness.

She shook her head at me. "She can't. The Marines know that they're riddled with moles. They know they're weak and can't survive an uprising. They cut off electronic communication with Kanaris."

"Oh, shit!" I exclaimed. "Oh shit! How are they communicating then?!?"

"If I have to pass something up the chain..." Biragor paused to collect her train of thought. "...I have to get a ride to the Phoenix and brief them in person."

"Are you going up there soon?"

The agent turned her head to look at all the dead bodies littering the hallway. "I'm pretty sure Commandant Taillur is going to want to know all about this shit show."

Before Biragor's lights went out, I grabbed her by the collar and shook her awake. "Get the activation message from Gyanis and make sure it gets sent out across the entire network up there! Tell Elia I told her to give it to you! Our code word is 'Cupid!' Do you understand me?"

"Uh huh," Biragor said as her eyes started to close.

"Come on, Eamon," Black Francis said as he limped over to me. "We gotta go."

"Give me a second...."

"We don't have a second!" Haeli snapped. "We have to get moving!"

I shook Biragor awake again. "Hey!" I shouted at her. "Hey! What's the password!"

"Huh?" Biragor asked.

"The password! What is it?"

The agent's eyes fell closed again as more blood began rushing from her nostrils. "Cupid," she groaned. "It's fucking Cupid."

As Biragor faded away, Deena Vulk crawled out of the room she had tortured me in. She was only using her arms. Her limp legs dragged behind her. "Help!" she gasped. She tried to scream, but the best she could muster was a coarse whisper. I would have loved to have done to her what she had to me, but it would have been a futile exercise, considering the woman was incapable of feeling pain.

Even though I knew Deena Vulk hardly registered it, I still departed Narman's Pyke a happier man for having shot her through the head before I left.

●●–◈–●–◈–●●

Agent Biragor afforded us a considerable head start, but it was barely enough. I had been wounded in the buttocks, while Black Francis had sustained a fairly serious injury to one of his legs. Even in our compromised states, we had to drag Francis through fifteen kilometers of drainage pipe while he did his best to help us by hopping on one foot. When we were on the home stretch, less than a kilometer from the ledge, we detected a squad of Marines closing in on our six.

Reaching for the rifle slung across my back, I turned to Haeli and said, "Get Francis outside! I'll hold them off."

"Look at me!" Haeli snapped back. "I'm half his size! I can't carry him by myself!"

"Drop me here!" Francis pled. "Give me your weapons and I'll stop them! I'm just slowing you down anyway!"

Haeli let go of Francis's arm and unslung her weapon. "Go on, Eamon! Get him out of here! I'll watch our backs! Nobody needs to get left behind!"

While Francis and I struggled to get each other out of the pipe, Haeli walked backward behind us with her rifle pointed at our rear. As slow as Francis and I were, Haeli was even slower, and the distance between us kept increasing. "Goddammit, Haeli!" I whispered, trying to be loud enough for her to hear me but not so loud that I gave away our position. "Keep up!"

Haeli would not answer me. Nor would she pick up her pace. Frustrated, I turned my head to call out to her again, only to be stopped by Francis. "Mission, Eamon. Mission. We have to get out of here and send out our distress beacon, or we're all dead."

I let out a long string of curse words and started limping even faster than I already was. Francis was right. We had an insurrection to run. As much as it hurt me, I could not let my relationship with Haeli jeopardize it more than it already was.

A few minutes later, the tunnel erupted with the sounds of automatic gunfire — a lot of it. I craned around to see what was happening, but the fighting was too far away to make out anything but muzzle flashes. When the shots died down, the racket of combat was replaced by the screams of wounded men. Then, there were reports of single rounds being fired to silence the shriekers one by one. "Haeli!" I called out.

Black Francis slapped me across the face. "Shut the fuck up! What are you doing?!? Keep walking, Eamon! Remember the mission!"

A couple of minutes later, Haeli caught up to us. "Go, goddammit!" she said as she pushed me forward. "Go!"

Hearing more voices running our way from behind, I told Haeli, "You didn't get them all!"

"Not yet," she said, just before I heard several loud explosions erupt in the distance. Shortly afterward, a rush of warm air and dust blew past us, followed by the sound of the ceiling caving in beyond our backs.

"There," Haeli told me. "Now I got them all." Breaking into a smile, she added, "With their own grenades!"

Francis looked at me in disbelief. "Eamon, I think she's a keeper."

"Tauk!" I heard someone call out from the opposite direction. "Is that you?!?"

I recognized the voice as one of the *Hornet's* sentries, Jonas Braiqer. "Yes! It's me!"

Before I knew it, we were surrounded by Je'Sikka Albarn's security contingent.

"We figured you were in trouble," Braiqer said as he and his comrades started throwing us over their shoulders to run us out of danger. "We detected a trio of Haiv fighters racing to your extraction point. We took 'em out, but we're betting we'll soon have to deal with a lot more if we don't skedaddle the hell out of here!"

"Yeah," I said as I was spirited toward daylight. "I think it's safe to say we've worn out our welcome in Narman's Pyke."

•●⬗●⬗●•

Chapter 49

THE FALL

When Elia Gyanis opened the door to her barracks room, Nala Biragor collapsed into her arms. She was not wearing the black fatigues she was typically clad in but a set of soaking-wet hospital pajamas. Even without the medical garb, Elia could see the woman was hurt. The entire left side of her face was one big bruise, and her eye was swollen shut. As soon as Elia laid the agent on her rack, Nala told her, "We captured Eamon Tauk. He was trying to see you."

"WHAT?!?" Elia screamed as she started to shake.

"It's okay," Biragor mumbled. "I helped them escape. They got away. He told me to tell you it's go time."

"Oh god," Elia said as she placed her hand over her mouth. "Now?"

Biragor nodded weakly. "Now."

Elia's knees went weak. She knew this was coming, but now that it was here, everything suddenly became very overwhelming. She did not know where to begin. Biragor could see Gyanis starting to fall apart. "What are you doing? What's our first step?"

"I-I-I have to get to th-th-the messaging center. It's important that everything begins simultaneously. If Narman's Pyke mutinies, they'll destroy us from orbit. If the Phoenix goes first, the Pyke could move against us before we move against them! We...."

Biragor shook her head. "The command severed all electronic communications between the mothership and Narman's Pyke. They know they have mutineers, but they're in denial about the scale of it. They're more worried about saboteurs.

I'll have to take it up there myself when I brief Taillur on Tauk's escape."

Elia's jaw dropped open. She trusted Biragor mainly because the agent had never asked anything of her. Biragor always pumped information her way and never requested any back in return. The message that Gyanis had to transmit held the identity of every recipient in its distribution file. Biragor was not only asking to help deliver a message; she was asking for the entire operation to be placed in her hands.

"I-I'm the only person who's supposed to handle this message."

Biragor nodded. "I know. But now you're going to need help."

Elia shook her head. "I need to clear this with Tauk."

"Cupid," Biragor told her.

"What?"

"Cupid," the agent repeated. "Your code word. It's Cupid."

A smile crept across Elia's face as she opened up her footlocker, retrieved a small device, and plugged it into Biragor's tablet. As she downloaded the activation message, she said, "We got this, don't we?"

"We sure do," Biragor said as she smiled back. "You have any idea what we're going to do when this is all over."

"Nope," Elia replied. "I only know what we're not going to do."

Biragor lifted an eyebrow. "What's that?"

"Evil."

Two days later, the Section 615 agent stepped off a Wasp transport and marched aboard the *Nebulean Phoenix*. She was greeted by Commandant Taillur personally. Looking over his subordinate's injuries, he asked, "You sure you're well enough to travel, Nala?"

Biragor shook her head. "I thought the Gs we pulled lifting off were going to kill me."

"I imagine. I'm glad you're here. They tell me you have good news, but I'm struggling to guess what that could be. I understand you had Eamon Tauk in your custody, but he got away."

Biragor nodded. "Yes, sir. That's correct."

"I also heard that Kryndil died while under interrogation. Is that true?"

"That's correct, sir."

"And did that son-of-a-bitch tell you the location of Xaramika before his heart exploded?"

Biragor shook her head.

"Okay, we lost three hundred thousand troops at Kryndil's Lair. All we have to show for it is a massive hole in the ground and an entire ecosystem rotting away from radiation exposure. Our entire Harnillium mining industry has collapsed, and though we had one of the leaders of the Narman insurgency in our custody, we somehow let him slip through our fingers. What do you have that could possibly be construed as good news?"

Biragor pulled her tablet from a cargo pocket and placed it into Taillur's hand. "I have the name of every turncoat hunkering in our ranks, waiting for the signal to rise up and kill us in our sleep."

Taillur looked at the tablet in disbelief. "What? How?"

"I was at the front when the Satapadaya rising occurred. I learned then that the scale of our infiltration problem far exceeded the resources we had to expose them. Even if I had a success rate twice what you would consider a win, I would have hardly even put a dent in it. Even if I captured the people who curated all the names of our traitors, it still wouldn't help us. They could delete the database, destroy it, or make us chase our tails by leading us to one full of false data. In order to get the entire thing and keep it reliable, I had to join them, sir. I had to gain the trust of one of theirs."

"You infiltrated the infiltrators?!?" Taillur gasped.

Biragor shrugged. "It wasn't all that hard. We're dealing with Marines, sir, not spies. My contact was stuck in the Pyke, all by herself, with little espionage experience, backup, or support. She was vulnerable, and I was able to slip into the void she needed filled. I protected her, earned her trust, and became above reproach after I let Tauk go."

The color rushed into the Commandant's face. "You let Tauk go?!?"

Biragor grinned. "I did. It didn't matter. I knew where he was going."

"What?!? Where?"

"He's going to Xaramika."

"And you know where that is?"

"I do."

"But I thought Kryndil died before...."

"He did, but I didn't need him. When Tauk liberated the Harnillium mines, they encountered a problem at Anga-Iskalei. The inmates generally hijacked freighters from the mines to make their escape, but at Anga-Iskalei, they ran into some sort of complication and had to send a vessel from Xaramika to bail them out. As luck would have it, our Marines managed to shoot it down. It crash-landed against the mine and burned, but the navigation recorder was intact. We had a record of everywhere that Warp Haug had been and where it had been hiding since it was stolen from Razbauten. Sir, we know where the fucking Morghul live."

●•⬦⬤⬦•●

"Unbelievable," General Kroaht said as he bent back into the cushions of his couch. "That woman's a bloody hero."

Commandant Taillur nodded as one of the general's mechanical servants poured more whisky into his glass. "Yes, she is."

"When all this is over, Biragor's going to end up being your boss."

Taillur grinned. "Yes, sir."

Kroaht leaned forward and rested his forearms on his knees. "I'm not exaggerating, Nilton."

"I know you're not."

"We're going to destroy this mutiny before it even gets started, take Xaramika, and exert our full control over that planet only to come out of it still looking like chumps who had their asses saved by a junior 615 agent."

"We will if Biragor controls the narrative, General."

Kroaht cast his gaze at the deck. "You think she'd be open to reporting all this shit from our perspective?"

Taillur sighed. "She'd tell you she would be if you asked her. Nala Biragor is every bit as ambitious as she is smart, though. Her official report, which will not be submitted before she's free of our influence, will emphasize all this command's shortcomings and highlight everything she did to save us from ourselves."

"So, after three hundred thousand dead Marines, my legacy will still end up mud."

"Very few leaders send that many troops to their deaths and have history remember them fondly, General. You're the first one to confront a technologically advanced alien race, however. If not for Biragor, we could spin this in a much more flattering direction."

"Is there anything we can do about her?"

Taillur took another drink of liquor and smacked his lips. "Is there anything in particular that you're suggesting, General?"

"Do you want me to come right out and say it?"

The commandant laughed. "Of course I do! There's nothing I enjoy more than watching a man of mine come to terms with his dark side."

"Could you kill her?"

"I could. It's not like I haven't done it before."

Kroaht's face turned red as he grew angry at Taillur's little games. "Will you kill her?"

Taillur finished his drink and set it on the end table. "That depends. What are you going to do for me?"

The general smiled and began undoing the front of his pants.

The commandant laughed. "You've got it backward, Druze. You're the one asking *me* for a favor."

Chapter 50

A Final Farewell

Elia Gyanis thought that it would be Agent Biragor knocking on her door. When she answered it, however, the fist of a burly Section Kommando sailed through the opening and smashed her in the jaw. The sergeant was sent staggering backward onto her bunk while a couple of other brutes pounced on the dazed armorer. While Elia struggled to come to terms with what was happening, Taillur's goons pulled her arms behind her back and slapped restraints on them. Gyanis was then yanked to her feet by her hair and thrown into the hallway. She was not alone. All around her, doors were being kicked in while her comrades were dragged from their bunks, shackled, and, if they resisted, summarily executed.

On Elia's floor, more armorers than not were taken into custody and herded into the stairwell. Their numbers only grew as they descended toward ground level. When they were outside, they joined the throng of Marines that had been seized at the barracks. Then they mixed with the thousands of convict laborers being forced toward the landing pads, where a fleet of Wasp troop transports was standing by to spirit them off Kanaris and place them in cells aboard the *Nebulean Phoenix*.

At one point during their chaotic exodus, Elia found herself beside the colonel she spotted at the enlisted club a few days before. "What do you think they're going to do with us?" she asked him.

"If we're lucky," Pursair told her, "they'll take us aloft and jettison us into space *en masse*."

"And if we're not?"

"They'll hold us in the cargo bay of the mothership until they gain control over the Morghul, then use us to replace the Portunese they lost when they reopen the Harnillium mines."

It felt like an earthquake. We were all recovering in Xaramika's medical facility when the entire settlement shook. The lights flickered, the hum of the ventilation system went suddenly silent, and the corpsmen who were tending us looked at each other in fear. They had no idea what had just happened, but they knew it wasn't good. Half an hour later, a Narman soldier ran into our bay, calling my name.

"Here!" I shouted back at her. "Eamon Tauk is over here!"

The woman ran over to me and saluted. "Sir, I know you're hurt, but I've been instructed to help you and Ms. Deboara to the council chamber. The Duvani has called an urgent meeting."

"What happened?" I asked, sitting straight up in my bed.

"The Marines nuked our hangar bay, sir. It's gone."

"Oh my god!" cried Haeli. "Je'Sikka!"

Haeli and I were the last two to walk into the Council Chamber. Melki was pacing around the room with his hands behind his back. The others were conferring among themselves. When we arrived, no one bothered to call order. The Duvani just turned to everyone and declared, "It's over."

"W-w-wa-what?" I gasped.

"The Marines know where we are, Eamon."

"So?" I argued. "We're going to rise up and...."

"No, we're not," Bengin Meinhopf declared. "The bastards sent me a copy of your activation order, Tauk. With the entire distribution on it. They got hold of it before it went live and rounded up all your assets, both in Narman's Pyke and on the mothership."

I felt my hands starting to shake. "H-h-how?"

Governor Ghona shrugged. "It doesn't matter. It only matters that it's over. Bengin confirmed that our infiltrators have been identified and sent off-planet. Narman's Pyke is practically a ghost town right now."

I started pacing as I tried to rationalize what was going on. Rubbing my temples was not helping me think any clearer. "Okay, admittedly, this is a setback."

"It's more than a setback, Eamon," Meinhopf told me. "It's the end."

"It's not over!" I shouted at the intelligence chief. "We can still fight them! Do here what we did at Kryndil's Lair! If they rounded up all our assets, they'll be coming at us with no more than eighty-thousand troops! After all the deserters we absorbed before we vaporized the Mathusala Corps, we're practically even now! They don't have the three-to-one ratio that...."

Melki sighed. "The *Admiral Phranqen* is now on station with a half million fresh troops, Marines we have not even begun to approach. Eamon, we did not call you here to ask your counsel. We called you here to inform you of our decision. We're going to surrender."

"You're going to what?!?" I exclaimed. "They're going to kill you, Melki! All of you!"

"Not if we have something to offer them," Melki said. "The League will soon be confronted by a threat unlike anything they have ever faced. We know the Morghul Empire far more than anyone else they have access to. If we help them against the Empire, they'll...."

"...fucking slaughter you slowly the minute they've exhausted whatever use they can get out of you."

"It's the only choice we have," Melki pled.

"What about my people?" Haeli asked the Duvani. "What do you think is going to happen to them? I'll tell you what their fate is! They'll be rounded up and sent back into those camps to pull Harnillium out of the ground!"

Melki's shoulders slumped. "I won't let that happen, Haeli. I need you to trust me."

"Trust you?!?" Haeli gasped. "Trust you?!? How can you expect me to trust somebody who trusts them?!?"

"Please listen to me," Melki begged as he dropped to his knees before us. "Duvanis are ancient beings. Timeless. This one has survived not years, not decades, not centuries, but millennia! Ages, even! As hopeless as all this seems, I can promise you that this Duvani will figure a way out of it. He always does."

I sighed in frustration. "You might believe your own bullshit, Melki, but don't expect me to." With that, I turned on my heel to walk out of the chamber. Haeli turned to leave with me.

"You can't go, Eamon."

"The hell I can't!"

Calling to the praetorians in the darkness behind him, Melki shouted, "Guards! Seize him!"

Before I could even turn around to face them, one of the bastards hit me with a bolt of energy that ripped through my muscles, causing them all to seize up and sending me crashing onto the deck.

As my body convulsed upon the floor, I wanted to spit something at Melki that would make him realize how unforgivable his betrayal was. I longed for him to know that he was now every bit the enemy to me that the League was and that if I ever earned my freedom back, I would hunt him down and deal with him without mercy. I would avenge not only what would eventually become of me but all the Portunese he delivered back into the grasp of the Marines.

Unfortunately, the electricity they pumped into my body scrambled my brains a bit. The best I could come up with was, "You dick!"

When Commandant Taillur stumbled into Kroaht's suite aboard the *Nebulean Phoenix*, the general had difficulty determining if his lover was injured or intoxicated. Blood was streaming from his nose, but he reeked of stale brandy. The Marine commander eventually decided the man was probably a little bit of both. "What happened to you?"

Taillur grinned. "Nala fought back. The bitch is tough. She knocked the shit out of me."

"Did you do it, though?"

"Of course I did it. If I hadn't, she'd be standing here in front of you instead of me."

"What about the other thing?" the general asked.

"The Mogs? They're surrendering. We've got Wasp dropships transporting them all to Narman's Pyke as we speak. From there, we're bringing them all up here."

"To the *Phoenix*?" Kroaht asked. "Who gave that order?"

"I did. On your authority, of course."

"Why would you bring them here?"

Taillur staggered to the window overlooking the surface of Kanaris. In the space between the planet and its ringed moon of Gaiomedi was another dreadnought, the *Admiral Phranqen*. "I didn't figure you'd want to make General Sqaar's life any easier by leaving all this free labor behind. I also didn't want him using them to harm you."

"Harm me? How?"

"The video of all that horrible shit that went down in Razbauten is still generating rage and unrest back home, Druze. Sooner or later, the League's going to have to reckon with it. They're going to need to hold someone accountable. You know General Sqaar would love to collect all kinds of testimony from those poor Portunese souls and use it to make you the face of what went on down there. As long as we have control of those prisoners, though, we control the narrative."

Kroaht smiled at his lover. "I can't tell you how happy I am to have somebody around me who can think that far ahead. How can I ever repay you?"

Taillur took the general by the hand and led him toward his sleeping quarters. "I have something in mind."

I could not believe my eyes. As the Marines were pushing me off the dropship at Narman's Pyke, I was relieved beyond belief to see a familiar face in the crowd. "Albarn!" I screamed. "Je'Sikka!"

"Tauk!" my pilot shouted back.

A nearby Marine struck me in the back of the head with the butt of his rifle. "Shut the fuck up!"

"Okay. Okay," I said as I struggled to get up. "It won't happen again."

Albarn was not in restraints and, being as short as she was, managed to make her way through the crowd without attracting the guards' attention. Surprisingly, Haeli got to me at almost the same time to help me get back to my feet. Luckily, she had the presence of mind to keep her voice down. "Je'Sikka! We thought you were dead!"

Albarn shook her head. "I was in Xaramika when the nuke hit the hangar cavern. Everybody was. After the Marines nuked Kryndil's Lair, the Duvani wanted everyone kept underground unless preparing for a mission. Eamon, what do you think they're going to do to us?"

Looking up and seeing scores of Killbillies lining the path to our staging area, smacking their lips at all the fresh meat being paraded past them, I said, "The unspeakable."

I spotted Gunny Malcolm among the Qilkorian Death Squad men. Then he spotted me. Breaking off from his squad of killers, he pushed through the sea of Portunese to get to us. "What do you want?" I asked him.

"Some fucking rest, you miserable son-of-a-bitch!" Malcolm snapped at me. "Yet every time you get away, they make me go looking for you. This time, I ain't leaving your side until I'm sure you're on that bird to the mothership!"

When we were captured by Malcolm beneath Narman's Pyke, Haeli's eyes had been locked on the pistol Deena Vulk held pointed at her forehead. Without that distraction hanging over her, she was now able to get a good look at the old gunnery sergeant. As a spark of recognition flashed across her face, she scowled at Malcolm and said, "I think I know you."

"Oh yeah?" Malcolm asked. "From where?"

"Kusan Plaat."

Gunny Malcolm suddenly went white, stopping in his tracks. The three of us stopped with him. Looking at Haeli, he said, "You don't look old enough to remember Kusan Plaat."

"Do you think that's something someone could possibly forget?"

Malcolm swallowed hard. "I suppose not. I've been pumping shit into my veins for years trying to erase those memories."

"Obviously, you haven't been pumping enough of it, you son-of-a-bitch! Try a double dose next time! Maybe a triple dose! That woman was my aunt!"

"Which one?" Gunny winced as soon as the question slipped out of his mouth. He was not trying to be flippant. He was genuinely curious about who he was being confronted about.

Haeli glared at him in revulsion. "They were all somebody's aunt! Or mother! Or wife! Or sister! Or...."

Gunny placed his face in his hands, reeling as visions of what he had done in the village once again flooded his memory. He no longer seemed to be in Narman's Pyke. He was back on Portuna. He had to get out of there. "Fuck it," he said to me. "There's no way you're getting out of this one, Tauk. The Marines'll make sure you make your flight. Believe it or not, I'm sorry things worked out like this. In some sort of twisted way, I was actually kind of rooting for you."

"Go choke, you fucking monster!" Haeli snarled. "Do the right thing for once in your life! Go die, you piece of shit!"

Malcolm retreated to the sidelines under a barrage of venom spit from the mouth of Haeli Deboara. I watched him walk up to a ghastly-looking Killbilly wearing a bandolier fashioned from tattooed human skin. It was a Qilkorian I had seen once before, a lifetime ago, back in Camp Taarlak. I watched as the gunnery sergeant pulled out his tablet to transfer a sizeable amount of credits to the freak and received a big bag of brown powder in return.

It looked big enough for several of the triple doses Haeli had recommended to him.

••‹•›‐●‐‹•›‐••

Chapter 51

A Toast of Death

With Kanaris now pacified and emptied of malcontents, General Kroaht had a reason to celebrate. So did the eighty-thousand loyalist Marines he still had under his command. With their mission now accomplished, they were going home. Whatever came next was not their problem anymore. It was the concern of General Sqaar and the troops aboard the *Admiral Phranqen*.

On the *Nebulean Phoenix's* departure day, a jailorbot opened my cell door and ordered me to my feet. "Prisoner 8425603," it announced in its coarse, electronic voice. "You've been summoned by General Kroaht. Produce your hands for restraints."

There was no resisting a Sikario-Class jailorbot. You could either do what it told you to, or it would shackle you by force, and likely rip your arms out of socket in the process. I showed it my wrists and allowed it to activate a set of magnetic cuffs around them.

As I marched down the corridor, I passed Black Francis, who was being paraded in the opposite direction, surrounded by more than a dozen mechanical guards. I was relieved to see him. I had not laid eyes on the man since we were in Xaramika and, up until that point, had no idea if he was alive or dead. "What did you do to earn such an entourage?" I called out to him.

"Silence," my jailorbot ordered. "Communication between stockade inmates is unauthorized as per Article 678906."

Violating that specific article, Francis smiled at me and answered, "Apparently, General Kroaht thinks I'm a very dangerous man." When he finished speaking, the gunnery sergeant's guards issued him the same warning I had previously received.

A quarter kilometer down the corridor, another robot led Melki into step right beside me. I shot him a look of furious contempt and continued walking in silence. A little while later, we were joined by Governor Ghona. Then Bengin Meinhopf. Then Leila Hyfer. Finally, as we neared the end of the cell bloc, Haeli Deboara joined our procession. Careful not to make any actual sound, I looked at Haeli and mouthed the words, "Francis is alive."

It did not matter. I got a second warning from my robotic escort about communicating with prisoners. It assured me that a third offense would have consequences.

After exiting the stockade, we were herded onto a shuttle that transported us forward, toward the bow. We began to slow as we approached the launch bay, where it appeared nearly all eighty thousand of General Kroaht's surviving Marines were assembled to hear him speak. I spotted the commander through the window near the rear of his bridge, but the troops below were watching a five-story-tall hologram of him being projected above them. Our shuttle was soundproof, so I could not hear what he said, but I could see by the man's waving fists that he was delivering a very bombastic performance.

When the shuttle came to a stop, we were wrenched from our seats by a half-dozen belligerent Marines and manhandled onto the bridge. After we were thrown to the deck at the commander's feet, General Kroaht paused his speech to smile menacingly at us. "And here they are!" he laughed as he strolled over and grabbed Melki by the throat. He then dragged the alien to the speaking platform and tossed him onto it.

"Behold!" Kroaht shouted to his troops as the hologram outside now showed the red-eyed Duvani. "This is the face of our enemy! This is what we're up against, Marines! They don't look so fearsome now, do they? The truth was, they never were! These puny little pug-faced aliens were barely even a factor in the fight for Kanaris! Your real enemy was never extra-terrestrial in nature! It was treason!"

General Kroaht shoved Melki off the projection platform, knocking him face-down onto the deck while the Marines in the debarkation bay cheered. He then dragged me up to the stage so I could take the Morghul's place. "This is your true enemy! This is the real threat to our way of life! This is the man who has sworn to rob you of your power, your riches, your rightful place in the Samaari pecking order!"

General Kroaht was the highest-ranking officer aboard the Nebulean Phoenix, but Admiral Stiiger was a close second. While Kroaht was responsible for the mission, Stiiger was in command of the itself. When Kroaht mentioned the Samaari pecking order, the general caught Stiiger's attention. The Navy man began paying closer attention to his counterpart's speech.

"Yes! This is the man who wants to tear down everything we've built! He wants to stop us from looting far-flung places full of ungrateful, subhuman degenerates like Portuna and Terrakand! He wants our industry to actually pay for the labor it uses to produce its wares! He wants to stop you from molesting your convicts! Deprive you of your sex slaves!"

While the Marines below began looking at one another quizzically, Admiral Stiiger leapt to his feet and shouted, "Kroaht! Have you lost your fucking mind?"

Spinning to face his counterpart, the general flashed him a maniacal smile. "As a matter of fact, Michal, yes! I have! And I mean that quite literally!" Turning to the duty engineer, Kroaht then said, "Launch Operation Zero Fury."

Stunned, I turned my back on the aft window to face the commander. "Zero WHAT?!?"

Before Kroaht could answer, the energy field separating the Marines from space dissipated, flooding the debarkation bay with a lethal vacuum. Many were sucked out into the void, while those who managed to stay aboard writhed on the ground in agony as their blood started to boil.

Stiiger sprinted to the engineering console, but the captain manning it drew his sidearm and shot the admiral through the head before he reached it. Our Marine escorts then raised their rifles and executed the two other duty officers whose loyalties remained faithful to the League.

Shifting his attention to the weapons officer, Kroaht barked, "Initiate Phase Two!"

With the flip of a switch, a barrage of nuclear anti-ship missiles was sent hurtling at the *Admiral Phranqen*. The dreadnought, and the half million Marines she carried, was blown to pieces and sent diving into the Kanarisian atmosphere before she even knew she was under attack.

With the *Phranqen* destroyed, the general patted the weapons officer on the shoulder. "They never saw it coming." Directing his attention back to me, Kroaht said, "When I was still Biragor, I scrubbed the Navy's names off our infiltrator list. They remained above suspicion. I then did what I could to get Narman sympathizers on bridge duty before I set Zero Fury into motion. It worked like a charm, didn't it?"

I was gobsmacked. "What do you mean by, 'When I was Biragor?'"

Ignoring my question, Kroaht returned to the command console and picked up a microphone. "Black Francis, give me a status report."

"Armory is secure and the prisoners are released. We have control of all weapons and the engine room. If you have the bridge, it's safe to assume the ship is now completely under our control."

"Eamon," I heard Melki call to me. He was still lying on the floor. "I have a confession to make. I'm not the Duvani. I never was."

Melki rolled over and pointed his chin at General Kroaht. "I'm pretty sure he is."

Kroaht smiled at me and nodded. "For the moment. At least, I'm the Duvani until I can find a new body to slip into."

I was reeling, but everything started coming together. "You wanted to see the universe through Akkam's eyes. You possessed him?"

Kroaht shook his head. "No, sir. I let him become me."

"I...you...what?"

The general laughed. "It's complicated to explain, sir. A Duvani doesn't possess its hosts. It's absorbed by them. When that happens, they do not become the Duvani, but it's more like the Duvani becomes them. The Duvani gets a body, and the being inhabiting that body gains the experiences, wisdom, knowledge, and memories of all those who hosted it before them."

"So now you're Kroaht?"

The general laughed. "No, Kroaht is not my host. He's my victim. As was Commandant Taillur and Agent Biragor before him. I took over their bodies and robbed them of their memories, but I never became them."

"Then who are you?"

"Sir," the general said as he placed his hands on my shoulders. "I'm Akkam Lumuk, and after this, I'm going home to make sure my momma's all right!"

••-•-●-•-••

When the Marines rounded up all the 247th MEF's traitors, they collected all their weapons, ordnance, and ammunition. They abandoned all their personal gear, however. Their clothing, rations, and comfort items remained right where they left them. That included their tents, giving Gunny Malcolm plenty of options to sleep in after twisting his mind so hard on Kan Qui Radix that he was unable to find his way home.

Had Malcolm actually made it back to his own shelter that night, someone would probably have woken him up in time to catch the last shuttle back to the *Nebulean Phoenix*. Gunny was so deep into one of the most deserted areas of Narman's Pyke, however, that there was nothing within a half kilometer that could have disturbed him. He stumbled out of his tent the following day heart-breakingly sober and burdened with the sickening realization that he had missed ship's movement. Though for all practical purposes the man had retired, he would officially remain a Marine until he was discharged from his home base. Therefore, he was still subject to the Uniform Code of Military Justice, and getting left behind by one's command remained a very serious infraction.

Malcolm spent the entire day frantically trying to hitch a ride up to the *Phoenix*, but every outbound bird was headed for the *Admiral Phranqen*. After the sun went down, he had no choice but to approach his Killbilly friends.

"No can do, Gunny," Buster Hoarase, the pilot of the rust-bucket trawler *Down and Dirty*, told him. He was hanging out of the ship's starboard access hatch, a meter above Malcolm's head. "They ain't lettin' Qilkorian craft on the dreads no more. Ever since one of our trawlers caught fire and exploded on the *Quantum Annhilator* a couple of years back, the fleet thinks we's all safety hazards."

"Just get me close," Malcolm begged. "We'll shoot them a message and have them send a pod for me."

"It'll have to wait for tomorrow," Buster told him.

"I can't wait until tomorrow!" Malcolm snapped. "They might already be gone tomorrow!"

"Gunny, my guys are all already fucked up three ways from Sunday. They ain't in no shape to operate anything more complicated than a twist-off bottle cap."

"Gaaaah!" Malcolm shouted in frustration. "What the hell am I going to do?!?"

Buster grinned as he reached one of his tattooed arms into his back pocket and pulled out a flask of Killbilly hooch. Offering it to the Marine, he asked, "How's about you join us?"

Malcolm let out a long sigh and hung his head in defeat as the realization sunk in that he was going nowhere that day. Reaching his hand out to take the Killbilly up on his offer, he said, "Sure. Give me a drink."

As Malcolm reached for Buster's flask, he saw a bright light flash through the clouds above him. He first dismissed it as lightning, but it was followed by a spectacular light show as a billion pieces of debris burned up in the atmosphere in a dazzling shower of fireballs.

"Wow," Buster said as he looked toward the heavens. "That sure is pretty."

"The fuck it is!" Malcolm replied as he threw the flask back to Buster. Sprinting toward the colony's landing pads, he shouted, "That's a dead dreadnought! I don't care how messed up your men are, Buster! Get those killers ready to fly!"

Chapter 52

CLARITY

"We couldn't tell you, sir," Kroaht said to me. It was surreal having a four-star Marine general repeatedly referring to me as a 'sir.' "I couldn't tell anyone. Had Melki not been critical to my plan, I wouldn't have told him, either. If you had been captured and tortured, as you actually were, and broke, all would've been lost."

The Duvani was right. I had never experienced agony like what Deena Vulk had inflicted on me, and I was not sure what I eventually would have told her. To be honest, I suspect the main reason I did not give up any information was that my tormentor had not actually bothered to ask for any. That sick little bitch was not interrogating me. She was entertaining herself.

Turning to Melki, I asked, "Did you know the Duvani was in charge of the mothership?"

The alien nodded. "I did after they nuked the aircraft hangers. That was our signal. The Marines could never have gotten coordinates that precise from Kryndil."

Kroaht grinned. "That was actually the weak link in my plan. I was certain that Section 615 knew we irreversibly dismantled the navigation recorder of any vehicle that goes to Xaramika. I expected Taillur to call me on that when I told him I got it from the downed Warp Haug at Anga-Iskalei."

"You mean when Biragor told him?" I asked.

"I *was* Biragor," Kroaht reminded me.

I shook my head in disbelief as I glanced around the dreadnought's bridge.

"Did you go to Narman's Pyke with me, as Akkam Lumuk, intending to get captured?"

Kroaht shook his head. "Nah. I was planning on slipping away, though. I was going to take over the highest-ranking officer I could get my hands on, then work my way up the chain of command. My biggest danger was trying to figure out cover stories for all the brainless bodies I was going to leave in my wake."

"Out of curiosity," asked Meinhopf, "how did you get away with that?"

The general shrugged. "Luck. I left my body, my Akkam Lumuk body, behind by shooting it in the head after I took over Biragor. Had you spent more time looking around that room, you'd have seen an awful lot of blood, but no brains."

"Don't you think the investigators would have noticed that?" asked Governor Ghona.

"If there was actually an investigation, probably. At that point, there was just too much going on and not enough resources to deal with it all. Before the MPs could even begin looking into what went down at the sanitation complex, all hands were called on deck to round up deserters. As far as I know, no one even went back to clean up the crime scene."

"And Biragor?" I asked.

"Easier still. Nobody pokes around Section 615 business. That was close, though. Having access to Biragor's mind, I knew how depraved our intelligence service was, but I never saw Taillur coming. Before I even had an inkling that something was wrong, the man shot me twice in the chest. Luckily, I can survive days inside a dead body, and as long as there are nerves leading to them, I can still control the corpse's limbs. I was still able to overpower the commandant and get into his skull when he went to check my vitals. Once I made the transition, I shot Biragor in the head like I did myself, then had Taillur's valet droids take care of the body."

Before anyone could ask the next question, Kroaht said, "If anybody's wondering, Taillur's body is still lying in the general's bed."

While Kroaht explained how he would no longer be sleeping in that stateroom, my head spun in circles, trying to figure out everything that had to come together to put the Duvani where he now stood. I had so many questions. "Kryndil's Lair," I said to him. "That was where it all fell into place. It was Deena Vulk who led them there. Did she really escape?"

The general shook his head. "No, it was Kryndil who arranged to have her set free. It was even his idea to bring the young man who freed her into his lair and Kryndil's people who put the bug in his ear about how to break his girlfriend and Vulk out of that place. They even arranged for that kid to keep capturing Demon Root to 'bribe' the guards. That poor fool fell for all of it."

"I'm kind of surprised Deena Vulk did," I said.

Kroaht laughed. "The funny thing is she didn't! She knew we were setting a trap for the Marines, and so did Agent Biragor." The general paused to point at his temple. "The truth is, Kroaht knew it, too. He was just so desperate that he had no choice but to march right into it."

"And the Harnillium bomb? Was that always in the equation?" I asked.

The Duvani nodded. "Yes. We've been collecting Nexilium fuel for it since before you got here. Our plan was always to draw our enemies right to where we wanted them and then break them down on a molecular level. Your filtering technology allowed us to save the Marines on our side while we lured the Mathusala Corps to their doon. If I failed to assume command of the *Phoenix*, it would've been up to you to initiate your mission to assault the mothership with that three-to-one advantage you were striving for."

Something still did not make any sense to me. "How did Kryndil getting captured fit into all this?"

Kroaht shook his head. "It didn't. That was a stroke of luck on our enemy's part. His capture caused the death of Dimitri Naktada, and that was a crippling price to pay for our freedom."

I nodded sadly in agreement. It certainly was. "What happened to Kryndil after he was captured?"

"I killed him while I was still Biragor," the Duvani confessed. "Both to put him out of his misery and to end his legacy of savagery. Kryndil was a sick, sick individual, Eamon Tauk. He was the kind of terror that needed to be left behind on Kanaris."

As Kroaht finished speaking, the bridge doors slid open and let Black Francis in. With him was Elia Gyanis, who screamed my name and jumped into my arms. Trying to mask the discomfort she felt watching me embrace another woman,

Haeli wandered over to the weapons officer's console and pretended to look engrossed in what Captain Jaem was doing.

"I'm sorry!" Elia sobbed. "I'm so sorry! I shouldn't have trusted that bitch! I didn't know she'd...."

"Shhhhh," I hushed, trying to settle the armorer down. "It's okay. I trusted her, too."

"Actually," Kroaht said, "both of you trusted me. I know it's confusing, but I was the one who betrayed us all and had everybody rounded up. I thought we'd suffer fewer casualties being brought aboard the *Phoenix* as prisoners than fighting our way onto a dreadnought as insurgents."

"So what side was Biragor really on?" asked Meinhopf.

"Her side," answered the general. "She was going to flip toward whoever looked like they would end up on top. In other words, even she didn't really know who she was working for."

Elia looked around the room and caught a notable absence. "Where's Captain Naktada?"

I shook my head sadly. "He didn't make it. Of course, he died a hero." I decided to wait until I could be alone with Elia before I told her about the rest of our platoon getting shot down over Anga-Iskalei.

Shocked, Gyanis buried her face in her hands. "Oh no! Naktada was a man who could never be replaced."

"I wouldn't be so sure about that," I told her. "I've already got someone in mind as my technical warfare specialist. Someone Dmitri highly recommended."

"Really?" Gyanis asked. "Who?"

"You."

Elia flinched. "Me? Why? I don't have half of Naktada's brains!"

"Which means you still have twice as much as anyone else I can think of."

"You can say that about balls, too," Black Francis added. "I loved Dimi, but he would never have survived in the Pyke so long doing what you did."

"General," Captain Jaem called from the command console. "What about Phase Three?"

Kroaht sighed and looked out the window at the wreckage of the *Admiral Phranqen*. "We've already killed a half million people today, Captain. Do we really need to incinerate a hundred thousand more?"

Jaem shrugged. "If the shoe were on the other foot, they wouldn't think twice about incinerating you."

"I'd like to think we're better than they are," Kroaht told the weapons officer. "Is Phase Three ready to go?"

Jaem nodded. "Everything is armed, locked, and loaded. All I have to do is press the red button."

Kroaht's shoulders slumped as he turned to Ghona and me. "Are the Marines on Kanaris any threat to this vessel?"

The governor and I looked at each other. I ended up shaking my head. "They don't have anything down there that can touch us."

Kroaht bobbed his head. "In war, opposing sides tend to try to outdo one another with cruelty. It's a vicious circle that's very difficult to stop. I'd like to show the people down there that we're not the beasts they've portrayed us as. I'm inclined to show them mercy."

I glanced over at Captain Jaem to gauge his reaction but instead caught sight of Haeli Deboara standing behind him with a look of pure horror on her face. Struck with a sudden premonition of what she was about to do, I lunged for the weapons console and screamed, "HAELI! NO!"

When Jaem looked up to figure out what I was yelling about, Haeli clocked him in the jaw with her elbow, sending him tumbling out of his seat. The instant he was out of her way, she smashed both hands down against the red launch button.

The bridge fell silent as I skidded to a halt to look outside the window. I saw two dozen missiles speeding through space, heading toward Kanaris's surface to obliterate Narman's Pyke and everyone in it. Unable to believe what had happened, I turned to the woman I shared my bed with and asked, "What have you done?"

Tears were streaming down Haeli's cheeks as she shook her head from side to side. "It was the Marines that came to our planet, Eamon. They killed our leaders, our thinkers, and our neighbors. They slaughtered men, women, and children. They looted. They pillaged. They destroyed everything they got their hands on. They humiliated us. Beat us. Raped us. Enslaved us. They were so much stronger than we were. They still are. Those of you who haven't ever been crushed under a

Marine boot may not realize it, but we don't have the luxury of being merciful to these animals. I am NOT going to spare them so that they can do to others what they've done to me."

•• -•- ● -•- ••

Heeding Malcolm's advice, Buster Hoarase had the *Down and Dirty* ready to go long before he saw Malcolm sprinting back their way. "WE GOTTA GO!" the Marine was screaming. "WE GOTTA GO NOW!"

"What the hell happened?!?" Buster asked as Malcolm jumped into the access hatch and struggled to buckle himself in.

"Those fucking traitors still must've figured out a way to take over the *Phoenix*!" Malcolm snapped. "They destroyed the *Admiral Phranqen* and there's thousands of dead grunts floating outside the *Phoenix's* debarkation bay!"

"What?" gasped Buster. "How?!"

Malcolm smacked the pilot hard atop the helmet several times to get him to focus on lifting off. "It doesn't matter! Get us in the goddamn air!"

"Okay! Okay!" slurred the co-pilot. Grabbing his microphone, the Killbilly said, "Pyke Tower. Pyke Tower. This is D&D5478, requesting permission to...."

Malcolm popped out of his restraints, grabbed the co-pilot by the helmet, and began bouncing the man's melon against the auxiliary control console. "FUCK THE TOWER! FLY GODDAMMIT! FLY!"

More to piss Malcolm off than out of any genuine sense of urgency, Buster threw maximum power to the thrusters, lifting his ship off the ground and tossing the gunnery sergeant to the deck. The Killbillies then directed the burners to burst forward and made for the top of the wall with everything they had, letting inertia roll Malcolm ass over elbows toward the stern while the drunken Qilko-rians rolled with laughter. Only once they rose above the canopy and leveled off was Malcolm able to get to his feet and strap himself into a seat. The Killbillies were still giggling.

"That was a feckin' riot, Gunny! But what did you think was going to happen to us back there?"

Haeli Deboara answered Buster's question with an enormous fireball that suddenly appeared where Narman's Pyke once stood. In the blink of an eye, the colony had been blown to pieces by a massive missile barrage wiping it, and any hope of the League fortifying the planet before the Morghul arrived in force, off the map forever.

Unlike the League, the Duvani did not use nuclear weapons. He instead used the most powerful conventional explosives in his arsenal. With the exception of radioactive fallout, the effect was largely the same. The inferno left few survivors, and the shockwave leveled the rainforest surrounding Narman's Pyke nearly to the horizon.

When the explosion went off, Buster Hoarase's *Down and Dirty* escaped the fireball, but it could not outrun the shockwave. The ship was ripped off its trajectory, tossed high into the air, and forced down into the destroyed forest below. Miraculously, Buster kept *D&D's* nose up as it crashed to the surface and saved it from disintegrating on impact. Instead, the vessel skipped several times over all the fallen timber, ricocheted off a pair of hillsides, then careened into a massive boulder before taking to the ground for good and rolling over a half dozen times before it finally came to a halt.

When the craft stopped, most of its occupants were catatonic with shock and terror. The co-pilot, whose stomach was already soured by all the rotgut hooch he consumed before take-off, was projectile vomiting into his crotch. Judging by the overpowering smell wafting through the cockpit, Gunny Malcolm also suspected that one of the *Down and Dirty's* passengers had soiled themselves.

And he hoped it wasn't him.

Chapter 53

TRANSITION

General Kroat circled the gurney and looked down upon his prey. "I know you," he told the doomed man.

The convict tried to shake his head, but every part of his body was immobilized. "Know me?!? I ain't ever seen you before in my life!"

Kroaht smiled as he pulled the curtains closed around the section of the *Phoenix's* medical bay we had taken over. "You've never seen me like this, no. You're from Gorsu Qat?" he asked, confirming the information he had read in the inmate's file.

"Yes." Heisu Tris looked like he was from Gorsu Qat. He had the dark skin, a head full of thick curly hair, and the stature the planet's people were known for. Though he was not nearly as tall as Akkam Lumuk, he still towered half a head above anyone else I knew. The man was stocky, too, but unlike my beloved giant, Heisu was covered in solid muscle. There was not a gram of fat on him, and he looked like someone very capable of inflicting a great deal of damage with only his bare hands.

"You worked for one of the produce brokers. Mr. Rudaul. You were one of his stooges."

"Yeah, that's right."

Kroaht laughed softly. "You came to my house once. You climbed off your land speeder with that big old club in your hand, lookin' like you was going to put my momma on the business end of that thing. Then you saw my humungous ass walk out of our dwelling. You dropped your shit and ran."

Tris blinked in disbelief. "Akkam Lumuk?"

The general nodded. "Yes. I'm Akkam Lumuk — among others. Tell me, Heisu. How does a broker's goon end up a Class One convict in the Kyperion League Space Corps?"

Tris scoffed. "You know, they paid me a pretty penny to do their bidding. They sent me to break bones, remove digits, murder, rape, and pillage. Whatever was needed to protect their wealth. As long as it was their dirty work I was doing, I was a valued employee. The minute I used my talents to collect what they owed me, though, I was considered a psychopath. A menace to society."

Governor Ghona, the one person besides myself who was invited to witness the Duvani's transition, took a step back away from the gurney, not comfortable being so close to such a person.

"It's fun doing the master's bidding until the one the master is imposing his will on is you." As Kroaht spoke, he crawled upon the gurney beside his victim. "Pardon me if I'm less than sympathetic to your sudden change of fortune."

"W-w-what are you going to do to me?"

"Don't worry about it," Kroaht said as a stream of blood started pouring from his left nostril. "It'll be over soon."

As Ghona and I watched, Kroaht's eyes began darting wildly about in their sockets. Then, the light in them appeared to go out as they sank deeper into the general's skull. The blood streaming out of Kroaht's left nostril turned into a torrent, while out of his right emerged something I at first thought was a large wad of mucus. As more and more of it emerged from the orifice, however, it took on the form of some giant slug. In shock, I looked up at Ghona, who had thrown her hand up over her mouth in an attempt not to vomit.

The creature slithering out of Kroaht's head kept coming and coming. When it finally finished extricating itself from the general's nose, it was about the same shape and size as my forearm.

"Oh, man," groaned Heisu Tris as the Duvani slithered across the gurney, over the prisoner's shoulder and up to his chin. "You all know how fucked up this is, right? Come on, man! Don't do this to me!"

Tris continued to beg as the slug worked its way up his face and began probing his nose. Once the creature was pushing its way through his sinuses and starting to burrow through his skull, the convict began to scream. Tris struggled ferociously against his restraints, but it was to no avail. Within a minute, the prisoner's eyes rolled back behind their lids, and he started to gag as he struggled for air.

"Should we do something?" asked Ghona.

I shook my head. "He made it very clear that we were not to interfere in any way."

"But it looks like something's going wrong!"

Glancing at the governor, I said, "He told us he's been doing this for thousands of years. We have to assume that if he wasn't very good at this, he wouldn't have lasted so long."

"My god," Ghona gasped. "There's so much blood coming out of his nose! How much does he have to lose before it becomes a problem?"

"I don't know," I confessed. "Tris is a big guy, though. He's got to have quite a bit in there still. Much more than you or I have."

By this point, the Duvani was completely inside the prisoner's skull. The body on the gurney started thrashing against his restraints once more, then Tris's eyes closed as he went completely still. Ghona and I stared silently at the convict for several moments before his eyelids suddenly popped open, causing the governor to practically jump out of her skin. Blood began pumping out of Tris's nostrils again.

"Are you okay?" I asked the Duvani.

Heisu Tris shook his head as a tear rolled down the side of his face. "My momma's dead. Heisu Tris watched it happen."

Ghona and I were quite shaken as we pulled back the curtains and walked out of the Duvani's space. Both of us were surprised to find Melki standing just outside. "How is he?" the alien asked.

"Fine, I guess," I answered. "He said he needs rest."

Melki nodded. "It's an exhausting process."

"Have you been out here the whole time?" Governor Ghona asked.

"Yes. Yes, I have."

"Then why didn't you come inside with us?"

The alien shuddered. "I have already seen the Duvani naked once. I would consider it a great privilege to go the rest of my life without seeing him that way ever again."

When the Duvani regained enough strength, he joined us for the meal we were having in the staff officers' wardroom. After assuring us that he was fine, he sat at the head of our table. "So, what do we call you now?" asked Black Francis as he pushed a plate of braised meat toward our newest guest.

"Akkam," the Duvani replied. "Akkam Lumuk. When he agreed to host me in his body, to see the world through his eyes, I promised to absorb his essence, to become him, so to speak. Good people, I *am* Akkam Lumuk and will be until he tires of the world and urges me to become someone else. Had I not learned from Heisu Tris's memories that my momma was no longer alive, I would be going to Gorsu Qat right now to care for her."

"So, where are we going then?" Governor Ghona asked.

The new Lumuk shrugged. "That's up to you. I'm not your leader."

"But you saved us all," Ghona insisted.

"No, I only reduced the casualty count. Eamon Tauk had a plan to get us off of Kanaris, and it would have worked had I not sabotaged it once I learned I could accomplish the same thing with fewer casualties."

"Then I vote we make Eamon Tauk our leader," Black Francis said.

"I decline," I told the crowd without hesitation. "Kanaris was my first war. I hope to make it my last." Looking at Haeli sitting by my side, I took her hand. Hoping to steer her off the path I could see her heading down, I said, "I just want to find a planet someplace where I can disappear and live in peace with someone special."

Haeli pulled her hand back and sadly shook her head. "I can't do that. Not while the Samaaris are ravaging Portuna unchecked. My war is just beginning, Eamon. If obliterating Narman's Pyke didn't convince you that I intend to see it through, I don't know what will."

Several former inmates of Kanarisian Harnillium mines agreed with her. "And don't forget Terrakand!" Someone called out from the aft end of the wardroom.

"I most certainly won't, Ansel!" Haeli called back with steely determination.

"You know," Francis said, "there are plenty of NEE planets in the galaxy that haven't been settled yet. We could take over one of those and train refugees from the League's conflict zones to fight back. If we can somehow manage to overthrow those fucking Samaaris, maybe we can sue for peace with the Morghul Empire and...."

"There is no peace with the Morghul Empire," said Arot, one of the marooned Turqs we had rescued from the Killbillies. "Once they find you, they will conquer you. That's just the way it is."

Melki agreed with him. "That's the way it's always been. We can't have peace without defeating the Morghul as well."

"Is there any discontent we could take advantage of there?" asked Francis.

Arot nodded. "Just like in your civilization, the Morghul always have planets that are more restive than others. It is also a slave society." With a nod to Haeli Deboara, the Turq added, "As we have learned from the mines on Kanaris, there is no one you can count on more than a slave to bite the hand that whips them."

"Come on, Eamon," Francis begged. "You're an Academy Marine. There's no one better equipped than you to turn broken people into warriors. Be our leader."

"Francis, I can not think of a worse person to lead a training camp than me. You need someone who knows how to keep the lights on and the water flowing. You need someone like Governor Ghona. I'm not any good at any of that shit!"

"Could you at least stay long enough to teach us what you *are* good at?" Haeli asked as she retook my hand.

I let out a little sigh after looking into Haeli's eyes. What I saw in them scared me. She was determined to strike back at the Samaaris and reclaim her planet. As a natural leader, I did not doubt she could do it. I also saw in her the potential to morph into a monster even more terrifying than the one she vowed to destroy. She needed guidance. Restraint. She needed someone to reign her in from acting upon her baser instincts, and I saw no one around her more capable of doing that than me.

"Sure," I said as I squeezed her hand. "I'll stay for a while. It's not like I know of anywhere else I can go at the moment."

Chapter 54

FIN

When the *Nebulean Phoenix* bombed Narman's Pyke, a few hundred Marines were sweeping the catacombs beneath the colony. They were deep enough underground to survive the attack, and once the fires died down, they emerged from the rubble to the realization that they were marooned.

That was the same conclusion reached by the brigade General Sqaar dispatched to Camp Taarlak. There was also a battalion of Marines that had just arrived at Camp Vayipar who had escaped the attack intact. Since the Qilkorians running the acclimatization course were the most adept at surviving the harsh conditions on Kanaris, Vayipar is where the roughly seven thousand remaining humans ended up gathering. Gunny Malcolm was not among them.

"What you got against Vayipar?" Buster Hoarase asked when Malcolm announced he was getting as far from the camp as he could.

"It's run by Samaaris," Gunny told him. "Who else would take every Marine on this rock and concentrate them in one spot?"

Buster shrugged. "There's strength in numbers."

"Yeah, well, for the enemy, there's also opportunity. That's how we lost two hundred thousand Marines at Kryndil's Lair."

"Yeah, but the Mogs is all gone! So is Tauk! There ain't no one left to attack us here but those giant centipedes out in the bush!"

As he continued to pack his things, Malcolm said, "The closest Space Corps facility to us is on Hunaa-11. That's where both the *Phoenix* and the *Admiral Phranqen* were based. There're no more dreadnoughts left there to deploy. The next closest military spaceport is on Lansiano. That's several months away, and, like Hunaa-11, there're only a pair of dreadnoughts based there. The League isn't going to send another Marine Expeditionary Force to this place after they just lost two of them. They're going to assemble a friggin' attack squadron. That means pulling craft from Portisbain, Qalidar, Marmoar Koak, and even Zaimiraldo. It could be a year before any sort of rescue mission gets here."

Buster ran his fingers through the white beard he kept cropped close to his jaw. His wrinkled face then winced at the thought of living rough out in the bush for months on end. "You know, Gunny, I'm an old man...."

"And you won't be getting much older if you throw your lot in with these idiots," Malcolm assured him.

Tuts Meehan was one of Buster's men. He was a morbidly obese individual and, like many Qilkorians his size, walked around in a type of canvas crop top that covered his upper chest but left his enormous, tattooed belly fully exposed. It made him look like he was wearing a bra. "Major Paatiq wants all Qilkorians to assemble down by the mess tent," Tuts wheezed as he lumbered into Malcolm's shelter to find his boss.

"For what?" Buster asked. "We's civilians. We don't work for his Corps."

"Well, it looks like we do now," Tuts answered. "The Marines ain't got no convicts down here to do the shit work, so they's gonna make us do it."

"The fuck they is!" announced Irnie Dax. Dax was a skinny man with big eyes that never seemed to be able to move in the same direction at the same time. That, in combination with his nervous demeanor, was why everybody called him Twitch. "I don't care if Paatiq's a Samaari or not!"

Qilkorians literally worshipped the Samaaris as their gods' chosen people. After several months of watching their revered idols destroy everything they interacted with, Malcolm noticed that Kanaris's Killbilly contingent was experiencing a collective crisis of faith.

Buster Hoarase turned to Gunny Malcolm. "Yeah, we ain't doin' that shit. Gunny, if you don't mind, we's comin' with you."

Malcolm smiled. "I figured you would be. Grab everything you can carry on a long hike right now. We'll come back to steal anything else we need after we figure out where we're staying."

••⊸⊸◗⊸⊸••

Four months later, Gunny Malcolm and Buster Hoarase were perched high upon a hillside, looking through optical amplifiers at an unhappy parade of captured Marines marching through the jungle with their hands atop their heads. Surrounding them were a few hundred Morghul warriors clad head to toe in black exo-armor.

"So, that's what the Mog army looks like, huh?" Buster asked.

Malcolm nodded as he zoomed in on the alien troops that had captured Camp Vayipar in a matter of minutes. "Check out their shells. They're all kitted out in the same general concept, but each is unique, with different options, decorations, and styles. No two of them are uniform. They're less like soldiers and more like knights."

"Except for they's eyes," Buster said. "They all got those red glowing eyes in they's helmets."

"Yep. The way I understand it is that they can't see very well in daylight. They're nocturnal or something."

Buster sighed and laid his head down into the mud. "Damn, Gunny. What the hell are we gonna do now?"

"The same thing we've been doing," Malcolm said as he scooted back into the bush. "Lie low. It's a big planet. We're going to hide as long as we can. Hopefully, when the Corps comes back, they bring enough boom to smack these fuckers sideways so we can go home."

"Amen to that," Buster said. "Let's get back to...."

When the men turned around, a dozen Morghul knights seemed to pop out of thin air with their blasters pointed at the pair's heads.

"Uh...uh...uh...what do we do now?" Buster asked Gunny as he threw his arms up into the air.

"Whatever they tell us to," Malcolm answered as he followed Buster's lead and raised his hands above his head. "At least we do until I can figure a way out of this mess."

••⊸⊸◗⊸⊸••

Author's Note:

First, thank you so much for reading the Kanaris Trilogy of the Eamon Tauk Space Odyssey! If you enjoyed it, please don't forget to leave a review on Amazon!

Let me assure you there is plenty more to come. This is an epic tale with a lot of moving parts. The next story to emerge from this series will be *The Waardan Reaper*. The original intent was for this to be a novella in the spirit of *The Nest*, but my outline says otherwise. It appears this will be a full-length novel following the story of Ritza Xi after she leaves Kanaris, intent on settling scores of her own.

I am setting the release date as October 2024 to ensure it is absolutely perfect before launch, but I hope to make it available well before summer arrives.

Eamon Tauk will make his next appearance in *The Haifuna Rift*, which I also intend to release in 2024, as I do *Escape from Kanaris*, which will follow Gunny Malcolm's attempt to flee from the Morghul menace invading the planet he finds himself marooned upon.

To keep up with news of upcoming projects, I invite you to like my Facebook page at **https://www.facebook.com/JEParkAuthor**!

Once again, thank you for choosing to read the *Eamon Tauk Space Odyssey*, and I hope to see you again soon!

THE END

My Sincerest Thanks TO...

No great task is ever undertaken alone, and this was certainly no exception. There were plenty of people who offered me their encouragement and support in getting this, and the subsequent books of this series, written.

The first people I have to thank is my family. This has been a LONG effort, more than two years in the making. There was a lot of time taken away from my wife and children to get this done. So, to Patrina, Regan, Mason, Carson, Fairen, and Linden, I love you and thank you for your patience, your enthusiasm, and support.

I also need to thank the authors of the Grand Blanc Authors Meetup, who have continually read, critiqued, and listened to my work for five years now. Doug Allyn, Kathleen Rollins, Gloria Goldsmith, Brenda Hasse, Richard Drummer, Jeanie Hunt and anyone else I may have missed, THANK YOU!

And finally, my beta readers! Beta reading is no easy task. It is a HUGE undertaking and requires a lot of time and effort to do. It also requires commitment. You really have to be dedicated to the project to see it through. There is no such thing as casual beta reading and these people are an author's most valuable asset in cultivating a story. So, Rich Sorgenfrei, Matt Shefke, Deann D'Onofrio, and Tim Geniac, thank you so much for your help and invaluable assistance in helping me get this done.

And, of course, to you, the reader, thank you for taking a chance on an unknown author and reading this work. I hope you enjoyed it enough to continue on with the following books in this series.

XI: The Waardan Reaper

Ritza Xi, Margi Gul, and Zubi Jenich returned to the League, ready to unleash hell upon those responsible for their enslavement. Seeking revenge against those who condemned them to such savage servitude with absolute impunity, the women embark upon a mission to show the League's elite what real power feels like.

As their quest leads them to Waardan, Margi Gul realizes that the family of an officer responsible for obliterating her village years before is within her grasp. Driven by an insatiable craving for vengeance, Gul descends down a path so dark even her closest confidantes can no longer follow her.

Refusing to let her comrade's thirst for wanton bloodshed destroy scores of innocent lives, Xi and Jenich are forced to intervene. They ultimately find themselves not only locked into combat with a former ally who knows how they think, but with the military operators, underworld killers, and government assassins she has drawn onto Waardan to stop her rampage.

With each page, J.E. Park's masterful storytelling unveils layers of conflicting loyalties, personal sacrifice, and the true meaning of survival. Buckle up for an adrenaline-fueled journey that will leave you breathless and begging for more!

About the Author

J.E. Park grew up in a suburb of Detroit, MI, where his efforts in seeking misadventures in the Motor City's punk rock scene and pursuing his vices dashed any aspirations in pursuing a higher education. They certainly did not help further his aspirations for a career in politics, either.

After graduation from high school, J.E. Park joined the US Navy and spent the next six years bar-brawling his way across the Far East, gaining the experiences that formed the foundation for his first novel "Tequila Vikings", a tale of a troubled young man navigating the military politics, violence and wanton hedonism woven into the naval culture of the early 1990s.

J.E. Park was a former contributing writer to the now-defunct comedy website Zug.com where he was best known for penning an article on harnessing the hallucinatory experiences of the smoking cessation aid Chantix for recreational purposes, positing that whether a condition is considered a side effect or an unintentional source of amusement depends largely upon the patient's attitude about the whole thing.

J.E. Park currently lives in a suburb of Flint, Michigan with his family where he has successfully used the region's suspect water quality as an excuse to stop neglecting his drinking.

Also By J.E. Park

The Tequila Vikings Series
Tequila Vikings
Olongapo Earp
Neptune's Martyrs

The Eamon Tauk Space Odyssey
Narman's Pyke
Moloch's Garden
The Morghul
The Nest

Novellas
Acid and Ozymandias: Notes from Skid Row

www.ingramcontent.com/pod-product-compliance
Lightning Source LLC
Chambersburg PA
CBHW051525250626
47156CB00001B/230